"Don't you get the message, Brice? We had a fling. That's all. It happens to people all the time."

"Not with you, Belinda," he said softly. "I don't think you have too many flings."

Brice moved closer to her and, gripping her shoulders, he forced her around to face him.

"Look me in the eye, Belinda. Look me in the eye and tell me all we had was a fling. Tell me you haven't thought about that night we had together a thousand times, just like I have."

She looked back at him and prepared to tell him just that, but she had barely begun when his mouth was on hers.

Instead of pushing him away she drew him closer. The sheer power of his heat seemed to suck her into a whirlpool as all the suppressed desires and yearnings forced her to him.

"We've had this date for a long time, Belinda," he said, gently loosening the silk cord that held her robe closed.

The robe fell to the floor in a pile of black silk . . .

THE TEXAS GARLANDS

Born To Be Rich

SARAH GALLICK

PINNACLE BOOKS
WINDSOR PUBLISHING CORP.

PINNACLE BOOKS

are published by

Windsor Publishing Corp.
475 Park Avenue South
New York, NY 10016

First printing: December, 1989

Printed in the United States of America

Prologue

Galveston, Texas

Galveston Island has always drawn the cannibals. The Karankawa Indians, despised by all other tribes, were the first, but by the time Jean Lafitte and his pirate brothers arrived they had been wiped out by the white man. Then came the traders and hustlers who made nineteenth century Galveston the Wall Street of the West. Some people thought that the Hurricane of 1900 had washed away all that and that Galveston would go the way of Sodom and Gomorrah, but that was not to be. These days, the cannibals come dressed as land barons and speculators, men who take their opportunities and took them, and the women they have taken. And the latest of these was Buster Garland . . .

It was shortly after dawn when Big Buster Garland, his black Labrador Lyndon on the seat beside him, paused in his daily drive around the parameters of the Sand Castle Ranch and brought the red Range Rover to a stop atop a wooded crest within sight of the main house, the Sand Castle, which soared above the flat terrain of West Galveston Island like a shipwrecked pirate's mirage, a four-story pile of limestone and granite glittering with a kind of magic, the magic perhaps that had protected it from hurricanes and depressions and countless Garland family quarrels.

With the Rover's air-conditioning set to near freezing,

7

Buster was insulated from the scorching July sun, but as soon as he set foot outside, the heat hit him like an oven blast. Lyndon followed behind in three-hundred-pound Buster's generous shadow.

The old man made his way quickly to the shade of a palm tree. At sixty-three Big Buster was still ramrod straight, his better than six feet in height allowing him to look down on most men. His steps were brisk and sure. Truth to tell, he felt no different now than when he was twenty and washed up in Galveston right after the war, but he had begun to pace himself. If there was any justice, he reflected, he should live another thirty years, but one thing he'd learned in the oil patch was that there was no justice. There was money and luck—both of which a man made himself. And then there was power. A man had to reach out and grab power and Buster Garland had grabbed his share.

He took off his white Stetson and used it to fan himself as he looked up at the cloudless sky. No rain today, for sure, he decided. His son Cordell would be happy, this Fourth of July barbecue was his idea.

A sudden, shooting pain gripped Buster Garland and he leaned against the trunk of the palm tree and struggled to catch his breath, glad at least that he was alone. His time was running out and he knew it. This would be his last Independence Day. He'd never been a religious man but lately he'd been recalling the Bible stories of his childhood. The one about the rich man and the eye of a needle, and one about the Prodigal Son.

Yes, it was time to sit down with Myles McLean and start putting his affairs in order. The doctors said he had a year. A year to make up for the mistakes of a lifetime.

From the top of the crest he could see most of the two-hundred-acre ranch, a ranch in name only, of course. Galveston had always been cash and cotton country. Ahead of him was the sprawling granite Sand Castle. Just beyond was the paddock where the ranch hands would soon be setting up the great bluebonnet canvas tent that would shelter his two hundred guests from the unremitting sun. Behind him was the beach where tons of pure white sand, mined in Florida and barged across the Gulf, had

8

been laid down to create a decent beach on Galvez Bay, a fresh-water lagoon and a twelve-foot waterfall. He put his Stetson back on.

And every one of those two hundred guests would be looking for something, Buster reflected, not without amusement. He looked down at Lyndon, then picked up a fallen branch, broke off a stick and tossed it a few feet. The old dog ran for it. Poor old Lyndon was the only one who just wanted his company. Not that Buster Garland was feeling sorry for himself, far from it. He relished his power, and what was power but allowing someone to believe he needed you?

Soon the guests would be arriving. His family was already there. Lyndon had brought back the stick and he tossed it for him again.

Time soon to go back and get his morning eggs.

Above all things, he wanted to believe that the Garland empire he'd built from nothing would live after him. Chuckling to himself, he called Lyndon back and the two of them got back into the Rover. He must begin now, to be sure, and it was time for a few surprises—it was the unexpected that made life worth living.

Part I
Summer 1984

Chapter One

Belinda Garland was thinking that the problem with being brought up a princess is that you never learn to ask for anything, so she was having some trouble asking her father just what was going on. But she was determined to know.

She managed to corner Buster in his study where he had retreated to get a fresh Macanuda cigar from his humidor and, taking no chances on interruptions, she slammed the heavy oak door behind her. The study was a large tower room, with circular walls punctuated by casement windows that were closed tight because her father liked his air-conditioning frigid.

From his great oak desk in the middle of the floor, Buster could look out in all directions at his two hundred acres, but now he looked up, startled, and smiled benignly at his daughter.

With his great, puffy face, Buster Garland looked like a crafty Santa Claus, or even more, like Santa Claus's younger brother, the black sheep who went off and made a fortune wildcatting in the oil patch.

Buster looked at his daughter with pride. Belinda had polished good looks, today her long honey-colored hair was swept up loosely, her white voile summer dress exposing a long neck and fine, soft shoulders. Two weeks earlier they had celebrated her thirtieth birthday, but there was still a fragile girlishness about her. He just wished she would get married again so she would be off his hands. He had enough problems with his business and his granddaughter Tammy Lynn. He waved his paw impatiently for Belinda to sit down and get whatever it was off her chest.

"You know, Daddy, I've had a funny feeling you've been avoiding me," she said as she seated herself in the worn green leather wing chair. Buster had made few changes at the Sand Castle since her mother's death, and in the five years since then some of the furnishings had begun to look a little worn. These days it looked more like the cozy lived-in country houses Belinda had visited in England than the glossy new money mansions of Houston.

"Now, darlin', you know that isn't true," Buster assured her. "Maybe I've been busy, but I'm never too busy for you. I only hope you're not going to keep me from my guests. That would be rude." He paused to light the cigar, sparking his match on the side of his white lizard boots.

Belinda smiled and her blue eyes glittered. She had the Garland eyes, dark Galway blue and fringed with thick black lashes. "No, Daddy. I won't be rude and I won't keep you from your guests. But I've been expecting you to talk to me about the Maison Rouge since my birthday and you haven't said a word."

He looked at her blankly. "What are you talking about, darlin'?"

Now it was Belinda's turn to be annoyed. Had he really forgotten, or was he just playing games? "It's been a year, Daddy. I've been running the the hotel for a year. But we've never made it official. I thought today at the barbecue you could make some kind of announcement."

Buster stared at her without blinking. "Have you and your brother been quarreling again? Is that what this is about?"

"No, things with Cordell are fine," she answered. "But I've been thinking that we should formalize our arrangement. A lot of people still think of me as some society deb playing hotel with my daddy's money. But you know better. You know I've turned the Maison Rouge around."

Had it only been a year, she wondered. Just a year since Arden Yates's Mercedes went sailing over the seawall taking him to a watery grave and leaving her a widow. Poor Arden. His luck was bad right to the end. He wasn't even driving. He was too drunk.

Buster couldn't help himself. He started to laugh, a great, lusty bellow that petered out into a wheeze. Belinda never cracked a smile. She didn't find it amusing at all.

14

"Now, darlin'," he said smoothly. "I know what you're up to. You want me to sign over that hotel to you, don't you?"

She wasn't going to fall for that trap. "I don't need anything in writing," she answered. "Your word is good enough for me."

He nodded in agreement.

"You've given me a free hand all year, and I appreciate it. But now you've seen what I can do, and I'd like to make it official."

"A year isn't a very long time, Belinda. You've done a good job, sure. But you haven't had any emergencies. Why you haven't even had to deal with a good hurricane! How much do you really know about hotels?"

"After a year of running the Maison Rouge I know more about hotels than you knew about newspapers when you bought the *Sentinel-Wave*," she snapped. "Besides, you told me once that you didn't need to know how to run a business—you just needed to hire people who knew."

"And what do you know about hiring folks?" he said. "What do you know about budgets and planning and all of that stuff."

"I learned from you," Belinda said coolly. "I've seen how you built up Garland, Inc. I admit I didn't have much business experience before I took over the Maison Rouge," she added. "But I did run a household with a full-time staff of five and I raised almost a million dollars for the Galveston Fund."

"That was charity," he snorted. "Business is different. Nobody gives you money without wanting something back. Remember that Belinda: everyone wants something."

Belinda was in no mood to be distracted by the Wisdom of Buster Garland. "It's not like I'm asking to come into Garland, Inc.," she said. "I wouldn't dream of crowding Cordell."

Buster looked more alert and his fine blue eyes narrowed. "What's that? What about your brother?" He'd suspected from the beginning that Cordell figured in here somewhere.

Pleased that he had risen to the bait, Belinda went on smoothly. "Just that I know Cordell's in charge of the Garland papers and you're grooming him to run Garland, Inc., someday. He dropped in at the Maison Rouge the

15

other day and mentioned that he should know more about what's going on there. He has lots of ideas, he said. He wants the Maison Rouge to reflect Garland, Inc."

"Oh, he does, does he?" Buster snapped. "Well, it just so happens that your brother may think he's going to run Garland, Inc., but that's no sure thing. I'm still in charge and I make the decisions."

"Well, of course, Daddy. Everyone knows that you're still in charge. And Cordell is doing a wonderful job with the *Sentinel-Wave.*"

"A wonderful job? With advertising down thirty percent? I've been letting that boy have a free hand, but it looks like I've given him enough rope to hang himself. No, ma'am. If that's how he runs the *Sentinel-Wave,* there's no way he's getting his soft white hands on Garland, Inc!"

Belinda looked down at her own manicured hands. The ruby-and-diamond ring glittered on her right hand and a gold Tiffany sports watch was on her wrist. Her left hand was bare. She had stopped wearing Arden's wedding ring the day of his funeral.

"Really, Daddy. I didn't come here to put down my brother. I'm sure he's doing the best he can," she added primly. "Did you say advertising was down?"

"In the cellar and still sinking," he grumbled. "Cordell's so busy hobnobbin' with celebrities and getting his picture taken with the governor he's forgotten that ads are where a paper makes its money. I hear weeks go by when nobody in the ad department even sees that boy."

"I don't understand that," she said, her blue eyes widening in amazement, a particularly useful technique perfected by her sorority sisters in Kappa Kappa Gamma. "I used to love selling ads. Remember I worked there every summer when I was at Ursuline? Advertising sales was always my favorite department."

Buster looked at his daughter with speculation, as if he had a sudden thought, then quickly discarded it in favor of another. "Cordell's sniffing around the Maison Rouge, is that it?" he pressed. "And you want to get rid of him?"

Belinda hesitated, obviously reluctant to start criticizing her brother when he was already in disfavor with Buster. But he *had* been rude to her when he came by, pointing out all the ways she could cut costs. And the Maison Rouge, unlike the *Sentinel-Wave*, was making money. He had no right to tell her how to run it. She was as much a Garland as he was.

"Well, yes," she admitted at last. Cordell had been very clear about "the lines of succession," as he called it. Namely, that with their older brother long ago banished to New York, he was the heir apparent. No matter how much of a success she made of the Maison Rouge, she was still only a daughter.

Buster slammed his paw down on the desk. "Damn that boy! I make the policies around here. Forget about him meddling in the Maison Rouge. It's yours until I say different."

"What abut Cordell?"

"What about him? I'm still running this show, thank you. And I'll just remind him of that fact. And I'll give you a deed to the Maison Rouge in writing, just to show him so."

Belinda stood up and ran to the other side of the desk, giving her father a big kiss.

"Oh, thank you, Daddy," she bubbled. "This is just a wonderful surprise!"

"Now get downstairs and start kissin' my guests," he said.

So Belinda descended the great oak staircase and floated outside to the star-spangled tent where Buster's guests had begun to gather, smiling sweetly and enormously pleased that the dreaded encounter with Daddy had gone exactly according to her plan.

By three o'clock, the barbecue was well under way. Buster stood in the center of the enormous air-conditioned tent, center ring, as it were, under the big top, in a great white Panama suit, one big paw extended to greet friends and supplicants, the other gripping the chili pepper red-wrapped rump of the latest Miss Galveston *Sentinel-Wave*. Although he allowed his son Cordell a free hand with editorial policies, he reserved for himself the selection of the weekly beauty queen who decorated page 3. As far as he was concerned, that was what sold the paper.

Moving through the crowd, Belinda alternately embraced old friends and scanned the tent for a sign of her brother.

17

She had also promised to look out for her niece Tammy Lynn because Tammy Lynn had a new beau she especially wanted Belinda to meet. But Belinda felt like celebrating. She couldn't wait to see Cordell's face when he learned she had outmaneuvered him.

"Darlin', did you see that earring?" a voice whispered, and Belinda turned to find her aunt, Miss Carrie Clinton. "The earring on Tammy Lynn's beau. Don't tell me you didn't notice? That diamond's the size of a garbanzo bean!"

"No, Aunt Carrie, show me," Belinda said, because she was in a good mood, flushed with the small but significant victory over her brother. Besides, she had always been fond of her eccentric aunt. As a child, Belinda had found something mysterious about Aunt Carrie living alone except for her servants, in a big gingerbread mansion on Sealy Avenue. Now that she was grown up, Belinda admired Carrie's dotty independence.

Carrie discreetly nodded in the direction of a tall, well-tanned man in his early thirties, standing by the barbecue pit. He was thin, almost haggard, with prominent cheekbones and a long, angular nose. His dark brown hair was long and brushed back into a pony tail. (How had Carrie missed the pony tail? Belinda wondered.) In his right ear he wore a diamond stud that glittered in the sunlight streaming through the star-shaped vents in the tent roof.

He was standing beside Tammy Lynn Garland, a petite girl with close-cropped black hair and a nervous, frenetic energy about her. Tammy Lynn was quite pale, except for her bright red lipsticked mouth. She was wearing heavy gold earrings that bobbed as she talked. Tammy Lynn, pale and tense, and her sun-bronzed and languid boyfriend made a handsome couple, Belinda thought, as the man, as if sensing that someone was watching him, looked up and caught her eye. He stared at her, openly and boldly, like a cat.

At that moment a waiter went by with a tray of salt-rimmed margaritas, and Belinda helped herself to one. The man kept staring at her, then she saw him whisper something to Tammy Lynn. Her niece's face lit up and she nodded, taking him by the arm and walking toward Belinda like a little girl with a new doll.

"Aunt Belinda, I want you to meet Brice de Young. Belinda's my favorite aunt, and I want the three of us to be best friends." She had to raise her voice to be heard over the din of the crowd and the music of the strolling mariachis.

Belinda looked into Brice de Young's deep-set brown eyes and saw them full of gold and laughter. Something about the party or Tammy Lynn's introduction, or maybe even Belinda herself seemed to strike him very funny.

"What about me?" Aunt Carrie piped in. "Don't I count for something?"

Tammy Lynn had accidentally overlooked Carrie, but she introduced her great-aunt now without apology.

"I'm just so happy you've found our Tammy Lynn," Carrie gushed as she shook Brice de Young's hand. "This little girl has had her share of trials."

Tammy Lynn cut her off. "Brice already knows all about me, Aunt Carrie. I told him the whole tragic story about how Daddy ran off with Zena Pickens of the black Pickens's when I was four and how Granddaddy disowned him and took me and Mama in and then Mama took me off to live on a commune but Granddaddy tracked us down and got custody of me and took me back and how I grew up at the Sand Castle just like a typical Texas debutante." She winked at Brice when she finished up and caught her breath.

Belinda wondered if he knew about the five boarding schools, the expulsion from Sophie Newcomb, and the stints at Hazelden and Silver Hill, but she said nothing. If Tammy Lynn had found a nice man and was ready to settle down, the Garlands could all breathe a sigh of relief—even if he did wear an earring and a pony tail and had a discomforting stare.

Brice winked back at Tammy Lynn as they shared some private joke, and the sight of that filled Belinda with sadness and even a twinge of jealousy. There must have been a time when she and Arden exchanged covert glances like that—the private language of lovers—but if there had ever been, she couldn't remember it. Their marriage died a long time before Arden's accident.

She tried to think about something else. Anything else, but unsettling thoughts about Tammy Lynn's new boyfriend kept intruding. Right now she couldn't help wondering what it would be like if Brice de Young took her by the hand down to the grotto on Galvez Bay with the white sand from Florida and made love to her all afternoon. He was staring at her again, with those mink-brown eyes that seemed to laser through to her soul. She only hoped he could not read her mind.

Belinda looked away, anxious to move on and talk to someone else, anyone else, while Aunt Carrie held tight to Brice and Tammy Lynn and made her pitch for them to live in Galveston after the wedding. She regarded anywhere else, especially mainland Texas, as unsafe and unhealthy.

Tammy Lynn looked uncomfortable. "Really, Aunt Carrie, it's too soon to talk about a wedding!" she said.

"Nonsense," the old lady prattled on. "If you're living together you can talk about a wedding."

"I guess first I'll find a job," Brice said smoothly. In the background, the boisterous mariachis were playing "La Paloma Blanca."

"And what do you do, young man?" Carrie asked. "Cash, cotton, or crude?" As far as she was concerned, those were the only three ways to make a living in Texas, especially if he expected to support her grand-niece.

"None, ma'am," he said. "I'm a cook."

"Oh, I see," Carrie said, her voice barely a whisper.

"Brice is a chef," Tammy Lynn hurried to add. "He's one of the best in New York. You should see the stories about him in the papers. I'm going to talk to Aunt Belinda about giving him a job at the Maison Rouge."

Brice was uninterested in Carrie's opinion, but he looked to see Belinda Garland's reaction.

"I'm afraid we already have an excellent chef," she said. "He used to work at Maxim's in Paris. But you're welcome to come by the hotel tomorrow," she said, trying not to show her annoyance at Tammy Lynn. It was just like her niece to bring up a sensitive matter at a time like this. Well, she would put him off somehow. Let her manager, Wiley Muehl, give him a tour and a free lunch, and then get rid of him.

With relief, she noticed Myles McLean and his sister Fayette Cramer and slipped away to join them.

Myles embraced her and kissed her on the cheek. Belinda

had always liked him. Myles had been her escort the year she made her debut at the Artillery Club Ball. A girl never forgot something like that. And the night of Arden's accident, Myles had been there for her, staying with her all night, assuring her that it was not her fault, that nothing she could have done would have saved Arden from himself.

Now Myles was Buster's lawyer, handling her father's personal affairs, and Belinda suspected that Cordell resented his influence. Myles wasn't family, but she knew her father trusted him completely. So did she.

She trusted his sister Fayette, too. They were old Kappa Kappa Gamma sorority sisters. After three divorces and several careers, Fayette had settled down with an eccentric midnight talk show on KGAL-TV. *Fayette's Corner* had made her a local celebrity.

It was strange, because Myles had been like a rock for so long, and he had been such a comfort to her in the aftermath of Arden's death, but she could not feel any passion for him. She knew that marrying him would score points with Buster, but even that wasn't temptation enough. Somehow, she still hoped to find the kind of happiness she'd shared with Arden in the early years of their marriage. Before the drinking and the drugs and the other things—the things she didn't want to think about—got out of hand. Not even Buster knew the real reasons she had refused to press wrongful death charges against Arden's best friend, Senator Aynsley Adder, who had been driving the car the night of the accident. Yes, Adder could have saved Arden if he hadn't panicked, but for some reason she couldn't bring herself to go after him. Not that she didn't thirst for revenge, but she preferred to wait. Another lesson she had learned from Buster.

As Belinda thought about her encounter with her father, she was pleased it had gone so well. She manipulated him into agreeing to tell Cordell to keep his hands off the Maison Rouge. Soon she would have her control in writing. No matter what happened to their father, Cordell would not be able to touch her hotel.

And it *was* her hotel. The Maison Rouge was just a seedy old beachfront dinosaur when Buster had picked it up for a song, intending to build condos on it eventually. He was not

21

the kind of man who lost sleep over landmarks. Belinda was different. She saw the potential in the hotel's glorious past, and in the past year had turned it into a tourist attraction, lovingly restoring every architectural detail, capitalizing on every bit of Island history associated with the building.

No matter what her father hinted at, Belinda was sure that when he passed on, control of Garland, Inc., would pass to her and Cordell. There was their cousin Lamar, of course, but he was out in Hollywood and had never demonstrated any interest in the family business. He was happy to cash his checks every month. And of course their brother Buddy long ago ruined his own chances to share in Buster's estate. No, it would be between her and Cordell. She hoped the day was many years off, but when it came, she intended to exercise every bit of her control. She already knew that Cordell would resist. It would not be easy, but she had faced this first skirmish and won.

Later, much later, Belinda would come to recognize that she hadn't even understood the battle plan. But for now she was looking forward to her next encounter with her brother.

All afternoon the crowd inside the tent was so thick and giddy that by the time Belinda found Cordell the strolling mariachis had long since disappeared and a country western band was setting up. The leader, a husky redhead with a thick Hill Country drawl and embroidered western shirt and jeans, announced that Miss Valdene Sykes would join them onstage for a number. Everyone applauded wildly, well aware that Valdene Sykes had not sung in public for a year. Not since the sudden death of her husband, televangelist Prescott Sykes.

Belinda watched as Valdene, who was just a few years older than she, tossed her tangled and teased black hair and took center stage. Belinda noticed the diamond brooch clipped to Valdene's red halter top, almost buried in the deep cleavage between her breasts. The diamonds were real, were the breasts? Belinda wondered. In any case, Valdene and her late husband had certainly done very well in the God business. Belinda had priced that brooch herself at Walzel's and knew it cost seventy-five thousand dollars.

As Valdene finished up "Falling Through the Bottom and Working My Way Down," she beckoned Buster to join her onstage. Buster leaped up on the platform with surprising agility for a man his size. He was laughing and he kissed Valdene on the cheek before turning back to the audience of his friends and motioning them to be quiet. He grabbed a microphone with one paw and held Valdene with the other. He beamed. "I think we can all agree that this little lady is one huge talent," he drawled into the mike, drawing renewed applause from the crowd, well primed on margaritas and longneck beers.

At that point, Cordell turned up and stood beside Belinda. Her brother was slim and fair, so that he seemed less than six feet tall; he had the Garland blue eyes, but his face was lean and hawkish, and his eyes held a perpetually wary look.

He watched the stage intently even as he spoke to Belinda. "They look good together, don't they?" he said.

"Daddy and Valdene Sykes?" Belinda said, paying more attention to the interaction on stage. Her father and the singer were certainly laughing a lot. "Who invited her?"

"I did," Cordell said with satisfaction. "He's known her for years. And now that she's a widow . . . Lord knows old Buster needs to think about something besides business all the time. And Valdene's a handful. Once she gets him up to Nashville, he'll never want to leave. Could be wedding bells, Sister."

And wouldn't you love that? Belinda thought. But she was sure she had nothing to worry about. Unlike his sons, Buster Garland had never confused business with pleasure, and he wasn't likely to be taken in by a cheap Bible belle.

Yet, that night, as the last of the musicians packed up and the last helicopter lifted guests out of the pasture, Belinda was seized with an odd premonition. Watching the great blue tent come down, she felt as if some part of her own world were coming down with it. She had not spent a night at the Sand Castle in years, preferring these days to stay in her penthouse apartment atop the Maison Rouge, and she was glad to be heading there tonight. As Myles McLean took her home, she was unusually subdued.

Brice de Young was also unusually subdued as he and Tammy Lynn prepared for bed in the guest cottage of the Sand Castle. At least it had been built as a guest cottage, but Tammy Lynn had made it her clubhouse for the last year.

They were discussing the barbecue. Brice had found the food satisfactory. The first decent food he had on the Island.

"Well, honey, you're back and you're gonna change all that, aren't you?" Tammy Lynn said. "You're going to make the Maison Rouge the Maxim's of the Gulf Coast!"

"I've been to Maxim's, Tammy Lynn, and the food sucked there, too."

"See? There you are. You'll show what real home cooking is all about. They'll be lining up to get a table at the Maisonette."

"There's a limit to what you can do in a hotel dining room, Tammy Lynn, even at the Maison Rouge."

"It's a start. And you're home, where you belong."

"You sound like my agent."

"I should be! Every time I read about Wolfgang Puck or Paul Prudhomme, I say to myself, they don't know a thing! They've never sat down to a meal cooked by Brice de Young. And now everyone in Galveston will know."

"Yeah, Galveston," he said dryly.

She looked at him sharply. "You don't know, honey. Galveston's changed. This Island's hot. Wait till you see downtown. Granddaddy and the Luries and the rest are falling all over themselves to show who can do more to bring this island back to life. Why do you think Aunt Belinda is going to hire you? Honey, you make the most of this season and by next year you'll have your own restaurant on the Strand!"

"And you can be my hostess. We'll have Victor Costa do up your wardrobe."

Brice shook his head, but he was enjoying himself for the first time in months. His luck was back, no doubt about it. Two weeks ago he'd been so broke he'd been sleeping on the beach. He'd been reduced to palming cash from the can for Jerry's Kids at the 7-Eleven when he ran into his old friend Tammy Lynn Garland. He had never had much use for

24

spoiled rich girls, especially possessive ones like Tammy Lynn, but this time she had proved her usefulness right away, when he told her he was down in Galveston on a quick vacation from his busy New York schedule. He gave her a line about how good it was to be home, and how he was thinking about staying on, if only he could find a job.

"That's great!" she'd said at once. "My aunt Belinda runs the Maison Rouge. She'll give you a job."

So she had said, but now, after meeting Belinda Garland at the barbecue, he wasn't so sure. She didn't sound real enthusiastic, and even said she already had a cook. He reminded Tammy Lynn of this fact, but she was undiscouraged.

"Don't worry about it," she assured him, speaking with all the confidence of a Garland. "Belinda's crazy about me. If I tell her you're good, you've got the job. When she finds out you can do more than boil shrimp and crayfish, she'll be thrilled. To tell you the truth, I think everything else is microwaved anyway."

Tammy Lynn was a good old girl, no doubt about it. And a rich one, too. And sleeping with her in the Sand Castle guest house, with her granddaddy's servants at his beck and call, sure beat fighting off the fire ants on the beach.

While Brice showered and prepared for bed, he mused that servicing Tammy Lynn was a small price to pay for such a setup. And she certainly had one good-looking aunt. Yes, he looked forward to being alone with Miss Belinda Garland very soon.

"Darlin', your problem is you've just never learned not to piss where you eat," Tammy Lynn said sharply, bringing Brice back to real life with a crash. It annoyed him that she seemed to be able to read his mind. "But it's all going to be different now."

"Who was that on the phone?" he asked, drying himself with a thick terry-cloth towel. A rich man's towel.

Tammy Lynn looked smug. "That was Wiley Muehl. Aunt Belinda just lost her chef. Immigration came around and took him away in a van."

"Mexican?"

"No, French. It turned out he'd been a tourist on a French cruise ship and just got off when they docked in Galveston

25

and never wanted to go back. He told me so himself, only the other day. You know, Brice, it's like my granddaddy says. Always take the time to get to know people. You never know what kind of valuable information they're going to hand you."

"You little devil," he said, grabbing her and pulling her down on the bed. What the hell, he told himself. Even if Tammy Lynn did nothing for him sexually, she'd earned this one.

Later that night, as Tammy Lynn slept, Brice walked to the terrace and savored the breeze that ruffled the palm trees outside. At times like this it felt good to be home, and Galveston was as near to home as any place he had ever lived.

For the first time in a long time he thought about his parents, Colette and Beau de Young. Beau, with his dreams of striking it rich . . . Whether he was selling cars or managing mud wrestlers, Beau never lost his touching faith in the Big Score. But he never found it, either. The de Youngs lived like Gypsies, but they had stayed in Galveston the longest, four years, long enough for Brice to finish high school. Then poor old Beau's luck ran out all together during a tonsilectomy. At least Colette made a bundle on the malpractice settlement. She finally got Beau's Big Score.

Colette was another matter. She was always Colette to Brice, never Mom. Colette said "Mom" made her feel old, and after all she was barely thirty-nine. Colette had been thirty-nine for as long as Brice could remember. Madame Colette, the gifted psychic. She'd supported them by giving psychic readings through Beau's dry spells or his occasional "retreats," as in "Your daddy's gone on a retreat for a spell, Brice, don't you worry about him." Later, Brice understood that the retreats were spent in the penitentiaries of states where Beau's particular brand of imaginative salesmanship had not been appreciated.

Colette was no mere fortune-teller. She now lived in a penthouse on Lake Shore Drive in Chicago and wore couture clothes. She wouldn't even discuss her closely guarded client list with Brice, but hinted that it included oil barons, movie company presidents, and royalty.

Brice was genuinely fond of Colette, he liked her guts and her nerve, but he could not think of her as his mother. She was a force of nature, not a mom. A mom ironed your clothes, made you vinegar pie, and nagged you about staying out late. Brice knew from personal experience that he could disappear for days without Colette even noticing. Until he started cooking their dinners, supper was likely to be a can of unheated Campbell's gazpacho or catered by Colonel Sanders. Colette never did appreciate his skill in the kitchen. She didn't understand it. She didn't consider cooking a career.

She considered pyschic reading a career.

Brice and his mother did not have much to say to each other. Colette had never liked Galveston, too small for a lady with her big dreams. She'd left the Island right after him, and maybe for her it had been a good thing. But he was back now and he had a feeling in his pocket that this visit would bring him luck.

This might be his last chance to make it into the four-star ranks. He was thirty-five and not getting any younger. Most chefs had their own restaurants by now. In New York, after the restaurants closed, he would often go to an after-hours bar the French chefs had made their New York club. They all seemed to own condos in Alsace and Roven, while Brice could barely pay his rent. He never stayed at a job long enough to build up that kind of nest egg. He was getting a reputation for temperament and nobody needed that.

And now there was a whole new element coming into the business: yuppies looking for a cash write-off and the glamour of owning their own restaurant. His life had begun to follow a pattern. He would be contacted by one of these overnight millionaires who heard he was "available"—and lately he was "available" a lot. The yuppie, a nerd-turned-moneymaking-machine, would have a beautiful model on his arm. He was married to the model and he wanted to name his restaurant after her. Fine. The three of them would toast the restaurant with Cristal and open it two months later. It always started out with a bang: Brice de Young was the best chef in New York—even the Alsatians were afraid of him.

But the model would start coming around during the day with suggestions. Suggestions for Brice de Young! Did they make suggestions to Rembrandt? To Picasso? So he did the only thing he could to get her off his back: he gave her what she was really after and fucked her. Fine for a few weeks until she found out she was not the only woman in his life, she'd complain to the nerd and he'd be fired. The restaurant would coast, then close. They couldn't live without him. But they couldn't live with him.

Brice's last backer, a broker later indicted for inside trading, had gone a little further and hired somebody to take a shot at him on West Broadway. That was when Brice concluded it was time to say *Au Revoir* New York and Howdee Galveston, Long Time No See!

After he scored this summer in Galveston he planned to conquer Houston. That was where the big money was. He had not yet decided what to do about Tammy Lynn.

Chapter Two

Charlene Lurie was thinking that it was tough to break into movies when you were mainly known as a high-spirited Texas debutante, especially when your debut was more than ten years behind you and mostly what you had done since then was get married and divorced three times and have a daughter and get your face in the supermarket tabloids a lot.

Hollywood was proving a lot harder to crack than Galveston, where she had grown up, or Houston and New York, where she had partied heartily in years past.

At least she had an agent and a manager and an acting coach now, and they all told her the way to get acting jobs was to be out and be seen, so she had spent the Fourth of July at Harold Harris's Malibu bash, where *toute* young (or youngish) Hollywood was supposed to gather.

And she'd come home with a door prize, Harmon Lane. Her daughter Chandler and the girl's nurse, Miss Ruby, were away for a few days, which left Charlene free to party with Harmon, Nashville's finest guitar picker and star of *Breakout,* currently in national release.

Now, as morning dawned in Beverly Hills, sunlight streamed into the bedroom of Charlene's small, rented bungalow, just across the road from where Grace Kelly used to live, and smooth, pink-and-gold Charlene, and dark, bearded Harmon stirred reluctantly among the Frette sheets and down pillows.

Charlene tried to hide from the sun by putting her head under a pillow, but Harmon was too fast for her and

29

playfully pulled it away, slapping her backside so hard she screamed.

"Easy, Tex," he growled, his voice hoarse from a twenty-year diet of tequila, tacos, and trouble.

"I can't help it, that stings," she said, jumping from the bed and drawing the curtains. There was no point in giving the gardener a free show.

The main reason Charlene was avoiding the sun, however, was because Harmon looked so terrible in it. Like the women he sang about, Harmon was a lot more appealing at sundown than in the cold light of dawn.

He was thirty-five, had been on the road with country western bands for two decades, and although he had racked up five platinum albums in the past six years, Harmon looked like ten miles of bad road. His face was lined, his scarred body tattooed. Yet he had just appeared in his first movie, an action adventure saga set in Hong Kong, and it had grossed thirty-five million dollars, making him as hot a property as Stallone or Eddie Murphy.

At the Malibu party, Charlene's agent had seen her talking to Harmon, and whispered that if she played her cards right she might get a role in his next picture.

Charlene was trying to decide if it would be worth it, for Harmon Lane was crude, uncouth, and had no class. Harmon was a redneck, and here she was trying to make it in a town that considered him a sex symbol.

Did the women who paid seven dollars to see Harmon on the screen know that he wore his socks to bed? Or that he passed wind in his sleep?

Why, back home in Galveston, she would never have had anything to do with the likes of Harmon Lane. Forget socially! Her daddy, Claiborne Lurie, wouldn't even hire such white trash to clean his pool!

Probably for many of the same reasons, Harmon was smitten with her. She could tell. That slap on the backside was his idea of affection. She watched him from the window as he reached for the Baccarat glass beside the bed. It was full of plastic straws and he took two, handing her one. He had already laid out two neat lines of white powder on the mirrored top of the nightstand.

"Go ahead, Tex," he said, indicating the lines. "Be my

30

guest."

Charlene joined him on the bed. There were some perks to this starlet business after all, she decided. But after she had hoovered up her share, she rose again. Harmon reached for her, but he had barely cupped her round pink bottom when Charlene pulled away, wrapping the buttercup-strewn top sheet around her.

"Hey!" screamed Harmon, who was a guitar picker, not a songwriter, and lacked a writer's facility with words.

Charlene ignored him and slipped on her high-heeled mules before stalking off to her bathroom. She did not believe in coddling men and had more on her mind than Harmon's pleasure. After last night's party, she was sure she had gained five pounds and she sought her reflection in the mirror with dread.

Her neck and breasts were covered with hickeys. Wouldn't you know Harmon would be a biter? She had been so high last night when they made love she hadn't realized what he was doing. Oh, God, they were even on the inside of her thigh! Some other time Charlene might have laughed, but now she only hoped they would fade by the end of the week, when she was due to fly to London for her mother's latest wedding. She stared at her image in the mirror.

Actually, there was no single mirror in the bathroom, for, except for the pink-tiled floor and Kohler fittings, the walls and ceiling were completely paneled with mirrors. It was part of Charlene's campaign to maintain her beauty regimen. It was the one area of her life in which she exercised strict discipline.

She and Harmon had been so drunk on champagne the night before that she'd forgotten to throw up the meal, and now it was too late. She would just have to put in an extra hour with her trainer this afternoon — after she got rid of Harmon.

She would be thirty soon and she couldn't afford to let up now. She stared at herself as she was reflected from four walls and the ceiling: she was five seven, with long legs, slim hips, and firm, high breasts. The breasts were a problem: now that she was pursuing a career as an actress, she wasn't sure they were enough. She was considering getting them enhanced. Everyone else was doing it, even Morgan Fairchild, and people told her she looked a lot like Morgan Fairchild.

The rest of her was fine, as far as Charlene was concerned: generations of Luries married and reproduced with just such a genetic triumph in mind, for the Luries bred their women like they bred their horses, for show and speed. Charlene had the looks of a Thoroughbred and she intended to go the distance like one.

Daddy would want it that way.

The Luries were an old Texas family with roots in Galveston that predated the Revolutionary War. Theirs was not the kind of new money that could be wiped out by some little old real estate crash or nasty oil boycott. Like the looks of their women, Lurie money had a certain timeless quality.

Timeless, but not patient, and Charlene had demonstrated this lack of patience in three hasty marriages repented at leisure. Her first and longest union, an elopement with a handsome rich boy named Cordell Garland, had lasted two years, long enough to produce her daughter Chandler. Although her father loathed the nouveau riche Garlands, he doted on Chandler.

Unfortunately, the marriage ended when Cordell came home early one day and found Charlene in bed with the Vietnamese pool man. She had tried to explain that it was really Cordell's fault since she had begged—*begged*—him to hire a woman for the chore, but he didn't see her reasoning and filed for divorce. Until then Charlene had not realized how narrow-minded and possessive her new husband was and she was glad to be free of him.

The second was the dress designer she met in New York. Their relationship started out as a business venture. She was supposed to invest in his couture house, but it quickly escalated into a full-blown affair. He was a Brazilian loaded with machismo, and if she hadn't seen the videotapes herself she would never have believed he was interested in anything but women. She might even have been able to forgive a fling with a man, but not the scenes with the German shepherd. Those she could not forget. She was a Texan, after all, and believed in treating animals with respect.

The third was a writer whose play was being produced at the Glaveston Opera House. Charlene met him at the opening night and when the Island bars closed they eloped to Juarez. Two months later she had the marriage annulled. When he got drunk he kept rambling on about winning the Pulitzer Prize, and he never did explain what that was.

As a three-time loser Charlene had decided to cool it. What did she have to marry for anyway? With the fortune she had inherited from her grandfather and the even bigger fortune she expected to inherit from Daddy Claiborne Lurie she certainly didn't need to marry for money. And she'd never had any problem finding a lover. Harmon, for example. Sure he was white trash, but she had seen the other women stare with envy when she left the party with him. That turned her on, even if Harmon himself didn't.

Sometimes little Chandler asked Charlene about her daddy and Charlene would find herself recalling how different things had been with Cordell. How stupid and naive she had been! He had taken the best years of her life, marrying her went she was an innocent girl of eighteen and casting her off two years later. If she hadn't managed to get pregnant, he probably would not have married her at all. She hated and despised him.

Yet, sometimes, when she was under a major, world-class star like Harmon, she would see Cordell's face, feel Cordell inside her, and it was the only way she could come.

It made Charlene hate him even more.

None of Charlene's marriages or relationships had brought her the same satisfaction as her marriage to Cordell Garland. They were like Romeo and Juliet. Her daddy loathed his daddy, Buster Garland, and they moved in different circles. She was old Gulf Coast money, the Garlands were new rich oil people. But she and Belinda Garland, Cordell's sister, had become best friends in boarding school and used to run off to New Orleans together every weekend in Belinda's little MG (Charlene's own license had long since been suspended). They even made their debuts together at the Artillery Club, although Daddy was a tad annoyed about that, since he'd fought for years to keep Buster Garland out of Galveston's most exclusive club. There wasn't much he could do about Buster's children, since they were half Clinton and the Clintons went back even further than the Luries. And Miss Carrie Clinton wielded more social clout than God.

Then Belinda brought her home to visit the Sand Castle, Buster's big ranch on the Galveston Bay, and she met Cordell. He was four years older and at twenty-two totally uninterested in her. How could she resist a challenge like that?

By the end of the day, when most of the guests had departed, the Mexican houseman she always called Ricky Ricardo found them down by the manmade waterfall where she was giving Cordell head like he'd never gotten at SMU. After that, he would have followed her anywhere.

Too bad, Charlene thought. She and Belinda had some good times together. But since Cordell had betrayed her by filing for divorce, she had not seen Belinda. That hurt Charlene. Just because Cordell hated her didn't seem reason for his sister to cut her dead. Charlene consoled herself with the thought that some people were just not as flexible as she was.

Outside she could hear Harmon singing along to a Jerry Lee Lewis tape. Oh, well. Her daily workout at the sports club wasn't scheduled until three . . . which left them four hours to play. Harmon always played the Killer or Bob Wills and the Texas Playboys when he wanted to make love. The Playboys meant it would be a quickie, but with the Killer they might go for hours. Charlene sighed as she sprayed a bit of Poison at her knees and thighs, then flung open the door.

Some men were so predictable.

Chapter Three

By one o'clock Buster Garland was alone in his office at the top of the twenty-two-story Garland Tower, the pink granite monolith that his detractors liked to call "Big Buster's erection." He knew Belinda was expecting him at the Maison Rouge, but he was in no particular rush to go. He leaned back in the brown leather chair, a half-smoked Macanuda in his paw, a half-empty fifth of Jack Daniel's and a glass tumbler on the great desk in front of him. His eyes were closed and his mouth was open, and his big, beefy face was serene as he snored loudly and with great contentment.

With the blinds drawn against the afternoon sun, the office was dark and the air-conditioning was frigid, just the way he liked it. He spent one day a week here, not so much to conduct business as to assert his territorial rights. He did not want his son Cordell, operating the Garland News Syndicate twenty stories below, to get the idea that he owned the building. No, and he did not want Cordell to gain the misapprehension that he ran Garland, Inc., either. Cordell was the heir apparent by default and a poor substitute for his older brother.

On Buster's crowded desk was a small, framed photograph of his granddaughter Tammy Lynn that had been taken one summer when she was at Camp Waldemar. She had not changed much, still ready to battle over the dumbest things, and now she wanted to marry this Brice de Young character! And yet she left him to his own devices while she went off to some ashram for a week. That had to be her dumbest idea yet.

35

It was not that way with Belinda, he reflected. The sly fox was her father's daughter, all right. Getting him to agree to turn the Maison Rouge over to her, lock stock, and driveway. Now that his head had cleared, however, there was no way on earth he was going to do that. Handing her a deed to the Maison Rouge would be the first step to dismantling Garland, Inc. No, he wanted the company he built to live after him, and in one piece. For now he controlled it. He controlled it all.

But he did not look forward to telling her that she wasn't getting the Maison Rouge after all. No, he did not look forward to that.

Buster got up from the big leather chair and walked to the window, raised the blinds and gazed out. One advantage of being this high up was that he had an excellent view of most of the Island. To his left was the ANCO Tower, which belonged to the Moody family. Off to the right he could see the squat redbrick United Shipping Company Building. It was a good-looking building but too old-fashioned, he thought, just like the Luries who owned it. The Luries, he snorted. Jesus Christ, deliver him from fine old families that wouldn't know a good deal if it walked up and pissed on their boots.

He would never forget the time when he and Bubba, let him rest in peace, turned to Claiborne Lurie to beg him — practically beg, since a Garland never begged — to put some cash money into their fledgling parts business that year, 1953, when they almost went under. They survived, but no thanks to that cold fish Claiborne Lurie, who never gave them a dime. They ended up having to take the company public — sell stock to raise cash — and even though that parts company was just a little piece of the great edifice that was Garland, Inc., the idea of even that little old business being publicly held rankled like a burr under his saddle.

He had his revenge a few years later, though, when he outbid old Lurie for this very parcel of land. Buster snickered at the memory. Lurie wanted to build some kind of park, no doubt, named for his dead, distinguished ancestors, but he lost out. Served him right. If he wanted to play, he'd have to pay. Then Lurie'd tried to fight the

36

building itself—claiming it was going to be too tall—
meaning taller than his—and of course there were still
folks on the Island who worried about tall buildings in
case of a hurricane, but Buster got them to step up into
the modern world. Finally, Lurie claimed that the pink
granite tower would be an eyesore. A lot of good it did
him. The day was long past when a Lurie could stop a
Garland.

Buster went back to his desk and refilled his glass with
bourbon, sipping it slowly and savoring that victory once
again. If only his own family was as easy to control as
outsiders like the Luries. He looked at the photograph of
Tammy Lynn again. That was how Buster liked to think
of his granddaughter: cute as a button and anything her
granddaddy said was law. How times had changed!

Buster wondered if he should have allowed Tammy
Lynn to move this boyfriend into the guest house. He
knew what she was up to. She thought he'd get used to
him. Build up a tolerance. Imagine that! The day Buster
Garland tolerated a man with a diamond in his ear!

Tammy Lynn claimed de Young was some kind of
cook. Fine occupation for his granddaughter's future
husband! Did Tammy Lynn think he didn't know that this
de Young didn't have a pot to piss in and had been
sleeping on the beach just weeks ago?

It was just like that girl to take up with another bottom
fisher. She had informed him of her latest discovery in
typical Tammy Lynn style, turning up at the Tower office
one afternoon when she was supposed to be in New York,
and after minimal small talk getting right to the point. "I
want to open a restaurant with Brice," she announced.

"Go ahead and open a restaurant, no one's stopping
you," he assured her.

"You know what I mean, Granddaddy. I'll need money
from my trust."

"If your restaurant's so good, you don't need money
from me," he said.

"It's not from you," she said. "It's my money."

"Not until you're twenty-five, darlin'. That's the terms
of your grandma's trust. And even then I have final say. It
would pay you to stay on my good side."

Buster had her there, and Tammy Lynn was speechless for a few seconds. He enjoyed recalling the scene. He always enjoyed a good negotiation, even with his granddaughter. He could see her mind working as she measured her options. A true Garland, he noted with pride.

"Brice is a great chef. When he gets his own restaurant, you'll see." Her blue eyes were starting to fill with tears, and her small hands opened and closed as she nervously clenched them into fists.

Buster remembered chewing on his cigar then and looking at her, this little itty bitty thing. He knew a lot more about time than she did . . . But her blue eyes looked up at him soulfully and he exploded. "Damn— you're all alike. Can't tell you anything. Go ahead and do what you want. I won't stop you. I don't know how much I'll be able to help you, though, darlin'," he told Tammy Lynn. "This oil depression has hit us all pretty hard."

Tammy Lynn didn't believe that for a minute, but she let it pass. She had what she wanted. Her granddaddy knew what he wanted, too however, and Buster Garland had no intention of supporting some pretentious little poseur. He had seen too many second- and third-generation fortunes squandered on gold diggers to let it happen in his own family. But Tammy Lynn was thick-headed and ornery and stubborn as her daddy. There was no changing her mind.

The best he could hope for was to get a look at this de Young character up close and stall for time to figure him out. Know your enemy, that was the trick. As for Tammy Lynn, this rushing off to her ashram made him wonder. Was she going to end up like her mother, jumping into one cult after another? One year it was a hippie commune and the next a Hindu retreat. Now Tammy Lynn was going off to meditate for a week and leaving this boyfriend on his own.

Buster didn't have any illusions about men, especially his granddaughter's new boyfriend. A man was a man and he needed tending. But he wondered if there was some way old Brice's free time could be put to some productive use. Perhaps throw him together with some young ladies. De Young looked like a man who would never pass up attractive female companionship. It should not be hard to team him with some former Miss *Sentinel-Wave,* then arrange to have Tammy Lynn find out about it. Yes, that was one possibility. Buster mused on, considering other options to rid himself of this latest irritant.

Plotting such schemes filled him with warmth, like the smell of warm bread fresh from the oven in the Rosenberg Home for Boys where he and Bubba had spent some painful years. He had not done too badly for an orphan boy. The orphanage still stood on Broadway but it had been empty for years. Orphanages were out of style, he supposed, and people didn't die off the way his parents had, in the flu epidemic of 1939, with the Sand Castle auctioned off to pay their debts; leaving him and Bubba at the mercy of Galveston charity. At the mercy of philanthropists like the Luries, he thought bitterly.

He and Bubba never asked for a break and never got one. But after the war they saw that Galveston had little to offer them and set out for the Houston oil fields. It was a good time to be young and hungry in the oil patch. Together they learned everything they could about the oil business, and diversified, expanded, ever on the lookout for a new opportunity. Even now, when Garland, Inc., meant not just oil-drilling equipment but banking and real estate, hotels and factories around the world, he kept track of it all. Details, details. He kept them all in his head and shared his knowledge with no one.

In his whole life Buster Garland had trusted two men: his brother Bubba—poor old Bubba, who'd survived poverty and combat and countless barroom brawls to choke to death when he swallowed a Lone Star bottle cap he had just removed with his teeth, just days after Buster had managed to buy back the Sand Castle. Bubba's only fault had always been his will to make a spectacle of himself. The other man was Buster's oldest son Buddy, but Buddy had messed up.

He had such plans for that boy. Things he'd never even told Buddy about. He could have been a senator or even President. Instead, what was he doing? Building high-rise hotels and condos with other people's money. Of course, Buster only knew about Buddy what he read in the papers, but he was shrewd enough to read between the lines. Lots of publicity, but mortgaged to the hilt. A paper billionaire, but if one project failed the whole house of cards would tumble. How often he had toyed with the idea of bringing his renegade son down like that! How sweet it would have been to see that boy brought to heel, coming back to him, hat in hand, begging for his daddy to bail him out. Only the thought that Buddy, like his daddy, would sooner die than beg kept Buster from acting on that pleasant daydream. No, there would have to be another way to corral his maverick son.

Buster put the bottle of Jack Daniel's away and left the empty glass tumbler out for the cleaning woman, then called Myles McLean and told him to meet him at Gaido's. He locked the office door and headed for the elevator. He was tired of being alone.

As Buster steered his big sunshine-yellow Cadillac into the parking lot of Gaido's, the sight of the huge fiberglass softshell crab outside the restaurant reminded him of how he used to have little Buddy convinced that the crab was real and his Uncle Bubba had caught it. Those were the days! What good times they used to have!

He missed his oldest son. He hadn't talked to Buddy in fifteen years, but he never stopped missing that boy. Sometimes Buster wondered if he was to blame for the break. He never should have let Buddy marry that flighty little Wynn Ann but Buddy had insisted he was in love with her and she was in a family way. What was he supposed to do? He let Buddy drop out of SMU and marry the girl. A big June wedding at St. Mary's Cathedral with all the trimmings.

They had moved into the Sand Castle with him and Buddy went to work at Garland, Inc. Four years later the whole thing exploded. It was one of the few times in his life Buster felt he didn't have a choice, but damn, he had expected more from his own son. Hadn't Buddy learned his lesson the first time he knocked up a girl? No, not Buddy. Married four years and already cattin' around. Never even waited for the seven-year itch. No, not Buddy.

And leave it to him to do it up brown: taking up with a little colored girl Buster himself had hired as a copy girl at the paper. A smart girl, too. Buster had expected more from her. He supposed she'd started listening to Buddy's problems and instead of making things better, that only made them worse. Much worse!

And there was a child involved. If he'd taken Buddy's side he would have lost his grandchild. In a rare moment of tenderness he'd taken the little girl into his arms and promised her she'd never have to leave the Sand Castle. Her idiotic mother had already told the girl everything — how could he trust her with custody? Tammy Lynn was a Garland and had to be raised like one. He didn't like to think about the bastard his son had sired on the colored girl.

Buster had to choose between his son and his granddaughter, and since Buddy had already demonstrated such poor character, Buster chose Tammy Lynn. Since then, he and his oldest son had not exchanged a single word. Their paths rarely crossed and when they did they avoided acknowledging each other. Texas was a big state in a big country.

He and Buddy never had a written contract. It had always been understood that Buddy would be taking over Garland, Inc., one day. Once that was out of the question, Buster felt he owed him some kind of settlement, and through Myles McLean he offered it: one million dollars cash and another million toward any business Buddy might want to buy or start up. That was in 1969, Buster recalled, when a million still meant something. Buddy sent back word he wanted no part of it.

Damn, he missed that boy! Some boy! Buddy was nearly forty now; making a name for himself. The real-estate market in Texas had collapsed, but he was thriving up in New York. Buddy had always had his daddy's nose for an opportunity.

He'd even married the colored girl after she had his son. Buster snorted at the thought of that. At least Buddy always did right by the girls *after* the damage was done. Buddy moved in different circles now — maybe they didn't blink at a mixed marriage but it would never go over in

Galveston. But then Buddy didn't seem to give a damn what went over in Galveston anymore.

And that, more than anything else, marked him as his father's son.

Buster kept track of him, of course. It was hard not to. Buddy Garland's picture seemed to be everywhere: *Texas Monthly, Ultra, Fortune, Business Week*. He wondered where Buddy had found the money to get started again.

He knew all about Buddy's mansion in Palm Beach, in fact he'd even had his pilot fly over it when he was in Florida. He couldn't see much from a plane but it seemed a good enough spread. And there was the penthouse in New York—Cordell had shown him pictures of it from *Architectural Digest* magazine. Buddy and Zena had two children now—the boy who had caused all the trouble and a little girl born two years later, since their marriage. At least they were legitimate now.

He was always hearing about Buddy Garland, but who knew for sure how well he was doing? These days in Texas even the mighty were falling: Connally, Murchison, Davis, even a Moody—all millionaires who ended up in bankruptcy court. There was no telling how Buddy would end up, Buster told himself, or why he should even be considering taking his son back into the fold.

Buster was not sentimental, but as he entered Gaido's big old-fashioned seafood hall and headed for the table where he used to lunch regularly with his favorite son, he felt a great wave of sadness and regret wash over him like a Gulf Coast wave.

He remembered them playing baseball together and him teaching Buddy how to shoot at the cabin on Bull Bayou and the first time the boy got a duck on his own. Not like his tenderfooted brother! No, Buddy always killed like a man.

After that year at prep school—his mother Mona's idea—Buddy had taken up a little too much polish to suit Buster, but he'd always been a good old boy at heart.

The maître d' led Buster to his usual table, the one with a view of most of the room and, from the window, a good look across the street to the Gulf. The table was prominent, but there was no need to worry about being overheard; it was a nice distance from any of the others. As he made his way he nodded and waved to diners at other tables, for Gaido's was always crowded at dinner.

Myles McLean was already at the table, waiting for him and halfway through a Pearl beer. The waitress, who knew Buster well, immediately brought over a platter of cold fresh oysters and Buster dived right in.

The two men made an odd pair. Buster was a good twenty years older and looked his age. McLean was tall and lanky, in his early forties now but with a kind of boyishness about him made even more acute by his soft laconic drawl. His country demeanor was deceptive, and Buster knew well that McLean possessed one of the sharpest minds in Texas.

"You know, Myles, if it wasn't for lawyers, we wouldn't need lawyers," he began, after he had gobbled up three oysters. Myles might just possibly be the third man in the world that Buster trusted. He was about Buddy's age—he and his sister Fayette had been friends of his—but Myles lacked the drive—the killer instinct—of a true Garland.

"Exactly my thinking, sir," Myles said affably. He was used to Buster's opinions and in this case, at least, he agreed with him.

Although their table was out of earshot of those around it, Buster still lowered his voice. "Did you ever think about what will happen to Garland, Inc., after I'm gone?" he asked, then signaled their waitress to bring more beer for both of them.

"No, sir," Myles drawled, unsure of where this conversation was going. "But let's hope that day is a far way off."

"It ain't," Buster snapped. "It ain't far off at all. It's around the goddamn corner. My doctors tell me I'm a walking dead man."

Myles slipped easily into his trial lawyer's posture, his face betraying no surprise at this bombshell. "Doctors can be wrong, sir," he said.

Buster snorted. "I expect more sense from you. When I tell you I'm a dying man, do me the honor of assuming I know what I'm talking about."

"Yes, sir." Myles McLean's placid temperament was

never affected by Buster's outbursts. It was the thing that kept him his own man and what had held Buster's respect over the years.

The waitress arrived with their orders: oysters skewered with bacon and grilled onions and peppers for Miles; fried soft shell crabs for Buster. He waited until she went for more beers before he resumed.

"I want Garland, Inc., to stay in one piece and in the family," he said. "But who'll run it after I'm gone?"

"Well, sir, I'm sure old Cordell feels the same way as you do about keeping it all together."

Buster made a face and stabbed his crab with such force it almost slid off the plate. "That boy is a pussy. If he couldn't handle his own wife, how can he handle my company?" An odd glint flickered in the old man's blue eyes. "Just 'cause he plays in my corral don't make him the only horse in my stable, you know."

Myles was used to this, too, and to Buster's hints about other progeny who didn't play in his backyard. Given the way Buster's grown-up children had turned out, he supposed it was natural for the old man to wish for others.

"You know that boy actually told me he was publishing the *Sentinel-Wave* as a public service? I said, 'Excuse me, son, I thought I bought it to make some money.' I never gave a goddamn what people like the Moodys and the Luries thought. Went my own way. Always."

"I saw your nephew Lamar this morning at the yacht club," Myles put in. "He's always been interested in the business."

Buster snorted again. "You better stop putting away all that beer, boy, if you think I'd ever give that playboy a piece of my action. I got to take care of him 'cause he's my brother's boy, but he's got no more sense than my dog Lyndon. And at least old Lyndon's loyal. First thing you know, Lamar'd sell out to some Japs."

"There's always Belinda."

"Ah, Belinda Sue . . ." The old man paused and sighed. "It's just too bad she wasn't born a man."

Myles McLean had always thought Belinda Sue Garland was pretty perfect as a female and he told Buster as much. The old man looked at him sharply. "Still carrying

44

one for her son?" he said. "I told her when she married Arden Yates she was picking the wrong man, but she wouldn't listen to me."

Myles felt any response would be an admission of guilt, so he said nothing.

Buster went on. "Now she's all wrapped up in that hotel! Imagine! Working too hard. She's making her brother Cordell nervous. Trouble is, that was only supposed to keep her occupied a few months, till she got over Arden. I never expected her to turn the hotel around. She's not going to like it when I tell her the old building has to come down."

"You're tearing down the Maison Rouge?" Myles said with surprise. "When?"

Buster shrugged. "Sooner or later. Imagine what a highrise I could put up there!"

"But the Maison Rouge," Myles said. "It's a landmark. People love that building."

"Listen to me, Myles," Buster said, his genial tone never wavering. "Never, ever, fall in love with a property. It's the road to ruin. There's no reason to get sentimental in business."

Myles moved to change the subject. "How about this de Young? Is it serious between him and Tammy Lynn? Has he shown any interest in coming into the business?"

Buster had finished his meal and grimaced as he lit up a Macanudo. "Phew. In a year I'm going to be in my grave, Myles, and I want to rest there. You suppose I'd lay easy knowing my life's work was in the hands of a man with an earring?"

At that moment there was a rustle in the dining room and then a silence. Both men looked up and saw Fayette Cramer leaving the rear dining room. She was with a tall rugged-looking man Myles didn't recognize at first, but the stillness in the room and the way heads turned to their table made him realize it was Buddy Garland. Fayette nodded at them and smiled but didn't approach their table, heading quickly for the exit. Buddy Garland and his father carefully avoided eye contact. As soon as Fayette and Buddy Garland were out the door the room seemed to heave a collective sigh and resumed the hum of conversa-

45

tion just as Buster resumed his without missing a beat.
"I'm not interested in past history, Myles, and I've got no future. All I care about now is Garland, Inc.," he said.

Myles felt that at this point all Buster's obvious heirs had been exhausted and he was relieved that Buster saw the folly of appointing family members to run the company. "It seems to me that what you're talking about, sir, is professional management. You can organize Garland, Inc., into a family trust and bring in professional managers to run it. Put your heirs on a board of directors and they can hire or fire the managers. Like the King Ranch."

Buster waved a paw in the air. "Don't want no pussies that can't bake their own pie cutting into mine." He shook his head. "No, boy, you know as well as I do that the only man who could carry my pickax has to be a lowlife sumbitch like yours truly. Ain't that right?" Buster's blue eyes were shining.

Myles made one last stab at the answer. "How about going public? Sell shares in Garland, Inc. You'd make a fortune and you can get out. Divide up the cash among your heirs and you're home free."

Buster motioned for the check and stood up, tossing several bills on the table and muttering. "Years ago when Bubba — God have mercy on him — and I were strapped for money we sold shares in one little old company. That was Lone Star Tool and Die. And damned if that little old company hasn't been a thorn in my side ever since."

Myles was starting to feel like he had lost a war without even knowing he was in it, but he was used to Buster and his ways. The method to the old man's madness would be revealed soon enough. Meanwhile, as usual, lunch with Buster had been far from boring. Myles rose to follow him outside.

They walked to the parking lot together where Buster's yellow Cadillac was beside Myles's blue Ford. Buster told McLean he was heading home to the Sand Castle, but when he reached the west end of the Island he pulled to the side of the road and made a call from the car phone. After that, he kept going several miles farther, until he was in the swampy area known as Bull Bayou. He'd kept a hunting cabin there for years. It was where he'd taught his

46

sons to shoot. It was almost dark by now, but it was too early for a moon. The only illumination came from his Cadillac's headlights.

The clustered cabins were little more than shacks, built on pilings that extended out over the bayou. It was off season, and Buster knew the other cabins would be deserted. He noticed with pleasure that a light was on in the Garland cabin and a sleek brown Mercedes was parked outside. He cut off his car lights as he neared the car and approached the cabin as quietly as he could. He would have enjoyed taking his guest by surprise. But as he gently pushed open the door, his son was already standing, a glass of bourbon in one hand, a lit cigar in the other.

"Hello Daddy," said Buddy Garland. "Long time no see."

The two men, father and son, shook hands stiffly as Buster entered the cabin. It was small and tidy, three rooms furnished with an old leather office couch, cast off-tables and chairs, and a fold-up card table. One wall was taken up by a fieldstone fireplace.

Buddy was already halfway through a fifth of Wild Turkey, and he poured out a glass for his father. Up close, Buster could see that his son had aged. His dark hair was starting to go gray and his tanned face was lined. People used to say the boy looked like his father and now Buster could see it, although Buddy was leaner and there had always been something a little more refined about him. Buster supposed that was Mona's Clinton blood in him.

Buster, never at a loss for words, was suddenly searching awkwardly for something to say and wondering if it had been a good idea to suggest this meeting after all. At last he managed to take charge. "Well, son, how are you?" he asked.

"Fine as frog's hair," Buddy said, handing his father the glass of bourbon.

The glass almost disappeared in the grip of Buster's paw as he tossed it down with a gulp and handed it back to his son. He settled in a leather wing chair near the fire that

47

Buddy had started. Without a word, Buddy refilled his father's glass and handed it back, then sat down where the base of the fireplace jutted out, forming a stone bench at his father's feet. He put the bottle to rest beside him.

"Since you were on the island, I thought we should talk," Buster boomed, having regained some of his bravado. He was both pleased and uneasy with this mature, confident Buddy. Buster had expected his son to have changed, but the mature Buddy was less son and more man. He saw that he would have to revise some of his strategy.

Buddy Garland was also taking in the situation. His open face had hardened, and his eyes narrowed, taking on a shrewd expression. Maybe that was the look he brought to the table when he did business, Buster thought. He had heard Buddy was quite the wheeler-dealer these days. What made his son think he needed that look here, Buster wondered.

Buddy Garland was also doing some recalculating now that he was seeing his father up close for the first time in fifteen years. In the restaurant and on the car phone he had been the old Buster—big, loud and bold—but here he looked his age, his face was deeply lined and there were liver spots on his face and hands. He still stood erect, though, and his sharp blue eyes had the calm, unnerving focus Buddy remembered so well.

"You're looking good, Daddy," he said.

"I'm so-so," Buster answered, taking more time with his second bourbon.

He wanted to know exactly where Buddy stood. He was his son, but what Buster had in mind was not a sentimental matter. There was no room for sentiment in business.

"I hear you're buying KGAL," he remarked casually, and was pleased to note the surprise that momentarily flickered across Buddy's face. The sight of it brought out Buster's big, booming laugh, the first time he'd laughed since entering the cabin.

"Now where did you hear that?" Buddy answered. "I'm talkin' to Fayette about syndicating her show."

This made Buster laugh even more. *God damn, he'd trained this boy well. How had he ever let him go?*

48

"When I seen you with Miss Fayette Cramer, I supposed something was up! Is that what you're doing on the Island?" Buster saw that Buddy was irritated and, as a peace gesture, he took the bottle and poured refills for the two of them. They said no more about business that night. Instead, he brought up the subject of Buddy's daughter.

"I guess you've heard about Tammy Lynn's boyfriend?" Buster remarked.

"Is he all right?" Buddy asked. It was awkward to ask about the daughter he hadn't seen in fifteen years, or, to be honest, given much thought to. "And how is she?"

"Headstrong like her daddy," Buster answered. "Looks like a Garland but takes after her mother in other ways. Right now she's off at some ashram mediating."

"Is she pretty?" Buddy asked.

"Not bad. The way they dress now—all black and hair short as a boy's—doesn't help. A little featherheaded like her mother."

"And the boyfriend?"

"We'll just have to see about him," Buster answered. "Not someone you'd want to make a deal with," he added.

Buddy Garland knew that his father was never at ease discussing sentimental things and he was enjoying Buster's discomfort immensely. He was still irritated that Buster had tricked him into tipping his hand about Fayette Cramer's show. It was the kind of stunt he'd pull on a kid just out of Harvard.

When Buddy had walked into the cabin after so many years and was engulfed in the warm, fetid smell of old times and shrimp and oysters and the swampy bayou, he'd felt like a boy again and was filled with dread at the idea of seeing his father. Would Buster start up again about his past mistakes? But now that the old man was here, Buddy felt more at ease.

"And how's Cordell?" he asked.

"He'd like me to retire," Buster answered. "Go on a world cruise." He stretched out the word so that it sounded like something full of *ooze* and not like anything Buster Garland would be caught dead on.

"Maybe he's right," Buddy ventured. "You've made

your pile. Get out and leave some opportunities for the rest of us."

Buster looked at him so sharply that Buddy wondered if he'd gone too far. *Damn, I've made my pile, too. I shouldn't have to pussyfoot around my daddy at my age,* he thought with sudden anger. *Besides, he's the one who called me.*

"Yes," Buster agreed, taking Buddy by surprise. "I ask myself what I'm going to do about Garland, Inc. I'm not going to live forever, you know."

Actually, Buddy was among those who did expect his father to live forever and this kind of talk disturbed him. He could no more imagine his father out of Garland Inc., than he could imagine him out of the Sand Castle. Was that why Buster had invited him here? Did he want to sell out? Buddy was successful, but he still measured his net worth in millions. There was no way he could buy out his father—that was talking billions.

Was it possible that his father was lonely? Did he just want to talk? Was Buster going to become one of those garrulous old hogs who rambled on about the good old days? But Buddy had seen Buster eyeing the waitresses at Gaidos—there was nothing old about him then.

From Buster's point of view, however, this little reunion was going as well as he had expected. It was good to be with a man he trusted—and he still trusted Buddy, in spite of his past mistakes. He couldn't talk to Belinda about the price of oil. He wasn't about to discuss real estate or banking with Cordell. And as for Myles McLean—the lawyer could get awfully Methodist when it came to Buster's more creative business practices. No—Buddy and only Buddy was his favorite companion: he understood Buster's disgust at Shean Moody's trial, his sadness at J.R. McConnell's bankruptcy . . .

This tentative reunion suddenly gave Buster hope that his life's work might survive him after all—but it would have to be with Buddy's cooperation.

Buddy Garland was a good listener. He watched Buster's face, nodding or asking a pointed question once in a while, without disturbing the smooth, steady flow of the old man's thoughts.

That was how they passed the night until Buster dozed off, and when dawn came to the bayou Buddy surprised his old man with a breakfast of ham and eggs and grits with red-eye gravy before they shook hands again, and, without making any promises, got into their cars and headed off in opposite directions.

Chapter Four

While Tammy Lynn was off at her ashram meditating for a week, she had generously allowed Brice the use of her Porsche, and as he pulled to a stop at the circular drive of the Maison Rouge, he took in the old building with interest. It certainly looked a lot better than the last time he had seen it. Although it had always been a landmark, no one bothered much about keeping it up for years. The name was an oddity, for the Maison Rouge was neither red nor a mere *maison*, but a sprawling Spanish-style pile of white stucco walls, red tiled roofs, countless wrought-iron balconies, and a wide sweeping green lawn that ran practically all the way to the Gulf of Mexico.

A white-uniformed valet who recognized Tammy Lynn's car raced to open the door. He looked surprised when Brice stepped out and handed the keys to him. Brice enjoyed that. He planned to be driving his own Porsch up to the door very soon.

Brice walked through the hotel's bustling atrium lobby, noting how well the old building had been restored. Somebody seemed to appreciate its history, and instead of attempting to turn the old mausoleum into a sleek, modern monstrosity, they had lovingly restored the old paneling and murals to their former grandeur.

He had been told that Wiley Muehl's office was near the kitchen, and he headed in that direction, recalling the days when he and his buddies would help out there in return for the chance to clean the giant vats of ice cream. He had one pal whose father was the house detective and they managed to filch his keys and copy them so they had the run of the hotel. Brice thought he probably knew a lot more about the Maison Rouge than Belinda Garland, even after all these years.

Funny, he thought, he'd only come back to the Island because he was broke, and he had no intention of staying. Yet in the past few days, Galveston had crept back into his blood. Twenty years ago, he'd been on fire to leave, lighting out for New York right after Ball High School graduation, carrying nothing more than his father's boundless optimism and his mother's faith in the future. He had no idea what he would end up doing in New York, but he had to try to make it there.

He had no trouble finding the kind of work that would keep him alive, once he got to New York. He was a waiter in an Italian restaurant on the East Side, a Click model; he even got a bit part in a movie shooting in Little Italy. He shared an apartment in a run-down building on Riverside Drive with a rotating slate of waiters—Italians, Yugoslavians, French, and Taiwanese. He discovered he had an ear for languages and began to pick them up from his roommates. There were plenty of girls, too: models and actresses he met on assignments; girls he picked up in Central Park; women in smart suits who would watch him with hungry eyes and slip him their business cards.

He went everywhere on foot or on his ten-speed bike. And he discovered food. He became fascinated with cooking techniques, and with his gift for gab he managed to talk his way into Chinese noodle factories on Mott Street and rib parlors in Harlem. He started getting standby gigs as a cook. He never claimed any formal training, no Cordon Bleu, no diplomas from any fancy Swiss hotel school, but there was no doubt he had a natural gift. He took his dates to the Four Seasons and Lutèce. They were expensive, but he examined each course like he was Sherlock Holmes, trying to determine ingredients and cooking techniques. He was a man obsessed, who thought nothing of dropping in on the kitchens of four-star restaurants like Mon Chou and Solange, just to observe the master chefs at work.

They recognized one of their own and allowed him to watch all but their most secret processes.

Imagine! A kid raised on SpaghettiOs preparing entrees at Mon Chou!

He developed his own style: a sophisticated American style based on America's great range of fresh produce but with a continental touch. He discovered that there were others doing the same thing in small, exclusive restaurants around the country, but he didn't feel competitive: the time was right.

In those days, the late 1970's, New York was restaurant mad. Restaurants were suddenly show business and everyone wanted to follow the hot ones. He had no trouble finding backers to set him up in a restaurant of his own, and when they got bored or went broke, he could always find others.

Meanwhile, he was determined to learn all he could. Having grown up on Eggo-s and Velveeta, he had a lot of catching up to do.

He sighed at the thought of all he had learned. New York and those days seemed very far away now.

Being back in Galveston, even temporarily, was going to take some adjusting.

Belinda Garland was getting a manicure at the Maison Rouge beauty salon. She had imported a hairdresser from Rome to manage the place, and it was a point of pride with her that women came down from Houston and up from Corpus Christi just to have Lucio or one of his assistants cut their hair. She had a feeling that Lucio and his team of handsome Italians were providing more personal services as well, but that was their business. She never interfered with her employees' personal lives. And there were a lot of lonely women out there.

"We have a new color I think you'll like, Miss Belinda," the manicurist told her. "Hurricane Red."

"Sounds stormy," Belinda said, and allowed Honey to coat her nails with the new red. To her it looked exactly like all the previous reds.

Belinda always made it a point to stop in at Lucio's. Men could joke about hairdressers and beauty salons, but there was no telling what kind of news you could pick up there. And running a hotel as big as the Maison Rouge was like being mayor of a small town. It paid to keep an ear to the ground.

She looked up at the clock. It was almost two and no sign of Buster. She'd called the Sand Castle and his houseman had assured her he'd left. At his office downtown they said he was in a meeting and couldn't be disturbed. Where was he? And where was her lease? She decided to call him again. But not from the salon. She'd wait and use a house phone. She was there to pick up gossip, not to provide it.

On his way to meet with Wiley Muehl, Brice passed a tall, beautiful blonde. She smiled at him. He smiled back but kept moving. Galveston was crawling with beautiful women. In fact, the entire state of Texas was infested with beauty queens. Brice could always tell them by the pageant walk: head up, neck elongated, eyes bright and smile dazzling. After fifteen years in New York, he couldn't get enough Texas smiles, but at this particular moment he was not looking to make new friends.

When he was ready he intended to go to Houston. Galveston was just the beginning. He would make a name for himself this summer, then he could get the kind of investors he would need to open big in Houston. Right now, all he had to do was make it.

The beauty queen was still flirting with him and he realized he had been staring. He moved on through the atrium, watching the milling crowd. The Maison Rouge drew a mixed bag of guests, but they all looked rich. There were piles of Gucci and Vuitton moving on carts pushed by bellhops, and even the plainest women were decked out in casual clothes from Missoni and Calvin Klein. He wondered if any of them were available to invest in his restaurant.

Tammy Lynn was a lifesaver for now, but all her money was controlled by her grandfather. It was great staying in her grandfather's guest house, and driving her car, but there was little more she could do for him now.

He noticed Belinda Garland standing by a potted palm

55

and talking into a house phone. He recognized her from the barbecue yesterday. Tall, honey-blond, and aloof. She looked back at him without a sign of recognition.

What the hell. It was going to be a long summer. He smiled at her.

Deep in thought, Belinda Garland frowned and turned away.

Later for you, Miss Belinda, he thought. It was going to be a *very* long summer.

Belinda Garland had recognized Brice de Young, but she had other things on her mind. She was in the middle of preparations for a major banquet honoring the fashion designer Ciprianna that was just days away, and her chef had just been picked up by immigration. She'd even called Myles McLean to try to bail the poor man out, but it was no use. Jean Claude was already on a 747 back to France. She had just reluctantly ordered her manager to give Brice de Young a tryout in the kitchen, but she would let Wiley Muehl handle the details. The less she had to do with de Young the better. She could not forget the way he had stared at her at Buster's barbecue and she could not forget the way it made her feel.

Still, she tried to push such thoughts from her mind. She had more important things to think about, such as where was her father and the lease he'd promised her?

It was almost one o'clock by the time Belinda finally got Buster on his car phone. "Weren't we supposed to have a meeting today?" she demanded.

"Now, darlin', what's your hurry?" he chided her. "Why don't you go swimming or something? You don't get enough fun."

"I have a hotel to run," she reminded him. Funny, she thought, how her work consumed her, while Buster, with his myriad enterprises all over the world, seemed to thrive on it and never passed up the chance for a good time. He made it all look so easy!

"Now, Belinda, I appreciate everything you've done for the Maison Rouge, but you have to remember that it's a little old fish in a great big pool, and I do have other things on my mind."

Yes, Belinda could not help thinking, and lately most of them seemed to concern Valdene Sykes. Now that she knew her brother Cordell was promoting this relationship, she couldn't regard Valdene as just another one of her father's flings. Suppose Buster decided to marry her? Suppose they had children? What could Cordell be thinking of?

Cordell, who was always so concerned that Belinda would somehow edge him out of his hard-earned position as Buster's heir apparent, had introduced this woman into the family. Was it possible, she wondered, that Cordell had something up his sleeve? Or was he just a fool?

The funny thing, Belinda told herself, was that she did not care if Cordell ended up with all of Garland, Inc., someday. Once she had control of the Maison Rouge she would be very happy.

But Buster still owned the property and, technically, she still answered to him. She wanted to talk to him about her plans. And she wanted to get that deed in writing.

"Is this the way you treat a trusted executive?" she demanded.

"There's no such thing as a trusted executive," he snapped back. But he got her point.

"Then when can I see you?"

"How about dinner tomorrow night?" he asked. "At the Maisonette. That way you won't even have to leave your precious hotel."

"Of course," she said, ignoring his little dig. Maybe she did spend too much time at the hotel, but she couldn't help herself. She'd failed in her marriage, she'd failed Arden, and in the year since his death the hotel had become her obsession. Her lover. Her child.

Wiley Muehl, manager and general factotum of the Maison Rouge, was a tall, craggy-faced man of about fifty. He had none of the oiliness of some hotel managers and could have easily passed for a wheeler-dealer himself. He got a kick out of it when visiting tourists mistook him for Governor Connally, but that was about as far as his sense of humor went.

His steel-gray hair was slicked back and his steel-gray eyes missed nothing. He was a man who had learned to trust nothing but his judgment. And he did not like the looks of Brice de Young, even if Miss Belinda had said to give him a chance. The way he figured it was that Miss Belinda didn't have much choice. Her spoiled little niece had taken this stray dog in and the rest of them were going to have to see that he got fed. What the hell, he told himself, struggling to be philosophical. The Maison Rouge needed a cook anyway. Might as well give this one a try.

Brice asked Muehl if he wanted him to prepare something in the kitchen.

"That won't be necessary," Muehl assured him. "Miss Belinda says you come highly recommended." Privately he was thinking that Miss Tammy Lynn's recommendation on a bed partner might not have much to do with the quality of his cooking. And they had the big Cirprianna bash coming up in a few days. Miss Belinda expected that party to finally put the Maison Rouge on the Texas map. He sure hoped this guy knew more about food than just saving his own bacon. "How long you known Miss Tammy Lynn?" he said coolly.

Brice looked at him but did not answer. He considered the question inappropriate, an invasion of privacy. It was amazing what two weeks with an heiress and a twenty-minute ride behind the wheel of a Porsche had done for his confidence and self-esteem.

Changing the subject, he asked to see the rest of the hotel, especially the kitchen where he would be working. He was anxious to get the names of the hotel's suppliers, too. There were opportunities for kickbacks there and he was anxious to get to them. The sooner he got his stake together the sooner he would be out of there.

Muehl was only too glad to show Brice around, and he seemed to take an owner's pride in the operation.

A born lackey, Brice thought, as he listened to Muehl sing Belinda Garland's praises and extoll her restoration of the hotel.

58

Chapter Five

The next morning, dawn found Buster Garland relaxing in his king-size bed in the tower bedroom of the Sand Castle and enjoying himself immensely. Looking down he could see the tousled black curls of the multi-talented Valdene Sykes.

Valdene Sykes. Widow of televangelist Prescott Sykes, who had been killed in the crash of his private plane just a year earlier. Buster had been a great admirer of Reverend Sykes's business acumen, at least, although he was indifferent to the reverend's preaching. Buster had even had Sykes and Valdene down to his annual Fourth of July barbecue a few times and made it a point to send a fine arrangement of yellow roses to Sykes's funeral in Memphis.

Buster had not seen Valdene since then, until she turned up at a horse auction in Victoria just a few weeks ago. His son Cordell had invited her to join them, and to Buster's surprise and pleasure, Valdene had been buzzing around him like a May fly on manure ever since.

When Valdene confided she would be spending the summer in a beach house Sykes had left her in Galveston it seemed natural that they ought to get together, and get together they had, over and over for the past weeks. She had practically moved into the Sand Castle, and the little beach house had been forgotten.

"Easy, easy," Buster whispered. "I don't want to go the way of old Prescott."

Valdene lifted her head and pouted prettily. "Now, Buster, you know old Prescott died in a plane crash. I had nothing to do with it."

"Be that as it may, darlin', you're a handful, and no doubt about it."

Together Valdene and Prescott Sykes had built up one of the most popular and lucrative televangelism systems in the country. They'd made a great team, with Prescott's hellfire preaching and Valdene's earthy sex appeal. She still had the look of a country music star, with great masses of black hair, a strong-boned face, and good features accented by heavy makeup.

"I just love these curls," Buster laughed, ruffling her elaborate coiffure.

"And not fake, either, like Loretta and Dolly," she had hurried to show Buster. "Go ahead, pull it."

He insisted on taking her word for it, but he demonstrated his appreciation for the whole package. Valdene's oak-brown eyes and high cheekbones hinted at her Indian blood. Her generous breasts had been enhanced by silicone implants (although she did not tell Buster). At thirty-five, the rest of her was long and rangy, the kind of body that could easily go scrawny if life got hard. Fortunately, Prescott Sykes had always pampered her and now she was expecting the same from Buster Garland. She sat up and began to lick his nipples. He gently pushed her head away and kissed her on the forehead.

"Enough, darlin'. Old Buster's got to get up and start dragging his pickax."

"Ah, Buster, I thought we were gonna play all day. It's Saturday!"

It took a minute or two for Buster to shift his great bulk into a sitting position. Then he reached for the in-house phone and alerted Luz in the kitchen that there would be two for breakfast and they would be down in twenty minutes. Luz was also getting used to having Mrs. Sykes around.

"Twenty minutes?" Valdene purred. "You spoil all my fun."

He pushed her out of the bed. "Come on, my little firecracker. Get in there and make yourself respectable for my cook."

"Oh great! Now I'm dressing up for a Mexican."

Buster ignored her sarcasm as he lumbered into his shower. The master bedroom had baths and dressing rooms on either side, one for the master and one for the mistress. He had explained all that to Valdene the first time she stayed at the Sand Castle.

"Does that mean I'm your mistress?" Valdene had asked.

But Buster knew better than to encourage her. "Now, darlin', that just means I want you to have a nice little powder room all to your own self."

"I still don't know why I have to rush off," she pouted when she joined him on the terrace that overlooked Galveston Bay. As Luz silently served them breakfast, (pancakes with bacon for Buster, toast with marmalade for Valdene), Buster turned from staring out at the Bay to look at Valdene appreciatively. Her black hair was tousled and she was wearing tight jeans and high white boots, but she had not put on a shirt, merely wrapped a short red silk kimono around her, barely covering her breasts. He recognized her little defiance and was amused by it. He liked a woman with spirit, and Valdene Sykes certainly had that in spades.

"Now you just go home, darlin'. And we'll get together tomorrow," he said, as soon as Luz left them alone.

"Oh," Valdene said, sticking out her bottom lip the way she had seen Tanya Tucker do it at the Country Music Awards. "Why can't I come to dinner tonight?" she demanded. "You disappeared last night, crept in at dawn like I was a wife you were avoiding. Do you want me to go back to Nashville, Buster?"

"No, darlin'. Of course not." Buster regarded Valdene as a smart lady, but there were times when she could be downright dense. He had already explained to her that he and Belinda had to talk about business today. He didn't want to discuss yesterday's meeting with Buddy with anyone else, especially not Valdene.

There would be plenty of time for her to get to know his children, when and if he decided to bring Valdene into the Garland family circle. Meanwhile, he had to find out if that circle even existed anymore.

"My, my, darlin', you look good," Buster Garland boomed as he kissed his daughter. He had been waiting for her in the small bar off the Maisonette, trying to recall if he and his brother had ever dreamed they would own such a fine a hotel.

Buster Garland and his brother Bubba, were born on Galveston Island in the 1920's, shortly before Texas and the rest of the country were plunged into the Great Depression. Times were hard and few people were generous, and when their parents died of influenza the boys went to the Rosenberg Orphanage, which was full up with boys just like them.

By the time they were old enough to be on their own, war was heating up in Europe and the Garland brothers enlisted in the Navy, mostly because Galveston was a port town and they were familiar with ships. They washed back up in town after the war, but recognized that opportunities lay a little farther north on the mainland, in the oil patch, where the two of them launched a booming business in drilling supplies, then diversifying into other businesses all over Texas and what would come to be called the Sun Belt. They were all over the Southwest, but their home remained Galveston . . .

Especially when Buster wedded Miss Mona Clinton, daughter of one of the mercantile families that had run Galveston since the Revolutionary War. The old families had always snubbed him and Bubba, but they could hardly do the same to his children: they would belong to the Pelican Yacht Club, make their debuts at the Artillery Club.

Mona bore him two sons: Buddy, his oldest and his favorite, and Cordell, who now looked to be his heir. And then there was Belinda who seemed to have inherited her mother's looks and her daddy's brains.

"Don't try to put me off with flattery, Daddy," Belinda said, smiling sweetly and coaxing him toward their table in the dining room the way she might have once coaxed him to look at a pony she had trained. Her excitement about her new project had been simmering for days and Buster's delays had only sharpened her desire. A deed to the Maison Rouge was just the beginning of her plans. Once she had undisputed title to the hotel, she would be able to get financing to expand onto the other side of the Island. The difference would be that the next property would be hers.

"Well," he said as they were seated in a quiet corner of the busy dining room. "What is this big deal you've got going?"

Now it was Belinda's turn to be cool. She looked at his empty glass. "Let's get you another drink first," she said. Her nod was almost imperceptible, but in seconds a waiter had swept away their empty glasses and returned with a fresh glass of chardonnay for Belinda and a tumbler of Jack Daniel's for her father. She wondered if he was impressed with how well drilled her staff was but refused to give him the satisfaction of asking. She was sick of always needing his approval.

"Well?" Buster said. He was enjoying her little game, for he certainly recognized it as a game. In fact, he was pleased. The girl had learned a lot in the past year.

But, he reminded himself, she had a lot more to learn, and he had no time to teach her. Besides, she would never be another Buddy. He only hoped Buddy would come to his senses and forget the past. He was willing to.

"Well, Belinda," he repeated. "What is it you're so excited about?"

Belinda took a deep breath. It was now or never. "Did you know the Delancy Street warehouse is coming up for sale?" she said.

Buster cocked a bushy white eyebrow and his blue eyes narrowed with sudden interest. "That's been tied up in court for years," he said. It was well known that the feuding Delancy heirs had tied up the estate in the Texas courts from Galveston to Amarillo. One of the casualties was the enormous redbrick Victorian warehouse on Delancy Street downtown which had been sitting empty and abandoned for the last ten years. "What makes you think it's for sale now?" he asked.

"I heard about it in the beauty salon yesterday. One of the heirs was having a manicure and I got to talking with her. You always told me to talk to everybody. In fact," she

63

added, "it's a good thing you stood me up yesterday. Yesterday I just wanted a deed to the Maison Rouge. Today I have much bigger plans."

"Oh," he said. "And what might those plans be?"

"I want to renovate that warehouse. I want to turn it into a hotel-spa-restaurant complex with luxury shops. I've been thinking about it for a while, but the location had to be just right. And Delancy Street is the perfect spot. It's in the Historic District. It's close to the cruise ships. It's got a great view of the channel . . ."

"Whoa there," Buster said, raising his big hands as if to ward off her onslaught. "What about the numbers?"

She smiled. "I knew you were going to ask me that," she said. "But I've only had twenty-four hours to work on this. The property is going to be listed at seventeen million dollars, but I think we can get it for fifteen if we offer cash. And I've called a few architects and contractors to see if they can get us some estimates."

"Us?" he repeated.

"Of course. I want us to go into this together. Think of it. Just what downtown Galveston needs: a year-round attraction. What do you say? Will you help me buy the land?"

Buster had listened to her proposal with interest. It wasn't the first time he had been impressed by Belinda's imagination. She was just like Buddy.

He had never expected this. When he suggested she run the old Maison Rouge a year ago, he had only been thinking of some way to keep her occupied until she came to terms with her grief. He knew she blamed him for Arden's death, or at least for not doing anything about it, and she never understood that it was part of something bigger. Much to Buster's surprise and pleasure, his inexperienced daughter had demonstrated a real feel for the hotel business. He had bought the sprawling white elephant just for the land, planning to hold on to it for a few years and sell it at a profit as values went up. But Belinda had turned the Maison Rouge into a real little gusher. If only some of her brother Cordell's acquisitions for Garland, Inc., were as profitable!

He was beginning to wonder if the wrong child was

64

sitting in the offices of Garland, Inc., and to consider the possibilities of bringing Belinda into the real business. As lucrative as the Maison Rouge had become, it was just a grain of sand in the great sunny beach that was his conglomerate.

When Mona was alive it had all been so different, Buster reflected: he made the money and she dealt with the children. She seemed to be good at it, but when they grew up things started to go wrong. Buddy—his favorite, the one who was most like him—taking up with that colored girl and running off.

And Cordell marrying that spoiled little Lurie tramp. Cordell and Mona and everyone else was impressed with the girl's bloodlines, but he always knew she was a tramp and he was proved right. And Belinda, marrying into another fine old family and getting nothing but heartache. Buster did not regret Arden Yates's death at all, and although he had nothing to do with it, he considered Arden's fate good riddance to bad rubbish.

If only his daughter could see that.

There was a small commotion in the dining room, and Buster was much surprised to look up and see Valdene Sykes in jeweled and fringed white buckskin minidress and white boots being led to a nearby table, followed by a tall, distinguished-looking gray-haired man. She smiled brightly at Buster when she saw him looking, waved, and turned her attention to her escort.

Galveston was a small narrow island, physically and socially and Belinda recognized Valdene's escort at once. "Isn't that Claiborne Lurie with Valdene Sykes?" she asked. Had the relationship between Buster and Valdene cooled so soon? She could only hope.

Buster hid his annoyance well, but he was extremely irritated by Valdene's behavior. She was obviously still pouting because he had refused to take her to dinner with Belinda. But to show up here with Claiborne Lurie? She could do better than that bloodless stiff, he thought. Had she been seeing Claiborne all the time she had been sleeping with him?

Not one to be taken by surprise, Buster motioned for the maître d'.

"Is everything all right, Mr. Buster?" the man asked with concern. Usually Buster Garland did not like to be disturbed during his meal.

"I was just wondering, Wilson, if that might be my old friend Claiborne Lurie with Mrs. Sykes?" he said smoothly.

"Yes, sir. Yes, that's Mr. Lurie, sir." Wilson was uneasy. He knew very well that Garland and Lurie were far from friends. For one thing they had once been in-laws and the marriage between Mr. Buster's son and Mr. Lurie's daughter had not been a success.

But Buster was booming with good cheer. "I insist they join Miss Belinda and me. You go tell those two I insist on it."

Wilson was not the only one who was uneasy. Belinda recognized the horse-trading gleam in her father's eye, and she saw he had lost all interest in her Delancy Street deal. His attention was on Valdene and Lurie. She just hoped he was not going to make a scene. "Now, Daddy," she said. "If you really want to chat with Charlene's father, can't you do it during business hours?"

"Darlin', don't you fret. This is an excellent opportunity for you to get to know Mrs. Sykes. A lovely woman, and a most talented singer, I might add. You ought to talk to her about working your lounge."

"I've heard her sing at the barbecue, Daddy." *And I'm sure she knows all about working a lounge,* Belinda thought nastily, but that was still not the kind of thing she could say to Buster, not when she had an awful suspicion that her father was actually serious about Valdene. "Are you seeing her?"

Buster tried to look innocent. At such times his great, puffed face took on the look of the fattest boy in the choir denying he knew what had happened to the sacramental wine. "Mrs. Sykes is an old friend, and I hope that in some small way I have been able to comfort her."

Belinda thought for just a moment of how little he had comforted her when she lost Arden, but she quickly pushed the thought aside. If she dwelled on it too long she could easily hate her father. Too easily.

Arden Yates had been all her father was not, and

everything her mother wanted for her. As tall as Buster, he was reed slim, with black curly hair and chestnut eyes he had inherited from some long-forgotten Mexican great-grandmother. His roots went back as far as the Republic and his family's fortune had the fine patina of old money that long ago lost the taint of commerce. It no longer mattered where the Yates money came from, only that there was plenty of it.

And Arden had loved her. Of that Belinda was sure. Her mother had been all for it, although Buster had for once joined with the Yateses in objecting to the wedding. It did no good. The wedding went through with six bridesmaids and three flower girls at St. Mary's Cathedral.

Arden had no interest in working, and in those days Belinda had no interest in doing anything without Arden, so they had traveled around the world, sometimes just the two of them, sometimes joined by Texas friends, especially Aynsley Adder, son of Senator Adder. Aynsley liked to joke that every day he spent out of Texas translated into more votes for his daddy.

Finally, they had returned to the island, buying the run-down old Cutlass mansion and carefully restoring it. But Arden started to change. She blamed Aynsley Adder for that. The two old boys were inseparable and their antics got wilder and wilder until one night she got the call she had been dreading.

Totally drunk, Aynsley had driven Arden's Mercedes over the sea wall and into the Gulf. He had managed to escape, but his best friend, passed out drunk beside him, did not make it. Belinda always believed that Aynsley could have saved Arden, but he never even tried. Aynsley Adder was as responsible for her husband's death as if he had put a bullet to his head, and no one cared. Aynsley Adder was the son of a senator, with powerful connections throughout the state and the country, and he seemed to be immune to justice.

But she was Buster Garland's daughter, and she expected Aynsley Adder to pay.

To her surprise and rage, Buster refused to help her. He advised her to drop it. Gradually, as her anger and pain subsided, she came to suspect that the Adders had something on Buster, something that had kept him from doing the right thing. Her father had disappointed her for the first time in her life, and there was nothing she could do about it . . .

Nothing but wait, as he had taught her. There would come a time when she would settle that score. Aynsley Adder would pay for killing her husband.

It took less than a minute for Valdene and Claiborne Lurie to accept Buster's invitation and join Buster and Belinda at their table. Valdene was all exaggerated surprise at the tremendous coincidence of finding Buster having dinner with his daughter in the dining room of the hotel he owned and Belinda ran. If Claiborne Lurie was embarrassed to bump into Buster Garland while escorting Buster's new lady friend, however, he gave no sign of it.

Belinda noticed that Valdene's heavy lip gloss reflected the chandelier overhead. But although Valdene looked like a road house singer she also had a country girl's shrewdness and there was a hard, appraising look in her eye as she sized up Belinda.

Yes, Belinda could see how such a woman could appeal to her father. Valdene Sykes was no fool.

"Wow! This is a pleasure!" Valdene drawled breathlessly. "I'm just thrilled to meet you. I told Buster to introduce me to you at the barbecue, but you know what a rascal he can be. Old Buster talks about his little girl all the time."

Belinda managed to be courteous, although she was frustrated that Buster was evading discussing the deal with her. Now that Valdene and Lurie had joined them, there was no way she and Buster could talk business.

Valdene quickly managed to work in that Claiborne Lurie owned her late husband's record label, leaving the question open about whether theirs was a social or a business meeting. With an air of celebration, Buster ordered champagne.

"It's good to see you, Mrs. Yates," Lurie said smoothly, taking the seat beside Belinda.

"I'm back to Belinda Garland now," she corrected him.

"Of course."

68

The exaggerated courtesy was what Belinda had always remembered about Claiborne Lurie from the first time she met him, during the season she and his daughter Charlene came out together at the Artillery Club. Although the Garlands and the Luries moved in different circles, Belinda and Charlene became close friends and she often spent weeks at the Claiborne ranch on the Rio Strega. She never knew who else might turn up there. Like her father, Lurie had financial interests in broadcasting, entertainment, publishing, and real estate, as well as cotton and crude.

Belinda remembered coming down for an early swim at the Lurie ranch one morning and discovering a former governor passed out drunk on the pool chair. Charlene's mother, an heiress from the East, had taken off years earlier, and in those days Lurie's longtime mistress was a well-known photographer, but there was always a steady parade of beautiful and sophisticated women who were obviously there to pleasure him too.

"My Daddy sleeps with everyone but Mother," Charlene once confided.

Belinda sympathized with Charlene in those days, and she had been grateful her own father never seemed to get seriously involved with any of his women.

That was then, this was now, she thought glumly. And Valdene Sykes seemed different from the others. For one thing, Buster had always kept his love affairs away from his family. Cordell kept track of all his father's mistresses and kept Belinda informed with morally outraged bulletins via the telephone or their occasional dinners together. But here was Buster with Valdene, showing her off like she was a blue ribbon he picked up at the county fair.

Belinda wondered if Cordell even recognized how serious a rival Valdene could prove to be.

She certainly did, but there was no talking to him. He was so patently jealous of her success.

Cordell had not been pleased when Buster announced that Belinda was going to run the Maison Rouge. He turned her over to Wiley Muehl, the longtime manager of the hotel, who recognized her eagerness to learn. Although Cordell had told Muehl that Belinda would merely be a figurehead, Wiley soon learned otherwise, and he gladly shared all he knew including the finances of the operation.

She was at the hotel twelve hours a day. She sold the house she and Arden shared, and moved into the hotel penthouse.

When Cordell heard that he hit the roof. "We need to rent that out," he insisted. "We need the money to keep the operation in the black!"

"If that's what you're worried about, I'll lease the penthouse myself and pay out of my own pocket. The hotel will come out ahead."

"You're no businesswoman, Belinda," he snapped.

For the first time in her life, Belinda decided to stand up for herself, without Buster's help.

"It's my understanding that Daddy gave me complete charge of the Maison Rouge. If I want to be here twenty-four hours a day, that's my business."

"You're running this hotel into the ground," Cordell insisted.

She laughed. "Really, Cordell. This hotel was ready for the wrecking ball when Daddy gave it to me. I know neither of you expects much, so why don't you concern yourself with some of your really worthwhile properties and leave me alone?"

She fended him off that time, but she never got over it. Imagine! Cordell was jealous. He considered her a rival. That was the biggest surprise of all.

Belinda tried to concentrate on the menu. "We're trying out a new chef," she said, winking at Buster. "He comes highly recommended."

"Can he cook Texas?" Buster said, being perfectly aware that Belinda had hired Tammy Lynn's boyfriend. "That's what you need, darlin'. Home cookin'."

"People can get home cooking at home, Daddy. They come here for something special."

But Belinda was looking at the carefully calligraphed menu with mounting disbelief. She had not discussed the menu with Brice de Young, but the understanding had been that he would take over and execute Jean-Claude's sophisticated, continental menu. Now to her horror, she saw the menu she was holding began with chicken fried steak and went downhill from there. Her expensive new chef had come up with a menu that belonged in a roadside diner. In the brief silence as the three others made their choices, she noted the rest of the atrocities. How had this happened?

She was not surprised that Valdene and Buster were pleased. They were debating whether to have fried oysters or boiled crayfish. So that explained what they have in common, she thought bitterly. Yes, Valdene would look right at home under a sign that said "Eats," but she expected something more. *Where were the wonderful dishes Jean-Claude had created? Where was the salad of poached radishes with basil and black currant vinegar? Where was the matelote of sea bass that Jean-Claude had been marinating for days in red wine and green peppercorns until the exterior was as rich and dark as mahogany? What was chicken fried steak doing on her menu?*

It was ridiculous, but she could feel that she was on the verge of tears. This was the last straw. Here she had planned to impress her father with how well she was running this white elephant, and her centerpiece, the crown jewel of any hotel, her kitchen, was putting out white trash cooking.

To her surprise, it was Claiborne Lurie who seemed to sense her distress. He reached over and patted her hand, obscuring the light of her ruby-and-diamond ring. She looked up into his faded gray eyes and was surprised to find sympathy there. Perhaps he wasn't so cold and ruthless after all, she thought. He could see this menu was a disaster. He held her hand, and she realized that this was more than a gentle pat of reassurance. She did not pull her hand away, but stared at it as if it was a stranger's. An odd feeling came over her, a feeling that she had not experienced in years.

She knew that if Claiborne Lurie asked her to leave with him that minute, she would have. That was the way it had been with Arden and she was surprised that she could feel that way about anyone again.

Belinda was relieved that at least the food was good, although it was not what she had expected, and her father

71

and Valdene seemed delighted.

"Do you ever see Charlene?" she asked Lurie at last. She only knew about her former sister-in-law from what she read in the supermarket tabloids.

Lurie shook his head. It was a brief but meaningful nod. His only daughter was an embarrassment to him. "Charlene lights down here or at the ranch occasionally," he said, smiling. "But I'm afraid getting married and divorced seems to consume most of her time. That and some idea she has about becoming an actress. She's in London now. Her mother is getting married again."

Belinda was barely listening. Her mind was on the kitchen. She would have to see Brice and straighten him out. Although the others seemed pleased with the menu, she was outraged. She tried to boost her spirits by drinking more champagne.

"This is an excellent meal, Belinda," Lurie was saying, as he refilled her glass. "My compliments to your chef."

Later, after Buster had excused himself and Valdene and the two of them had hurried off like a pair of teenagers, Belinda and Lurie finished the remaining bottle of Cristal and he ordered a nightcap of Grand Marnier. Belinda's head was spinning and she could see that the dining room was almost empty. It was time to leave. Lurie offered to escort her upstairs. She declined. He kissed her hand. "I enjoyed our conversation tonight, Belinda. I hope I'll see you again."

Belinda hesitated, wondering if she had been too hasty in dismissing him, remembering the touch of his hand on hers. An affair with Claiborne Lurie might make sense, it would certainly be a lot more sensible than the fantasies about Brice de Young that had been intruding on her dreams day and night since she met him. But at that moment, her elevator had arrived (she had insisted that the elevators in her hotel be prompt) and with a flourish Lurie kissed her hand and was gone.

Once Belinda reached the penthouse she regretted even more not asking Lurie to accompany her. As she put her key in the door, she sensed immediately that something was wrong. Yet she did not turn and run but stepped in and turned on the lights. Someone was sitting in the great leather swivel chair that looked out over the Gulf. The chair spun around.

It was Brice de Young. He was smiling.

"What are you doing here?" she demanded. She was still steamed at the high-handed way he had changed the menu, and she was also angry about the way he had broken in here. "You're lucky I don't call security."

"What for?" he said coolly as he rose to his feet. "If you're worried about Tammy Lynn, don't be. She won't be back until tomorrow. She's still in Taos, trying to reach a higher spiritual plain." He moved closer to her. "As for me, Aunt Belinda, I'm the more earthbound type."

He moved closer, and before she could step away he was kissing her on the neck. His lips, soft and warm on her neck. Involuntarily she arched her neck as the heat of him washed over her like sunlight. His mouth sought hers, but his conceit was so blatant she couldn't take him seriously for long. She started to laugh.

"What's so funny?" he demanded, his voice suddenly hard.

She struggled to break away, but she could not stop laughing. All that champagne and that awful dinner and now this. The idea that she might not be interested in him had obviously never occurred to Brice.

There was no denying his kiss had stirred up all the passion she had been denying herself for so long, but his arrogance canceled that out, and suddenly she was reminded of all the other men like him. Like her father and Cordell and Aynsley Adder. Not that Brice de Young was in their league, but his attitude, his cockiness, was more than she could bear.

And he was supposed to be her employee! Did he think she would really sleep with her niece's lover? Brice de Young was either the stupidest man in Texas or the cockiest.

"If you want me to leave, just say so," he said. But he took out a pocket handkerchief and offered it to her. "Here. You better use this."

She took it and dabbed at her tear-smudged mascara. "I always cry when I laugh," she explained.

Brice was still convinced that his first night as the

73

Maisonette's chef had been a rousing success, and success always made him horny. He had expected that getting Belinda Garland into bed would take some doing, but he didn't want to waste too much time. He had to be at the market early in the morning.

"Are you all right now?" he asked, trying not to sound impatient.

If Belinda had not been so high on champagne she might have listened to the warning bells that went off in her head at the note of sympathy in his voice. Instead, she yielded, acknowledging that this Brice de Young, who had already established that he was arrogant, obnoxious, and possibly stupid, radiated a kind of sexual heat that she had forgotten existed. This was not Claiborne Lurie's tender solicitude, this was an urgent demand. And yet, she found herself drawn to him like a tired plant is drawn to the sun.

She was still under the delusion that she was the one calling the shots.

"Are you seeing someone?" he asked. "I've been waiting here for an hour. I was almost ready to leave." Tammy Lynn had claimed that her aunt lived like a nun, but now he was not sure. These cold ones were always full of surprises.

Belinda shook her head, then wondered why she felt she had to tell him the truth. But she did. "Business meeting. I work for my father, you know," she said. "Tonight I'm feeling a little like a poor relation. I've got the name, but I don't have too much else."

This encouraged Brice. If there was one thing he knew how to handle, it was a vulnerable woman.

"You've got me!" he assured her, putting his arm around her and leading her to the couch. She turned to him, her head tilted upward, and he bent down and kissed her on the lips.

"This isn't right," she gasped as his warm breath caressed her ear, and his tongue began to trace a path down her throat.

"So what," he whispered. His hands, surprisingly gentle and warm, stroked her breasts, toying with the buttons as if waiting for permission to open her blouse. He was

74

teasing her, bringing her to the gates of pleasure, but he would not force her. If she wanted to go any further, she would have to say so.

Her hands caressed his head as he warmed her, and as her mouth met his she gave him her answer, silently but resoundingly, as he helped her out of her shirt, then she, in turn, helped him out of his clothes. Reading her willingness in every sigh, he led her to her bedroom and proceeded to awaken the long-dormant turmoil within her.

Chapter Six

Charlene Lurie arrived in England fresh from another career-threatening disaster and she blamed it all on her daughter Chandler. The hideous British press were waiting in droves at Heathrow to get more pictures of the two of them. And they all knew about the fashion show debacle in Hollywood.

It had looked like a great opportunity: an invitation to take part in a mother-daughter fashion show at DeMarco's, the town's hot new restaurant. A great place to be seen and photographed. Photographed, she thought bitterly. How could she have predicted how Chandler would behave?

All the celebrity mothers were there: Joan Collins, Jeannie Kasem, Jacqueline Smith. And at the last minute, when Pia Zadora canceled, Charlene had been invited to replace her. Of course she accepted, even though it meant delaying her departure for Mother's wedding by a day and getting on the telephone to Ciprianna Rivers, her father's mistress, to get the designer to provide her and Chandler with suitable mother and daughter outfits.

And Ciprianna had come through, Federal Expressing matching mother and daughter dresses of deep violet silk moiré. Maybe Chandler's was a bit young for her, Charlene admitted in retrospect. It had been a while since Ciprianna had seen her, and Chandler wasn't exactly easy to dress. If she had inherited blond good looks from her parents it was hard to tell because her features were buried in fat. Chandler was far beyond pleasantly plump, and the elaborate puffed sleeves and flouncy skirt ballooning out over a stiff black tulle crinoline only added more pounds.

But that was no excuse for what Chandler had done.

They had arrived at DeMarco's just a few minutes before showtime, and headed for the temporary dressing room for some last-minute primping. Charlene immediately got lost in conversation with a female studio head who was also in the show, and suddenly the announcer called for her and Chandler to start down the runway. She grabbed her daughter up and headed out of the dressing room. It was only when she heard the snickers of the crowd that she looked down and saw what her daughter had done.

Gone were the flat little Mary Janes and white lace tights that Charlene insisted she wear. Instead her daughter had donned black cowboy boots. And the dress. What she had done to Ciprianna's dress! It was slashed to ribbons, still ballooning out over the black tulle crinoline which now looked like a balerina's tutu, and as she moved down the runway the shreds of purple moiré waved like pennants.

Her beautiful blond hair, which had been sweetly braided when they arrived, was now moussed up into ugly spikes and her eyes were heavily made up with black eyeliner and mascara. She looked more like Charlene than ever, but as if Charlene was made up to play some fat psychotic punk rocker.

Suddenly, Charlene understood exactly how Joan Crawford felt! And all she could do was smile and pretend that she thought this was adorable and listen to the commentator describe Chandler's personal fashion statement as if she knew a thing about it.

Somehow she made it through the fashion show without killing her daughter, but the worse was to come. The newspapers and *Entertainment Tonight* all carried pictures of Chandler's altered Ciprianna gown, and Charlene dreaded the designer's reaction. Fortunately, she had already gotten the dresses they were going to wear to the wedding, but would she ever get another freebie from Ciprianna again?

And if Ciprianna was angry, would she complain about it to her father? She didn't care too much about Ciprianna's feelings, but Daddy could make life very unpleasant when he got angry.

She was relieved to be out of the U.S. for a week, and hoped that the story of the fashion show would die out by the time she returned from Mother's wedding.

She had not reckoned on the British press. They were waiting for them outside the Connaught, obviously hoping to get more photographs of Chandler in one of her costumes, but when they saw that she was only wearing jeans and a T-shirt that said "Don't Mess with Texas," they contented themselves with demanding Charlene's comments about the whole business.

How Charlene loathed England. She hated the lurid papers that would print anything. She hated the Connaught, where she was booked into a suite with little Chandler and Miss Ruby, because it was stuffy and crawling with Arabs. She missed California already. She missed Harmon Lane. She missed the sun.

This was the first time she'd been back to England since an incident at Heathrow when she was just a kid and customs discovered marijuana in her luggage. Since her mother Amanda was married to the American ambassador at the time, the press blew the whole thing out of all proportion and she ended up barred from the British Isles for ten years. Small loss, she thought, and she hadn't been back since.

Charlene had tried to make the best of the trip and had borrowed her father's Gulfstream because the idea of taking Chandler and Miss Ruby on the Concord was beyond considering. And she had the foresight to stash her cocaine in her shoulder pads. She didn't want another ugly encounter with British customs.

It was just too bad she couldn't do anything about Chandler, Charlene decided, as they arrived in their suite and she eyed her chubby and sullen daughter with disapproval. Frankly, she could hardly bear to look at her and was only dragging her to England because her mother had

78

insisted on it. Otherwise Chandler would be in a weight-loss camp where she belonged.

Chandler's nurse, Miss Ruby, was little help and Charlene only kept her on because she was the only one who could handle the girl's tantrums. Actually, Charlene had no choice. Miss Ruby had been working for the Luries since Charlene's father, Claiborne, was a boy. In fact, Charlene suspected Miss Ruby was a spy for her father. But since Claiborne Lurie controlled her allowance, there was little Charlene could do about it. Charlene was sure that Miss Ruby was slipping the girl snacks and sweets every time her back was turned. When Chandler was sixteen Charlene planned to sit her down and tell her the facts of life. She would tell her then about the tongue trick.

Charlene was a little awed by Miss Ruby, a large woman of great presence. Her skin was smooth and black as ebony and she liked to wear bright green or red calico dresses with matching kerchiefs. Charlene was too intimidated to point that she looked like Aunt Jemima. And lately she'd been finding odd little gris-gris bags around the house in Los Angeles and in Chandler's drawers. She was torn between a desire to confront Miss Ruby and demand to know what kind of voodoo she was up to and gratitude that someone could control her difficult daughter.

Charlene was not thrilled to be traveling with Chandler and her eccentric nurse, but her mother wanted Chandler at the wedding and so Charlene didn't have much choice. She was on a spendthrift trust from her grandmother and she had her alimony from Cordell, but for extras she still had to go to Amanda or Claiborne.

Although Charlene was always tagged as the "Texas Deb," her mother Amanda came from the Long Island Gold Coast. Marrying a Texan, even a Galveston millionaire like Claiborne Lurie, was as close to rebellion as Amanda ever came. A few years after giving birth to Charlene, Amanda tired of Claiborne's demands and left him, but not before lining up his replacement: a Detroit auto tycoon who was subsequently named ambassador to the Court of St. James. Amanda was in her element in

London, but Charlene was not and after the Heathrow incident she was sent back to her father's ranch and became his responsibility.

The ambassador had recently kicked the bucket and Amanda, a woman born to be a wife, had moved up quickly to number three: the twelfth Earl of Ormsby. Charlene had not yet met her stepfather-to-be, but she expected him to be as awful as the ambassador. Was it possible that Amanda had been getting it on with Lord Ormsby even while the ambassador was alive, she wondered. What a delicious thought. But she dismissed it quickly. Not her mother. Not Amanda.

On the other side of the world, Claiborne Lurie watched the sun set over the water from his gulfside mansion, then returned to the auction catalogue he had been studying earlier that day. Booth's had a sale of first-rate paintings coming up and he had his eye on a pair of Watteaus in the collection. He put it aside and picked up another Sotheby's catalogue for jewelry from the estate of "a collector." He had been assured by his man at Sotheby's that the "collector," who remained anonymous for security reasons, had been the favorite mistress of the late Shah of Iran and the jewelry reflected the ruler's Arabic taste.

Yes, he considered that any of these ornate pieces would be appropriate for Ciprianna. Like most adventuresses, Ciprianna loved opulent jewelry. Such pieces were far from Lurie's own disciplined, classical tastes, but he had never felt compelled to inflict his own taste on his mistresses. Let a thousand flowers bloom—that was his philosophy. And Ciprianna, who had been his mistress for almost ten years, was a very special flower: a lush crimson rose in full bloom.

Imagine! Lurie would often ponder the wonder of it. How many of his ancestors must be spinning in their graves at the prospect of Claiborne Lurie taking Ciprianna as his bride. With her dusky skin, full-blown lips, and curly black hair, there were times she looked—almost—Negroid. Yet, Lurie was enough of a horseman to appreciate the jolt that raw and lusty Ciprianna could give the Lurie bloodlines.

Early in their relationship she made it clear that she was perfectly willing to leave Carl Rivers, the man who had taken her out of a Juárez brothel and turned her into something like a lady, but only if Claiborne was ready to make her his bride.

And this Claiborne Lurie was not prepared to do. As a mistress, hot-blooded Ciprianna was a delight. As a wife, well . . . He offered instead to set her up in luxury wherever she wanted to live, if she would only leave her husband.

Ciprianna was not interested. "You don't understand, *chico*," she explained so many times that he had stopped asking. "I am a respectable married woman, not some *putana*. I am not going to live like a mistress."

"But you *are* my mistress."

Ciprianna merely shrugged her lovely shoulders. "Just because I am your mistress does not mean I have to live like one."

Perhaps it was such petty bourgeois principles that gave their sex that extra *frission*—for he had never known a more sensual woman. She was Aïda and Cleopatra, with just a dash of Eva Perón. Certainly not the sort of woman he considered spousal material.

And so they had continued their affair for years, with Criprianna still married to Carl Rivers.

As a couple, the Rivers had often joined other celebrities on his annual spring cruise, and he found the financier great company. Surely Rivers knew by this time what was going on, but he chose to ignore it.

Well, Lurie told himself, he had had enough. It was time to present his bid to Ciprianna. He was still a virile man, and with any luck he would be able to father another heir. The Luries had not done well in that department, in spite of his and his father's concern for bloodlines. His daughter Charlene was a magnificent physical specimen, but an intellectual and moral disaster. And her poor daughter Chandler wasn't even attractive. Just a fat and sullen lump. He hoped to father another heir before it was too late.

Lurie settled on a gaudy brooch, then cast the glossy

catalogue aside. Although exquisitely conscious of his position—in society and in Texas history—Claiborne had never been afraid to flaunt convention when it was to his advantage. Such a time was now. Ciprianna would be coming to Galveston in two days for the launch of her new perfume "Ciprianna," and Carl Rivers would be with her. He would give her what she wanted all along.

He was ready to remarry, and ready to make Ciprianna Rivers his bride.

Chapter Seven

Belinda woke, half convinced that last night had all been a dream, until she saw the note on the pillow beside her.

Dear Belinda—
   Had to run to the market. See you later. Thanks a million.

B.

Oh, God, she thought with a sinking heart. She did not know which was worse. Sleeping with Tammy Lynn's lover was merely disloyal, but sleeping with a Garland employee was downright stupid. Brice de Young had already gone too far when he rewrote her menu. What kind of weight did he plan to throw around now that he thought he was her lover?

She tore the note to bits. There was only one solution: Brice de Young had to go, immediately.

Dear Mr. de Young—
   You're not going to fit in after all. Good-bye and good luck.

Sincerely,
Belinda Garland

Brice looked at the note and the check for one week severance pay, then he looked back up at Wiley Muehl.

"Does this mean I'm fired?" he demanded.

"I'm afraid so, son. Miss Belinda hired you to produce a Continental menu and you came up with something else."

"But everybody loved it!"

Wiley shrugged. He was trying to figure out how to replace another cook this late in the season. And he had the party for Ciprianna to worry about.

"Don't ask me to explain Miss Belinda," he said. "I only work here."

Wiley Muehl was almost as confused as Brice. He had worked for the Garlands for most of his life, and for the last year he had seen Belinda grow into the job of hotel manager. He had taught her a lot about the day-to-day details, but he couldn't deny that she had good instincts. Original ideas. She was her daddy's girl, no doubt about it. Which was why this sudden order was so disconcerting. He kind of liked the new cook and thought he had done a good job, coming into the kitchen with barely a day to prepare. But Miss Belinda had a streak of ruthlessness in her just like her daddy. You couldn't cross either of them.

Funny. This morning she was looking softer and acting tougher. Go figure.

"How soon do I have to be out of here?" Brice asked.

Wiley coughed nervously. "Miz Belinda wants you out by noon. Otherwise she'll have the guards toss you out, and I'm sure you wouldn't want that."

"No," Brice snapped. "I wouldn't want that. And where is Miz Belinda anyway."

"She's gone fishing."

"Oh yeah?" Brice stood up, and began tearing the check to bits, then tossed it to Wiley. "Let her use this for bait."

Belinda was on her way to the Pelican Yacht Club for her fishing date with Myles McLean. She sipped a Coke from the can as she drove. She wondered how soon it would be before Wiley was on the phone to her father to discuss her high-handed firing of de Young. Or had she broken him of that habit? She didn't care; by now she was confident that Buster would back her up. Buster wanted to make money and the way she was running the Maison Rouge was making lots of money for him.

Unlike the rest of the Garland enterprises, she thought dryly, but that was none of her affair. It was enough that she had the hotel and her own plans for the future. At least she *thought* she had the hotel, until last night. Now she wondered about the future.

It meant so much to her to be good in this business. She had been so inadequate in her marriage.

She thought again of watching as the police lifted Arden Yate's Mercedes out of the Gulf, then removed her husband's body. She had since learned that most drowning victims looked terrible, but not Arden. He looked like he was sleeping. Only he would never wake up. Ever. A wrongful death. A totally unnecessary death. If Aynsley Adder had had the courage to go for help her husband would be alive today. Instead, he had killed Arden and gone unpunished.

And her father had allowed it. She would never understand why, just as she would never allow herself to be distracted by another man until she had achieved justice for Arden. Last night had been a foolish mistake. She had had too much champagne. It would not happen again. And in twenty-four hours Brice de Young would be out of town and out of her life as quickly as he came in.

"If you go looking for revenge, you better dig two graves," Aunt Carrie Clinton always said. But Belinda did not care. She sipped the Coke to convince herself it was helping her hangover.

But it wasn't the hangover that was bothering her. It was the nagging feeling that last night when she allowed Brice de Young to make love to her, she had felt more alive than at any time during five years of marriage to Arden Yates.

The more she tried to push that thought from her mind, the worse her headache got. And she still had to go fishing with Myles McLean. At least *he'd* be fishing, the only fishing she'd be doing would be for information about Buster's plans.

Chapter Eight

Charlene considered herself a good mother. She had raised her little Chandler on Baby Dior and Florence Eisman, but unfortunately Chandler was a monster. A fat preteen monster. They were on their way with Ruby to Amanda's wedding and Charlene dreaded encountering her mother. She knew Amanda blamed her for the girl's weight problem, and she considered the whole fashion show disaster Charlene's fault.

Why did Amanda have to be so perfect? At fifty her complexion was still flawless; her weight hadn't varied since her debut at the Mayflower Ball in 1953 except for a few months out of the social ramble to give birth to her daughter. Charlene had never seen Amanda with a hair out of place. For that matter, she had never seen her mother without makeup. Amanda's bra straps never showed, she never caught the heel of her Jourdan pumps in the hem of her Givenchy gowns. Charlene couldn't imagine Amanda ever resorting to the tongue trick.

Her mother was the sort of woman for whom crowds parted like the Red Sea; designers begged her to wear their clothes; the sun shined for her as it did today. Charlene hated her.

Yes, facing Amanda was definitely going to require medication, Charlene decided as she headed for the Magic Box, the Vuitton makeup case she had fitted out with her prescription drugs. There was even a place for her to keep the prescriptions to present to customs. She didn't want any more incidents. The cocaine in her shoulder pads could wait until later. With any luck she'd find a guest who would share his stash with her and she wouldn't have to use her own at all.

She took a Quaalude and washed it down with water, wondering if tranquilizers had calories. Were Quaaludes more fattening than Thorazine? She would have to ask Dr. Zbgny when she returned to Los Angeles. He had a big clientele among the stars and if anyone knew the answer he would.

Too bad there wasn't a medication to control Chandler. She would have to talk to Chandler's pediatrician about Ritalin. Better yet, have Ruby do it. That was what she was paid for.

The following night, the only reason Claiborne Lurie was at home, reluctantly watching a special live edition of *Lifestyles of the Rich and Famous* was because Ciprianna was being interviewed about her new fragrance. She looked particularly beautiful, Lurie thought, posed against the lights of Acapulco Bay. Afterward, Robin Leach announced that later in the week he would take his audience to a typical wedding among old English aristocracy. The twist was that the bride was an American, Lurie's own ex-wife, Amanda.

Lurie sat upright, curious to see how Amanda had aged. They had parted company under difficult circumstances and, although they stayed in touch over the years, most of their contact was by telephone. The Amanda he saw now only vaguely resembled the young debutante he had eloped with thirty years ago. She was still a damn attractive woman, though, he had to admit.

If you liked frigid blond bitches, he added bitterly.

Although the snob in Lurie was impressed that Amanda had managed to snare an earl he consoled himself with the thought that Lord Ormsby was probably bisexual. All those English peers were kinky. And if his lordship wasn't bent already, a few months in the icy arms of Amanda would surely bend him.

Lurie thought again of Ciprianna. His slum goddess. Her earthy beauty, her untiring zest for life. If only he had been able to come up with a woman who combined Ciprianna's sensuality with Amanda's patrician beauty and aristocratic taste. Ciprianna had gone from the slums of Juárez to the highest realms of wealth and power, but she never lost that touch of the mud.

He found himself thinking of Buster Garland's daughter. Strange, when she was around the ranch during Charlene's debutante days, he had scarcely noticed her, for his tastes did not run to very young women, no matter how beautiful. Since encountering her at the Maison Rouge, however, he had thought of her often. How had an oaf like Buster produced a work of art like that?

Belinda Garland was fortunate, he mused. She seemed to have inherited her father's brains and her mother's beauty. And in spite of her cool facade he sensed there were still some smoldering embers there. It would be tempting to stir them up a bit.

The Luries and Garlands did not mix, and he wondered if he would see her again. Then he realized they would be thrown together at the launch for Ciprianna's fragrance. Perfect! He had nothing to lose by toying with Belinda Garland, and it would not hurt to shake Ciprianna's confidence a bit.

Either way, he would end up in bed with a passionate woman.

Lurie would have liked to have ended his evening on that note, but such peace was not to be. At the very moment he was about to turn off the television, he noticed that Robin Leach was interviewing a blond butterball in a purple-and-black Halloween costume. She looked vaguely familiar.

He realized with disgust that it was his granddaughter Chandler Lurie. The sight of her on international television in that outrageous getup appalled him. Did Charlene have no shame? Did she have no sense? Now every potential kidnapper and opportunist in the world had a look at her!

Lurie angrily disconnected the television and placed a call to his daughter's suite at the Connaught. Of course she was out. He was so angry he almost attempted to reach her at Ormsby's, but decided he did not want to tangle with Amanda. Instead, he left word for her to call him immediately on her return.

Chapter Nine

Tammy Lynn confronted Wiley Muehl in his office at the Maison Rouge as soon as she heard the news. Only that afternoon she had returned from Taos to find a good-bye message from Brice on her answering machine and his few possessions gone.

"How could you fire him?" she demanded. "Why didn't you talk to me?"

Wiley glared at her. It was bad enough that he had to take orders from Miss Belinda. He had no intentions of catering to Buster's spoiled granddaughter. "Now, Miss Tammy Lynn," he started. "It was your aunt's decision. Why don't you ask her?"

Tammy Lynn shrugged and sank back in the chair. "She won't tell me anything. She acts like it's none of my business."

"Then maybe it ain't."

The girl glared at him. "Brice was a star in New York. He had his own following. And he threw it all over to come down here. And everybody liked him. You told me yourself you got nothing but compliments last night." Tammy Lynn had been so anxious to see her Brice succeed she had taken a break from meditating to sneak out of her ashram in Taos and call the hotel. Now that she was back, however, everything had gone wrong.

Her voice was starting to shake and Wiley had the awful fear that Tammy Lynn was going to cry. *Please Lord,* Wiley silently pleaded. *Anything but that. At least Miss Belinda never cried.*

Tammy Lynn started groping around in her oversize

Vuitton satchel and brought out some crumpled tissues. She dabbed at her eyes.

Brice was so furious after his session with Wiley Muehl that he jumped in his battered Buick and started driving toward Houston before he even had time to consider other options. By the time he reached the outskirts of Houston it was almost noon, and he was already regretting the cavalier way he had torn up his pay check. The sun was blazing overhead, and the air of the city was fetid. His car had no air-conditioning, and even with all the windows open the inside was hot and miserable. He had no idea where he was going or where he would stay.

So much for his comeback. He probably should have waited for Tammy Lynn, maybe even told her the truth about her aunt, but he couldn't stand to be on the Island another minute. He had forgotten something crucial about Galveston: it was run by a few powerful families and if they turned on you, you were dead. And Miss Belinda Garland had certainly turned on him. He could not help wondering why. After they made love last night, he was sure he had her around his finger. She was a confusing, mixed up dame who had no idea what she wanted. He was better off getting away from the whole mixed-up Garland family. He had to get off the Island.

He did not even bother looking for another job there now. The bitch had probably blacklisted him with all the better hotels and restaurants and he wasn't going to take some job frying up po'boys at a beach shack at this point in his life. He'd have to line up something in Houston and fast.

He didn't know many people in the city, just his old friends Jan and Kukla. He laughed. Maybe he should call his mother in Chicago and ask her what the stars promised for him. Maybe he should have called her before he took the job at the Maison Rouge.

Tammy Lynn was sure Belinda was avoiding her, but that afternoon she finally managed to corner her aunt in the garden where she was making an inspection tour with the

90

head gardener. When Belinda saw the angry look on her niece's face she quickly dismissed Felipe and led her to a stone bench in the shade of an ancient live oak tree.

"What's going on?" Tammy Lynn demanded. "What happened to Brice?"

Belinda sighed, trying to sound patient while she groped for just how much to tell Tammy Lynn about her latest disastrous boyfriend.

"I'm afraid he just didn't work out, honey," she said. "We had different ideas about the kind of food that should be served at the Maisonette."

"So you fired him? Just like that?"

Belinda blinked her blue eyes at Tammy Lynn. The girl noticed how different her aunt looked. Something had changed about Belinda, but she wasn't sure what it was. She had never thought of her aunt as a particularly sexual woman before, but suddenly she was aware of a sensual quality about Belinda. Men, she was sure, must find her very attractive. Certain men, that is. Not sophisticated, super-hot types like Brice, but the more reserved traditionalists like Myles McLean.

That was it, she decided. While she was away, Belinda and Myles McLean must have finally decided to end her period of mourning. Belinda was back in the real world. For that Tammy Lynn was glad, but she was still furious that Belinda had fired Brice.

"You don't understand. I love Brice!" Tammy Lynn screamed. "And you made him leave!"

"Nobody made him leave, honey," Belinda said. "He's probably just embarrassed because he has no job. But honey, he's not for you. Take my advice. Find someone else. Someone from your own world."

"Someone like Arden Yates?" Tammy Lynn said nastily.

Belinda paled just a bit and she clenched her hand. "That was really uncalled for, honey," she said. "Trust me, you'll get over him. Don't let him come between us. He isn't worth it."

Tammy Lynn jumped up. She was crying and her usually pale face had turned red. She was one of those unfortunate plain women who became even less attractive when they cried. Belinda knew as well as she did that Tammy Lynn was hardly going to attract a man on the basis of her good looks and charm.

"I won't get over him. Poor Brice got a raw deal from the Garlands and I'm going to find him and make it up to him. You just wait, Belinda. He'll be back and you'll face him and admit you made a mistake."

Belinda was dearly hoping that day would never come, but all she said was, "I'm very sorry about your boyfriend. Maybe that just shows what happens when you try to do a relative a favor. Now, if you'll excuse me, I have a hotel to run."

But Tammy Lynn beat her to an exit, turning her back on her aunt and storming through the garden. As Belinda watched her niece's fading back, she realized her own hands were white and shaking.

Brice replaced the pay phone and stared at it for a while. Miss Belinda Garland was not taking his calls. It looked like that was the end of her. Maybe he was better off. If he was ever going to see her again he didn't want it to be when he was broke and jobless. Better to save the get-together for when he was back in the money. Then she'd be sorry.

He struck oil on the next call. Kukla and Jan insisted he come right over.

Chapter Ten

By midafternoon, Belinda was out on the Bay in Myles McLean's cruiser and she was feeling much better. She had put thoughts of Tammy Lynn and Brice de Young well behind her. She was much more concerned with Valdene Sykes.

She couldn't believe she had let Valdene get to her at dinner last night. The woman was nothing, just another of her father's tarts. There had been many before Valdene and there would surely be many after. There was nothing to worry about, Belinda assured herself. She had caught Cordell's paranoia, and in the light of day she saw how silly it all was.

Belinda smiled in spite of herself. If only Cordell had some of their father's zest for life, instead of carrying a torch for his ex-wife all these years. She wondered if Cordell even had dates. He was so wrapped up in Garland, Inc., she doubted it. Now their brother Buddy was more like Buster: he had as much zeal for making love as for making money.

What about her? Thoughts of Brice de Young kept intruding and she struggled to push them away. Yes, she had been a bitch to fire him. Good chefs were hard to come by and it was possible she could have talked to him and worked something out. In her heart Belinda knew she had rushed to get rid of Brice because she was afraid. He had come too close. They'd come too close. And she had no time for love — or anything like it — right now.

Poor Tammy Lynn. She had every right to be furious about Brice (and she didn't even know the whole story), but Belinda was confident that her niece would get over it. She was also sure that Brice would never tell Tammy Lynn about their night together. Belinda was a Garland after all, and she could take the measure of a man. According to Wiley Muehl, Brice had been in a rage when he left the Maison Rouge, but she was sure their secret was safe.

She called out to Myles. Something was tugging at her line. She knew Myles would help her land it.

Buster Garland was an early riser and he nudged Valdene awake. She slowly came to, shaking her tangled black hair and blinking her eyes as if to make sure where she was before she said anything that could be embarrassing later.

Once she got her bearings, she looked up at Buster and smiled. He was already out of bed, wrapping his massive frame in a crimson silk robe. Valdene stretched out a long leg and caught the end of the sash with her painted toenail.

"Look, Buster honey," she teased. "Your robe and my toenail polish just match. Doesn't that mean we go together, too?"

Buster gave out that great, hearty laugh that so suited a man of his size.

"Now, darlin'," he chuckled. "That just means you and me are both red-blooded. That's all that means."

Valdene puffed out her lower lip in a girlish pout. It was a particularly sexy pout that had always sent contributions soaring when she exposed it on the *Happy Heart Hour*.

"Ain't you comin' down to breakfast, darlin'?"

"Now?" she whined. "I thought we had some time to play a little, Buster."

He shook his head like an ancient and wise old buffalo. "No, darlin'. It's the early bird that gets that old worm. Time to rise and shine and get out in the fields."

"Oh, all right," she said, tossing a pillow at his back as he retreated from the room.

Fishing was a sport that suited Myles McLean. Tall, lanky Myles, with his laconic James Stewart air, could be a killer in the courtroom, but he also had the patience to spend a whole afternoon on the Bay.

Belinda did not, and she was getting restless.

94

"I think this sun's too much for me," she said. "It's time to get back to the Maison Rouge."

"Whatever you say, Belinda," he said mildly. "But if you got out in the sun more often, you'd remember how to relax. Look at how pale you are. And in the middle of summer."

Still, he started up the engine and headed back to the Pelican Club Marina. On the way back she tried to pump him about her father's plans, but he was betraying no secrets.

That was probably why her father trusted him so much, she acknowledged to herself. She liked Myles, if only because Cordell loathed him. Her brother was jealous of anyone else who claimed their father's attention. Yet the fool had encouraged Buster's newest affair!

"Do you think my father is planning to marry Valdene Sykes?" she asked at last.

Myles paused for a few seconds before answering. It was one of the things Belinda liked about him. Myles always thought before he spoke and didn't speak at all unless he had something to say.

"I can't honestly tell you what old Buster plans, Belinda," he said slowly. "But I do think it would be a good idea for you to get to know the Widow Sykes. She's not like the others, you know. She's a gal who gets what she wants, and she wants Buster."

"And what about my father?" she demanded. "What does he want?"

"Well," Myles drawled. "I do believe he wants Mrs. Sykes."

By the time Valdene had showered and dressed and come downstairs to the terrace, Buster was finishing his last cup of coffee. He drank a special chicory blend he had sent over from New Orleans. Valdene had never had it before coming to the Sand Castle, but she had begun to develop a taste for it.

Buster had a mug in one hand, his cellular phone in the other, and *The Wall Street Journal* spread out in front of him, but he was alert to Valdene's approach and looked up as her high-heeled mules clicked on the slate terrace. He put down the phone and cup and opened his arms wide.

"It's about time, darlin'. I thought I'd have to leave without saying good-bye," he said, greeting her as she kissed his plump cheek and tried to sit on his lap.

He pushed her away playfully. "No time for that, darlin'. Daddy's got to make some money today."

"Are you going to see Belinda?" she demanded, sounding harsher than she meant to. She took her seat next to him and helped herself to his toast, loading it with marmalade and biting it fiercely.

Buster eyed her with caution. He had noticed that Valdene and Belinda had not hit it off. Odd, even though Cordell was downright rude to Valdene she didn't seem to care a bit what he thought. She seemed to sense a rival in Belinda. He nudged her playfully under the chin.

"Calm down, darlin'," he said. "Don't go getting jealous of my little girl. She's had a hard time, you know, and she's just coming out of it. I hope she'll meet someone soon who'll take her off my hands."

"Didn't her first husband die on her or something?" Valdene asked.

"There was an accident. You know they lose about five cars a year over that seawall. They get loaded and drive right off. Poor old Arden was just another summer statistic."

"Maybe it was suicide," Valdene said, her voice full of spite.

"Oh, no, darlin'. The poor boy wasn't driving. His best friend was. And he lived. Imagine having to live with that on your conscience. Terrible pity."

"Yes," Valdene said smoothly. "Wasn't it?"

As soon as they hit the dock, Belinda started making calls from the pay phone. She had no luck getting her father, so she called Wiley Muehl.

"Have you found a new chef yet?" she asked.

"Have mercy, Miss Belinda," he said. "it's only three o'clock. I've got a few calls in, but we're going to have to get by with just the sous chef for a while. Most folks would have lined up a replacement before they fired their chef."

"Oh, Wiley, I though you knew!" she purred. "I'm a Garland, we're not like most folks." She knew she wasn't making his job any easier, but what was done was done. "Do you have anyone who looks good?"

"A few. We'll probably end up with a gal from New Orleans. You like blackened redfish, don't you?"

"A woman?" she said. "That'll be different."

"She's been working at the Ponchartraine and has a following. But I don't want to talk about it; it might jinx the deal."

"What about de Young? How did he take the news?" she asked.

"He was upset. Confused. Wouldn't you be?"

"We've all been upset and confused a few times, Wiley. And we all got over it."

Belinda put down the phone and went back to join Myles for a late lunch on the club deck. She tried to ask him more questions, but she couldn't concentrate. She still felt guilty about canning Brice. What had he done but remind her she was a woman?

There was nothing wrong with Brice de Young and quite a lot that was right. It was just that he was the wrong man for her.

Right now any man would be wrong for her.

That night, Belinda tried to amuse herself by calculating what Valdene Sykes's weekly cosmetics bill must amount to. It was the only way she could get through dinner with Valdene and her father. Tonight Valdene seemed to be wearing the entire Ultima line. Buster had suggested the Wentletrap, and for once Belinda had been delighted to get away from the Maisonette and the overworked sous chef who was filling in until Brice de Young's replacement arrived.

Throughout dinner Valdene had been making catty remarks, as if she wanted to lure Belinda into a quarrel. But Belinda recognized Valdene's strategy: She wanted Belinda to snap at her so she could get Buster's sympathy. Well, it wouldn't work.

What really bothered Belinda about Valdene was her pretensions. She pretended to be this religious innocent, this helpless widow, and she was not. Belinda was sure Valdene was probably the brains behind the famous Happy Heartline ministry. Did her father see it? Buster was a shrewd trader, but dealing with a woman was different. Especially a woman who had so obviously set her cap for him.

Desperate situations demanded desperate measures. Belinda's chance came when Valdene announced she was going to the little girl's room. In fact, that's what she called it, thereby sinking any lingering respect Belinda had for her. Belinda passed up her chance to join Valdene for some "girl talk" and grabbed the opportunity to have a private conversation with her father. They seemed to be a rare luxury these days.

"What do you think of Valdene?" he asked as soon as they were alone.

"I think she's very attractive," Belinda said. "But I'm surprised to find you with someone in the religion business. You used to call them all hypocrites. Are you planning to join her in the ministry?"

Buster looked startled, as if he hadn't thought about the Happy Heartline factor in quite that way. Actually, Valdene was so much woman with him that he rarely thought about her religious side at all. Before he could reply, however, he could see Valdene making her way back to their table.

Belinda saw her, too, and smiled. How Valdene must have raced through her visit to the "little girl's room," once she realized the two of them would be alone together. Had she even stopped to wash her hands? Well, Belinda had made the most of what little time she had. She was satisfied that she had planted a seed of doubt in Buster's mind. Let it grow and prosper.

Then Valdene was on him, kissing Buster like they'd been apart for days instead of minutes, and Belinda's private conversation with her father was over.

Chapter Eleven

In Houston, Kukla Trumbo greeted Brice with a big bear hug. He hadn't seen Kukla or Jan in almost a year and he wouldn't have recognized either of them. A year ago the Trumbos had been living in a rat-infested loft over a Chinese restaurant on Pearl Street. The loft was full of plants and Kukla's giant paintings, but the clouds of incense that Jan kept burning day and night could never quite cover up the smell of rotting garbage from the alley downstairs. They were scraping by on food stamps and what Jan got waiting on tables in a Soho art bar two nights a week, but they were the happiest people Brice knew.

Now they were rich. Kukla's grandfather had died and Kukla's share of the Trumbo fortune was kicking in two million American dollars a month. They were living in a River Oaks mansion, but Kukla quickly assured Brice it was only their Houston place.

"We're building a villa in Acapulco that will be a real palace," he explained. "And we're spending most of our time at our ranch in Santa Fe. I'm going to do a lot of painting out there, I know it."

"Have you been painting, then?" Brice asked. He was eager to see Kukla's newest work.

"Not really," his friend shrugged. "Settling the estate and all the lawsuits have taken up most of my time."

There followed a long and elaborate education in Texas inheritance laws and how Kukla's uncles were screwing him out of his rightful share of his grandfather's estate. This was punctuated by Jan's encouraging asides.

At appropriate intervals a dark-uniformed maid would

come in with a fresh bottle of José Cuervo and limes piled in a silver Buccellati bowl. Brice finally figured out there was a buzzer beneath the hammered silver coffee table between him and Jan, and she used it to signal the maid to keep the tequila coming.

He'd had about all he could take of his friend's estate talk. "It sounds like this case has become a full-time job, Kukla," he said. "Aren't you the guy who would never take a straight job because it would keep you from painting?"

"It's my money, Brice," Kukla said with a wounded look. "Sure, I could take the millions and Jan and I could live well. But why should my relatives have the rest? It's my money."

Actually, Brice thought, the money was Kukla's grandfather's, and in the Pearl Street days Kukla had made it clear how much he despised the old man. But Brice didn't feel like arguing. The whole business was turning him off.

As the afternoon rolled by, Brice grew more depressed. Not even the Trumbo cook's excellent guacamole and nachos helped. He was surprised and disappointed by how much his friends had changed. What had happened to the fun-loving couple he'd known in New York. They were obsessed! He didn't think he was going to be able to handle this much longer. Fortunately, Jan came to his rescue.

"Did you know your mom's in town?" she said.

The clouds parted. "No kidding? Have you seen her?" Once, when Colette was visiting New York, he had taken her to the Pearl Street loft. Colette liked eccentric places. Now that he thought about it, she'd told Kukla that night that he and Jan would come into money.

Jan shook her head. "Not yet. There's a rumor the defense brought her in for the Starsund trial. But it's just a rumor. I don't think she wants anyone to know she's here, actually. I just ran into her at Elizabeth Arden. She was in the next booth, all hush hush, but I'd know her voice anywhere."

Ah, yes. Colette's New Orleans accent. That peculiar combination of Brooklyn and Scarlett O'Hara. Colette's version of it was unmistakable. And if she was in town, maybe she'd help him out. It was humiliating to have to ask his mother for help at his age, but anything would be better than having to ask Kukla Trumbo for money. His pride wouldn't let him.

Besides, Colette owed him.

Cordell Garland slowed down his coffee-brown Mercedes XL as he reached the seedy neighborhood at the end of Desranes Street. It would have surprised him to know that the regulars—pimps, whores, and drug dealers—all knew him by sight. In a dangerous life like theirs you have to have a memory for faces, and an instinct for self-preservation. Not that they regarded this rich boy as dangerous. They knew he was rich because of his clothes and his car, and they figured he was married or a politician or both because he was so afraid of being recognized. He was known among them as "the one who likes to take pictures."

That's what he was doing with Rhonda at the Breeze Inn that evening. Rhonda regarded him as one of her regulars and although she was pretty sure that "Sam" was not his real name she went along with it. She kind of liked the guy. He was good-looking and clean and it meant an easy fifty bucks twice a week, Tuesdays and Thursdays, like clockwork.

"You know, Sam, we don't have to come here," she said, lying back on the red plaid bedspread the motel supplied.

"What's wrong with here?" he asked, removing the dark glasses and heavy jacket that were supposed to disguise him. He started rooting around in his camera bag.

"I mean, it would be nice to go for a drink up the road or something, sometime. I feel like we've got something going, you know?"

"Of course I know, Rhonda," he said, staring at her with those sincere blue eyes. They were kind of like Robert Redford's but not really. Darker. "Do you have the teddy I told you to buy?"

"Sure do," she said. "And the receipt, too, just like you said."

He took the receipt and looked satisfied. "Thirty dollars, that sounds about right."

She was already out of her street clothes and slipping into the lacy black lingerie.

"Don't forget to keep your high heels on," he reminded her.

She turned to him, hands on her round hips, with the teddy open in front, revealing her full breasts. "Now, Sam. How

101

long have you been coming to me? A year? Have I ever forgotten?"

He grinned sheepishly, then returned to his stiff demeanor. "Back on the bed, Rhonda. I don't have all afternoon."

She leaned back and began the series of poses. Sometimes Sam let her try something new, like holding up a tube of Crest and pretending she was a professional spokesmodel, but mostly they stuck to the same old script. He rarely wanted to have sex with her. He just liked her to strip and put on some of his ex-wife's jewelry and then he'd take pictures. Sam was really a boring guy. The kind of guy who'd make a good husband.

"You know, Sam," she said at last. "I have an idea. It *has* been a year that you've been coming to me and I think we should celebrate. I want to buy you a drink."

He smiled. Rhonda thought he looked even more like Robert Redford when he smiled. Then he shook his head and looked sad. "No, darling. I'm the customer. I couldn't take advantage of you."

"Come on, Sam. I insist. We could go downstairs. The Sea Breeze has a little bar and we've never been there. I'm sure none of your snooty friends will be there, either."

Sam shook his head and nervously began to pack up his camera.

"Are you ashamed of me?" she said.

"It's not that, Rhonda," he assured her, then looked into her eyes for maximum sincerity, the way he'd learned in business school.

Unfortunately, Rhonda's green eyes were filled with tears and one round, glassy drop was already spilling down her plump pink cheek.

Even Cordell Garland had a heart, and he could not resist a woman's tears.

"Oh, all right, Rhonda. One drink." What could happen? he asked himself. Rhonda was a good old girl and he might as well keep her happy. And quiet.

The Voodoo Lounge of the Sea Breeze was a straw-lined former pantry with four minuscule tables and a bar. They did most of their business in room service, but Rhonda had decided not to mention the room service to Sam. She wanted to pretend they were on a real date. She even changed into a conservative green linen dress that flattered her red hair. Her only jewelry was plain gold earrings and the gold charm bracelet that used to be her mother's. It had always brought her luck.

"What'll you have?" the burly black bartender who doubled as a bouncer growled when they entered. He was usually alone at this time of the day and liked to watch Oprah Winfrey in peace. Sam called for Stolichnaya on the rocks, but Rhonda asked for a Singapore Sling.

"It seems to go with the decor," she explained, secretly hoping it would come with a little umbrella. She wanted to treasure every nuance of this. It was their first date.

Cordell felt suddenly awkward. He was a man who only felt comfortable behind a desk or in bed. Social situations were agony for him, and one of the reasons he and his ex-wife Charlene had never gotten along. Part of the reason Rhonda appealed to him was that when she was stripped and lying naked on the bed, wearing Charlene's jewelry, she looked a lot like his former wife. She was heavier, and of course without Charlene's breeding and class. And without Charlene's demands. No, he told himself, he did not want to lose Rhonda. But here in the freezing bar, with Oprah Winfrey talking to transvestite overeaters on the television, he felt like a fish out of water, gasping for air.

"So. Rhonda." Sam said after the surly bartender brought their drinks. "What are your goals?"

Her heart fluttered at the sight of the little turquoise paper umbrella at the top of her glass. It seemed like a good omen, and she toyed with it thoughtfully as she considered her answer.

Brice was getting desperate. He'd been listening to Kukla and Jan giving him career advice for at least three hours while he left message after message for his mother at the Four Seasons. That was where Colette always stayed, but this time the hotel wouldn't even confirm that she was registered. That left him pretty sure she was, otherwise wouldn't they just say she wasn't there?

He didn't know how much longer he could put up with the Trumbos. He was considering just crashing in the lobby of the hotel when Kukla jumped up.

"Oh, my God! It's five o'clock!" he said.

"What does that mean?" Brice was afraid they might be tossing him out and he still hadn't reached Colette or lined up a place to stay.

Jan pressed another button under the silver coffee table and a Monet on the opposite wall began to rise to the ceiling, revealing a jumbo television screen.

"Time for our latest sensation, the queen of the five o'clock news," she said.

"She's a hoot," Kukla chimed in. "You've got to see this. She can mispronounce Nagadoches more ways than a stuttering Gypsy."

"The only reason she got the job was because her boyfriend owns the station," Jan added, but was interrupted when the phone rang. She picked it up, spoke briefly.

"It's your mom," she announced, handing it to Brice. "Don't be too long, darlin'. You don't want to miss Lauren Armour."

He took the phone.

"Brice! Mon *chéri!* What are you doing in Houston!" she trilled. "What a coincidence! It seems we were fated to meet!"

"Yes ma'am. When can I see you?"

"*Chéri!* I want to see you, but not a soul is supposed to know I'm in Houston. It's very confidential, but I'm testifying in court. That's all I can tell you. The defense brought me down and ordered me not to talk to no one."

"Not even your son?"

"How were we to know my son would turn up in Houston?"

Because you're supposed to be a psychic, he almost said, but pulled back. He wasn't always sure she couldn't read his thoughts, even over the telephone.

"Are you all right, *chéri?*" she asked. "I thought you were in New York."

"Didn't the stars tell you? I was in Galveston, but the job didn't work out. Now I'm looking again."

"Have you ever thought of law school, *Chéri?*" she said.

104

"I'm sure Bernardo would help you get into a good one."

"Bernardo? Bernardo O'Higgins? That's who brought you down here?" O'Higgins was a flamboyant, irreverent attorney in the grand Texas tradition of Joe Jemail and Racehorse Haines. Using a psychic to testify for the defense would be just his style.

"Oh, dear. That's why I shouldn't be talking to you. I can't keep a secret. Promise me you won't say a word."

"Sure, Mother. And you promise me you won't nag me about law school."

"Nag?" she repeated in a wounded tone. "I don't nag."

"No, ma'am," he sighed. "You don't."

"I prod. I encourage. I don't nag."

"Yes, ma'am."

"When you said you wanted to be a cook, did I try to stop you?"

Brice had been through this with her before. His mother had a gift for seeing the future, but she tended to wrap their personal past in a rosy mist. Maybe it was all that Velveeta she ate.

"Wait a second. I have an idea," she said suddenly. "Remember Aunt Tootsie?"

"Aunt Tootsie and Uncle Harris? From the circus?" They were no relation to Brice, but when he was traveling the circuit with his parents, all the circus people were his aunts and uncles.

"Yes. They have a playland in Houston. Tootsie just sent me a postcard of it. There's a carousel and a roller coaster and a snack bar. She said they can't keep a cook. Maybe they can use you. I'll give them a call."

Brice felt his last shred of his pride slowly slipping away. He couldn't go back to New York and he couldn't go back to Galveston. He was broke, with only the clothes on his back and a rusting fifteen-year-old Buick. And now he was going to work for Circus People?

Biology was destiny after all. He was going back to a carnival, just like his father.

He took a deep breath and tried to think of the great Texas heroes. Sam Houston. Davy Crockett. H.L. Hunt. Hard times had never fazed them. At least a job with Tootsie and Harris would get him on his feet. They'd probably even give him a place to stay so he wouldn't have to put up with Kukla's bitching about his pathetic two million a month.

"Great, Mama," he said. "What did you say their number was?"

All the time Brice had been talking to Colette, Kukla and Jan had been laughing it up at the KLMN-TV reporter's expense. Now that he was free to join them, they explained she was Lauren Armour.

"But how did she get the job if she's so dumb?

Jan sneered. "Our Lauren's got herself a twofer. She's having an affair with Aynsley Adder."

"Sounds like a snake," Brice said.

"Close enough, honey," Jan said. "His daddy was Senator Adder and he's a regular star these days down in Austin. They say he could be the next governor. I'm chairing a fund-raiser for him here next month. He wants to reform the Texas inheritance laws."

But that brought Kukla and Jan back to their favorite subject: their lawsuits.

Brice sank back and listened. He had nowhere else to go.

Lauren Armour was at her dressing table while the studio hairdresser fussed with her do. She had completed the news, but she wanted to fresh up a bit before taping some promos.

She was pleased with what she saw in the mirror. She always liked to make love before going on the air because the afterglow of sex, even sex with Aynsley Adder, left her especially photogenic.

She was wishing, though, that Aynsley would find something else to do besides hang around her dressing room. Maybe he wanted to remind her who had gotten her the job . . .

Which wasn't fair, she thought, since with her credentials and background in television news she would have gotten the spot sooner or later. It was just luck, really, meeting Aynsley at a fund-raiser while she was just a press assistant in Washington. And Aynsley was the most connected man she had ever known. Some women went for athletes or rock

106

stars, but Lauren could smell power two rooms away. Aynsley had it and he was crazy about her. And Aynsley was not like most men she knew. He understood politics and strategy. Naturally, she had not shared her entire five-year plan with him, but he was most definitely a part of it.

Step one had been the introduction. Step two was the job. Step three would be marriage. Lauren saw the two of them as a professional team. Aynsley was only a state senator now, but everyone expected him to follow in his daddy's footsteps and run for the U.S. Senate soon. Once Aynsley was elected to Congress, Lauren was sure he would be ready to leave Carola Lee.

Yes, the wife was a problem, Lauren acknowledged to herself, but a small one. Aynsley had assured her that he and Carola Lee only stay married because of his public image and once he was safe in Washington he would dump her.

After that, who knew? Maybe even the White House! *Eat your heart out, Diane Sawyer!* Lauren thought.

Of course, they couldn't go public with their romance just yet, but she could be patient. By this time all of Aynsley's aides knew her and knew what was going on, but nothing had ever appeared in the press. And it never would.

Aynsley's car was waiting to take them back to her hotel after the taping. She leaned back and turned on the Sony Watchman in the backseat while his chauffeur guided the car through Houston's late-afternoon traffic. Aynsley reached over and squeezed her hand.

"You were wonderful," he assured her. "You're brilliant, and sexy and talented."

"Yes," Lauren mused. "I am, aren't I?"

Chapter Twelve

Every employee of the Maison Rouge was caught up in preparations for the gala to launch Ciprianna Rivers's new fragrance, Ciprianna. The official occasion was a benefit for the University of Texas Medical Center, of which Claiborne Lurie and his family were major benefactors. The entire hotel was blanketed in creamy white double peonies, Ciprianna's favorite flower, and the Grand Ballroom, where the banquet would be held, had been entirely remodeled to resemble the decorator's idea of an Aztec palace, in homage to Ciprianna's alleged ancestors. Between Ciprianna's perfume company and her couture clients, as well as the many University of Texas Medical Branch benefactors, every celebrity in the Southwest was expected to be there.

Belinda was delighted that things were going so smoothly. Ciprianna's decision to have the gala in Galveston had been a lucky break for her and the Maison Rouge and Belinda was going to make the most of it. The hotel might even lose money on the affair, but it was worth a fortune in publicity. She knew that once exposed to the ambience of the Maison Rouge most of the guests would be back. They would want to have their own parties and debuts and weddings there and that was where the money was for a hotel like hers.

This gala was an occasion to flex her muscles a little, too, Belinda reflected, because it was exactly the kind of affair that her father loathed and wanted nothing to do with. "Empty-headed celebrity chasing" he would say. She had gotten him to agree to come, and she regarded that as a small victory, even if he did insist on bringing Valdene Sykes along.

Belinda only hoped Wiley Muehl's new chef would live up

to her advance billing. Not for the first time did she regret her hasty dismissal of Brice de Young.

Belinda had ordered a new dress for the evening: a surf-green crêpe de chine that looked perfect with her emerald earrings and hammered gold necklace. Arden had given her the earrings for their fifth anniversary, just weeks before he died.

At the Sand Castle, Valdene Sykes was also thinking about what she would wear. Buster had insisted she stay for the Ciprianna party and she considered that a good sign. He was hooked, that was for sure. Now it was just a matter of reeling him in and that called for real artistry. Not unlike bringing in lambs to the Lord. Only this lamb was for her alone.

Valdene was having a little trouble making up her mind about what to wear. She had no desire to look like Buster's prim and proper daughter, but she wouldn't give Belinda the satisfaction of showing up like a tart, either. Besides, why should Ciprianna be the only star? Too bad her best clothes were home in Nashville, Valdene thought with annoyance. She even considered calling Reba Twining and having her ship some dresses down on the Happy Heart jet, but discarded the idea. She didn't want Buster to think she was extravagant. Fortunately, she had found a good dress shop on the Strand and settled on a black-and-yellow sequinned lace sheath that made her look young, hot, and sexy. Well, she smiled to herself, two out of three wasn't bad.

Later that night, as Valdene was dressing, Buster came in and asked her to fix his tie. She liked that. It made her feel like he needed her.

"You're gonna miss me when I go home," she teased him.

"Oh, now, darlin', I hope that won't be for a while yet," he said.

"Oh, go on, Buster. You know I got to go home sometime. I'm supposed to make another gospel album soon. The ministry wants me to do a tribute to Prescott. Cover all his hits."

Buster sniffed his disapproval. "Sounds like grave-robbing to me. Next thing you know they'll be sighting ole Prescott in the parking lot of Six Flags."

She put her arms around him, or as far as her slim arms could reach around his great bulk. "Now you go on. I think you're jealous of a dead man."

"Not jealous of a dead man. Jealous of a live woman. I don't like sharin' my gal with anyone."

"I've got to take care of myself, Buster," she said, caressing his cheek. "I'm alone in the world now and I've got to look out for myself."

"Never alone, darlin'," he said, kissing her on the mouth and clutching her plump backside with his big paw. "Never alone."

As the guests assembled, Ciprianna Rivers prepared to make her entrance. She shimmered like an Aztec goddess in a gold lamé gown wrapped around her voluptuous body in the Grecian style, leaving one tawny shoulder bare. Her sleek black hair was gathered up à la greque, in a style so severe only a woman with a perfect profile would dare to wear it. A few tendrils escaped and trailed down her neck. She smiled, she turned, she dazzled. Waiters and busboys paused and stared. If she caught a busboy's eye her smile was just as dazzling as it was for Carl or Claiborne. She was incandescent.

Lurie fingered the gaudy brooch in the pocket of his tuxedo. Tonight, when she came to him after Carl went to bed he would present her with what she really wanted: a proposal of marriage.

Chapter Thirteen

Charlene Lurie had been partying with friends at Crackers, a private club on Berkeley Square, when a tall blond man as wide as a refrigerator walked in, surrounded by photographers, beefy security guards, and television cameras. He was wearing a white satin track suit that glowed under the black lights of the club. He was surrounded by a quartet of black men, all as big and imposing as he was, dressed in identical Saville Row business suits.

"Who is that?" Charlene asked her escort, Viscount Gaffney, who explained that the jolly golden giant was Sven Petersen, aka the Great White Hope, who was expected to be the next heavyweight champion of the world.

"The wogs are his bodyguards," young Gaffney added.

Charlene knew nothing about boxing and didn't see anything good about being a heavyweight, but she had spent enough time at her father's ranch to recognize a fine animal when she saw one. And Sven Peterson was one fine piece of beef.

"Have him brought to me," she ordered.

Sven was soon presented to her and he seemed equally thrilled to meet a rich and beautiful Texan.

His Norwegian accent was too thick for Charlene to understand much of what he said, but he did keep repeating something about "fashion show" and "new styles." It seemed that everyone in the world had seen the pictures of her and Chandler, Charlene thought with a sigh. Ciprianna and Daddy had been telephoning from Galveston and New York, but, taking advantage of the time difference, Charlene had so far managed to avoid their calls. Still, if the publicity from the fashion show helped her get an acting job, it would all be worth it.

Meanwhile, she beckoned to handsome Sven, encouraging him to take a seat on the banquette beside her. His long blond hair kept falling into his pale-blue eyes and he was constantly brushing it away in the most endearing gesture. The four bodyguards silently took up their posts around Sven and Charlene, freezing out young Viscount Gaffney. Charlene hardly noticed, her attention was elsewhere.

After months of pale, battle-scarred Harmon, the sight of Sven affected Charlene like a big thick hamburger might affect a starving man. She caressed his rock-hard bicep, then moved her soft white hand to his rock-hard thighs.

"Hard?" he said. His pale Nordic blue eyes clouded with the struggle to come up with just the right word, but it satisfied Charlene.

"Yes, honey," she whispered, continuing to stroke his thigh as his four bodyguards gazed off sullenly in different directions.

Sven Petersen turned out to be an excellent lover. Although he lacked imagination, he more than made up for it with his amazing endurance. He was a perfect physical specimen: massive biceps, a stomach as hard as a rock. With the golden hair and the contrast in their size — he was so wide and she was so slender — they turned heads wherever they went. Charlene loved it.

Chandler thought her mother's new beau looked like Hulk Hogan and she hated him. She called him the Swedish meatball although he patiently explained he was Norwegian. When he was nice enough to prepare his special vitamin drink for her, she spit it out and claimed it tasted like bull piss. Once she deliberately spilled Orangina on his trademark white silk running suit. He almost hit her but then he remembered that for a fighter to use his fists was considered assault with a deadly weapon. Instead, he sent her off with Miss Ruby and five hundred pounds to Sextasy, the hottest new boutique in London, so he and Charlene could be alone.

"I don't understand what I'm paying Miss Ruby for," said Charlene. "She's taught Chandler nothing. The child's a little savage."

Sven suggested boarding school. There were some fine ones in the north of Norway where they specialized in lots of exercise and cold showers, but Charlene couldn't bring herself to send Chandler that far away.

"Besides," she said, "Chandler's daddy would never allow it."

On the day of Grandma Amanda's wedding Chandler refused to leave her room at the Connaught. Miss Ruby couldn't do anything with her and turned to Charlene in desperation, informing her that Chandler refused to wear the lovely pink-and-white lace frock Charlene herself had ordered from Ciprianna's collection.

"I don't want to go to a stupid wedding," Chandler was screaming. "I hate Grandma. And I hate this dress."

"But, darling, it's exactly like mine."

Charlene looked at her daughter, then she looked at the frilly dress that her mother had had delivered to the hotel. It was really quite pretty, with puffy sleeves, lots of lace and ribbons, but perhaps it was a bit more flattering for Charlene's lean body than Chandler's chunky, squarish one. But Ciprianna always let her have clothes free, because she wanted to keep her good will, and, besides, they looked so cute together, dressed as mother and daughter. They were sure to get their picture taken. And with Chandler's white lace tights and flat Mary Janes, Charlene was convinced she could easily pass her off as ten.

"I want to wear my new black dress," she screamed.

"You can't wear black to a wedding," Charlene said. "It's out of the question."

"Then I'm not going!" Chandler sat back on the bed, folded her arms in front of her, and jutted out her double chin belligerently.

In that moment, she looked exactly like a young, fat version of her father, and the very idea of taking orders from someone who looked like Cordell was enough to give Charlene the strength to cut this arguing short.

"Look, sweetie," she said, sitting beside her daughter on the bed and taking her in her arms. "You know how much Grandma Amanda wants to have you at her wedding. And if you're a very good girl I'll take you to Sextasy tomorrow and

113

buy you a new outfit."

Ruby sniffed eloquently. She didn't approve of Chandler's taste for black leather and biker gear. She didn't approve of bribing a child to behave, but she was used to Charlene.

Charlene got up from the bed with a look of smug triumph. "There, Ruby, I think everything's all right. Now hurry, Sven's waiting downstairs in the limo."

Amanda's new home was in Kent, only about thirty minutes from London, but it seemed a world away. The country was lush and green and the Earl of Ormsby's ancestral hall was a huge Georgian structure set back in a landscaped park. As their limo made its way along the tree-lined corridor to Ormsby Hall Charlene noted with interest that there were television crews on the scene. In her own discreet way her mother was just as publicity conscious as she was. Charlene hoped this exposure would help her career.

As soon as they arrived, Chandler announced that she had to use the bathroom and disappeared.

"Don't forget there'll be photographers," her mother warned her.

"Oh, Mama, I won't."

Was that a wicked gleam in her daughter's eye? Charlene barely had time to consider it when she and Sven were accosted by Robin Leach, who wanted to get her perspective on this happy occasion. Just as she expected, he looked thrilled to see them and wanted Charlene and Sven to share all the details of their new affair with his viewers. Since Sven's English was limited mostly to gym terms, Charlene got to do most of the talking.

"And how do you like being back in Merry Old England?" he asked her, rather tactlessly reminding his viewers of her last appearance at Heathrow.

Before Charlene could answer, there was a terrible scuffle and Leach and his crew abandoned her to head for the source of the excitement. Charlene followed. Something, a mother's instinct, perhaps, drew her to the center of the crowd.

The guests buzzed among the morning coats and flowered hats of a peer's country wedding. The British had a tradition of ignoring eccentrics, but even a few of them were sneaking sidelong glances at the spectacle Miss Chandler Lurie Garland offered.

In just a few minutes, Chandler had gutted her couture dress the way her grandfather Buster might have gutted a building. Gone were the puffy little-girl sleeves and the high neckline. She had ripped out the sleeves but cut out most of the bodice with a manicure scissors, which was all she could find in the bathroom of Ormsby Hall. She had also cut off six inches from the front of the skirt, so that her bare legs (the white lace tights long gone) were exposed to the top of the thighs, while the back formed a kind of train. Her blond hair was moussed into frightening spikes, and her blue eyes were almost lost in a pitch-black frame of kohl and mascara.

Chandler had also gotten rid of the flat white Mary Janes and replaced them with a pair of her mother's high heels that she had sneaked out of the Connaught. Unfortunately, they were gold, adding to the entire aspect of a Soho tart. Two Arab gentlemen, business partners of Lord Ormsby's, were enchanted, and deep in conversation with her. Being her mother's daughter, however, Chandler quickly abandoned them at the approach of Robin Leach and his camera crew.

"What a unique gown, Miss Garland," said Robin Leach.

"Thank you," said Chandler, blushing girlishly as she addressed his millions of viewers via satellite. "It's a Ciprianna original."

Chapter Fourteen

"Fasten your seat belts. It looks like it's going to be a bumpy night," Belinda whispered to the handsome gray-haired man seated beside her. He turned to face her: it was Claiborne Lurie. She was surprised. Just that morning she had reviewed the seating plan with Ciprianna herself. Buster and Valdene were supposed to be at her table. Looking around the grand ballroom, she saw that Buster and Valdene had somehow ended up at the table meant for Claiborne.

This was no ordinary gala. Tourists and Islanders never mixed, but this evening hordes of them had lined up in the driveway of the Maison Rouge, braving the steamy summer heat, to gawk at the parade of bejeweled women and their tuxedoed escorts. The invitees, who had given at least three thousand dollars a person to the UTMB—University of Texas Medical Branch—and then paid an additional five hundred dollars a ticket to celebrate their own generosity, swept through the lobby of the hotel and up the marble staircase to the Grand Ballroom in a steady stream of glamour.

The room was heavy with the fragrance of thousands of creamy white double peonies nodding over the gold lamé-draped tables. The ballroom chairs had been slipcovered in more glittering gold lamé, and at exactly eight-thirty the lights dimmed and white-gloved waiters lit the vermeil candelabra at every table. A thirty-piece orchestra played a society band's version of Bruce Springsteen and Billy Joel standards while the waiters moved through the crowd bearing magnums of Taittinger's which, Belinda had been informed, was the only champagne that Ciprianna would drink.

Lurie glanced at Belinda blankly, and barely seemed to recognize her. At first she was annoyed, especially after the way he had flirted with her just a few nights earlier, but then she saw that his chilly gray eyes were focused on the dais where Ciprianna Rivers, ravishing in gold lamé, sat flanked by officials of UTMB and representatives of the Sealy, Kempner, and Moody fortunes. Somewhat farther down the table of honor sat Ciprianna's gnomish little husband Carl. So, Belinda realized, it must be true that Claiborne Lurie was having an affair with the Mexican designer.

On Belinda's left, her brother Cordell was fuming. Valdene had secluded his father at another table, and now he was going to have to look at his ex-father-in-law all night. He and Claiborne had exchanged cold nods when they first sat down and now they pointedly ignored each other, Cordell chatting with his partner Tammy Lynn, and Claiborne staring at Ciprianna, which meant Belinda was virtually forgotten and could concentrate her attention on the party favor: a gold-plated basket filled with a small flacon of Ciprianna, the fragrance.

Ciprianna had overseen the decorating, and she had gone overboard on the gold. Yes, Belinda repeated to herself, it was going to be a long and bumpy night.

At another table, Buster Garland was enjoying himself immensely. Valdene was nibbling on his ear as he debated Dallas Cowboys strategy with the director of the Houston Space Center.

Valdene took a deep, satisfied breath, inhaling the rich mix of hothouse flowers and Gulf air and two-hundred-dollar-an-ounce perfume.

"I just love the smell of this room, don't you, Buster honey?" she purred.

"Sure do, darlin'," he answered. "It smells like money."

Valdene was delighted. She had switched the place cards to get Buster away from his annoying children and to give them some time alone before she had to return to Nashville. And sweet old Buster hadn't even noticed. Didn't that show just

117

how much he wanted to be with them?

She lifted her jeweled compact and restored her lip gloss, giving her a chance to check out Cordell and Belinda in the mirror. She was pleased to see that they were ignoring each other. Divide and conquer was one of Valdene's golden rules.

Buster was enjoying himself, and more than that, he was enjoying Valdene. He usually found these affairs boring and he felt trapped and restless in his black tie. Tonight was different. She was a beautiful gal, and tonight in those black and yellow sequins she looked like a brunette Dolly Parton. Valdene was so frisky, he told himself, she could have a good time anywhere. She could be a handful, no doubt about it, but he had never shrunk from a challenge. One thing was for sure: she was plenty of fun.

For several days he had been thinking about getting married again. Valdene pampered him like a killing hog, bolstering his ego at every turn and lavishing him with affection. That was on the plus side. On the negative side was the fact that his children, especially Cordell, would probably be very upset by any such move.

Yet he could not help wondering what marriage to Valdene would be like. Since their first night together she couldn't seem to keep her hands off him. Sometimes it became downright embarrassing, such as when she wanted to cuddle up to him while Cordell or Belinda or Tammy Lynn was around. But Buster craved just that kind of attention. He needed a strong and loving woman. A woman like Valdene Sykes.

He watched Valdene now as she playfully flirted with the other men at the table, never going too far, never losing eye contact with him for more than a second.

Damn. He had a right to a wife, a right to the steady companionship and devotion of a beautiful woman. If his days were numbered the way the doctors said, that was all the more reason to make every one of them count. Cordell would be riled as all getout. Belinda Sue would not be happy, either, and there was no telling what this would mean to Buddy. Tammy Lynn would go into a decline and Carrie Clinton would give him hell!

Great God Almighty! Who was the head of this family anyway? Mona Clinton, his first wife and the mother of his children, had been a fine woman, but she had been in her grave for more than five years. He had lived alone since then and he had shown Mona's memory more than enough respect. It was time to respect himself.

Valdene noticed Buster's pensive expression and reached over to caress his plump cheek. "What's the matter, honey? Ain't you having fun?" she asked.

He grinned with satisfaction. "Darlin', I'm havin' a heap of fun. I'm just making up my mind about some property I intend to acquire."

Valdene's brown eyes glittered. Like Buster, she appreciated a good acquisition. "Oh?" she said. "And what did you decide?"

"I'll make my bid tonight." He winked at her, but before she could ask any more about it, the crowd was being silenced and the speeches had begun.

There was a speech from the head of UTMB, and from the governor and from Carlo Rivers who was donating one million dollars to the medical center in honor of his wife, and finally from Ciprianna herself who, despite her slight Mexican accent and flirtatious sexuality, came across as surprisingly demure.

Then dinner was served, beginning with smoke salmon followed by chateaubriand, green salad with brie, all accompanied by a seemingly endless shower of Taittinger's. While dabbing at the dessert: chocolate meringue swans stuffed with white chocolate mousse, Belinda tried once again to engage Claiborne Lurie in some kind of small talk. Maybe it was the effect of the red meat, or maybe it was the champagne, but he began to loosen up and take his eyes off Ciprianna long enough to compliment Belinda on her dress.

As coffee was brought out, the gorgeous Ciprianna stood and made her way toward the rear of the ballroom where her models were waiting to demonstrate her fall line. Her gold lamé shimmered in the candlelight as she paused at Belinda's table, pointedly ignoring Claiborne Lurie.

But he was too fast for her, jumping to his feet and

119

catching her arm, as if to save her from tripping. "Not so fast," he whispered. "Why have you been ignoring my calls?"

"I have nothing to say to you!" she snapped, her dark eyes flashing with anger.

"I just want to know why you've been avoiding me since you got here. I have something very important to discuss with you. I've got the *Lone Star* waiting in the harbor with the crew standing by."

"I don't care about your yacht, Claiborne, and I don't care about you," she said. "How could you allow your grand-daughter to make a fool out of me?"

Claiborne sighed. So Ciprianna had seen Amanda's wedding, too. "Is that what this is about? You blame me for Chandler's little episode?"

"Is that what you call it? *An episode?*" Ciprianna said, as she struggled to escape his grip. "The girl has made my clothes look ridiculous. Those photographs are running in trash magazines from Stockholm to Costa Smeralda. I should sue!"

"Now, Ciprianna," he said.

"It's no use, Claiborne. We're through!"

She broke away and headed for the stage to take her anger out on her models. Lurie knew that it was pointless to try to explain to Ciprianna that he had no control whatever over his daughter and granddaughter. Being a Mexican she could never understand. He sat back down on his gold-covered chair.

"If it's any consolation, Claiborne, I think your grand-daughter improved on Ciprianna's clothes. Chandler's got a great future as a designer." Belinda had been trying not to eavesdrop, but it was impossible not to pick up the gist of the conversation, and she, too, had seen the photographs of little Chandler in her customized versions of Ciprianna's gowns.

"That is none of your affair, I'm sure," he said. His rage at Ciprianna was only made worse by the knowledge that Belinda Garland had seen his humiliation. Fortunately, everyone else at the table was deep into their own conversation. That consoled him, and he recovered his good graces. "You'll have to excuse me, there's nothing worse than being misunderstood."

"Tell me about it," Belinda sighed, moved by a sudden sympathy for a fellow sufferer, and possibly by the quantity of champagne she had consumed.

An idea began to form in Lurie's mind, a way out of this situation Ciprianna had brought him to. After all, Ciprianna was nothing more than an ambitious Mexican whore who got lucky. And he'd been prepared to make her a Lurie! Belinda Garland, while hardly in the same league as a Lurie, was half Clinton, and besides that she was a beautiful and intelligent young woman. Younger than Ciprianna.

"You know, Belinda, I think I've had enough of honoring the Rivers family for one night. I was thinking of taking a little sail to clear my head. Would you care to join me?"

His direct approach took Belinda by surprise, but she was bored with the endless speeches about how wonderful Ciprianna was and furious at Buster for stringing her along on the Delancy Street project. At the same time, she was intrigued with Lurie. Once upon a time, he had been her best friend's remote and worldly father. Now he was a charming and handsome man who was clearly interested in her. Very interested.

She took up her fichu wrap and instinctively Lurie helped her swathe it around her shoulders.

"You know, Claiborne," she said smiling. "I think a sail on the Bay would be just the thing to clear my head."

After the festivities, Cordell Garland had invited a small group of notables to a private party in honor of Ciprianna and her husband at his home on Oak Park Circle, the house Buster had bought for him and Charlene as a wedding present. Buster scowled as he watched his son moving through the assembled guests with Ciprianna on his arm. Cordell's face was flushed from drinking and excitement and he had uncharacteristically loosened his tie. The boy was star struck!

Fortunately, Buster had little time to brood about Cordell or wonder where Belinda had gone to. He was constantly being approached by a steady stream of supplicants who wanted his advice or aid or just to be seen in intimate conversation with the infamous Buster Garland. "You're like

121

the pope, Buster honey," Valdene teased him during a rare minute when they were alone. "Everybody has to get your blessing."

"I'm not the pope, Valdene, and you're not the Virgin Mary," he said, scowling.

Valdene was unruffled. She playfully straightened his black tie. "Would you want me if I was, Buster?" she said.

"What I'm sayin', darlin', is that I think you and me are two of a kind. We came up the hard way, we know what we've got."

"I've got you, Buster, that's all I care about," Valdene assured him.

"All these people here, Cordell's friends," he waved his chubby paw around the stockyard-size living room. "They all want something from me. They're like a pack of fire ants looking to suck this poor boy's blood."

"Now, Buster, don't talk like that," she chided him. "You know I don't want anything from you."

"I know, darlin', and that's what I wanted to talk to you about. Remember that acquisition I was talking about?"

Valdene sensed what was coming. She was pleased yet surprised that he had chosen this moment to make his pitch. She had imagined he would choose a more romantic setting when they were alone. On the other hand, there were plenty of witnesses here, so it would be harder for him to back out.

"Yes?" she said, trying to put an innocent Loretta Lynn-type throb into her voice.

"Well, darlin', it's not so much an acquisition as a merger. What do you say?"

"Buster, are you asking me to marry you?"

He shifted his weight and looked uncomfortable. He had only proposed once before and that was more than forty years ago. "You're not going to make me get down on my knees at my age, are you?" he asked.

She suddenly put her arms around him, or as far as her slender arms could make it around his tuxedoed bulk, and kicked up her heels behind her. "That's your answer," she squealed.

With that, Buster gave out a Rebel yell, and the heads of Cordell's important guests turned in unison. Cordell rushed to his father, suspecting a heart attack or indigestion, when

122

Buster told him the good news. Somewhat glazed, not quite registering, but ever the Galveston gentleman, Cordell led his father and Valdene into the center of the huge living room.

"Friends," he shouted above the din. "I want to make an announcement. My daddy here is taking himself a wife and we couldn't be more proud."

Valdene noticed that Cordell's hand was trembling and she grabbed it and before Buster could notice, held it up in a triumphant gesture.

Claiborne's chauffeur was waiting for him and Belinda outside and quickly moved the pearl-gray Bentley through the crowd of gawkers who were still hoping to catch a glimpse of a famous face. Belinda noticed that none of them recognized tall, patrician Claiborne. They were waiting for someone colorful and notorious, someone like her father.

The car headed to the opposite side of the narrow island toward the marina, and when Lurie remarked about all the development downtown and in the Historic District as they rode through, Belinda found herself telling him about the Delancy Street warehouse project and her ideas for it. To her surprise, Lurie insisted on detouring to take a look at the abandoned redbrick warehouse and he seemed genuinely interested in her plans as she described them, listening intently until they reached the Pelican Yacht Club.

Lurie's yacht, the *Lone Star*, all one hundred and fifty feet of her, was too big to be actually docked at the marina and instead was anchored farther out on the Bay, lit up like a Christmas tree and looming like a pirate ship. There was a Donzi speedboat waiting to take them out to the yacht. It was oddly quiet at this time of night, with only the sound of the waves lapping against the sides of the boat.

The sight of the *Lone Star* was frankly so awesome, that Belinda could not resist teasing him about it a little.

"Claiborne. You surprise me," she said. "You're such a traditionalist, I pictured you sailing a three-master topsail schooner."

He sniffed. "I get enough hot air in business, Belinda, I don't need it when I'm at sea."

Even in the moonlight, Belinda could appreciate the

123

perfection of the *Lone Star* as Lurie yielded to her request for just a brief tour. The saloons were vast and the decor was opulent yet simple. Walls that were not lacquered were paneled with bird's-eye maple; the sofas and banquettes and ceilings were padded with soft gray leather, and the carpets, too, were gray. Lurie was leading the way to the master stateroom when Belinda pulled back, her hand on the lucite handrail.

"Is something wrong?" he asked with concern.

She shook her head. "It isn't that, Claiborne, and I'd love to see your sauna, but not tonight. I hope you understand."

He looked grave, but relented. "Of course I understand," he said brusquely as he led her back up the stairway to the small, intimate library which was his own favorite place aboard the ship. "You need more time. Very well."

He prepared drinks for them himself at the small bar fashioned of elephant tusks and encouraged her to talk abut the Delancy Street project, and then the hotel and then, finally, Arden. All the time he listened. It was seductive, and as Belinda joined him in a toast to the dawn before they returned to shore in the Donzi, she wondered if she would be seeing Claiborne Lurie again. He could be good for her, she suddenly realized. With his money and power he was certainly a great catch and he seemed genuinely interested in her.

The moonlight shimmered on the water and the Bay was so quiet it seemed as if they had it all to themselves. The silver-splashed water lapped softly against the Donzi as they moved forward in a fine mist. Claiborne stood erect and handsome at the wheel of the speedboat, a man used to power and comfortable in command. This was the sort of man she should be seeing, Belinda told herself, not an oversexed drifter like Brice de Young.

Now what, she asked herself with annoyance, had brought thoughts of Brice de Young into her mind at a time like this?

Chapter Fifteen

Once upon a time, a trip to Tootsie's Funland meant a day in the country for Houstonians, but in recent years the city of Houston had grown and spread, encroaching all around Tootsie's until the little park was surrounded by the new Houston of glass-and-concrete high-rise buildings. Harris and Tootsie were sitting on a million dollars worth of land, but they refused to sell.

All the years they'd traveled with the circus Harris yearned to be a ringmaster and now he was one. The former barker was a local celebrity and he never forgot that the thousands who came to Tootsie's for a good time.

He explained to Brice that most of those who stopped at the snack bar would be happy with a Frito pie or some nachos, but if Brice was willing to provide plenty of those old favorites he'd be happy to give him a free hand with the specials.

Brice shrugged. What choice did he have?

The biggest surprise was yet to come: in a matter of days, word spread about the great new cook at Tootsie's Funland.

After more than ten years of cooking in some of the finest restaurants in New York, Brice de Young was an overnight sensation at a Houston hot dog stand.

The cars lining up for parking spaces outside Tootsie's Funland could hardly get past the pedestrians lining up to get at the eats.

Food critics from *Texas Monthly* and the *Houston Chronicle* had come with photographers to do major stories on the phenomenon of fine cuisine at a roadside amusement park. Offers poured in from hotels and restaurants trying to woo

125

Brice away, but he wasn't interested. The wounds hadn't healed. And Harris and Tootsie let him run the snack bar his way. There was no contract, no paperwork. They had a handshake agreement and Brice had a home.

He started small, giving the daytime customers, mostly families, exactly what they asked for, which meant things like Frito pies (melted cheese over Fritos, served in the bag), and corn dogs. But at night, he noticed, Tootsie's got a more sophisticated crowd, college kids on dates and, soon, River Oaks friends of Kukla and Jan. Word spread around Houston, and no night of hard partying was complete without a stop to refuel at Tootsie's. Some of the customers lining up hadn't been near a roller coaster or a merry-go-round since they were in high school. They discovered they liked that part, too. It was all part of the Tootsie's experience.

But most of all they came for the food.

Jan Trumbo suggested Brice and Tootsie let her redecorate the place. She offered to bring in some track lighting instead of Harris's carnival neon and replace the old freak show posters with modern art. Brice wouldn't have it. He was superstitious.

He thought about Belinda Garland sometimes and wondered when she would hear about Tootsie's. Everyone else in Texas had.

"I just wish you'd told me, that's all," said Rhonda Perillo. "I mean, I thought we were friends."

"Aw, honey, don't be that way," said Cordell. His life was complicated enough without Rhonda getting ideas. He was jockeying with his sister for his daddy's favor, he was floundering at the *Sentinel-Wave,* and his daddy was planning to marry greedy, ambitious Valdene Sykes. The last thing he needed was Rhonda giving him problems.

How he looked forward to their photo sessions. How he loved the way she sweetly posed for him, never questioning his instructions, obediently following his orders.

"Why, if I hadn't read the society page in the *Sentinel-Wave* and seen that picture of you at that ball for Ciprianna Rivers, I wouldn't even know your real name!" Rhonda went on.

"I'm sorry about that, darlin'. I did sincerely mean to give you my real name. In fact, I planned to tell you today. It's just that my daddy's such a terror, and my sister's so wicked, I got to protect myself. In Daddy's eyes, I'm still married to Charlene, you know."

Suddenly Rhonda's face softened. Poor Cordell! Sometimes she forgot how hard his life was. He was so rich, but as he had told her so many times, he was exploited by his family. How she wanted to help him. That was why she read the society pages faithfully. She wanted to learn how to behave. To be the kind of woman who could make him happy.

"You do want to make me happy, don't you, girl?" he said, as if reading her thoughts.

"Oh, yes, Cordell. Very much."

"Well then, just lay back on that bed and lift your leg just a bit."

He took out his camera and started snapping his pictures. Just the sound of the camera rewinding made him feel better.

"I want to talk to you, darlin'," Buster said, when he cornered his daughter in the atrium lobby of the Maison Rouge.

"I've already heard your news," Belinda answered coolly.

"I've been calling you all morning," he said. His usual genial manner seemed strained, and he had removed his Panama hat and was waving it back and forth to generate a breeze. The lobby was air-conditioned, but anything less than Polar was a trial to him. "I had to get in my car and drive over here just to corner you. Are you hiding from me, Belinda Sue?"

Belinda had just returned from a tennis game with Fayette Cramer and was still in whites, her blond hair held back by a red hairband. She shrugged. She hated it when he called her that. It made her feel like a little girl again. Which, of course, was exactly why he was doing it. But she'd be damned before she'd ask him to stop.

"I was out, Daddy. Congratulations. What else can I say?"

Buster shook his head. "I'm glad you're getting out, darlin'. I worry about you. You work too hard. You've got to slow down."

"And you've got to stop telling me what to do."

He gave out his big, booming laugh. Heads turned in the lobby, then the visitors returned to their business, pleased that the famous Buster Garland was to be seen on the job at the hotel he owned. *Wasn't it nice,* they would say, *that old Buster lets his little girl run it for him? But he's checking up on her just the same.*

"Now there, Belinda Sue, I know when something's bothering you," he pressed.

"Bothering me? Should I be bothered that I have to hear from Cordell that you're getting married again? Couldn't you have told me yourself? Or is that none of my business, either?"

"I can see that the Garland family grapevine is flourishing," Buster said. "I been getting calls all morning from your relatives. Carrie Clinton. Cousin Lamar." He toyed with the big black Macanuda. "Come on, darlin'. I been calling you with the happy news all morning. You're the one who's harder to get than a bank loan."

"I'd just like to hear it from you," she said.

"Honest to God darlin', I thought you were in the room when I made the announcement. How was I to know you sneaked off with that snake Claiborne Lurie?"

She glared at him, unwilling to let him know he'd taken her by surprise. Now how in the world had he known that? It was classic Buster Garland: the man had eyes so sharp he could catch a cricket.

He grinned, enjoying her discomfort. It paid to remind her that she could never put one over on him. Nobody could. Then he shook his head. "I cannot imagine what you would have to say to that old goat, darlin'," he said. "You just watch out for those Luries. Isn't it enough what his daughter did to poor old Cordell?"

"Cordell's a fool."

"That's no way to talk about your brother," he said. *Even if it's true,* he added silently.

Belinda could read his unspoken reservation and just glared at him. It was bad enough that she had to deal with Cordell. But if Buster really planned to add Valdene Sykes to the family, where would it leave her?

Claiborne had brought her back to the Maison Rouge at

dawn and there had been an urgent message from Cordell waiting for her. "Call me right away no matter what time you get in," it said. She was afraid something had happened to Buster, and in a way something had. The second worst thing imaginable. Belinda's only consolation was the Cordell was even more upset than she was. And anything that riled Cordell couldn't be all bad.

A crowd of people had started to discreetly circle around Belinda and her father in the lobby. It was always like that with Buster. His size, his presence, always attracted stares. Most of the gawkers would never dream of intruding on his private conversation with his daughter, but it made Belinda uncomfortable to be at the center of this kind of attention.

Her father seemed to sense her discomfort and suggested they go up to her suite where they could have some privacy. Instructing the desk to hold her calls, she led him upstairs to the penthouse. They sat out on her terrace overlooking the Gulf. On the wicker table was a fresh bouquet of pink roses that must have arrived while she was out. Her maid had unwrapped them and placed them in a Lalique bowl, leaving the unopened card propped up beside them. Belinda picked up the card and read it. It was from Claiborne Lurie.

"I see you've got yourself an admirer," Buster said, eyeing the flowers.

Belinda shrugged. "They're from Ciprianna," she lied. "Thanking me for everything."

"She ought to thank you," he said. "You did a first-rate job. Your mother would be proud of you."

"Thank you," she said coolly.

He looked around the terrace with annoyance. "Can't a man get a drink around here?" he scowled.

She went to get him a bourbon and water. She took the card with her, much to his annoyance.

When she returned, Buster had settled his bulk into the wicker sofa and she handed him the glass, taking a seat in a chair opposite him and sipping her chardonnay.

"Now, darlin'," he said. "I'll admit it is inconsiderate of me not to tell you that I was planning to get married again. I should've told you before the rest of the world. No doubt about it."

Belinda hated this. She felt he was treating her like an

129

immature child. Like Cordell.

"I know I hurt your feelings. And I apologize. I ask your forgiveness."

"You don't need my forgiveness," she snapped.

Buster started to laugh. "Old Cordell was right on this one. He said you'd be jealous and he was right."

"Oh, please, Daddy. Jealous of Valdene Sykes? Not hardly!"

"That's all right, darlin'," he continued, ignoring her protests. "It's only natural. You've had the run of the Sand Castle and the Maison Rouge all these years."

The Maison Rouge? Was he actually thinking of bringing Valdene into the business? she wondered. *No wonder Cordell was worried.* She tried to tell herself that anything that was bad for Cordell could only be good for her.

"I just wanted to be the first one to congratulate you," she said bravely.

"Of course you did, darlin'," he said, rising awkwardly from the couch. He had finished his drink and settled things with her, and, after all, he had a business to run. "Now, if you don't mind, I'll be getting back to my pickax."

"Wait! What about the Delancy Street project. We haven't talked about that," she said. "You have to give me a decision."

He only shook his head. "All I have to do now is get out of here. We can talk about it when I get back."

"Where are you going?" she asked.

"Just up to Nashville," he said casually, avoiding her eyes. "Valdene wants to break the news to the Happy Heart Ministry in person. Doesn't want them hearing it on the evening news."

The ministry? Did Valdene plan to involve Buster in her late husband's ministry? Belinda couldn't imagine her father on television pleading for contributions, much less chastising viewers for their sins. She started to laugh at the idea.

"What's so funny?" Buster demanded.

"I just wonder if she's planning to groom you to take over for old Prescott," she said, wiping tears from her eyes. It was as hilarious as it was appalling.

"You know me better than that," he sniffed. "I'm just helping the little lady with her affairs. Happy Heart, Inc., is quite an operation."

"When will you be back?" she asked.

"Shouldn't be more than a week," he assured her.

"A week? But I need to know about Delancy Street!" she said, trying not to sound like a hysterical woman. "If we don't move right away, it's going to go public and the price will double!"

Buster was restless and eager to get to his plane. Valdene was waiting for him and, frankly, she and her thriving ministry held more interest than Belinda's real-estate project.

"Never let anyone rush you into a deal," he said coolly. "The minute they say you have to make a decision right away is the minute you should take a week off to go fishing."

"Thanks," she snapped.

"Not at all, darlin'. Nothing has to be settled immediately. Everyone knows I'm behind you. When I get back from Nashville we'll sit down and work out the details. You've got my word."

Belinda could hardly believe it. He was walking away from the biggest deal of her life.

"Is Cordell behind this?" she demanded. "Did he talk you out of backing me?"

Buster laughed. "Belinda Sue, you've got to stop seeing your brother in every woodpile. Don't ever get the idea that I take advice from Cordell."

Belinda could not believe it. First, he'd given her a run-around about the lease for the Maison Rouge. Now, he was walking away when she needed him most.

"Can't you give the go-ahead now?" she said, hating the whining sound that had come into her voice.

"I'll be back in a week," he said, gave her a big bear hug, and was gone.

Belinda walked to the edge of the terrace and gazed out at the turquoise gulf. The sun was fire-red and the sky was dark. A balmy breeze was bending the palm trees. It was still the middle of summer and yet she could sense the hurricane season already in the air. When you grew up on the Island you got a sixth sense for hurricane weather.

She only hoped the hurricane wasn't named Valdene.

Who was this woman anyway? It seemed as though

Valdene and her husband Prescott had captured national attention overnight, a few years earlier, with their televised *Happy Heart Hour,* a combination of revivalism, faith-healing, and feel-good religion. It was no secret that the generous contributions of their viewers had made them rich. But what else did Buster know about her?

She decided to check for her messages and learned Claiborne Lurie had called her several times and left word for her to call back. She smiled. Much to her surprise she had enjoyed last night. Claiborne Lurie was a sophisticated, sensitive man. And he had the right enemies, like her brother Cordell. It wouldn't hurt to have Claiborne on her side, especially if she was losing Buster's support.

Belinda stared at the pink roses. Each one was perfect, as she imagined everything in Lurie's life had to be. What a disappointment Charlene must be to him. She wondered why he had never married again and had more children. And did it matter?

She reached Claiborne on his car phone.

"I'm leaving for New York tomorrow," he said, sounding very pleased to hear from her. Even a little surprised. "But I look forward to dinner with you tonight."

Belinda looked forward to it too. Somehow, with Claiborne Lurie, she felt she was finally beginning to make the break from her family that she should have made years ago.

Heartland, the estate Valdene had shared with her late husband, the Reverend Prescott Sykes, was in one of the most exclusive sections of Nashville. The sixteen-room mansion was owned by the Happy Heart ministry, as were the five cars in the driveway and most of Valdene's clothes. As Reuben Twining, her chauffeur-bodyguard, drove them through the iron gates Valdene could sense that Buster was impressed.

The Twinings lived in one of the guest houses. Reuben Twining was a distant cousin of Prescott's and looked a little like him but wasn't handsome enough to take over the ministry. Instead, he spent most of his time removing devoted followers who were trespassing on the grounds of

132

Heartland.

His sister Reba Twining spent eight hours a day answering fan mail from viewers of the Happy Heart Club. Most of it just required the assurance that the Reverend Sykes would be praying for them, and enclosing an autographed photograph of Valdene and Prescott. A surprising number of letters were still addressed to Prescott although he had been dead for more than a year.

At first, Valdene made no effort to hide the fact that Prescott had been called home. The story had been in *Time* magazine, but the members of the Happy Heart Club were not heavy newsmagazine readers. She finally instructed Reba Twining to stop breaking the news to club members. The faithful just didn't want to believe it and, after all, Prescott was still with them in spirit.

Unfortunately, he wasn't with them in the studio and Valdene could not carry the show alone. She could sing and play the guitar, but there was no way she could tug at the hearts and pursestrings of the faithful the way Prescott used to.

The Happy Heart Club had been in syndicated reruns since Prescott was called home, and contributions had begun to fall off. Cash flow was becoming a definite problem.

Valdene truly believed that Prescott was a visionary, but he had not been much of a manager or a planner. The affairs of the Happy Heart Club he left behind were a mess.

Valdene was getting anxious. The money was running out. She knew she had to do something. She prayed. Then she went to a plastic surgeon and had an eye tuck. Then she started calling on old friends. She was thirty-five years old, and ready to get married again. At first she thought her husband would come from the music community, but no one there panned out. Maybe they still resented the way Prescott used to criticize their spendthrift, worldly ways. Then Valdene saw a story in *Fortune* about Buster Garland and she knew he was her man.

Buster had all of Prescott Sykes's charisma and even more money. And he was diversified, that was important. He didn't have all his eggs in one basket, like so many Texans who were wiped out when the price of oil slipped to thirty dollars a barrel. And Buster liked to live. Even though he smoked

133

and drank, two vices Valdene could not abide, she decided to put up with his tiny flaws until after the marriage. Then she would have the time to train Buster up right.

It was an easy matter to get Cordell Garland to reintroduce her to his daddy. At first, Cordell was so relieved that the Widow Sykes was not interested in him herself he would have fixed her up with the Pope. He simply saw that Valdene and Buster were thrown together on a few public occasions like the horse auction at Victoria, and let nature, and Valdene, do the rest.

It was a lucky break that Buster's daughter had been so wrapped up in running her silly old hotel she hardly noticed Valdene's affair with Buster until it was well under way. Now that Valdene had met Belinda Garland she recognized Buster's daughter would be a formidable rival. She'd definitely watch her back around that one.

Truth was, Valdene had targeted Buster Garland as an easy mark, but she had grown quite fond of the big old bear. He was old enough to be her daddy, true, but he was a lusty old boy. She appreciated a man with bulk, a good-size man who liked his feed. And to her relief he was a good lover, too. Those women who raved about Eyetalian lovers didn't know what they were talking about. Redneck boys like Buster Garland who learned to make love in the back of a Chevy sedan could pleasure a woman anywhere, anytime.

Yes, Valdene mused, Buster Garland was quite a catch and he was all hers. She had him on the line, now she just had to land him. This return to Happyland would give Buster a chance to see her in her own surroundings.

"Welcome home, Sister Valdene," Reba Twining said when she greeted her at the door. Reba looked Buster up and down with undisguised interest.

With a sincere smile, Valdene presented Buster Garland as "the Kingfish of Galveston." Buster laughed and took off his Panama hat. His sharp eyes had already caught the neglected state of the weedy gardens, but that could be because Valdene had been away from Heartland for most of the summer. It was a shame to let a property run down, he thought. That was the problem with absentee ownership. Yes, he could see Valdene needed help with her finances. She was just a little ol' girl after all.

"Is the chapel ready?"

"Yes, ma'am," Reba assured her.

Buster stared at Valdene. *Was she planning to drag him into her holy roller church? No way!*

She smiled. "Don't worry about it, sugar. I just want us to say a teeny little prayer because we got here safe and sound." She tugged on his arm and he followed her. He moved reluctantly at first, but as she rose above him on the great circular staircase, her fine, round backside bobbing, he succumbed to his duty as a southern gentleman and followed meekly.

"There are all sorts of reasons to marry, Belinda. We can never know what brings some people together and drives others apart," Claiborne Lurie was saying as he and Belinda Garland shared a late-night supper on the deck of the *Lone Star*.

"But," he added, "if you wait for the perfect man, you might wait forever."

He had dismissed his servants and most of the crew, and they were alone on the yacht. He picked up the bottle of Cristal and refilled her glass and his.

I had the perfect man once, Belinda thought. It made it that much harder to settle for less.

Claiborne seemed to read her thoughts. "I know you were in love with your husband my dear, but you were just a girl. If you think about it, your needs, your capacity to love, all that has changed."

"Have your feelings about Ciprianna Rivers changed?" she said, anxious to change the subject.

He looked at her in surprise. Claiborne Lurie had the titan's delusion that no one knew anything about him unless he wanted them to. He would have been surprised and dismayed to know that his longtime affair with the designer was an open secret in international circles. He disliked publicity and he was painfully aware of how ridiculous the whole Ciprianna situation made him look. Wait till news got out that she had dumped him because he couldn't control his granddaughter!

"I never discuss Mrs. Rivers. Or any woman friend," he

135

said smoothly.

"Well, I like a man who's discreet," Belinda said. She knew that Claiborne Lurie was out to seduce her, but somewhere during dinner she had begun to enjoy it. He was sophisticated, he was worldly, and she sensed that he knew how to treat a woman. He instinctively knew when to back off a subject — like the death of her husband — and when to press. He asked her about her plans for the Delancy Street warehouse and showed far more interest than Buster had. Nevertheless, she stopped.

"I'm boring you," she said.

"Not at all," he assured her. "But we can talk about whatever you like."

"I wonder why you've never married again," she said. The thought had been in her head all evening, and it just popped out. To her immense relief he did not seem at all annoyed by the question.

"I suppose that, like you, I was looking for the perfect mate. And, unlike you, I've made some big mistakes in the past."

Neither of them had to mention Amanda and Charlene.

"But you know, I think that I have finally found the right woman," he said. He stared into her eyes, his cool, icy blue eyes gazing at her, and she could feel her color rise. "You're blushing," he said, smiling.

She shook her head, unwilling to admit it. "I'm just a little chilly," she insisted.

He stood up at once. "Then we'll go inside. I can't allow you to be uncomfortable. There's some brandy in my cabin."

He led her to his cabin below deck, but did not turn on the light when they entered. The only illumination was the moonlight streaming through the portholes.

He took her in his arms and kissed her. She responded, gently at first, and then more passionately as his hungry mouth sought hers. Just as she was yielding to him, he pulled away and, taking her hand, he led her to the bed.

In the dim light, as he made love to her, she did not notice the huge nude portrait of Ciprianna Rivers that hung over Lurie's bed, and looked down on them now like an avenging angel.

136

Chapter Sixteen

Claiborne Lurie left for New York on business the next day and Belinda was relieved. She had enjoyed their night together aboard the *Lone Star,* but she feared getting too involved with him. Most of her life had been controlled by powerful men. First there was her father, then Arden. She had no desire to get involved with another.

Claiborne was not discouraged. A small bouquet of perfect pink roses arrived every day with his card, reminding her that even though they were separated he was thinking about her. It was very flattering.

But she couldn't develop Delancy Street on flattery.

Buster was pleased with the setup at Heartland although he didn't much care for the Twinings, who always seemed to be lurking around corners and creeping up on him. Valdene took him out to see the great Happy Heart cathedral that Prescott had been building when he was called home. She showed Buster the plans for the Bible-theme park they had been working on together.

There was a religious meeting in progress, and Valdene and Buster sat in. He was impressed, but she insisted that this guest preacher did not have Prescott's old fire. "It's impossible to replace him," she sighed. "Folks just don't want to believe he's dead."

"They'll get used to it," Buster snorted. "Haven't you told them about us?"

Valdene shook her head. "I haven't had the heart to tell them. I want to break it to them gently, on the air, so everyone hears it all at once. I don't want them to hear it from anyone else. Just be patient."

That was okay with Buster. He hated to be rushed and he liked the idea that Valdene was in no hurry to announce their engagement to her flock. It meant she wasn't desperate.

Valdene could teach Belinda a thing or two about patience, he decided.

Yes, he mused, his daughter could learn a lot from her new stepmother.

"How could you, Valdene! Buster Garland! That man is a no-account wastrel!"

"Reba Twining! *That man* is one of the richest men in Texas!"

"What does it profit a man if he gains the whole world and loses his own soul? That man is sipping whiskey in your bedroom. Don't tell me he isn't."

"Now, Reba, have you been snooping in my bedroom? What were you looking for?"

They were in Valdene's bedroom at that very moment. She was sure part of Reba's outrage was due to the fact that Buster was occupying the late Prescott Sykes's adjoining bedroom, although he hadn't spent a night in Prescott's old bed, preferring Valdene's and no wonder. Valdene fussed with her hair as she stared in the mirror and watched her friend and confidante pace the floor behind her angrily.

"All that man cares about is making money!" Reba sobbed. Her eyes were filled with tears and her pale, upturned nose was turning an unattractive crimson.

"Oh, Reba," Valdene purred. "Prescott was just as good as Buster at making money. I just wish Prescott had been as good at keeping it. Then we wouldn't be in this fix."

"Prescott Sykes was a man of God. A holy man. How can you compare him to that . . . that . . . animal!" She helped herself to a tissue from the ceramic holder on Valdene's vanity table and gave her nose a hearty blow.

Valdene stood up and put her arm around Reba's narrow shoulder. "Calm down, honey," she said gently, tilting her friend's sharp little chin up so that she had to look into her eyes. "I do believe you're jealous of Buster and you know you've no cause to be."

She kissed her gently on the lips, then held thin, little Reba tight against her as she sobbed loudly into Valdene's motherly bosom.

Belinda was furious. It had been more than a week since her father left for Nashville and he hadn't even called. She knew Buster's office and Cordell had been in touch with him, but he'd left no messages for her. Damn, he knew how important this Delancy Street property was to her and he was deliberately sabotaging the deal. She had not even tried to line up any other backing because she had expected him to jump in, and now it was too late.

The Delancy lawyers had already hinted that other buyers were interested, possibly Arabs or Japanese. One of them, Belinda was sure, was her own brother Cordell. Maybe Buddy, too. Or maybe she was just being paranoid.

She suspected that if Cordell went to Buster for financing, he would have no trouble getting it, either.

Why couldn't Buster acknowledge that she was a grown woman with a right to her own projects? She had never insisted on a say in running Garland, Inc., but this whole idea to buy and develop the Delancy Street warehouse was all hers. All she needed was his backing. He could afford it.

The Houston lawyers were saying that they couldn't put off the deal any longer. Some faceless outside developer, American Holding, had stepped in with an all-cash offer, topping her bid, and the lawyers closed the deal.

Belinda called Buster in Nashville from her private phone in the penthouse. "The deal's off. They couldn't wait," she said.

He didn't even say he was sorry. "It's just as well, darlin'. I got enough on my plate as it is."

"Enough on *your* plate?" she said into the phone. "This was my deal! I could have gotten the financing somewhere else, but I waited for you. And now it's over because you'd rather fiddle in Nashville than build something down here."

"Fiddle," he repeated. "Very funny."

"If this was Cordell or Buddy's deal you would have

rushed to help them," she said.

There was silence at the other end. In her anger and pain she had gone too far. They both knew that what she said was true.

"I'll call you when I get back, darlin'," he said at last, then hung up.

Belinda stared at the silent phone, then out at the angry gulf. She felt like crying. She hadn't felt so helpless since Arden died. All her work turning the Maison Rouge around suddenly meant nothing. She wasn't a real Garland because she wasn't a man. She was just another employee like Wiley Muehl or Brice de Young, and she'd be out just as easily.

She was fed up. Maybe she'd just walk. She had her own money—her trust fund from her mother and what Arden had left her. But she hadn't stayed with the Maison Rouge for the money. She had brains and wanted to use them. If Buster didn't know how to make the most of his own daughter, she'd do it on her own.

Right now she just wanted to get away from the Maison Rouge and away from Galveston. Far away.

Chapter Seventeen

Tootsie Bright was delighted to relinquish control of the Funland kitchen to Brice and happy to share the secrets of her success. "If it ain't broke, don't fix it," she warned him. "You can play around all you want with the menu as long as you don't scratch the old favorites. Folks have been coming here for the corn dogs for twenty years and they'll be coming long after you're gone."

She advised Brice to bring the public along slowly. "You know what the most important thing in a restaurant is, Brice?" she asked him one afternoon when the crowd had thinned and they were preparing for the evening's onslaught.

"What?" He sure didn't know, as his miserable record would attest.

"Be dependable. It's better to be bad all the time than good somedays and terrible others. You just confuse folks."

"I'll remember that, Tootsie," he said, grinning. But maybe she had something. He never expected to learn the fine points of restaurant management from a former trapeze artist, but he had to admit she knew what she was talking about.

"You know who's our best customer?" she asked another time. "The folks who come back."

He understood. There were lots of folks who would stop in just to try something new, but Tootsie's had stayed around because two generations of families were devoted to the place.

"You can learn a lot in thirty years on the midway," she

said more than once.

And speaking of the carny circuit, Colette was traveling, too, and called Brice once in a while. After her sensational appearance at the O'Higgins trial in Houston she had tripled her fees and her bookings.

"Guess where I'm calling from, *chéri,*" the conversations would usually begin.

"I can't imagine," he would answer. Did she expect him to have her psychic powers? he wondered. He hated playing these games.

"The Beverly Hills Hotel pool," she might answer. "And Clint Eastwood just walked by."

"I'm really impressed," he said without enthusiasm.

Colette always wanted an update on the progress of his restaurant, although he suspected she wasn't as interested as she pretended. Maybe he did have her power to read between the lines after all. He sensed that in spite of her indifference, she feared he would get too close to Tootsie and Harris. He was her only son, after all, and she had a fierce Cajun tenaciousness about blood ties.

"You didn't tell me what you're doing in Beverly Hills," he said.

"Springer Rondello, the director, hired me as a consultant for the picture he's doing on a serial killer. The thing is I think he really wants to know if his wife is fooling around, but he's embarrassed to come out and say it."

"Is she?"

"*Chéri!*" she purred. "That's confidential! And I see Springer coming this way. Must go. *Adieu!*"

"Oh, Aynsley, you're too good to me!" Lauren sighed.

"Nothing's too good for you," he answered, leading her around the condo he had just purchased for her. The air was filled with the smell of fresh paint and Lauren's heels clicked on the marble floors. Until now, the station had been footing the bill for her at the Bayou Bend Hotel which was also owned by Aynsley's family. This would be a real home and also more discreet.

"I can't wait to fix this up," she said. "I'll have to talk to a decorator."

"You can use the gal who did my house in Austin. Carola Lee was very pleased with her work."

Lauren glared at him, then quickly softened. Did he really expect her to use his wife's decorator?

"I was thinking more along the lines of Mark Hampton or Mario Buatta," she said.

"Well, darlin', the thing is, Missey Holmes is a Texas gal, and she has a husband who yearns to be a judge."

"Oh, so she'll do the house for free," Lauren pouted. She hated the idea of using Carola Lee Adder's decorator, but Missey Holmes was one of the choicest decorators around and she had seen her work in *Architectural Digest* and *House & Garden*. She decided to let it go. After they were married she could hire Mark Hampton or Mario Buatta. There would be other houses. Maybe even the White House.

Aynsley's advance people had already been through the house, sweeping for bugs, and had thoughtfully left the refrigerator stocked with Lone Star beer and Diet Pepsi. Aynsley helped himself to a longneck and opened a soda for her.

It was rare for them to be alone like this. Even now, his driver was waiting downstairs in the limo. Lauren thought that for a man obsessed with his image, Aynsley could be awfully reckless sometimes. It was a good thing she was discreet.

There was also a pint of Aynsley's favorite rum raisin ice cream in the freezer and he reached for it. She tried to distract him. Aynsley had a tendency to put on weight and was heavier now than when she met him. His belly strained at the belt line and his beefy red face glistened with sweat.

Lauren couldn't help remembering the very first time he made love to her. As he undressed she noticed he was wearing a corset. For a second she feared he was some kind of secret transvestite, but he caught her looking at it and explained that the corset was just for his bad back. An old football injury. When he removed it, she saw that it also held back a massive beer belly. At the time, it was a turn-on for her actually. She liked a man with a little bulk. But this was getting ridiculous.

Her friend Whitney had confided that Aynsley Adder

was destined for a brilliant career in politics. Lauren thought theirs would be a perfect match: her contacts in the news business and his in politics. There would be no stopping them.

Sometimes, when she was alone at night, Lauren stared at a photo of Aynsley with his wife. Whitney said that she and Lauren looked like sisters. She would stare at the picture, but except for the fact that they were both pretty and blond she saw no resemblance at all.

"Lauren Armour's here," one of the new Vietnamese waiters whispered in the middle of the evening dinner rush. She had arrived with a film crew to do a story about Tootsie's. All through the taping, she was strictly business, but when she left, she slipped him a note with her home number. He felt very cool.

There were plenty of people at Tootsie's every night. Houston people, Galveston people. Texas people. Folks from all over the state were stopping in. Rock stars in town to·play the Astrodome. Food critics searching for something new.

Brice had had enough of that. Most of them knew nothing about food anyway. He concentrated on what Tootsie had told him: *keep folks coming back*.

As long as he kept the old customers coming back he was free to try new things. Every night was like being onstage. Afterward, he'd go out to a roadhouse where other late-night workers gathered and listen to a country western band. He would stand at the bar and think about Lauren.

He decided to call her. It was three in the morning and he must have taken her by surprise because she answered the phone herself. She sounded sleepy. And sexy.

"Hello? Hello?" she whispered. "Aynsley, is that you?"

"No, Lauren, it's me. Brice de Young."

"Oh, hi!" she said, sleepily. She sounded pleased and surprised. "It was so good to see you. When are we gonna get together?"

He wasted no time.

"How about tomorrow night?"

Chapter Eighteen

The minute Charlene walked into her daddy's New York town house she knew it had been a mistake. There was no point in staying there if he was going to be there, too. She immediately decided to look into buying a place of her own and that made her feel very smart indeed. Everybody knew that real estate in Manhattan was a good investment. Now she was thinking like a business person, not just another empty-headed debutante. Unfortunately, she soon discovered that the boards of most of the co-ops she looked at were very stuffy and leery about having anyone of her notoriety in their building. It was very annoying: if she wanted stuffy, she could have stayed in Galveston. So for the time being she was stuck at Daddy's town house on Sutton Place.

She tried to cheer things up by having the Iranian butler move some furniture around and rehanging the paintings, but when her daddy arrived he noticed the changes right away and ordered Reza to put everything back the way it was.

"You'd think this was a museum," Charlene pouted, but she didn't dare say anything to him directly. She was still a little frightened of her father. He was the only man who scared her. He had never hit her, but there was something about his mania for order and his unflappable composure that made her tremble. She could never measure up to his standards and she had given up trying long ago.

Chandler greeted him with open arms and a big kiss. Charlene sensed that he blamed her for Chandler's weight problem and the public destruction of Ciprianna's dresses.

145

She retaliated by encouraging Chandler to call him Grand-daddy.

When Chandler kissed him, he noticed her makeup. He took out a snowy white linen handkerchief and dabbed at his cheek with distaste, removing all trace of her lipstick.

"Did you bring me anything, Granddaddy?" Chandler chirped.

"Maybe I did, dear, but you'll have to wipe that paint off your face before I show you," he said smoothly.

Charlene stared openmouthed as her daughter blithely walked out of the room and returned a few minutes later, face scrubbed clean as a baby's bottom. *Now why wouldn't Chandler do that for me?* she wondered. *Did Daddy give such great presents?*

Claiborne produced a shopping bag from the Sharper Image. It was filled with gift-wrapped packages and Chandler squealed as she unwrapped each box. There was a Sony Outback Walkman, an Accusplit Pedometer, and a Dive 35 underwater camera.

"Oh, Granddaddy!" she said, rushing to kiss him again.

"This is all for your trip to the ranch," he explained.

Chandler looked at her mother with puzzlement. This trip to the ranch was news to her.

Charlene was getting a headache. By the time her daughter finally unwrapped the last box, a Gund stuffed bear, and carried on as if she'd never seen a stuffed bear before, Charlene had had enough.

"Now, darlin', thank Granddaddy and go play in your room," she said. Just to be on the safe side, she rang for Ruby, and the nurse stood in the doorway.

Chandler looked hopefully at her grandfather, but getting no encouragement, surrendered and exited with all the dignity she could muster, leaving Charlene alone in the drawing room with Claiborne. Such intimacy with her father demanded fortification, and not waiting for an invitation, she moved to the liquor cabinet and poured herself a Stolichnaya on the rocks, then sprawled on the sofa.

"How was Galveston?" she asked as she sipped her drink. "And Ciprianna? I guess she's really mad because Chandler tore up her dresses, huh?"

146

Claiborne stared at her. It was a wonder to him how his bloodlines and Amanda's could have produced such a gull head.

"You should have come to the dinner for Ciprianna," he said coolly. "UTMB is a family charity. You could have made some kind of apology to your mother."

"I had to go to her wedding. She's family, too, you know. Besides, Galveston is boring. And so is Ciprianna. How is Galveston by the way?"

"The same," Claiborne said. "I saw Cordell Garland at the dinner," he added.

Charlene's face formed a moue. She hated to be reminded of her first ex-husband.

"He looked very well," Claiborne continued. "He was there with his sister."

"Oh? Belinda?"

"She's his only sister, I believe," he said dryly.

Funny. She rarely heard Belinda's name anymore. They moved in different worlds. It was hard to believe there'd been a time when they'd talked on the phone twice a day, even if they were getting together that night. They used to have so much to talk about. It had been more than ten years since she'd even seen her. But Charlene was sure that Belinda knew all about her; how could she not when Charlene was in the *Star* and the *Enquirer* almost every week. There were times when such publicity could be very comforting, no matter what her daddy thought.

"So she never got out of Galveston," she said with undisguised pleasure.

"She's running the Maison Rouge for her father."

"I suppose that'll keep her busy until he decides to tear it down and put up condos."

"She's done quite a job actually," he said, and Charlene noticed with annoyance that he sounded impressed. Her daddy was rarely impressed with anyone. Why did it have to be Belinda Garland? "She's completely restored the building and the grounds."

"Decorating and landscaping, the ex-debutante's two favorite professions," Charlene snapped, completely ignoring that she was pursuing the other two: fund-raising and acting.

147

"Actually, she's very involved in day-to-day operations. You might almost say she works too hard."

Charlene got the point. Belinda worked hard and she didn't.

"I'd love to do something like that, but I have to devote all my time to Chandler," she said.

Her father looked at her, his thin lips forming a small smile. He said nothing, but his silence was eloquent. She couldn't stand it and turned away.

"Ah, yes, Chandler," he said at last. "This trip to the ranch will do her a lot of good. Fresh air and clean living. That's what the child needs. And you, too. We'll be leaving tomorrow at ten. I'll be here with the car."

Then he was off to some meeting, leaving Charlene alone in the drawing room to finish off the Stolichnaya. She didn't dare tell him she had no intention of going to Rancho Strega with him and Chandler. She loathed the ranch. Chandler would have Ruby to look after her anyway. Charlene decided she needed some time alone. While she was in New York she could go to a few acting classes, talk to a few producers.

No wonder Belinda Garland could run a hotel! She didn't have a spoiled, demanding daughter around her neck. It was too bad about Arden's terrible accident, but there had been no hint of a relationship for her since then. Belinda was probably frigid, Charlene decided. Of course she had free time; she didn't have to think about getting laid.

Charlene remembered the year they came out together at the Artillery Club Ball in Galveston. It was the most prestigious debutante ball in Texas and the oldest. Charlene had been the prettiest of the debs, too, although Belinda was the most popular. Belinda could have married anyone. And she chose Arden Yates. Charlene was just so jealous she seduced Belinda's brother and the rest was Texas divorce law history.

She could hear Chandler arguing with Ruby upstairs. Her daughter was screaming that she wanted to go out and skate in the park and Ruby was shouting that she couldn't skate because there was no ice.

Charlene sighed and looked at the ormulu clock on the

148

mantelpiece. It was nearly three o'clock. Maybe there was still time to get a facial at Georgette Klinger.

Belinda had made her decision but she wasn't sure what to do about it. She would leave the Maison Rouge. As long as the hotel was part of Garland, Inc., she would be under Buster's thumb. He had given her a chance and she had proved she could do it. But if she wanted more she would have to get it on her own. She still couldn't bring herself to tell him that on the phone. She would have to wait until he came back to Galveston. But he didn't seem in any hurry to come back.

The Island nights grew steamy and the days passed quickly in a welter of last-chance summer sprees, but as summer wound down and business slowed, she had more time to think. She had lost out on the Delancy Street deal and she had to start up another. This time she would not depend on Buster.

Leaving word with Wiley Muehl to call her the minute Buster came back, she called her friend Fayette Cramer and headed for the Golden Gate spa outside of Houston. During the week they were pounded and pummeled, massaged and ministered to, and fed only the finest in rabbit food. The best part about it was sitting beneath the glass dome around the pool and exchanging gossip with the other women there. Staying at the Golden Gate was always a little like a high-school reunion.

By the time the week was up she felt good, she felt strong, she felt ready to meet Buster on her terms.

"I've got to be gettin' home, darlin'," Buster said one morning when they were having grits and eggs in the big Heartland kitchen.

"Oh, Buster honey. You can't leave me now!" Valdene said. "You can see how lost I am. Besides, you're always on the phone here anyway."

Buster smiled. He did love his cellular phone, but there was no substitute for being on the scene. And he didn't trust Cordell out of his sight for that much time. Besides,

149

he'd been avoiding Belinda's calls for too long. It was time to go home and face the fiddler.

He got a kick out of Nashville, though. Meeting all the giants of country music made him feel just like a kid. Walking through the Country Music Hall of Fame and visiting backstage at the Opry tickled him pink. And he enjoyed being pampered by Valdene. He was wise enough to know she was on her best behavior because she wanted to get married, but he was man enough to enjoy it. At least she put herself out for him. What had his children done for him lately?

At the thought of his children, Buster felt a twinge of guilt. He had behaved badly to Belinda and he knew she would be steaming. But she had to learn that she wasn't going to run Garland, Inc. She was a smart girl, but she was a girl. And what man with two sons needed a girl to run his business?

That was something Belinda would have to learn.

Valdene had still not mentioned her plans for the ministry, but he had no desire to incorporate Prescott's church into Garland, Inc. She had mentioned that Prescott's younger brother Lydell might be interested in taking over. But Valdene seemed reluctant to tell the Twinings that she would be moving to Galveston.

Buster insisted and she finally broke the news to them over a family-style dinner at the Parkside Restaurant. In a moment of magnaminity, Buster told the Twinings that they'd always have a home with him and Valdene. They hardly reacted, but Reba Twining's pale cheeks pinked up a little and she exchanged looks with her brother.

"Wasn't that easy?" Buster asked that night as he and Valdene settled down into her bed. "Now I'll leave for Galveston tomorrow and you'll come with me."

Valdene looked horrified. "Oh, I can't leave Nashville yet," she said.

"What do you mean?"

She caressed his round cheek. "I just can't, Buster honey. You've only seen a teeny bit of the ministry. Things are a mess since poor Prescott passed on. The program's still in syndication, but the contributions are way down. I've tried to cut expenses and overhead, but I just don't have the head for all that stuff. I was hoping you'd help me."

"Is that all?" Buster said, putting a great arm around her and holding her close as they lay in bed. "Shucks, darlin', why didn't you say something sooner? We'll get this straightened out in no time. I'll get some of my cotton counters up here to look things over with you. They'll wrap everything up in a week and then you come down to Galveston."

"Oh, Buster, you're so good to me." She moved her hand down over his belly and began to caress him.

Buster leaned back on the pink satin pillows and allowed the minister's widow to minister to his needs.

"I thought that yellow dog would never leave," Reba Twining sighed after they had seen Buster off at the airport that afternoon. The Twinings and Valdene decided to celebrate her engagement with a stop at the Dairy Queen.

"Yellow dog is right," Reuben Twining agreed. "Valdene, you don't seriously intend to marry that rascal, do you?"

"That's enough, you two. You happen to be talking about my future husband."

The Twinings exchanged looks.

"Now, Valdene, we understand that you're a young and healthy woman," Reuben Twining offered generously.

"Thank you."

"And you certainly have every right to get married again."

"Of course I do."

"But why Buster Garland? The man is notorious! This could be very damaging to the ministry."

"Screw the ministry!" Valdene snapped. "I had ten years of the ministry with Prescott. Ten years of his bitchin' about the way I made coffee, complainin' on the air about my housekeeping, my cookin'. You think people sent in contributions because of Prescott's preaching? I've got news for you. They're sadists who got a kick out of watchin' Prescott piss and moan about me. Every housewife who watched sent in money to thank Prescott for marrying me and not her!"

The Twinings looked horrified. "Really, Valdene. You

can't mean that."

"Of course I mean it." She was sick of the Twinings and the whole cult that pretended to believe that Prescott had been a living saint. If anyone knew better, it was she.

"Buster Garland might be a rascal and a con artist, but he's no hypocrite. And you know what the Bible says: "Woe unto you, scribes and hypocrites!"

The trouble with the Twinings was they just didn't think big enough. They wanted to hang on to their ministry so badly that they didn't see the promise in Buster and his fortune. She had learned so much more from Prescott than they ever would.

Wiley Muehl's call reached Belinda at the Golden Gate. She had just finished a swim when a maid brought the phone to her at poolside. She dressed and was on her way back to Galveston in a half hour, ready to give Buster the news to his face: she was through with Garland, Inc.

Chandler Garland was not pleased when her mother informed her that she would be going to the ranch with Granddaddy Claiborne. In fact, she stamped her little Mary Janes on the Aubusson carpet so hard that a small bronze statue of Athena that rested on a Louis XVI cabinet toppled over onto the floor.

"I want to go to back to L.A." she whined. "I hate the ranch. I hate the animals. I hate you."

"If you hate me, then you wouldn't be happy with me in L.A.," Charlene said logically.

"But I hate the ranch *more*," Chandler cried.

"Quiet, please," Claiborne thundered as he retrieved his bronze statue from the floor and examined it for damage. He hated this kind of emotional scene for which his daughter was so famous and, unfortunately, he could see that his granddaughter had inherited his daughter's temperament. "What do you mean you won't be joining us, Charlene?"

"I have a reading in Hollywood," Charlene claimed. "I'm up for a part in Derek Halsey's new picture."

152

Chandler stopped crying, possibly hoping that her grandfather had suddenly become an ally, and embarrassed that he had overheard what she said about his ranch.

"Fine, Charlene. Chandler and I will go on to Rancho Strega without you. But I expect you to join us as soon as this reading is completed," he said.

Chandler felt a little better. She still hated the ranch, but she could tell that her grandfather was annoyed with Charlene. That meant he'd be nicer to her.

"Thank you, Daddy," Charlene said. "I'm glad you understand about my need for a career."

"Make sure you understand my needs, too. I'll be leaving for Europe in a week and I don't want to leave Chandler at the ranch alone."

"She has Ruby—" Charlene said, then stopped, frozen by the icy look in her father's eyes.

Miss Ruby was standing in the doorway. Claiborne's chauffeur was behind her, carrying her bags and Chandler's. The old woman was seriously corseted in a canary-yellow silk Liberty print dress. Her matching hat would have done the Queen Mother proud.

"Well, don't just stand there, Ruby!" Charlene said. "You know how much little Chandler wants to go to the ranch!"

"Yes, ma'am, indeed I do," Ruby answered, but her face was so solemn it was impossible to tell if she was being sarcastic.

Charlene looked at her, flashing for an instant on the odd tension that always existed between her father and Miss Ruby. But the thought, like most of the thoughts that drifted through Charlene's head, soon died a lonely death. Charlene had more important things on her mind, like getting back to Los Angeles in time for her reading. She kissed Chandler the way she supposed a loving mother was supposed to and gaily waved to the three travelers as they entered Claiborne Lurie's waiting limousine. The minute they were out of sight she heaved a sigh of relief and rushed to pack.

Charlene had arranged to take Regent Airlines to Los

Angeles. Next to Claiborne's jet it was her favorite way to travel. Sometimes she even preferred it. She always knew who would be on her father's plane, but Regent offered some surprises.

This time, for example, she ran into her old friend Harmon Lane, and together they adjourned to the bathroom to renew her membership in the Mile High Club.

By the time she landed in Los Angeles, Charlene Lurie was feeling young, hot, and sexy. Eager for her audition with Derek Halsey the following morning.

Chapter Nineteen

Rhonda Perillo was thinking that her relationship with Cordell Garland was moving along nicely. She had completely forgiven him for lying to her about his name and background and she was convinced that by clearing the air they had made their relationship stronger. She willingly donned the blond wig he liked to cover her red hair and he had taken to spending the night with her in her room at the Breeze Inn, although he always left at dawn, claiming that he had urgent business meetings. Such dedication impressed Rhonda although she thought he worked too hard.

Cordell was starting to have second thoughts about seeing Rhonda, but he could not stay away. She was a beautiful island in the middle of the aggravation and uncertainty that was his life right now.

He was worried about his father's wedding plans. Valdene had flirted with him like mad until he introduced her to Buster that afternoon at the horse auction in Victoria. Since then, Valdene and his father had been inseparable. The woman had used him to get to his father.

He told himself he wasn't one to dwell on the past. He was far more concerned about the real implications of this upcoming wedding and Valdene's arrival into the Garland family. The next thing you knew, Buster would be bringing back Buddy! Just what he needed. Cordell knew he hadn't been the most distinguished publisher in the history of the *Sentinel-Wave,* but it was difficult with his daddy always looking over his shoulder, second-guessing him.

He found himself telling Rhonda more and more about

his trials with the paper and the Garland News Syndicate and with Buster. Maybe Rhonda wasn't the most intelligent girl in the world, and maybe she didn't have Charlene's distinguished bloodlines, but she was a good and sympathetic listener. Not a bitch like Charlene or Belinda.

Cordell smiled at the thought of his sister. Belinda was fretting in the worst way over old Buster's wedding plans. He supposed she was afraid Valdene would take over the hotel. The thought of a conflict between his undesirable stepmother and his arrogant sister pleased him greatly. The sooner those two got into a genuine cat fight the sooner they'd kill each other off. Figuratively speaking, of course.

Brice thought Lauren was slightly paranoid about being recognized, but he went along with her and rendezvoused with her Mercedes to the Pasadena-Baytown corridor, home of Houston's industrial processing plants. They parked behind a darkened factory, and as he stepped out of his car and into hers he caught a whiff of the air which smelled like a mix of rotten eggs and Pine-Sol. Inside the car they could look out on a moonscape of endless glowing plants with chimneys spewing fire and smoke. Someday, one way or another, everyone inside those plants, and in the neighborhoods beyond, would know his name. Everyone in the whole state would know Brice de Young.

Secure now, Lauren took off the scarf and shook out her hair. She was thinner in real life, and her mouth was tight when she wasn't talking. He reached over, touched her cheek, turning her head gently, intending to kiss her.

"Don't," she said.

"No one can see us."

She shook her head. "It isn't that."

He grimaced. Was this another cock teaser? Dragging him all the way out here just to tell him she wanted nothing to do with him?

"I was surprised to hear from you," she said. "Surprised and happy."

"I'm glad you're happy."

He had had enough. He reached over and pulled her to

156

him. This time he wouldn't take no for an answer.

As Rhonda Perillo's relationship with Cordell progressed, he had hinted that she should stop seeing her other gentleman friends, and she was glad to do it. None of them had Cordell's admirable qualities. In spite of her sexual experience, she really knew little about men, and Cordell was one of the few that she had ever trusted totally. Yes, he had lied about his name and profession early in their relationship, but now she understood that he was only protecting his family name and saving his daddy from any hint of scandal. Now that Cordell knew her so well, he knew he could trust her completely.

Rhonda understood all about the importance of a family name and respect for your parents, mainly because she had never known her parents very well and her family was a modest, undistinguished one. Her mama passed on when she was two, although from the photographs she had left Rhonda could see that she was a pretty woman and Rhonda resembled her. It was sad to see the snapshots of her daddy and mama together. They looked young and happy and in love, kind of like Rhonda supposed she and Cordell might look if he ever took a picture of them together and allowed her to keep it. Instead, he just liked her to pose alone, and he always kept the cassettes.

Her daddy, a shrimper who worked the Galveston Bay, never remarried, but moved his sister Merle into their old-fashioned house on stilts. Aunt Merle, Rhonda recalled, was a deeply religious woman who was always taking Rhonda to Baptist services, especially after Daddy was drowned. After Aunt Merle was called home to Jesus, right after Rhonda finished high school, she was left on her own.

Even in those days, people told her she was beautiful, but she didn't feel that way. Beautiful was being like Cordell's ex-wife. Rhonda always studied the pictures of Charlene Lurie in the supermarket tabloids, trying to figure out what it was about her that held Cordell's heart. Imagine, Cordell's wife fooling around with a pool man! Rhonda found it hard to believe his wife could cheat on

157

him. She had never been seriously interested in pursuing a career as a model or an actress. She wanted to meet Mr. Right and get married. And as far as she was concerned, Cordell was it.

"That's it for the day, darlin'," Cordell said breezily as he gathered up his camera equipment.

Roused from her daydream, Rhonda was a little disappointed. In her castle in the air it seemed that something real nice was about to happen.

Cordell snapped his briefcase shut. "Did you give me all the tapes?" he asked.

"Yes, honey," she answered, as she took off the blond wig and shook out her own red hair. "When will I see you again?"

"You know I can't make plans," he said with the air of a man who had all of Garland, Inc., on his shoulder.

She stood up and walked with him to the door, wrapping her short robe around her as she went. She took his arm and held it as she looked into his eyes.

"Whenever you're ready, Cordell," she said gently. "I'll be here for you."

"Suit yourself, darlin'," Buster said affably as they sat together on the terrace of the Sand Castle, overlooking the grassy green lawns.

Belinda was stunned. It had taken all her confidence to come here and face him, to give him the news that she wanted to give up the Maison Rouge, and all he did was throw his plump paws up in the air, shrug, and say, "Suit yourself."

Buster was unflappable. He was glad to be out of Nashville and back on his own turf, with his own people. But he had businesses to run, people to see. He could only devote so much time to Belinda's female problems.

"You're a big girl, Belinda Sue. If you've decided that you want to resign from the Maison Rouge, you're free to do so. How soon will you be leaving?"

"So it's just like that, Daddy? You never did give me that deed you promised, you know."

158

His eyes narrowed with annoyance. "We still got things to work out, darlin'. You're in such a hurry to get out of here. What am I going to do? Who's going to run my hotel?"

"You've got Wiley Muehl. And Tammy Lynn would probably love to learn the business." Why, Belinda wondered, was she getting the feeling that she was losing control here? It was like wading into the Gulf late in the afternoon. Sometimes you could go out too far, enjoying the way the ebbing tide tickled your toes as it swept out to sea, and then all of a sudden the sand gave way beneath your feet and the water wanted to pull you out with it. Belinda had the uneasy feeling that she was no longer just wading. The tide was pulling her out into an unfamiliar area and there was no turning back.

Buster shook his head. It was clear that he was not satisfied. Something was bothering him even as an idea was forming in his head. "You know, darlin'," he said cheerfully, "this is all going to work out for the best, I'm sure. And I think you're making the right decision, walking away from here."

"You do?" Belinda said, with astonishment.

"Of course, darlin'!" he said. "Of course! Why it's only natural you want to spread your wings. I'm just proud that we can say that we gave you a chance to learn here, and make your mistakes at our expense."

Belinda's Garland antennae were up at once. "What mistakes?" she said sharply. "You never mentioned mistakes before."

He waved his hand in the air as if to dismiss any such notion. "Not at all, darlin'. Just a figure of speech. Forgive your old father. I'm just so proud of you . . . Why, I was just telling Valdene the other night about what a fine job you've done here. And how much she could learn from you."

"Learn from me?" Belinda repeated.

"Why of course, darlin'," he said, glad that she was seeing the light. "You've shown me what a little moneymaker this old white elephant could be. And I'm in no hurry to tear it down. There's plenty of time for that. Meanwhile, I need somebody to run my hotel. Someone as smart, as

159

classy as you. And that's Valdene."

Belinda almost choked. "Valdene Sykes? Running the Maison Rouge?"

Buster's blue eyes glittered above his pillowy cheeks. "You see, darlin'? It will work out perfectly. I never would've suggested it, except I know how much you want to be moving on. I just hope you'll be able to take the time to introduce the little gal around, show her a little about the business."

You must be kidding! was what Belinda wanted to say. Yet she couldn't help marveling at his resourcefulness. Buster had sandbagged her all right. He knew how much the hotel meant to her. He knew it would kill her to see it in the hands of Valdene Sykes. He fully expected her to back down, extend her stay and then call the whole thing off. Well, it was too late. Knowing he wanted to replace her with Valdene (*Could he really be serious?*) was painful, but it only strengthened her resolve. As long as she stayed in Galveston and worked for Buster she would be at the mercy of whims like this.

"I'm flattered, Daddy," she said coolly, looking into his eyes with a stare as wide-eyed and blankly innocent as his own. "But everything I know I learned from Wiley and I'm sure he'll be glad to work with Valdene. I think it's better to give somebody a chance to make her own mistakes, don't you?"

He glared at her, but refused to acknowledge that she had outmaneuvered him. That gave her the confidence to go on.

"You know, we never did get that deed in writing. And I'm entitled to something for what I put into the Maison Rouge."

"Funny, Belinda. I thought you were most generously provided for with a penthouse suite and your salary. Don't tell me you want to renegotiate that now." He wasn't usually so sarcastic, but he was still smarting from her rejection.

She smiled. She felt free already, free of all the burden of being Buster Garland's daughter. Now she could just enjoy the advantages.

"I'd like to have the jewelry that Mother left me," she said. "You've been holding it in your safe-deposit box, but I'd like to take formal possession of it. Don't you think it's time?"

He didn't bother to hide his annoyance. What did he care? Mona wanted her to have it and she was welcome to it. Family jewels, indeed! Mona Clinton's family hadn't had any real jewelry since the Reconstruction. Any of the good pieces were things he gave Mona after he and Bubba struck it rich.

Never mind, he consoled himself. There would be plenty more where they came from.

The affairs of the Happy Heart Club were a mess, his cotton counters informed Buster. In fact, they assured him, you could hardly call the Club an organization at all. The weekly mail had been bringing the Sykeses several hundred thousand dollars in cash, but they never bothered to keep accounts, much less draw up a budget. Valdene Sykes now owed the IRS half a million dollars. And with the current decline in contributions and her own expensive tastes, there was no way she could pay.

Buster talked to Valdene on the phone about it. She sounded genuinely surprised to hear how much money she owed. It just made Buster's heart go out to the poor little thing. It pained him to see a lady in distress.

"Prescott always said the Lord would provide," Valdene said, her voice trembling a little from the lump in her throat. In a sense, she felt the Lord had provided. He had provided Buster Garland.

"Well, don't worry your head about it, darlin'," Buster assured her. "My boys and I'll settle this thing."

"Now, you don't have to do that, Buster," she insisted.

"Consider it my wedding gift," he said gallantly.

"Oh, Buster, you're so good to me. I just know old Prescott is looking down on us from heaven and wishing us well."

That thought wasn't quite as comforting to Buster as Valdene meant it to be. He didn't relish the idea of old

Prescott Sykes watching him and Valdene in bed, for example, but he let her have it her way. Women got funny ideas and it was best not to mess with them.

Or push them, either, but he was getting restless and wanted Valdene to come down to Galveston, and soon. He didn't plan to stray, but he didn't like being alone, either.

"When you comin' down, girl?" he asked.

"Oh, darlin'," she purred. "There's so much to settle up here."

"What's left to settle? You just give those Twinings the keys to Heartland and get on a plane and come down here. Or I'll send my plane for you."

"I kind of thought we'd get married at Heartland."

No way! he wanted to shout, but caught himself in time. Next thing, she'd want to televise the ceremony and he had no intentions of getting any more mixed up with her Bible-thumping cronies than he was already.

"I was thinking about bringing Reba along. She's never been to Galveston and she's goin' to be my matron of honor."

"No problem," he assured her. "She can stay at the Maison Rouge. She can have the penthouse. Belinda's moving out." With Reba stashed at the hotel, he noted, she would be out of the Sand Castle and out of his hair. He didn't trust that woman. There was something off about her.

"Oh?" Valdene said, surprised but pleased at this bit of news. Belinda Garland had seemed so wrapped up in her precious hotel, so jealous and possessive. Here Valdene was expecting to have to do battle with her, and Belinda Garland was already deserting the field. How nice.

"Yes, ma'am," Buster went on. "Just up and announced she's tired of running the Maison Rouge and wants a change of scene. That's the problem with women in business. No staying power."

Valdene sensed he was only pretending to be indifferent, and that he was more upset than he appeared. Best to go slow, she decided.

"I'm so sorry, Buster. I saw how close you two were."

Valdene assured him she'd come down to Galveston real

soon, and as she hung up the phone and sank back in the pink silk pillows she smiled with satisfaction. She was more eager than ever to move to the Island, now that Belinda was out of the way. And it was nice to know that Buster wanted her so badly.

He was just like all men, she thought, give them good head and they'd follow you anywhere. A lesson learned early in life and still far more valuable than even the Golden Rule. You could even call it Valdene Sykes's Platinum Rule.

Valdene was the oldest of twelve children of an alcoholic refinery worker and his slatternly wife who ruled the household with the strap. She grew up in Merrywood, an improbably named shantytown east of Port Arthur. Her parents spent most of their married life feuding and reconciling and producing babies. Valdene was twelve when her mama found her with a neighbor boy and packed her off to a Pentacostal-sponsored children's home in Mesquite.

The home was an enriching experience for Valdene. She learned that cleanliness was next to godliness. She learned that God helped those who helped themselves. And she learned she could sing and play the guitar. The Pentacostals were very conservative, but not when it came to their church music, which was rousing and loud.

Her father was half Indian and Valdene inherited his dark good looks, but she grew up in a place where gentlemen and others preferred blondes, and it wasn't until the Pentacostal home that she learned that she was desirable. Praise the Lord, was she desirable.

With her looks and her musical talent, there was only one place for her to go: Nashville. At fifteen she ran away from the home and hitchhiked her way to the Oprey.

Stardom did not come easily, however, and the few talent agents and music publishers who would even see her were a much tougher audience than the Church. They were more interested in her breasts than her songs.

She was keeping herself together with a job at the Dairy Queen and sharing a tiny bungalow with four other girls when she met Prescott Sykes. By that time she was no kid, she had been knocking around Nashville for five years and

163

she was afraid she was becoming just another country music groupie. She could get into any concert and had even gone on the road with Harmon Lane and the Highlights but the closest she had come to a career move was her affair with a session man, Ricky Lee Wayne.

Ricky Lee wanted to marry her, but Valdene figured that if she had to give up her career and settle for marriage, it would be marriage to a star.

Then Prescott Sykes pulled into the Dairy Queen one afternoon in his turquoise Eldorado convertible with the top down and asked for vanilla. Her hands were shaking, so as she gave him his cone, she nearly dropped some on the zebra-striped upholstery. She had never come that close to a Living Legend before in her entire life. For the next few months, he brought her little presents and chauffeured her home from the Queen every night. To Valdene he was still a major, major star, but as they grew closer and she spent more time at Heartland, Prescott confided that his record sales were down, he was a quarter million dollars in debt, he hated going on the road, and sometimes, when he was alone at night and couldn't sleep, he could not decide whether to drink himself into oblivion or put a bullet into his head.

And right there Valdene saw it. She saw the light over Prescott Sykes's handsome head and felt the call. She explained it all to him and the light filled his eyes, too. That night, after she baptized him in his very own swimming pool, they made love for the first time. The next day, he announced that he had been saved. He had his managers call a press conference and he told the world that he was turning his back on the entertainment business and the music industry. He would no longer serve Mammon.

Prescott and Valdene were married beside that same pool just a week later and embarked on a national revival tour that raised enough money to pay off his debts and lay the foundation for the Happy Heart Cathedral. Soon he was on television, then in syndication. Together and apart they recorded albums of gospel music that went platinum.

Valdene thrived on their success, but she grew to resent the way everyone deferred to Prescott, calling him Reverend and acting like he was the second coming of Christ or something. If it hadn't been for her, he would be playing roadhouses in Amarillo.

She concentrated on her own album and she and Reba Twining discovered they were sisters under the skin. Not since the church home had Valdene been this close to a woman.

Praise the Lord that Reba had been there to console her in her widowhood! Only another woman could understand her needs. If only Reuben Twining weren't so ambitious and Reba weren't so attached to him. Oh, well, Valdene accepted that the Twinings were a package deal and if she wanted Reba beside her in Galveston, she would have to make Reuben Twining happy, too.

The morning after her confrontation with Buster, Belinda awoke sick to her stomach. This tension between her and her father was taking its toll, and had quickly erased all the pampering of the Golden Gate. She had some tea and toast sent up from room service, tasted it, threw up, then went back to bed. She decided that all this stress was making her physically ill and resolved to get out of Galveston as soon as possible.

Funny. Buster was always the one telling her not to rush into anything. The Delancy Street deal had fallen apart because he refused to be hurried. And here she was rushing to get away from the Island because she was upset and angry. But if Buster was going to marry Valdene Sykes and bring her in to run the Maison Rouge, there was no way Belinda could stay. The woman was dangerous. Why didn't her father see it?

She tried to tell herself that Buster was too smart a man to be fooled by a pretty face. And a sexy body. Don't forget the body. But he'd seen breasts before! She knew he hadn't lived like a monk since her mother died.

Belinda still hadn't thought about where she was going, and on impulse she took the phone and called her cousin Lamar in California. Lamar, son of Buster's brother Bubba, shared in the income from the Garland trusts, but he had demonstrated absolutely no interest in Garland, Inc. He seemed to know that the rest of the family regarded him as a lightweight. At one time he'd wanted to be an actor, and since moving to Malibu had taken to calling himself an independent producer. He always seemed to be in the middle of deals and dropped lots of impressive names, but so far no one had seen a finished picture.

Belinda liked Lamar, maybe just because Cordell and her father didn't. Besides, her cousin was a good sport and generous to a fault. He was always inviting her out to California, but the few times she had accepted she grew quickly bored with the cocaine-fueled Hollywood lifestyle. Lamar assured her that lately everything had changed and these days everyone was going to AA.

"What's this I hear about your daddy getting married?" he demanded when he came to the phone.

Belinda sighed. Buster was right. The Garland family grapevine was thriving. She assured cousin Lamar that the wedding news was true.

"That old dog! Who's the victim?"

"Have you ever heard of Valdene Sykes?"

Lamar's laughter boomed all the way from the Malibu shore to Galveston Bay. He finally managed to get control of himself. "You're pulling my leg, Belinda. Not the holy rolling Valdene Sykes from TV?"

"You got it."

"Don't tell me your daddy's been saved!" He started that laughing again.

Belinda was getting annoyed. "Not exactly," she said. "But I'm glad you find it so funny."

For the first time Lamar sensed that his cousin was upset and he tried to act more sober, but it was awfully hard. The idea of lecherous old Uncle Buster hooking up with tel-evangelism's First Widow was too rich. On second thought, he wondered if there was a movie in it. He'd have to shop the idea around after he finished talking with Belinda.

"I take it you know the Widow Sykes," Belinda said coolly.

"Darlin', everybody knows Miss Valdene. Loved to watch, mostly with the sound off. She's certainly Buster's

166

type. I can see the attraction. Both of them."

Belinda ignored his reference to Valdene's abundant breasts. "I was thinking of coming out for a visit," she added.

"By all means! You know you're always welcome! We'll have a party!"

"I don't know if I'm up for that. It'll be good just to get away."

Feeling a bit better as she hung up the phone, Belinda made another try at getting up, dressed, and went downstairs to begin her rounds. As summer faded, the crowds of beachgoers were thinning out, leaving the streets of Galveston to the natives who didn't bother to hide the fact that they were glad to have their Island back to themselves. It was a good time to catch up on the hotel's maintenance and inventory. Then she reminded herself that such things need no longer concern her.

She considered making a formal announcement, but people like Wiley Muehl already knew she would be leaving. The summer staff would be leaving, too, going back to school or winter jobs in Aspen and Telluride. And the old-timers had never considered her their real boss anyway. Just the boss's daughter. Just another rich girl.

Belinda thought about Claiborne and their night together aboard the *Lone Star*. He didn't seem so old anymore. He was ten years younger than Buster; twenty-three years older than she was. But he was in excellent condition and he had turned out to be a sensitive lover. And he definitely wanted more from her.

She thought of what he had told her that night on the yacht. That she could do anything. He really seemed to believe that.

Now, if only she could.

Chapter Twenty

The sun came up over Houston and Brice de Young felt like a new man. His ego was finally getting over the beating it had taken in Galveston. That whole fiasco was behind him now.

He showered and dressed hurriedly. It was Monday and Tootsie's Funland was always closed on Mondays for maintenance work on the rides. For the first time since coming to Houston, Brice welcomed the free time.

He fixed himself some coffee on the hot plate and turned on the morning news to watch Lauren Armour.

Being with her last night had restored his confidence. It wouldn't be long before they were together. He could feel it in his pocket. Sure, she claimed she had a boyfriend, but he could tell from the way her body responded to him that no one had satisfied her in a long time. She still needed him.

Brice had been sleeping in a little room in the back of Tootsie's and saving his money since arriving in Houston. Now suddenly he felt like spending. He would have driven by Lauren's house, but she wouldn't tell him where she was living. He would have surprised her at the studio, but she had gone slightly paranoid when he even mentioned it. No, Brice told himself, their relationship was still too fragile.

Lauren Armour did not share Brice's excitement about their tryst. For one thing, she hated making love at night: it left dark circles under her eyes which the morning makeup man always brought to her attention while he applied Erace. For another, that very morning, the lead videotape showed Aynsley Adder and his wife Carola Lee opening a new hospital in Austin.

That bitch, she thought. *What kind of emotional blackmail had she used on Aynsley to get him to bring her along?*

As she examined her face in the mirror, Lauren could not help thinking that Carola Lee was one of the reasons why Aynsley never spent the night with her. That usually allowed her to get a decent night's sleep before going on the air for the morning news. It was another reason, Lauren reminded herself, why her relationship with Aynsley was so good for her. And why starting up with Brice de Young would be so bad.

It was important for a young, ambitious, hardworking young journalist like herself to be well informed, aggressive, and witty on camera. But if her looks went and the television camera stopped loving her, she would be banished to PBS special reports before she ever got her network job.

No, Lauren told herself, there was no way she was going to take up with Brice de Young. No matter how much he bragged, he was just a glorified fry cook and he would only bring her down.

After the show was over she headed home for a meeting with her new decorator. She wondered if Missey Holmes knew about her affair with Aynsley. Lauren was tempted to drop some hints, because she was getting tired of the Carola Lee situation. Sometimes she was even tempted to get herself pregnant, but that would be a last resort. She was sure that Aynsley would divorce Carola Lee and marry her immediately, but there would be no way to hide it from the public and it would hurt her career. The men might come and go, but her career she would always have.

"Designing a living space for any public figure is always delicate," Missey Holmes said as they had drinks in the kitchen. Lauren wasn't thrilled to be serving her decorator in the kitchen, but it was the only room with a table and chairs.

"It's a matter of balancing your public image with your need for privacy," Missey went on.

Lauren softened a bit as Missey talked. At least the decorator understood that she was a public figure.

"I'm sure you have lots of ideas of your own," Missey said.

"Not really," Lauren answered. All she was sure of was that she didn't want anything like that Carola Lee Adder had. This apartment was a temporary stage set, someplace from which to give interviews and be photographed. Eventually she and Aynsley would buy a mansion of their own in River Oaks or Georgetown and entertains there on a grand scale.

Missey reached into her oversize Mark Cross tote bag and started to bring out fabric swatches and photos, laying them out on the kitchen table.

Lauren tried to concentrate, but the whole thing bored her. Her mind kept wandering back to last night's scene with Brice. How could such a jerk know so much about pleasing a woman? It seemed to be the only thing he *did* know. She was sorry she hadn't let him stay over, but that would have been self-destructive. Suppose Aynsley found out? She knew his handlers were jealous of her and resented the affair. How they'd love to give Aynsley the news. *Your mistress is cheating on you.* No, she'd never give them the satisfaction.

And if she did, it wouldn't be for a nobody like Brice de Young. She'd be the laughing stock of broadcasting.

"Lauren?" Missey was saying. She sensed that her new client's mind was wandering.

"Sorry, Missey. I don't know what I really want. I just know what I *don't* want."

"Of course. You don't want it too contemporary and you don't want it too traditional. That's just my style," the decorator assured her. "Each room has to have its own personality, but there had to be a genuine flow from one to another."

Lauren listened intently as Missey explained, lulling her with a siren song of marble consoles and lacquered terra cotta, buttery metal and crystal chandeliers.

That afternoon, when Brice got back from shopping, the phone was ringing. Sure it was Lauren, he raced to get inside, dropped the keys, finally managed to get the door open, just in time for the ringing to stop.

He sank down in a chair.

The ringing started again. It was Tammy Lynn Garland.

"Have you been out?" she said. "I've been calling all morning."

And probably tying up my line so Lauren couldn't get through, he thought bitterly.

"I've missed you, Brice," she said. "I'm sorry you were fired. It was all my fault. I never should have left you alone."

"Yeah," he said, hardly listening. He didn't want to be cruel and hang up, but he had nothing to say to her.

"I'm going to make it up to you, Brice."

"You don't have to, Tammy Lynn. Maybe it's better this way."

"No," she said firmly. "I want you to come down here Labor Day weekend. I've got a job for you."

He sighed, anxious to hang up in case Lauren was trying to get through. "I've got a job, Tammy Lynn."

"Not like this. Grandpa Buster's getting marred, and I want you to cater the wedding."

"And what does your Aunt Belinda say about that?" he asked.

"Aunt Belinda has nothing to do with this. Valdene, Grandpa's fiancée, and I are running everything. You'll get ten thousand dollars, for two days' work. How about it?"

First Lauren, now this. Brice could hardly believe it. His luck had changed for sure. He was on his way back to the top.

"Brice? Brice? Are you there?" Tammy Lynn was saying.

He looked at the phone. "Oh sure, honey. I'm here. And come Labor Day, I'll be there with you."

"Where were you last night?" Aynsley asked as he and Lauren lay together in bed. Not really a bed, actually, but a queen-size mattress on the floor, sans frame or headboard. The only other furniture in the room was the Sony Trinitron television. Aynsley had been watching Peter Jennings, but now he muted the sound so he could hear her answer.

"I went for a drive. I wanted to see Houston at night. You know I still haven't seen much of the city," she said. She was talking too fast and saying too much to cover up her lie.

Aynsley sipped his Lone Star and stared at her. "That's not what I heard," he said softly.

"Oh, really, Aynsley!" she said with exasperation. "Don't tell me you're jealous!"

The blow came out of nowhere, his meaty hand hitting her cheek so hard the sound cracked. Her tumbler of gin and tonic slipped from her hand and crashed on the bare floor. He stood up while she lay back on the pillows, rubbing her jaw, hoping he hadn't broken it. She was so shocked she was speechless.

"Don't ever lie to me, Lauren," he said as he stood up. He quickly laced up his corset, then donned his pants.

She tried to concentrate on how ridiculous he looked, hopping on one leg, then the other. At his size and in his condition it wasn't a pretty picture. Physical grace had never been Aynsley's strength and age, weight and beer had done nothing to improve him. His face was flushed red with anger.

Lauren wanted to say something, but she was afraid. She had never seen this side of Aynsley before, although she had heard the rumors for years. The idea that he could hurt her was appalling, but intriguing, too. Suddenly she didn't want him to leave. She told him so.

He shook his head. They both knew that his driver, a young campaign volunteer, was waiting downstairs.

"Have to. Carola Lee and I have an appearance together tomorrow." He leaned over the bed and kissed her, holding her cheek gently. It was starting to throb, but his touch

172

made her forget the pain. "You better put some ice on that," he said, then turned and was gone.

She stood up and went to the terrace, watching as Aynsley made his way out of the building and toward his waiting limousine. When it had disappeared down the drive, she picked up an ice cube from the puddle of gin and tonic on the floor and rubbed it thoughtfully against her chin.

The evening started out badly for Cordell and Rhonda. He had come to her late in the afternoon, still distracted, he explained, because of his daddy's wedding plans. To cheer him up, Rhonda offered to take him to dinner at Clary's where she had never been but which was out of the way and she knew that Cordell would like that. To her surprise, he liked the idea. It turned out that he loved Clary's grilled soft-shelled crabs.

She put herself together with special care in a short, strapless cotton floral dress she was wearing for the first time. Cordell said she didn't have to wear the blond wig, so she pulled her own red hair up into a chignon and put on the new real gold earrings she had just bought for herself. Not for the first time she wished Cordell would let her wear his ex-wife's jewelry outside once in a while, but he only seemed to want her to wear it when they had sex or he was taking his pictures. She settled for her charm bracelet and a splash of Poison. Cordell like her to wear Poison.

But when they left the motel, they discovered that someone had broken into Cordell's Mercedes and taken the radio.

This sent Cordell into such a rage that Rhonda almost thought he was going to call off dinner but instead he insisted she get in the car and he raced off to Teichman Road in such a fury that she thought they might be killed. All the time he stormed about her neighborhood and how awful it was.

"I'm telling you, Rhonda, that's exactly what I want to change. Bulldoze those places and bring some modern buildings to Galveston!"

Rhonda had never seen him so angry, and she was sorry about his radio, but she liked her funky neighborhood. It reminded her of the block where she grew up, which had long since been leveled by developers. "I guess those buildings aren't much, Cordell, but they are historic," she said meekly.

"Historic!" he snorted. "They're eyesores. And dangerous. Those people . . ."

By the time they reached Clary's he had calmed down some. After dinner and a bottle of burgundy, he was the same affable man Rhonda had fallen in love with.

Cordell himself could feel the difference as he looked into Rhonda's wide green eyes. She always had that effect on him. Just being around her was a calming influence. He saw himself as a man besieged on all sides, kind of like Sam Houston at the Alamo. Only his enemies weren't Mexicans but his own flesh and blood: his daddy wasn't happy with the job he was doing at the Garland News Syndicate and he kept carping about how advertising at the flagship paper, the Galveston *Sentinel-Wave,* was down; and there as this new bride on the horizon — Cordell was sure Valdene Sykes would not be satisfied to sit back and spend Buster's money. No, she was going to want a say in Garland, Inc., too. He could see it coming.

And Belinda — he didn't know if he should be relieved that she was leaving, or worried. There was no love lost between him and his sister, but at least as long as Belinda stayed in Galveston and at the Maison Rouge, he had been able to keep an eye on her. Now who knew where she was going or what her plans were?

Yes, Rhonda might be a tart, but she was an honest one and he had a great need for her. The need was especially great as they left the restaurant and he felt a stirring in his loins. They had never made love in his car and he was tempted to take her as soon as they hit the parking lot, but he thought better of it. The theft of his radio had rattled him and he would not feel secure. Damn! If a man wasn't safe in his own Mercedes, where was he safe?

174

"Rhonda, you've never been to Oak Park Circle, have you, darlin'?" he said casually, suffused with the warmth of a good meal and fine wine.

Rhonda's heart took such a leap that she was surprised it didn't jump right out of her mouth. Cordell knew very well she had never been to his home, the mansion he had once shared with Charlene Lurie.

"I think you'd like to see it. I've got a pool. We can take a little swim, and later . . ."

Rhonda's eyes sparkled. "Yes, Cordell," she whispered. "Later . . ."

Brice had given up on the answering service. He had left countless messages for Lauren and she still hadn't returned his calls. He couldn't believe that she didn't want to see him after the night they had spent together.

He started calling the television station and got the same runaround.

"Miss Armour has been given all your messages," the familiar voice of the receptionist assured him. "But she gets a lot of calls and she just doesn't have time to return them all. Can someone else help you?"

First he'd been dumped by Belinda Garland and now Lauren Armour. Was he losing his touch?

That night he curdled the hollandaise for the first time since high school.

He couldn't stop calling Lauren's number. He was like a junkie. He was on the phone more than at the stove, and the food that night showed it.

"Even I wouldn't eat this stuff!" Tootsie said. "Are you okay, honey?" She sounded genuinely concerned. Unlike Lauren.

At the end of the night he swore he would not call her again. Houston was his last chance, Tootsie's was his last chance. He was on the brink of something big and not even Lauren Armour was going to screw it up.

The house on Oak Park Circle was everything Rhonda had imagined, with fabric-covered walls and upholstered banquettes and Chinese porcelain and elaborately framed mirrors. Yet it was ghostly, too, as if Cordell had changed nothing since his wife moved out and her spirit still hung over the place.

They did not linger in the huge living room, and Rhonda was relieved because she was a little overwhelmed by the sheer size of it, not to mention the big oil paintings, pagodas, and porcelain parrots strewn throughout the room. Rhonda gladly followed Cordell upstairs to the master bedroom.

"Oh, honey, this is just grand!" she gasped, but Cordell didn't seem to hear her.

"I'll be right with you, Rhonda," he called from the small dressing room next door. She could see him in there, rooting around inside an enormous mahogany armoire.

As for Rhonda, she could not stop spinning around this beautiful room. It was like she had died and gone to heaven! At the head of the bed, instead of a headboard, there was an enormous Chinese-looking red-lacquer screen painted with thousands of flowers. Beside the bed was an elaborate dresser trimmed with gold and over it hung a mirror that was also trimmed with gold. She sat herself down on the bed to get a better look at the whole room. There were flowers everywhere: on the carpet, in an oil painting on the wall, on the sheets and the duvet, and on the upholstered loveseat and the chairs. None of the patterns matched and yet it was all beautiful. She sighed.

Cordell heard her as he came back in from the dressing room, a woman's sheer nightgown over his arm and some jewelry in his hand. "What's that, darlin'?" he said. "Everything all right?"

"Oh, Cordell, of course everything's all right," she gushed. "It's just that all this is so beautiful. The gold on the mirror—"

"That's not gold, darlin', it's ormulu."

She stopped, suddenly self-conscious. It was times like this that she was all too aware of the social gap between

176

them and all the things she didn't know or understand that he took for granted.

"Oh, Cordell," she sighed. "I hope someday I'll know everything about everything in this room."

He smiled. It was so relaxing to be with a beautiful woman who didn't think he was stupid. "We can start right now, darlin'," he said, handing her the nightgown. "Get yourself into this, it's from Ungaro in Paris."

Her face darkened slightly. She was used to his special requests, but somehow, doing it here seemed to spoil the mood. Nevertheless, she complied. The negligee fit perfectly and he looked on with approval. Then he added his former wife's pearl necklace, and pointed to their wedding picture which was in a silver frame on the bureau which he explained was actually an eighteenth-century bombé commode.

"She's wearing these pearls in that picture," he said. "And see if you can get your hair up like she has it there."

"Of course, Cordell honey," Rhonda whispered, her green eyes full of love and admiration. "Anything you say."

Chapter Twenty-one

Once Belinda Garland made up her mind to leave Galveston, she was anxious to make a clean break. She did not want to linger on the Island and allow Buster to manipulate her back into the fold.

Buster himself was back at the Sand Castle, but without Valdene Sykes. She was supposedly still in Nashville, assembling her trousseau.

"Aren't you going to help us plan the wedding?" Buster asked one afternoon when he found Belinda walking on the grounds of the Sand Castle.

"I'm sorry for intruding," she apologized, a little embarrassed to be found there. But the grounds, not the ridiculous waterfall with its imported sand but the gardens her mother had put in, rich with oleandar and azaleas, always soothed her in times of distress.

"Don't be silly," Buster insisted. "This is still your home, and don't you ever forget it! In fact, I'm delighted to find you here. I was hoping you would give us some help planning the wedding. Valdene wants to have it here, not at the Maison Rouge. Says it will be more private and personal that way."

And it will stake her claim to the Sand Castle, Belinda thought bitterly, but she said nothing. Her father seemed so genuinely content and ten years younger since he had returned from Nashville she didn't want to spoil his happiness. It was going to be short-lived, anyway, she was sure.

Belinda did not even want to attend this wedding, much

less have a hand in producing it. She had made up her mind that she was not going to do anything to help it along. Love or something had made Buster totally blind.

She refused to be lured into helping with the preparations and insisted he turn everything over to Wiley Muehl and Tammy Lynn. Poor Wiley was constantly on the phone with Valdene while Belinda concentrated on tying up loose ends at the Maison Rouge. When she turned over the keys to the hotel, she wanted to turn over the complete package, to walk away with a clear conscience and not look back.

She planned to visit cousin Lamar in Malibu, then go to New York for a while. So many of her old friends were living in New York now, they were calling it Texas on the Hudson. And Claiborne Lurie had even offered her the use of his town house. She was seriously considering taking him up on it. In any case, he said he would be in New York at the same time she was. All she would really be leaving behind was Galveston and the Garlands.

And that would be a pleasure.

Belinda and Buster dined at the Maisonette. He complimented her on the quality of the food.

"It's not my concern anymore. I'll leave that up to you and Cordell," she said. "And Valdene, of course."

"Oh, now don't go talking like that. You're the one who gave up on the game," he said.

"Gave up on the game? That's all any of this is to you, isn't it? One big game. Play me against Cordell and the two of us against Valdene."

He looked at her, his blue eyes wide and his great, puffy face taking on a wounded innocence.

"Now, darlin', you know how I feel about family," he drawled.

Belinda wanted to say more, but she stopped herself. She was not going to quarrel with her father now. You didn't win arguments with Buster Garland, you just wore yourself out. Like she'd worn herself out on the Delancy Street project. That still hurt.

179

"Yes, ma'am," he was saying. "No one can say that Buster Garland is not a family man."

"I've been worrying about you, Rhonda," Cordell Garland was saying as she posed for him in her motel room, wearing some more of Charlene Lurie's jewelry. Today it was an onyx-and-gold necklace and matching earrings. Except for her Bruno Magli pumps, also Charlene's, and the blond wig over her red hair, Rhonda was totally nude, reclining on the bedspread according to Cordell's directions.

"Ever since they stole my radio, I've been worrying about you," he went on. "This neighborhood isn't safe. I want you to move."

Rhonda's heart started to pound. This was the moment she had been waiting for. But was she ready for it?

"Oh, Cordell, I don't know about moving into Oak Park Drive. I think I'd be scared rattling around in such a big old house."

He laughed. How could he tell her the idea of her in Oak Park Drive was ridiculous? It was a nice place to have her visit, but he wouldn't want to have her live there. Suppose Buster found out?

"Well, actually, darlin', I was thinking of something smaller. There's some new condos going up down on the Seawall and I thought you might like it there. Wake up in the morning and look out at the Gulf. You'd like that wouldn't you?"

Rhonda hid her disappointment. Her eyes watered from the new blue contact lenses he asked her to wear. She had moved up from model to mistress, but she understood she was a long way from wife. And that meant a long way from Oak Park Circle. Then she reminded herself what one of her self-improvement book had said: "The longest journey starts with one step."

Valdene Sykes had her heart set on getting married in

180

white, but Reba Twining convinced her that antique ivory was a better choice. She always trusted Reba's judgment when it came to matters of taste.

She still could not bring herself to close down Heartland, so she had arranged to have it open a few hours a week for paid tours. The money raised would cover the maintenance. She had ordered some of the furniture, including her bedroom suite (a custom-made duplicate of the suite in Scarlett O'Hara's bedroom at Tara) and the urn containing Prescott's ashes, packed up and shipped down to the Sand Castle. Buster had promised Valdene that she could redecorate the entire mansion to her taste and she could hardly wait to get started.

Her bedroom at Heartland was almost bare now, stripped of draperies and rugs. Soon the furniture would be going too. She stood on a plain wooden chair to show off the creamy confection of ivory organza and antique lace that she and Reba had finally decided on. Reba oohed and aahed appropriately.

They made an odd couple: Valdene so dark and voluptuous, Reba so pale and . . . well, Valdene guessed there was no other way to describe it, poor Reba looked dried up. They were the same age, but Reba surely looked older. The old adage was right: still water ran deep, and Reba had a lot of deep torrents inside her that no one had ever brought out. Until Valdene.

"You're going to love Galveston, Reba," Valdene assured her friend as she stepped down from the chair.

Reba just shrugged her narrow shoulders. She had already made her feelings about this marriage known. No matter how much Valdene talked to her and tried to assure her that nothing would change when she moved to Galveston, Reba Twining clung to her misgivings.

"You know, Reba, Buster's daughter's been running his hotel down there and she's leaving. How'd you like her job?"

Reba looked down at the bare, stripped floor. The truth was, she would have taken any job that kept her close to Valdene.

Valdene was wriggling out of the tight wedding gown. "My goodness," she gasped, winded from the exertion. She put her hands against her chest. She was nude. "Can't wear a thing under that dress. Now you're sure you can't see nothing through it?"

Reba shook her head and looked away. Valdene touched her pointed chin and lifted it, gently forcing Reba to look into her eyes.

"Aw, what's the matter, Reba honey? Cat got your tongue? Things aren't going to change between you and me."

Reba's gray eyes filled with tears and her pale face reddened. "I just wish I could believe that," she muttered.

Valdene seemed so confident that she had Buster Garland wrapped around her little finger. Reba was not so sure. There was something about those glittering blue eyes and good-ole-boy manner that scared her. And even Valdene must see that Buster Garland didn't get where he was by letting his heart rule his head. His heart, she thought, or whatever other part of his body was tying him to Valdene. Even she knew it wasn't his brain.

"You'll be leaving old Reuben alone up here and we'll be together all the time," Valdene was saying.

"Almost all the time," Reba corrected her. "You'll be a married lady." It annoyed her that Valdene didn't even seem to consider that Reba might miss Reuben. Valdene never considered anything but what she wanted. It was one of the things that Reba admired about her. Admired and envied and loved.

The still air in the barren bedroom was suddenly broken by the sound of shattered china.

"Oh, Reba, those moving men are crashing my Lenox," Valdene moaned.

In a second Reba was out of the room and on her way to straighten out the clumsy movers.

Left alone, Valdene stared at herself in the mirror. She was still naked and pleased with what she saw. Now there was something right there Buster and Reba had in common, she thought, smiling at her reflection. They both loved her body. They were bound to get along.

In Galveston, Buster Garland was also thinking of his bride-to-be. He had never been without a woman in his life, but except for the late Mona Clinton, the mother of his children, he had never allowed any woman to come too close. And Mona had been so different from him. Her family was Old Galveston, the ones who still turned up their noses at him, the ones who associated with the likes of the Luries and the Moodys and the Sealys.

Valdene, he sensed, was more like him. Down to earth. And that thought both pleased and bothered him.

"Oh, Cordell, this is just beautiful!" Rhonda gasped, meaning every word of it.

Cordell Garland, who normally tried to present a gruff face to the world, couldn't help flushing with pleasure as Rhonda walked around the apartment he had rented for her. The Seawall penthouse had a spectacular view of the Gulf of Mexico.

"On a clear day, you can see Cancún," he said, repeating what the real-estate agent had told him. It had been a unique, unnerving experience, renting an apartment for his mistress, although he had assured the agent, probably overassured the agent, that this was to be pied à terre for advertisers and clients of the Garland News Syndicate. He would just have to be real careful to keep this information away from Buster.

Rhonda could not have been more thrilled. The whole feeling of the apartment was so sleek and modern. The soaring windows flooded the rooms with sunlight. As a native of the Island and the daughter of a shrimper, she loved the water and from now on she'd be living right on top of it.

"Careful, darlin'," Cordell warned, when he saw her staring out over the terrace. "That sun there will mesmerize you."

She turned to face him, her face suffused with happiness. "Oh, Cordell," she said. "I'm the luckiest girl in the world."

Brice couldn't believe it. Lauren had dumped him. He had taken to calling her at the station every half hour. The operators all knew the sound of his voice. And they all gave him the same answer.

"Miss Taylor has your message and she will return your call."

Sure, he thought. *When longhorns fly.*

He even tried to get Kukla and Jan to help him. They claimed they didn't know where to reach her.

"She's moved out of her hotel," Jan told him. "All her calls go through the studio."

"Can't you call her and tell her I need to talk to her?" Brice said, trying not to sound desperate.

"I have, honey, and she gives me the same answer. 'Oh, I'll call him back as soon as I can.' That's all she'll say."

Lauren had made a fool of him.

At the studio, Lauren's makeup man clucked significantly as he covered her bruised cheek with heavy pancake.

"Walk into a door, dear?" Spooner asked.

"Something like that," she snapped. That's all she needed, to have people know her boyfriend beat her up.

It wasn't so bad, she told herself. Spooner had done such a good job no one could tell anything was wrong. The ugly black-and-blue mark really *looked* much worse than it was. Aynsley had never meant to hurt her, he just had a terrible temper when he drank too much. She noticed that he drank less when he was around the aides she loathed and supposed that they managed to control him.

Lauren blamed the drinking on Carola Lee, Aynsley's alcoholic wife. Once he got out of that bitch's clutches, she was sure he could be a new man.

Her secretary was in the doorway, looking frantic as usual.

"What is it, Juanita? I'm going on the air in five minutes," she said, making no effort to hide her impatience.

"Lauren, you've got to do something about this de Young. He keeps calling. Could he be dangerous?"

"Don't worry," Lauren smiled. "He's a pest, but he's not dangerous. Now leave me alone. I have to meditate."

Juanita shut the door, and passing Spooner in the hall, she rolled her eyes. Lauren wasn't fooling either of them with her meditation.

Inside the dressing room, Lauren riffled through her purse until she came up with the small brown vial of cocaine. She screwed off the black plastic top and laid out two neat lines on the dressing-table mirror. There was a jar of striped plastic straws and she took one, using it to inhale the first line fast and neat. Then she hit the other nostril. Restored, ready to deal with the news of the day, she strode out of the dressing room.

"All right, folks," she smiled as she passed Spooner and Juanita huddled in the hall. "It's showtime!"

Dinner at Tootsie's did not go well that night. Brice even burned the popcorn.

"Isn't there something you can do about this?" Cordell asked.

Belinda stared at him. It was a fine time to be asking her for help. Had he cornered her in her soon-to-be former office at the Maison Rouge just to ask her that?

"I guess Daddy's old enough to marry without our consent."

"He must be senile," Cordell said. "He hardly knows her."

"You're the one who introduced them," Belinda said.

"She never said she wanted to marry him. She deceived

me."

Belinda laughed. Cordell was acting like a betrayed lover. Had he expected to manipulate Valdene all the way to the altar? Poor Cordell! His strategy had backfired, and now his Mata Hari was going to be his stepmother instead.

"How can he do this to me? He's making a fool of himself!"

"Oh, really, Cordell, Daddy has a right to get married again."

"It isn't that. I don't think he's even got Valdene to sign a premarital agreement. What about children? Do you realize that if they have children—revolting as that prospect may be—they'll share in *our* inheritance!"

Belinda didn't know whether to laugh or cry. And to think this fool was her brother! And Buster was grooming him to run Garland, Inc. Maybe poor Buster was getting senile after all. Everything Cordell said only made her happier to be getting out.

"This is exactly the kind of behavior that drove Buddy away," he said.

"Oh, Cordell. It was Buddy's hot pants that led him away, nothing else."

Belinda was becoming bored with this conversation. She was sick of Cordell's whining. In fact, she was sick to her stomach and wished he would leave so she could go into the bathroom and throw up in peace. This whole thing was ruining her health.

Cordell went to the door. "All right, Belinda. But remember, this marriage is just as much a disaster for you as for me."

At last he was gone. She just made it to the bidet.

Rhonda Perillo was so thrilled with her new home and so grateful to Cordell for his generosity that she felt the only way she could pay him back would be to become the kind of woman he could really love. A woman like Charlene Lurie. With that in mind, she continued to read her self-improvement books, but she added society columns and magazines like *Ultra* and *Town & Country* to her reading list. She signed up for a wine-tasting course at the Galvez Hotel and also intended to take riding lessons. She had seen photographs of Charlene Lurie riding a horse at her father's ranch in South Texas.

She had plenty of time to study such things since she had the days to herself, and she found living in her new apartment, beautiful as it was, a little lonely. There was none of the lively street action of her old neighborhood, that was for sure.

She liked to take breakfast on the terrace and just stare out at the Gulf. This morning, as she sipped her coffee, she read for the first time that Cordell's father was getting married. To Valdene Sykes! How often had she watched Valdene and Prescott and the Happy Heart Hour on TV with Aunt Merle! She felt as if she practically knew them. But it was awfully odd that Cordell had never mentioned it.

Poor Cordell, she thought. His daddy worked him so hard that he couldn't think straight.

Belinda had taken a walk on the grounds of the Maison Rouge, but she was still feeling weak and shaken. She was furious with herself for getting sick just at the time when she needed her strength the most. But another nagging worry bothered her more. She kept recalling her mother's illness. She could not remember any of the symptoms, only her mother's progressive weakness and retreat to her bedroom at the Sand Castle until one night they were called to her bedside to say good-bye. Was she going to die the same way as her mother?

The thought terrified her. She decided she could not afford to think about it. If she died, she died.

Aynsley came to Lauren's apartment at midnight, after his fund-raiser broke up. Once again he had promised to take her to dinner, then stood her up.

"Look, I brought you something," he said. He reached

187

into his pocket and pulled out two dinner rolls.

She stared at them in disgust. "Is this your idea of a consolation prize?"

He shrugged. He was wearing one of his fat suits, tailored to minimize his bulk, but it didn't disguise his beery complexion. He had been drinking heavily at the dinner and that always left his face flushed and his temper short.

Times like this, when Lauren started bitchin' and naggin', made Aynsley appreciate Carola Lee. She wasn't exciting or very bright, but she knew her place. And she didn't demand that he *talk* to her all the time.

Lauren was dressed for bed in a thin silk nightgown, and he could see right through it. She had a terrific body, slim, boyish hips and big breasts. Like something out of *Playboy* magazine. Just the kind he and old Arden Yates used to line up in quantity after the Aggie games.

Just thinking about Arden Yates made Aynsley suddenly sad and he headed for the kitchen to get another longneck. Lauren followed him, still bitching about the rolls, but he ignored her. He was anxious to get another beer in him before he got too sober. He didn't want to think about his good buddy Arden when he was sober.

The times they had! Before poor old Arden had to go and marry Belinda Garland. That was his big mistake. Belinda was no Carola Lee.

He knew that Belinda blamed him for killing Arden. Imagine! As if he would have deliberately killed the best, truest friend a fella could have! Next to his daddy, of course. Aynsley Adder, Sr., had saved his ass more than once. He understood about the whole stupid accident. His daddy didn't blame Aynsley for killing Arden. No, sir. He understood that it had been just an accident. If only Belinda could understand that.

He took two Lone Stars from the refrigerator and opened one immediately, chugging it down like a man dying of thirst. Refreshed, he realized that Lauren was still behind him, going on like a jaybird, and he hadn't heard a word she said. The buzz was irritating, and he reached out

188

with a beefy hand and swatted her one. In his stupor he hadn't measured his strength and the blow sent Lauren flying across the floor of the kitchen. Grabbing the other can, he turned his back on her and went into the bedroom. It was almost time for *Nightline*.

Chapter Twenty-two

At least Brice de Young was coming back to Galveston in style, he thought as he moved through the early-morning traffic. It was a clear September day with no sign of rain. No sign of hurricane.

This gig better be a success, he reminded himself, because he wasn't sure he could go back to Tootsie's.

Tootsie and Harris hadn't been thrilled when he told them he was taking off for Labor Day weekend.

"A weekend?" Tootsie said. "You know that's our busy time. How could you take off a holiday weekend?"

Brice had just shrugged and reminded Tootsie and Harris that they had no contract. Only a handshake.

"Besides, I'll go over the menu with Manuel and Ninh before I go, so they'll know what to serve."

Harris shook his head. "It won't be the same," he said.

Of course it won't be the same, Brice wanted to say. That's why Buster Garland's paying me ten grand to cook for his wedding. But he didn't need to give Harris Bright a hard time. It wasn't going to make any difference.

Tootsie was much angrier than Harris about Brice's sudden defection. "Call before you come back," she yelled as he was pulling out of the tiny parking lot. "In case we find somebody better."

"You won't," Brice yelled right back.

So here he was, cruising along the Seawall on his way back to the Maison Rouge, scene of his earlier triumph. The wedding was going to be at the Sand Castle and

190

Tammy Lynn was supposed to pick him up at the hotel and take him out there. He was anxious to get a look at the whole layout, especially the kitchen.

Tammy Lynn's call had come as a total surprise. Between his new job and Lauren he had hardly given her a thought. When he did it was only because he blamed her for introducing him to her aunt.

Oh, great. Her aunt Belinda would probably be there, too. Well, screw her, there was nothing she could do about this menu.

Maybe he shouldn't have left Galveston so soon, he thought. Tammy Lynn was still steamed about that. But it made no difference. He was coming back in a big way.

Brice reviewed the menu he and Tammy Lynn had discussed on the phone: barbecued shrimp, oysters on the half shell, Gulf crabmeat in phyllo pastry, and rack of lamb. He would be working with the Sand Castle staff and would be responsible for the wedding dinner Saturday and a small breakfast the following morning. A special pastry chef from San Antonio was bringing in the wedding cake.

A veranda wrapped around the back and sides of the Sand Castle and a flight of steps descended to an oleandar garden in the rear of the house. For the occasion, Valdene and Tammy Lynn had ordered a custom-built tent that covered the veranda, so that the two hundred-plus wedding guests would enter the house through the front door and then walk down the hall to the tent, which would seem to be just another room of the house.

On the morning of the wedding, the decorator's assistants were inside the tent, hanging baskets that would later be filled with gardenias. Workmen were setting up round tables that would be covered with ivory damask and peonies.

Tammy Lynn surveyed all this activity and was very pleased with herself. Everything was going according to schedule. And inviting Brice back to supervise the dinner had been an inspiration. She could not wait until Belinda saw him. She still had not forgiven her aunt for firing him so abruptly.

"Don't forget that we want the pool filled with gardenias, too," she reminded the florist's assistant.

"Of course, Miss Garland."

Tammy Lynn was discovering that she and Valdene had the same taste and she was looking forward to getting to know her new stepgrandmother better.

She consulted her Rolex. It was almost two and Brice should be checking into the Maison Rouge by now. She decided to leave. She did not want to keep him waiting. Brice got into trouble when left alone, as she already knew all too well.

Brice was checking in when he noticed his old nemesis striding through the atrium lobby. He had forgotten what a good-looking woman Belinda Garland was. But another ball buster. Why, he asked himself, was he always drawn to these women?

"What are you doing here?" she said coolly. "Don't you know you're not welcome?"

"Nobody told me at the desk," he smiled. "I've already checked in. I guess you haven't heard the good news."

Belinda stared at him. "What good news?"

"I'm back. I'm cooking for the big wedding."

Belinda tried to hide her surprise. But he wasn't fooled.

"Tammy Lynn didn't tell you, did she?" he laughed. "And I thought you two were so close!"

"We used to be, Brice," Belinda said coolly. "But something happened. You remember."

She turned and walked away.

Tammy Lynn Garland, who had been eavesdropping from behind a Corinthian column, saw all this, including the expressions on Brice and Belinda's faces. Now she knew for sure why her aunt fired him! She'd been after him all along. Fighting back her anger, she went to tell Brice she'd arrived.

Belinda was still shaking from her encounter with Brice de Young when she arrived at her doctor's office for a checkup. She had been putting it off for too long, and now that she was leaving the Island she decided to take care of it. Dr. Espey was downtown, near the Tremont Hotel. She avoided looking at the Delancy Street warehouse, but she couldn't help noticing that there was no sign of activity around the building. Not even a billboard announcing the new ownership.

Why hadn't Tammy Lynn told her that Brice would be staying at the Maison Rouge? Did Tammy Lynn know about them, she wondered. Or did she only suspect? Running into Brice had unsettled her, for she had managed to put him out of her mind totally, and now she was going to have to see him all weekend long. It was not a pleasant prospect. Nothing about this wedding was.

In his office across the street from the Tremont, Dr. Willard Espy put Belinda through a battery of tests. She tried not to show how anxious she was, but he had treated her mother and he knew her family history. He told her it would be at least a week before he had all the lab reports in.

"I'm going out of town," she said. "I'll call you for the results." In her mind, however, she was ready to forget the whole thing. If she was going to die, did she really want to know it?

Since returning to Los Angeles, Charlene Lurie had discovered a new path. A solar path. Her acting coach had told her that her body was an instrument and she had to treat it with care. And so she was working out regularly at the Sports Club. Her trainer, a former Mr. America, led her in a daily regiment on the turquoise-and-salmon Nautilus machines. It was hell, but it was wonderful. She had dropped nineteen pounds.

"You look anorexic," her acting coach said.

"Thank you," Charlene said.

She had stopped drinking, except for white wine.

She owed this new healthy way of life to her new lover. Speed Porter.

Since moving to Los Angeles she had quickly learned that all the serious casting was done at parties and she had made it her business to get around. Late in the summer, Derek Halsey had taken her to a birthday party for Howard Harlow, the agent. It was at Cary Grant's old house, on the market for twenty-five million. Speed Porter had been renting it since his split from Angelica Weston. This was the first time Charlene and Speed had met.

A week later, Speed, Howard, and his manager came to Charlene's fund-raiser to Save the Whales. Then Speed went off to the Philippines to make *Gorgon,* a movie about the Vietnam War, and had been calling Charlene ever since. By the time he came back to Los Angeles he couldn't wait to be with her.

He gave her an autographed photograph of his right arm flexing which was to be the *Gorgon* billboard on Sunset Strip.

All that fall, when he came home from the cutting room where he was editing *Gorgon,* they would spend their nights together watching movies in his private screening room, or having quiet dinners at Ivy at the Shore or Cinois on Main. They went shopping for matching Harleys in Culver City. Everywhere they went they traveled in Speed's black 560 Mercedes with the blacked-out windows. Speed's bodyguards followed in a brown Ford LTD.

Charlene decided she wanted to stay in Los Angeles forever. She didn't know what she was going to do about Chandler.

It had been understood that Belinda and Myles McLean would attend the wedding together, and as they arrived for the ceremony that would unite her father with

Valdene Sykes, she was relieved to be on the arm of someone she trusted. So many of the guests seemed to be friends of Valdene's she felt like a stranger in the house where she was raised. What did it matter? she asked herself. Her bags were packed and immediately after the wedding, she would be leaving the Island.

By the time she and Myles arrived at the Sand Castle, most of the other guests had already gathered inside Tammy Lynn's faux conservatory, but the pink-jacketed decorator's assistants were still jamming peonies into the centerpiece bouquets. The room seemed to be blooming with lush, full blossoms in every shade from pristine white to deep magenta, and the air was heavy with their fragrance. The tent poles were wrapped in baby's breath, the tables and chairs shrouded in ivory damask.

White-jacketed waiters moved through the waiting crowd with trays of shrimp canapés and flutes of champagne. Yet there was something odd about the whole setting. Belinda mentioned it to Myles.

"This doesn't seem like a wedding, does it?" she remarked.

"No, it doesn't," he said dryly. "More like the Dolly Parton Show, presented by Tammy Faye Bakker."

She realized for the first time that he shared her distaste for this whole shebang and was about to ask him about it, but at that point the sound of organ music floated through the room and they were asked to take their places. The boys in pink jackets herded them into an area where more damask-wrapped chairs had been arranged in a church setting, leaving an aisle for the blushing bride to proceed down. At the altar, banked with more peonies, stood Buster, looking more nervous than Belinda had ever seen him. Was it possible that he was actually in love with this woman? Belinda could hardly believe it.

Cordell was beside him, the best man by default, and the minister who would perform the ceremony bore a striking resemblance to the late Prescott Sykes himself. This must be his brother, Belinda decided. The seated guests had been creating a soft-anticipatory buzz, but

195

there was a sudden hush and then a few gasps, and suddenly Valdene herself was walking down the aisle on the arm of Reuben Twining, followed by Reba, who looked less plain than usual in a soft pink dress, and with her dark hair pulled up and crowned with wildflowers and roses.

But Valdene herself was breathtaking in her tight, antique ivory gown with the cascading lace. It was so elaborate it just missed being ridiculous, but only just. Her black hair was brushed up and held by two large white gardenias. Her bouquet was a cluster of more gardenias. Belinda had to admit Valdene was beautiful and sexy. And, she told herself, Buster was no pushover. Maybe, just maybe, he knew what he was doing.

Tammy Lynn, who had been lurking in the background, nervously surveying the crowd, quietly slipped into the seat beside Belinda as the minister began to read the ceremony. She tried to concentrate on the words, but for her they were just a prelude for Brice's debut as a caterer. She hoped that all these guests would go back to their cities and towns, mansions and ranches, singing the praises of an important new chef. She had big plans for Brice and this was just the beginning. She never should have left him alone the first time. After this wedding, she wasn't going to let him out of her sight.

The rest of the afternoon was a blur to Belinda. Once they were safely married, Buster toasted his bride, his children, his friends, and his future. The dinner was a rousing success and Belinda was happy for Brice and Tammy Lynn. Afterward, they threw birdseed at Buster and Valdene as they stepped into the Garland helicopter that would whisk them off to Cancún for their honeymoon.

As night drew near and storm clouds gathered, guests were still dancing under the lights at the beach as the breakers from Galveston Bay lapped at the shore, and after dancing with Myles McLean, Belinda made her excuses.

Belinda was relieved to sink back in the Sand Castle limousine for perhaps the last time and give Buster's chauffeur instructions to take her to the Houston airport. The sooner she was on her way to California, the better.

Chapter Twenty-three

"I'm going back to Houston with you," Tammy Lynn announced as Brice was packing up his knives. Most of the kitchen had already been cleaned and it looked as if nothing had ever happened there. The other servants had departed and they were alone.

Brice started to list all the reasons why she shouldn't. Starting with the fact that her grandfather had told her that she would get no more allowance if she wasn't in Galveston to collect it.

"I don't care. I'm sick of Galveston. And Valdene won't want me around."

Well, he didn't want her around, either. But maybe he owed her something. She had saved his neck twice this summer, and there was no doubt she was connected. After the wedding dinner, when he had been liberated from his kitchen duties, he had changed into a dinner jacket and the two of them had joined the other dancers down by the shore. He was impressed with all the people she knew.

"Kukla and Jan told me about Funland. Maybe I could help you there. Build up the catering end. It would be strictly business."

"Strictly?" he said, still skeptical.

"Sure, Brice. My family's got contacts all over the state. And we can get publicity in Grandpa's newspapers. Tootsie's Funland could be more than just a roadside cafe. Much more."

198

Brice was suddenly at a loss for words. None of this had occurred to him, but now that Tammy Lynn mentioned it, it seemed important. Maybe she could help him after all. He was moving up in the world.

"Partners?" Tammy Lynn was saying. For a second he thought she had been reading his mind. Well, he hadn't exactly been thinking of a partnership situation, but for the time being, why not?

"Partners," he agreed. "But remember, Tammy Lynn, when we get to Houston, you find your own place. This is a business relationship. Understand?"

"Oh, sure, I understand," she assured him. She was feeling in a generous mood anyway. She had won this battle with him and in time she expected to win the war.

It was an overcast morning in Los Angeles and a chauffeur and the white Rolls-Royce met Belinda at LAX and took her out to Malibu. The car pulled up at the gate, a man inside punched out a combination on the touchtone panel, a buzzer sounded, and the door opened. The man led her to the house, a modest two-story villa, and took her into the bright, spacious living room. Lamar was barefoot, in gym shorts, chomping away on a bowl of Granola. He put it down and came racing to her, arms wide open.

"Belinda! Welcome to L.A.!"

Like all the Garlands, Lamar was tall and fair, with memorable blue eyes. But his blond hair was long, pulled back in a tight Samurai-style pony tail. Although he was about Cordell's height and weight, he seemed stockier, because he had recently started working out.

He led Belinda out to a rear deck. A closed gate opened out onto Malibu Beach which she could see over the wooden fence.

"Sorry I couldn't make the wedding," he said.

"You missed nothing," she assured him.

Over tequila sunrises she poured out her heart to her cousin. The way she didn't trust Valdene and could not understand her father's infatuation with her. Just thinking about Buster's new bride made her so angry she got up and paced the deck.

"You should have seen her with Tammy Lynn," she said. "That poor little girl looks up to her. Valdene's got her wrapped around her little finger. I'm telling you, Lamar, I just don't trust her."

"Well, Belinda, that may be, but your daddy's old enough to know what he's doing. He's nobody's fool."

"You ought to see him with her, Lamar. The way he watches her."

"That'll pass," he assured her, a little sadly. "It always does."

"And then she'll take him to the cleaners."

"Maybe he'll think it was worth it," Lamar said softly.

Belinda looked at him, puzzled. "What are you saying?"

"Just that your father's not a kid and maybe he's lonely. Maybe Valdene gives him something that money can't buy. Besides, look at it this way. Can anything that upsets old Cordell be all bad?"

Belinda laughed in spite of herself. Leave it to Lamar to find the one bright spot in this.

Belinda stayed with Lamar for a week. He usually slept late and she got used to getting up early and walking the deserted Malibu beach alone. It was beautiful, but it wasn't the Gulf. Lamar took her to a few parties and introduced her to some movie stars. She even heard Charlene Lurie was in town, but their paths never crossed. Belinda wondered if Charlene knew that she was seeing her father. Claiborne called her a few times just to chat and it was understood that they would be getting together in New York.

She arrived a week later and checked into the Sherry Netherlands. Pink roses from Claiborne Lurie were already in her suite and there was a message from Dr. Espy to call immediately.

Belinda's hand started to tremble. This was just what she needed. She tossed the message away and went out for a walk. Once again, she had faced a bad situation by denying it existed. What good did that do? the adult in her wanted to know. But the frightened child didn't care, insisting that ignorance was bliss.

The adult in her won out for a change, and when Belinda returned to her hotel room, she found that the maid had been in to straighten up and had thoughtfully retrieved Dr. Espy's message and left it on the mahogany writing desk. This time she couldn't ignore it.

She placed a call to the good doctor in Galveston, hoping that perhaps he had left early.

He was in, and he sounded affable, no different than usual. But, she supposed, a doctor got used to delivering bad news.

"I have your message," she said coolly.

"Good, good. I never know if anyone gets a hotel message," he said.

Get to the point, she screamed silently. *You've got my life in your hands!* All she said, however, was "I hope you have good news for me."

"Indeed, indeed. Plenty of good news. That cyst is benign, and you're pregnant."

Belinda sank back into the chair. "I'm sorry, Dr. Espy. I think we've got a bad connection. Could you repeat what you just said."

"You're healthy as a horse, Mrs. Yates, and you're pregnant. Congratulations."

"Thank you," Belinda said, putting down the phone in a daze and settling back into the chair. Now wasn't that just great! No love for a year, she thought, and in July she made love to two men in two days. She would have to start considering some options.

That night, Claiborne Lurie insisted that she come for dinner at his town house. Belinda had always heard that he lived in baronial splendor and the house more than

201

lived up to her expectations. The butler, Reza, was on hand to serve dinner, assisted by a frightened-looking young houseman.

Claiborne was a fascinating host, but Belinda had trouble concentrating on what he was saying. She found herself going back to Dr. Espy's surprising news and measuring her alternatives. She had come a long way from her Ursuline Academy days, but not far enough to consider an abortion for longer than ten minutes. And having the baby on her own had the added advantage that it was sure to outrage and embarrass Buster. She wasn't exactly penniless, after all, and she could manage to get by on her trust fund . . .

But, Belinda reminded herself, just managing to get by was never what she was about.

After dinner, she and Claiborne moved on to a small drawing room where Reza or someone else had laid a fire and they sipped Grand Marnier while Claiborne told her about some of the paintings he had acquired on his latest trip to Paris. He invited her to look at his favorite, a small portrait of an Italian nobelwoman, and she admired it. Suddenly he took her in his arms and kissed her. It was the first time Claiborne had held her since that night aboard the *Lone Star* and she responded as she had then. Soon they moved on to his bedroom and he made love to her.

In that moment Belinda knew that he was going to ask her to marry him, and she knew that she would accept. The sooner they married the better. She had inherited her father's eye for a good bargain after all.

Part II
Winter 1986

Chapter Twenty-four

Young Dr. Thorne was shaking his head as he reviewed Buster Garland's latest test results. The old man sat across from him, beaming in his white Panama suit, an unlit Macanuda in his teeth. Dr. Thorne knew the minute Garland was out of his office he'd light the thing.

He was very annoyed at Buster. Young Dr. Thorne hated it when his patients made him look like a fool, and Buster Garland was making him look like a blue ribbon monkey. The man should be dead. He told him he was dying eighteen months ago, and he damn well ought to be dead.

Not that the young doctor wished any patient ill, especially not one he had inherited from his own beloved daddy (a man of moderate habits who had already gone to his untimely reward). *But his tests didn't lie.*

"I know what you're thinking, boy," Buster said. His blue eyes twinkled, and except for the usual signs of age—the lined skin, the gnarled hands—he did not look like a dying man.

"You're thinking that a big fool like me, who hears he's dying and just goes on smoking and drinking and taking a young bride, has no right to live, ain't you?"

Young Dr. Thorne had been having exactly that thought, but he denied it vehemently.

"I'm just concerned, sir, that a man lucky enough to get a second chance would be abusing it."

Buster just leaned back and laughed. "You got a lot to learn, boy. I wish I had the time to teach you, but we both know I don't. Your tests ain't lying."

Buster lived in his body every day and he knew that it was failing. He was on borrowed time. No, not borrowed. Stolen.

"When I'm called to my reward, I suppose I'll have to work this time off in purgatory or something, but until then I intend to make the most of it."

Young Dr. Thorne digested the interesting news that Buster Garland had no fear of going to hell.

"When a man's got as much on his mind as I have, son, even Heaven's got to wait."

Zenobia Pickens Garland was driving back to Manhattan from Connecticut in her Testarossa, a fifteenth anniversary present from her husband Buddy. Fifteen years. A milestone among their friends. Yet her own parents had been married for forty years and Buddy's parents for twenty-five. Only death ended partnerships like that. As for herself and Buddy, who could say? They had already confounded the skeptics who gave their marriage a year at best.

On the car stereo Placido Domingo had just begun to salute his African princess with "Celeste Aida." As his rich tenor filled the car, Zena noticed with annoyance that a highway patrol car was behind her. She liked speed, but she was not speeding, and the sight of the patrol car put her on edge. She had too many encounters with police who thought there was something suspicious about a beautiful black woman in couture clothes and serious jewelry driving an expensive automobile down the Saw Mill River Parkway a few days after New Year's 1986.

More than once, Zena had been pulled over while she was driving between the apartment she and Buddy kept in town and their country place in Connecticut. Buddy claimed she was overreacting, getting defensive and that New York and Connecticut were a long way from Galveston, but then Buddy was never pulled over.

Of course, as Buddy had wisely pointed out, she could stop all the unwelcome attention by dressing more conservatively, skipping the jewelry and trading the Testarossa for a Chevy van, but those were not options she was willing to consider.

She and Buddy had married in haste and thrived in leisure. Even those who knew she was pregnant at the time had expected that Buddy would dump her after the baby was born and go right back to the Garland family fold.

It hadn't worked out that way at all. Maybe Buddy felt he had to marry her sixteen years ago, but if he was asked now she was sure he would marry her for love.

At least, she had been sure until lately. They were so close that she could tell something was bothering him, and something was definitely bothering him these days. He was being uncharacteristically close-mouthed about it. Someone like Buddy, with so many deals going at once, always had a lot on his mind, but he usually shared everything with her. Zena was sure she knew more about the whole apparatus that was BGI—Buddy Garland International—than anyone but Buddy himself.

BGI—not to be confused with Garland, Inc. Not ever. She knew about Buddy's relationships with his investors, she knew when he was in shaky financial shape and when he was skimming enough cash to require yet another account in Geneva or the Grand Caymans. She knew the numbers of all the accounts, too, and she knew where he kept the keys to the safe-deposit boxes. She had never doubted that Buddy trusted her totally.

Buddy was in trouble, but he'd been in trouble before and they'd always come out of it. The Palm Beach house for which he paid a much-publicized six million was in her name, and she'd had to sign the twelve-million-dollar mortgage (not so well publicized) just weeks ago. If that

207

wasn't total trust, she didn't know what was.

She knew the conventional wisdom had Buddy lifting her, the poor little black girl, out of the ghetto and making a lady of her. As usual, the conventional wisdom was wrong. In her own circles, her father and mother had not sent her to Jack and Jill and paid for her debut at the Idlewild Ball for her to up and elope with the married son of the most notorious wheeler-dealer in Texas. As far as her parents were concerned, Buddy Garland's skin color was just the final insult.

No, she and Buddy had both burned their Texas bridges when they married. Zena knew Buddy's marriage was in deep mud long before they met, and it was his wife who left him. Took off for some commune in Oregon and disappeared for two years. All that Buster cared about then was getting his granddaughter Tammy Lynn back. No wonder the girl was so confused! Zena naturally felt some sympathy for her stepdaughter, but the fact was that she and Tammy Lynn had barely exchanged three sentences in sixteen years.

Zena could not help thinking of her own two children. She and Buddy had raised them right. Now fifteen and twelve, Clinton and Monica were everything she had wanted them to be. She knew Buddy was proud of them, too. Sometimes she worried that maybe they were too sheltered, though. They knew so little about real life. Too bad she couldn't keep it that way.

And now Buddy was up to something with his mysterious business trips and strange detachment. The obvious answer was that he had a girl on the side, but Zena could not bring herself to believe it. Frankly, she'd rather believe he had cancer.

Times like this, she thought of what her mother told her when she announced she was marrying Buddy. She was already four months pregnant and Buddy was getting his divorce. Her mother didn't want to hear about Buddy's crazy wife who abused and abandoned her own child, she didn't want to know how unhappy Buddy was

208

until he met her, or how much in love with Zena he was. No, all her mama could talk about was the seventh commandment. "Thou shalt not commit adultery."

"If he did it to her, Zenobia, he'll do it to you," were her mother's exact words, over and over. They rolled off her like water off a duck's back, until now. She had not thought about them for all these years, but the last few weeks she thought about them every day.

Was he cheating on her now? She stepped on the gas, impatient to get back to New York as soon as possible.

Chapter Twenty-five

Following the voluptuous curve of the Gulf Coast from Galveston, the traveler will reach South Texas, spacious and dry, no longer quite the open range these days but still the site of some of the greatest ranches in the world. Among these was the Rancho Strega, eight hundred thousand acres, bordered on one side by the Rio Strega and on the other by the King Ranch.

Because of the beauty of the land and the hacienda, a sprawling stucco main house with Spanish arches and red tile roof, Rancho Strega was considered the finest private ranch in the state. It had been in Claiborne Lurie's family for generations.

The manicured grounds around the main house sprouted elaborate cactus gardens and palm trees. The grass was as carefully groomed as a country club's and the nearby pond was stocked with catfish and bass. Peacocks, guinea fowl, wild turkeys, and an occasional elk roamed the land freely, and on the patio of the main house a myna bird insulted ranch guests in Spanish and Portuguese.

Down the road from the hacienda, a petting zoo that Claiborne had installed for Charlene when she was a child had grown to include three buffalo and a half-grown camel named Addis.

In the year and a half since their marriage, Belinda had shared this ranch with Claiborne Lurie and their infant son. And an array of exotic and domestic animals that included impala, elk, javelina, blackbuck antelope, and Mexican lion.

A full-time staff of twenty-six attended to every need. She felt pampered, protected, and extremely bored.

Sometimes she felt like she was just another prize in Claiborne's petting zoo.

Guests came and went, entertainers, royalty, and politicians. During hunting season, the tiny Barlow County Airport was jammed with sleek private planes bearing Claiborne's guests.

Belinda herself often took the guests on a tour of the ranch in her nile-green Range Rover, sometimes with Alexander strapped into the car seat. This week, for a change, the guest was an old friend of hers: Fayette Cramer. They were alone, crossing the mesquite-dotted expanse, and Fayette had just noticed that the Rover had a CB radio.

"That's so the cooks can radio me if they need a turkey or brace of quail for dinner," she explained. "They know I always carry my shotgun in the Rover and I'm a good shot."

Fayette could not help sensing that something was bothering her friend. Finally she decided to go for it. "Honey, is something wrong between you and Claiborne?" she asked gently.

At first, Belinda tried to brush her off. "Now Fayette, whatever gave you that idea?"

"Don't try to fool me, Belinda. Don't forget I've known you most of your life. And I know your husband, too. Everyone in Texas knows Claiborne Lurie's a hunting fool. And here it is the middle of the season, and, honey, where is that man?"

"In Paris on business."

"Look, Belinda, I don't want to make trouble between you and Claiborne, but what's he doing in Paris during

211

duck season?"

As they passed through the courtyard and into the hacienda, the two women passed Lourdes, the nurse, playing with Alexander. He was a fat, round, dark-haired boy with eyes as brown as Mexican coffee. He looked nothing like Belinda, or Claiborne either, for that matter. Fayette had noticed this, but said nothing. There were limits to even the oldest friendships.

Belinda suggested that they have the houseman set up dinner on trays in the living room. Fayette was all for this, because the grand dining room reminded her too much of Claiborne Lurie, a man she did not like, did not trust, and who, she was sure, could not sit down to a cup of coffee without candelabra. She, on the other hand, liked the informal living room which was big but cozy, and there was something warm and comfortable about sharing dinner in front of the fireplace, even if the heads of bears and other wild game shot by Claiborne in the past were mounted on the walls and looking down on them.

And it was, after all, the beginning of a new year, which was why Fayette held off raising the Claiborne matter again until the houseman had brought in their crème brulée and placed a fresh bottle of Cristal in the cooler, and steered the conversation instead to their hometown.

"Do you ever miss Galveston?" she asked.

"Sometimes," Belinda admitted. Lately more than ever. She had not been back in more than a year, and this time of year it was hard not to remember the good times and the holidays the Garlands had once shared at the Sand Castle.

"Have you talked to old Buster?"

Belinda shrugged. "We spoke on the phone at Christmas. He calls me every few months to talk about property because my name's on some of the deeds. Nothing personal. He asks about Alexander, but he's never seen him."

"Never seen his grandson?" That didn't sound like the Buster Garland she knew.

"Daddy's never forgiven me for marrying Claiborne. He can't forget that."

When she left Galveston, Belinda had intended a clean break and she had succeeded. For the last year she had devoted herself to her husband and her son.

Fortunately, Charlene Lurie, her former sister-in-law and current stepdaughter, rarely visited Rancho Strega. She was too involved in her much-publicized romance with Speed Porter and she knew that Claiborne disapproved of the relationship. Even Charlene's news that she had been cast in a small role in a television nighttime soap had not impressed him.

There was a silence between them, and then Fayette decided to take the plunge once more.

"I think it's time for you to find a new project," she said gently.

"I don't know—"

"You don't know? Belinda, honey, you ran a hotel. You run this ranch. If you don't know, I do. And anything you want, Belinda, you know you can get."

Belinda stared out at the sweeping grounds. She had been thinking about the Delancy Street warehouse again. According to Fayette, nothing had happened to the old redbrick building since she left Galveston. She could feel her interest growing keener. American Holding had paid more than fifteen million dollars for that property and then let it set in the sun for over a year. Not even Myles McLean had been able to identify the people behind American Holding. It was just a tangled web of faceless companies on three continents. Well, she told herself, there were plenty of other properties in downtown. She'd find another to develop. She missed the hotel business and the excitement of controlling her own organization.

She had her own money, but not nearly enough to acquire and develop the kind of thing she had in mind. Yet she wondered if Claiborne Lurie could ever under-

213

stand that.

"I want to go back to Galveston. I want something of my own," she said.

For reasons of his own, Claiborne Lurie had chosen to tell his wife that he would be in Paris on business rather than in the Swiss Alps getting intramuscular injections of fresh cells extracted from unborn lambs.

There was not merely the matter of privacy, but also the presence of his once and present mistress, Ciprianna Rivers, who had joined him on this rejuvenating retreat to Montreaux.

The room they shared was surprisingly modest, although it did have a sunken malachite tub and a terrace with a spectacular view of Lake Geneva and the mountains beyond. This morning, however, Ciprianna was not enjoying the scenery, but pouting as she watched her lover deep in discussion on the cellular telephone. The Clinique had strict rules forbidding telephones in guest rooms and restricting all contact with the outside world, but such rules were for ordinary people, not a man like Claiborne Lurie.

This was, she supposed, one of the things she loved about him. She, too, disliked rules, although her reaction to anything that impeded her will was to throw a screaming, cursing bilingual fit. Darling Claiborne was completely different. The angrier he got, the softer his voice grew, the more clipped his sentences became. Now, for example, his voice was so soft as he spoke into the phone that she could not make out a single word. It was most frustrating.

She was about to toss a small jar of face cream in his direction, when he finally finished giving instructions to whoever was on the other end of the line. When he put down the telephone, his face was still dark with anger.

"What's wrong darling," she said putting away the jar. "Don't tell me Texas is troubling you." That was about as

214

close as Ciprianna could bring herself to acknowledging Claiborne's wife. She had forgiven him for marrying the girl, but only because she did not expect this marriage to last.

"It's not Texas, dear heart, but these incompetent detectives."

"Detectives?" she repeated.

"Yes, dear heart. If I'm going to get rid of Miss Belinda, I would prefer to do it as frugally as possible. Then there is the matter of my son. When we divorce, I will of course retain custody."

"Of course," Ciprianna nodded. She fancied she understood Claiborne's attachment to his son. After all, she might part with Carl, but she would never give up her two Shih Tzus.

"So, first, I have to build a case."

Ciprianna took this in, although with less enthusiasm. She had met Claiborne's new wife when Belinda Garland was running the Maison Rouge, and the woman was no fool. If Belinda was having an affair, Ciprianna did not believe she would be easily caught at it.

Claiborne only shared a portion of his divorce plans with Ciprianna. Belinda had turned out to be a most frustrating conquest, for in spite of all the time they had spent together, in spite of the birth of their son, he felt no closer to her than the first night they made love aboard the *Lone Star*.

He was convinced that there was someone else, but who? After much study and thought, he had narrowed it down to Myles McLean. The Galveston lawyer was in touch with Belinda all the time, and Claiborne and his detective had reviewed the tapes of their phone calls and the photographs of their occasional meetings, but they were as chaste as children.

Until now. His detective had finally come up with something interesting.

Claiborne had told the detective to have the information waiting for him at the Plaza Athenée in Paris where he and Ciprianna were planning to celebrate their rejuvenation before rejoining their respective spouses in the States.

Chapter Twenty-six

"No," Tammy Lynn told the caller on the speaker phone. "Brice de Young is booked solid for months. There's no way he can consider another commitment until Texas Independence day."

"Please," the woman on the other end pleaded. "We'll redesign the kitchen just for him. We'll pay in cash. We'll pay in gold."

"I'm sorry," she hung up.

Moving to Houston with Brice had been the smartest thing she'd ever done, that was for sure. She had inherited her grandfather's business acumen after all, and she was pleased that she had developed Brice's name-recognition a thousandfold.

If he'd only dump Tootsie and Harris they'd really be going places, but to Tammy Lynn's chagrin, he remained loyal to the Brights. She would just have to be patient and wean him away from them gradually, the same way she was going to get him to marry her.

As it was, Brice hardly visited Harris and Tootsie anymore. He was traveling all over the state and the Southwest, sometimes as a celebrity chef for a debutante party or a fund-raising event; other times he was called in as a consultant for hotels or restaurants. He usually stopped in at Tootsie's Funland once a week to work out a menu and supervise the cooks he had trained. Tammy Lynn thought even that was too much.

Brice had to admit she knew what she was doing. She was getting him incredible fees for advice he would have given away free.

Tammy Lynn had become fast friends with Kukla and Jan, and through them she was developing contacts with most of the big money in Texas.

Unfortunately, Tammy Lynn wanted to get married. To him. And he liked her, he respected her brains, and he was willing to sleep with her. But he refused to consider what went on between them an affair or a relationship or any of those other words she liked to throw at him. He did not want to get married, and he did not ever intend to marry Tammy Lynn Garland. He had tried to tell her many times that just because they had sex a few nights a week did not make them lovers. She never listened.

Brice had always been vaguely sure of that, but a few nights before, when she unveiled her five-year plan for the two of them, in bed, he knew that he had to resist. He had insisted that they live apart, and she had found an apartment in a new high-rise, but it still seemed to him that she was in his pocket twenty-four hours a day.

Tammy Lynn went along. She loved Brice, but she agreed it would be best for the business. And for a true Garland, business came first.

Brice was with one of his ladies. Like most of them, she was rich and bored and surgically shaped to perfection. She might have been surprised at how familiar the routine had become to him. This particular woman had been introduced to him at the Houston Opera. Sometimes the ladies just called cold because they'd heard about him or read a story about him in the papers. This one was in the process of a divorce. Sometimes they were married or separated or widowed or single. This one had asked him to come and look at her kitchen, which she was about to have remodeled. Sometimes they claimed they wanted to discuss an affair (catered), sometimes they

218

claimed they were thinking about going into the restaurant business.

He enjoyed it. He had never found women exactly hard to get, but this was a whole new level. He felt like a rock star.

Suddenly, at thirty-six, Brice de Young was the flavor of the month and he was loving it. Marriage to Tammy Lynn—or even monogamy—was the farthest thing from his mind.

When he returned to his room at Tootsie's, the phone was ringing. It was his mother. Colette was reveling in his new celebrity, and shamelessly willing to use it to enhance her own.

"Chéri," she said.

"Yes, Mother?"

"I need your help. The *Star* is doing a story on me and they want to show me cooking something up. Can you give me some recipes?"

His laugh rippled through the room. When he let his guard down, Brice had a hickish laugh that declined into a good old boy's guffaw.

"Maman, I'd gladly give you recipes. But how would you find the kitchen?"

"Very funny, for a son to speak so to his mother."

"Cher maman, don't the stars tell you these things? Why do you want to start cooking now, anyway?"

"Oh, Brice," she sighed. "These are just small things. A baby custard, a porridge. The sort of thing I fed you when you were small."

Like pop tarts and Moon Pies? he wanted to say but held his tongue. He was after all, a Creole boy who respected his mother. But his *maman* had caught a bad case of star fever.

"Maybe you'd like to come by. I'm sure they would love a shot of the two of us together. I'm having Victor Costa make up the cutest little apron for me just for this. How about a picture of me stirring a pot for you?"

Not in this lifetime, he thought. He could just imagine

219

the shot: Colette spoonfeeding him SpaghettiOs. His mother was becoming a real publicity junkie if she was willing to be photographed in an apron.

There was no way Brice would join her in this. A photograph in *The Star* might be fine publicity for Colette, but he and Tammy Lynn were going for a higher end of the scale. *Town & Country, Ultra,* and *Vanity Fair* were the targets in Tammy Lynn's five-year plan, and Brice agreed completely.

Between the work and the women, he had little time to think about Lauren Armour. Lauren was a user and he was through being used. But he lived for the day he could tell her that in person.

There was another call. A divorcee was moving into a new house and needed him to consult. She suggested lunch. He suggested the Atrium. He was on his way.

"It's my father," Buddy was saying. "He wants me to come back to Galveston."

"And what do you want?" Zena asked. She had just discovered that her rival was no hidden mistress, but Buddy's father. This was going to be delicate. She was sure Buddy knew what *she* wanted, which was never to set foot on that sand bar again.

"Look, Zena, I know how you feel and I'm not going to force you to go back. Even if I do go back into Garland, Inc., it doesn't mean we have to live in Galveston."

"Oh yes it does," she snapped. "You know he'll want you right where he can see you. And me, too."

Buddy sighed. He had given this move a lot of thought. "The point is, Zena, that I'm in a serious cash-flow crunch here and Buster can help us out."

"How much do you need? I can sell my jewelry," she said.

He shook his head. "It's not that simple. This has to be done fast and it has to be done quietly. I borrowed

220

from the wrong people to finance that Ventura deal. I expected to pay them back fast, but things went sour in Texas. Buster found out about it—don't ask me how—and he called me. He says he considered the deal 'a window of opportunity'." Buddy grinned. "Now where do you suppose old Buster picked up a phrase like that, 'a window of opportunity'."

"Probably from your brother Cordell," Zena said.

"I have no doubt you're right, darlin'. And why should a fool who talks like that control all of Garland, Inc., I ask you? When my daddy has been wooin' me like a Sunday school virgin for two years to get me to come across."

"And what about the children?" Zena asked. Before they were married Buster had called the baby in her belly a half-breed and worse.

"He asked about them. That's a good sign. I showed him pictures. He knows what they look like."

"Were they color pictures?" she asked dryly.

He held his tongue. She had every right to be bitter, but he wanted her to come around. In time, he was sure, she would. She always had.

"He's aged quite a bit, Zena," he said.

"That new young wife of his must be working him hard," she said.

"No doubt. He says he's turned over most of the business to my brother, but he's not happy with the way Cordell's running it."

"How could he be?" She was intensely loyal and she loathed Buddy's brother. Cordell had done nothing to help them when they needed him, and he had gladly stepped into Buddy's place as heir apparent. But anyone could see he could never fill Buddy's shoes.

"I guess old Buster's thinking of what's going to happen after he's gone," Buddy said softly. "I think he's just discovered he's mortal."

Zena was unmoved. She had no desire to go back to Galveston. As far as she was concerned, the Island was

221

history, bad history.

On the other hand, why shouldn't her children get what was rightfully theirs? In New York they were merely rich, but in Texas they were Garlands. She loved her life in New York, but there was no reason she couldn't have both. Maybe she had become too comfortable these last few years. Secure in her love for Buddy and her children; content with her position in the society.

"Do Cordell and Belinda know about this?" she asked.

He shrugged. "I'm quite sure Cordell knows nothing. And I gather that Buster and Belinda haven't been real close since she eloped with Claiborne Lurie. I wouldn't wonder if that's what's aged him so."

Zena smiled. She had almost forgotten about Buster's bad heart. He had seemed so intimidating the few times she met him before she married Buddy. Now she pictured him withered and weak, a sick old man. A dying old man. A dying old man with one wish. To be reconciled with his oldest and favorite son.

"Let me think about it," she said.

Chapter Twenty-seven

As the taxi carrying Speed Porter and Charlene Lurie pulled into the driveway at the Avenue Montaigne, Charlene caught sight of something that warmed her heart. Ciprianna Rivers in violet St. Laurent suit, day-time diamonds, and, most marvelous of all, Charlene's own father Claiborne Lurie on her arm, standing beneath the zinc-and-wrought-iron canopy at the entrance to the Plaza Athenée.

Normally, the sight of Daddy leaving a posh hotel on the arm of any other woman, especially a cheap tart like Ciprianna Rivers, would have triggered familiar feelings of Oedipal rage, but this was different. For since her father's elopement with her former sister-in-law, Charlene had been consumed with jealousy and determined to break up the marriage. Now it looked as if events were out of her hands and being taken care of by a higher power. Maybe the rose quartz she was wearing had something to do with it. Speed Porter was a great believer in the power of crystals and had converted Charlene to the cult although he had yet to cast her in one of his films.

A doorman in Confederate gray with the bearing of a general opened the taxi door, helped Charlene out, then attended to their luggage. A small boy in matching gray spun the revolving doors beyond the black-iron fences and Charlene found herself in a vast, cool room with huge flower arrangements and impeccably dressed women.

The *functionaire* at the reception desk recognized her immediately, told her how sorry he was that she had just missed her father. Monsieur Lurie had just checked out minutes ago. Years of training in discretion kept him from mentioning that Madame Rivers had accompanied him. A page boy in gray showed Charlene and Speed to the suite her father had just vacated.

Charlene had mixed feelings about being recognized. It was flattering, especially coming on the heels of her humiliating experience with the producers of *Heritage,* who had fired her after only one episode, when the male lead, no Olivier himself, insisted she couldn't act.

But being recognized, and given her father's usual suite, meant the bill would come to her and she was really getting tired of paying her own way when she traveled with Speed. He was the cheapest man in the world. She even had to buy her own Christmas present and charge it to him. She wondered what he would say when he got the bill.

The suite's huge rooms were filled with Louis XV furniture covered in rose and blue damask. There was a deep blue Aubusson carpet on the floor. In the bathroom were thick white terry-cloth robes and towels warming on chrome racks. The tub was big enough for her and Speed to share. They would have separate sinks, however.

Next to the beds, on the wall of the bathroom and strategically sprinkled around the apartment, were little brown boxes, each containing a collection of bells. Next to each bell was a small drawing: a maid with an apron and feather duster, a waiter with a tray, and a valet with a pair of shoes for shining in his hand.

Between the bedroom and the bath the dressing room was fitted with hundreds of drawers and scores of closets.

Their bedroom was on the quiet inner courtyard.

From her window, Charlene could look down through the layers of bright red awnings and balconies festooned with red geraniums, to the tables, and bright red umbrellas in the courtyard.

Last time she'd stayed here with Chandler her daughter had spent most mornings dropping water balloons on those red umbrellas. Thank God she was now stashed at boarding school in Grenoble so that Charlene could have some peace. And that spying Miss Ruby was resting up in Santo Domingo.

Once inside the privacy of the suite, while Speed entertained himself by opening and closing the myriad closets, Charlene placed a call to Vermillion, society's favorite syndicated columnist, currently in winter residence at the Breakers in Palm Beach.

"You won't believe this, but Daddy and Ciprianna just finished a weekend at the Plaza Athenée," she informed her.

"Darling, does that mean it's splitsville with Belinda Garland?" Vermillion purred. She hated getting this kind of half-story, but anything involving Ciprianna was news. And if the Luries were breaking up after less than two years of marriage, it was delicious.

"I'm afraid you'll have to take it from here," Charlene said coolly. "And I'd appreciate it if you'd keep my name out of it."

"Of course," Vermillion assured her. As soon as the columnist hung up, she began placing calls to Paris and points west. But none of her sources in France or Texas could confirm the story. If Claiborne Lurie and Ciprianna were together again, they had covered their tracks well. On the other hand, as far as the gossips were concerned, it was possible that the whole story was just one of Charlene Lurie's drug-induced hallucinations. Vermillion decided to cover herself by running a blind item in her column, and spreading the details via the telephone. Many of her best sources, like the Cheshire Cat in New York and the Gusher in Houston, were delighted to get a tidbit that would never be seen in print. Who could sue over a phone call?

As Claiborne and his mistress rode to the airport, he studied the photographs that his detective had left for him at the Plaza Athenée. They were more innocent snapshots of his young bride with her friends. All completely useless. A waste of time and money! And yet, tucked in with them all was a smudged note from the little man himself, hinting that he had some more interesting information that was too valuable to send even by courier. He wanted to discuss it with Lurie in person.

Lurie leaned back and closed his eyes, pondering his next move and wondering if he was being taken for more than one ride.

Charlene was very put out when a week passed and nothing came of her call to Vermillion but a blind item that could have been about anyone. At least the column included a little mention of Charlene herself, and how she and Speed had been vacationing in Paris. Charlene loved to see her name in print. It made her feel like a star. It also made her feel better about her relationship with Speed. At least he was good for something, even though he had yet to cast her in one of his pictures.

Speed left to begin filming in Israel. She planned to join him, but first she wanted to do some shopping. One afternoon, after a particularly tiresome fitting at Dior, she walked back to the hotel. A news kiosk at the plaza had papers from all over the world and she picked up the International *Herald Tribune* and a French scandal sheet. What the doorman called a paper for concierges. Although the French was too colloquial for her to understand, she got a kick out of the pictures. She tucked the *Herald Tribune* into her Vuitton bag and started to riffle through the pages of the tabloid, then, stopped dead in the street.

There was a picture of Speed with Chandler! Horseback riding in the desert! The two of them on the same horse, Speed's thick arms wrapped around Chandler's small waist. The bastard was getting it on with her daughter. Her sixteen-year-old daughter!

"Merde!" she screamed, and for once didn't care about the stares she attracted.

"I know, Claiborne darling, they're awful." Belinda Garland was on the telephone, reassuring her husband that Chandler's episode was nothing but a teenage girl's hijinks, while at the same time she was looking at the tabloid photographs in front of her.

Claiborne was calling from the airport in New York and he sounded fit to be tied. No sooner had his private plane landed in Westchester than someone handed him a scandal sheet with cover photographs of his granddaughter cavorting in the desert with a movie star older than her father. Charlene and Chandler had embarrassed him again. He ranted on about the Lurie name, while Belinda listened patiently and assured him that the episode would soon blow over.

"Thank the Lord that little Alexander takes after you, darling," Belinda said smoothly.

"What's that? Oh yes. Excuse me, Belinda, our connection is poor."

He sounded distracted. Belinda cut the conversation short.

"When you comin' home, darlin'?" she asked.

"Not right away," he said stiffly. "Something's come up in New York. I'll have to stay on here for at least another week."

"Oh," she said, then quickly hid her disappointment. "Hurry home, darling," she said as she hung up, rather pleased on a whole with the entire episode, which had given her a chance to remind Claiborne how superior his second try at parenthood had been.

Buster Garland looked around the Galveston Opera House at the hundreds who had gathered for this benefit gala.

Since marrying Valdene he had taken on a new and unaccustomed role: Buster Garland, philanthropist and party hopper. It didn't set too well on his broad shoulders, but he kept telling himself he'd get used to it. Valdene had certainly got used to it quick enough.

For a year and a half he had been content to let Valdene lead him around to one party after another, like some kind of prize bull at a county fair. After all, his doctor had told him to slow down. Valdene had encouraged him to give Cordell a free hand. A last chance, Buster thought, although he never told Cordell that. He had lost out on Buddy, and he had lost out on Belinda. Cordell was the least of the litter but for a while Valdene and circumstances had convinced Buster that he would have to settle for him.

Now he knew different, and damn Valdene, every minute they spent at these wingdings was a minute away from serious business. A man who could not control his own sixteen-year-old daughter was not the man to control Garland, Inc.

Although he had his suspicions about her friend Reba Twining, and regarded her relationship with Valdene as downright unhealthy, he was not ready to send her away. At least Reba kept Valdene company when he could not be bothered.

Valdene was like a child, so transparent. He could see how happy she was that Belinda was gone and Cordell was mucking up. She wanted to be the center of his world.

The problem was that an old enemy had crept into the Sand Castle and begun to poison their marriage. Buster

228

saw it right away, but at first he dismissed it as merely part of growing old. Now he knew better: Buster Garland was bored. Marriage bored him. Valdene bored him. She was convinced that his children and his business were her enemies, but that was not so. Truth was that she was the enemy. She was boring him, and Buster Garland, a man who had tolerated poverty and pain, was not a man to tolerate boredom.

All evening long, he had been watching the guest of honor, a distinguished philanthropist and grand dame. He did not recognize her name, but all these people grew vaguely familiar after a while. Then, when she stood to receive her plaque and acknowledge the applause, Buster knew.

It was an old friend. Mozelle Bryant. Her figure had thickened a bit and the hair was a wilder red than he recalled, but Buster would have recognized those shrewd emerald eyes anywhere.

"Why, Buster," she smiled. "We've got to get together."

"Yes, indeed, Mozelle," he said. "We surely do." His blue eyes twinkled and he already looked fifteen years younger.

The more Belinda Garland studied the photographs of Chandler and Speed Porter, the more she saw that she had been thinking too small.

Yes, of course Claiborne would back her if she wanted to acquire and develop a building, which she did.

But that was no reason to close her eyes to another opportunity, and, being a true Garland, she most definitely smelled an opportunity in Chandler's disgrace.

If the incident had outraged Claiborne, she could only imagine Buster's reaction. It was a wonder she had not heard him ranting all the way down here.

Poor Cordell! He couldn't even raise his daughter right. While she, on the other hand, had not only married well, but produced a son, and she knew firsthand how Buster felt about male heirs.

If her father could only forgive her for eloping with Claiborne Lurie, there was a very good chance they could reconcile.

How nice! For her and for her Delancy Street project. And of course for Garland, Inc. It suddenly looked as if she might end up running Garland, Inc. after all.

True, she had already come up dry once when she asked Buster for his help, but this time was different. This time Cordell had really blown it.

It was just like one of Buster's old oil patch stories. Handling Buster was like drilling for oil, she told herself. No matter how much you knew, you could still go down for thirty dry holes. But when you hit a gusher, nothing else mattered.

She decided that while Claiborne was in New York, she would pay a call on Buster in Galveston.

Chapter Twenty-eight

Brice was demonstrating how to carve a turkey on the *Oprah Winfrey Show*. She had come down to Houston for the week and ended up asking him to do a cooking segment every day. Then he took viewer phone calls. The first call was from Colette. She wanted to know why he wasn't using her recipe for stuffing.

He explained that there was nothing wrong with her traditional combination of cornbread, peanut butter, and marshmallows, but that he liked to try something different. Soon Oprah was deep in a heart-to-heart with Colette about the importance of intuition in the kitchen.

After that he could handle any phone call that came his way.

When the week was up, Kukla and Jan threw a lavish party for him and Oprah. Kukla had settled his lawsuit against his relatives and seemed to be happy. Tammy Lynn had begun dating a real-estate developer who wanted to talk to Brice about going into the fast-food business.

Brice went home with a redhead and woke up with a hangover. She fixed them bloody Marys at a bar in her bedroom and then he left.

When he found Tammy Lynn at her apartment, she

was getting off the phone. She always seemed to be on the phone these days. She had news for him.

"How'd you like to go to the Mardi Gras?" she asked.

"In New Orleans? Great!"

"Brice, don't be silly. The Mardi Gras in Galveston. There's a celebrity cook-off at the Maison Rouge and they want you to be one of the chefs. You'd like that, wouldn't you?"

The Maison Rouge. That brought back memories. Of course, Tammy Lynn's aunt was long gone, but the way she had used him still rankled. It would be nice to return there in triumph.

"Yeah, sure," he said. "But make sure we get a limo to pick us up here and take us back and that they provide an assistant for me . . . well, you know. If I go, I want the works."

Tammy Lynn's blue eyes glittered. "Don't worry, honey. They want us, and they're going to pay for us."

Lauren watched the tape of the *Oprah Winfrey Show* in her dressing room. She had taped all Brice de Young's appearances that week and watched over and over. What was he doing? She was the one who ought to be interviewing him! How come he'd never offered to let her talk to him on the news? She needed something like that.

Things were not going well at KLMN-TV. No one took her seriously, although there was nothing they could do about it. By now everyone knew that she was Aynsley Adder's mistress, and since Aynsley's family owned the station there was no way they could get rid of her. She suspected her co-workers were sabotaging her work: giving her crummy assignments and lighting her badly. Of course they all denied it, but they made it clear they loathed her.

That gave Aynsely an excuse not to expand her role at the station. She had been in Houston for two years and he had still not come through with a show for her. But then he hadn't come through with the divorce from Carola Lee, either. And now her makeup man had passed on a rumor that the Adders might be selling the station to Buddy Garland.

She was no more than a glorified reader. She came in to appear on camera, but they wouldn't let her get near an important celebrity. How was she going to become the next Barbara Walters if they wouldn't let her interview anyone? And here was Brice de Young throwing himself away on Oprah Winfrey!

In her anger, Lauren conveniently forgot all the calls from Brice that she had not returned. Cocaine had sharpened her self-pity and dulled her detachment.

She knew that Aynsley was behaving strangely, too. She feared he was distancing himself from her. Was he planning to drop her? How could he? She had a contract! Lately one of his aides was always with her. Mostly the sleazy blond one. She thought he must be gay. He never even looked at her. Or maybe he wasn't gay. Maybe she was losing her looks. And if she lost her looks, where would she be?

She wasn't going on radio, that was for sure.

She laid out the lines and hoovered up. Something had to happen.

Photographs of his daughter with a movie star more than twice her age had outraged even Cordell Garland, distracting him from Garland, Inc., long enough to track down his ex-wife by telephone.

He found her at the Rancho Strega where he also had a conversation with his sister Belinda. Their first in months. Then she transferred his call to Charlene's wing.

The picture of her daughter with Speed had shaken Charlene to the core and stirred up whatever latent maternal feeling existed. She had rushed off to the

233

Golan Heights long enough to pick up a protesting Chandler and literally drag her back to the seclusion of the Lurie ranch. Miss Ruby had been summoned back from Santo Domingo for additional support.

It wasn't quite as isolated as she would have liked, because Belinda was there, but Charlene's wing was self-contained and she managed to avoid most encounters while she spent a few days giving Chandler the facts of life.

Fact one: her lover Speed could go to jail if he went near her again.

Fact two: Charlene and Granddaddy Lurie controlled the pursestrings and Chandler would not have a cent without their permission.

Fact three: Charlene could have her confined in a sanitorium or worse if she so much as went near Speed Porter again.

"You're jealous!" Chandler cried when she realized that there was no way she was going to get off the grounds of the ranch for quite some time.

For the first time in her life, Charlene managed to control her temper. Maybe she was growing up. Getting mature. In any case, although she couldn't bring herself to discuss such a thing with her daughter, what bothered her most about the Speed-Chandler thing was the idea that poor Chandler might think that he was a good lover. He was a lousy lover! He was so pumped on steroids that his organ, once celebrated as a baseball bat, had shriveled to a pencil. And her poor daughter probably thought that was the best there was! The beast had taken advantage of Chandler's innocence. And that was something Charlene could not forgive.

Now she had to listen to Cordell accuse her of failing as a mother. Threatening to sue for custody. She held the phone a foot away from her ear and could still catch every word of his parental tirade. He sounded more like her own father than her ex-husband.

"Great, Cordell, you do that," she said, determined to

call his bluff. "You take responsibility for a teenage girl."

"You make her sound like a monster," he said.

"When was the last time you saw your daughter?" she demanded. "Do you even remember what she looks like?"

"I'll have to check my calendar," he said, riffling casually through the date book on his desk. It seemed like he had only seen Chandler yesterday, but now that he looked he couldn't find any record of it.

"I'll tell you, Cordell. You haven't even talked to her since last Christmas. That's more than a year."

"Has it really been that long?" He was genuinely surprised. He considered himself a devoted father. "Well, Chandler has her own life. She knows I'm always here for her if she needs me."

In spite of conversations like this, Charlene found herself nostalgic for Cordell. There was something about his stiff-necked attitude, his narrowness, his solidity, that looked better and better after her experiences with men like Speed Porter.

Maybe Chandler's episode had been a blessing in disguise. "You know, Cordell, I don't think we should be having this conversation on the telephone," she purred. "When can I see you?"

She could feel him back off. "I don't know, Charlene. I'm waist deep in plans for this Mardi Gras thing."

"But that's perfect!" she breathed. "Chandler and I will come up and stay with you for Mardi Gras! Just stock Oak Park Circle with champagne, darlin', we'll be up there tomorrow!"

Chapter Twenty-nine

There were certain advantages to being notorious, Buster Garland reflected, and one of them was that you were seldom detained by even the border patrol caliber security of a building like the Valhalla Tower, which was how he managed to sail through the pink marble lobby, past the gold-braided, Uzi-armed guards, and into a bronze-paneled elevator that whisked him up fifty stories to the penthouse, thinking all the while how a place like this could only exist on Fifth Avenue, New York, New York, and thank the Lord for that.

In town to look over a potential acquisition and seized with good cheer, Buster had impulsively decided to pay a call and, stopping first at FAO Schwarz to make a few purchases, he had gone on alone to check out the territory. He knew it was in the possession of the enemy, but Buster Garland had fought German soldiers and oilfield roughnecks and he thought he could face Zena Garland, too, if necessary.

The butler who answered his ring looked just like Prince Charles of England and didn't show a trace of surprise at the appearance of this white-suited giant with the fuschia silk shirt and Panama hat.

"Is Mr. Garland at home?" Buster asked, removing his hat and handing it to the butler as he took in the onyx-and-brass inlaid floor and brown-satin-covered walls of the entrance hall, and wiped his brow with a fuschia silk pocket handkerchief.

"Yes, sir. What name shall I say, sir?"

Buster's blue eyes twinkled as he informed the Englishman just who it was he was dealing with. He then followed the butler up stairs lined with bronze mirror panels, running his paw speculatively along the sweeping brass banisters.

Buster's white lizard boots sank quietly into the ivory carpet as he followed his escort into the biggest living room he had ever seen — and he was from Texas! It looked like everything in the place was gold or glass. A gold leaf ceiling, two stories above him, that looked like one of Valdene's compacts, and a huge, ornate gold-framed whorehouse mirror, some kind of gold lamé on the sofas and the pillows, a crystal chandelier, and the wraparound windows that gave a panoramic view of the city skyline from the Willis Avenue bridge to the World Trade Center.

"They're in the park, sir," Prince Charles said and indicated a tan suede tub chair. "If you'll take a seat, I'll get them." Then he disappeared.

Buster was about to say that if the Garlands had gone up to Central Park he would come back some other time, but Prince Charles was already gone. His tub chair was quite comfortable, but the setting made Buster uneasy. All that bronze and mahogany and brown marble and the mirrors reflecting it gave him the feeling of suddenly entering a new century, a new age, which might not be quite the place for a Buster Garland.

He had nothing against flaunting wealth, and he was torn between pride that Buddy had done so well for himself and a nagging resentment that his son had done it with no help from his daddy.

Prince Charles came back and wanted to know if Mr. Garland would join the Garlands in the park.

Carrying his FAO Schwarz packages himself, Buster marched up another grand staircase and found himself in a glass-enclosed roof garden dense with potted palms

237

and birches, a gazebo and a carousel that could have come directly from Galveston's own Stewart Beach. There was a clay tennis court at one end, and Buddy and his son were playing against his wife and daughter. The whole family was in white, and Buddy and the boy were in shorts, Zena and the girl in short tennis dresses. The ugliest dog Buster had ever seen was keeping up with the ball, running back and forth along the boundary of the court and barking loudly every time the boy hit it.

When they had finished their set, they clustered together and watched him approach, Buddy with his hands on his son's shoulders, Zena holding her daughter close to her.

Near the tennis court, under a green-and-white striped awning, was a round wicker table surrounded by wicker chairs, and beside that a bar. On top of the bar was a tray with bottles of San Pellegrino water, a silver ice bucket, and crystal tumblers. The little family moved in one close group to the shade of the awning, and the mother began to pass out the tumblers of mineral water.

It took all of Buster's courage to approach that little domestic scene, but he went ahead, looking Zena directly in the eye. She stared right back at him impassively, as if to say *I've handled a lot in my life—I can handle you.*

In the minute it took him to stride through the gaudy park to the shelter of the awning and extend his free hand to his son, Buster called upon all the canny, daring, and intestinal fortitude that had taken him so far.

The dog, a Shar Pei named Mao, was the first to acknowledge Buster by sniffing around his white lizard boots. Descended from a breed that once guarded temples, Mao had a nose for the exotic and a genetically bred respect for power. Buster allowed the dog time to inspect both boots, and he expected that got him some points in the boy's eyes at least.

This ritual welcome over, Buster settled uninvited into a wicker chair that groaned slightly under his weight, and his two coffee-colored grandchildren, one on each side of his knee, stared at him in silence, never having seen anyone among their parents' friends quite so big, quite so fat, or dressed quite so flamboyantly. *With a diamond ring on each hand!* The little girl was particularly fascinated with the fuschia of Buster's silk shirt for only a few days earlier her mother had refused to buy her an Esprit dress in exactly that shade, saying that the color was "vulgar." *Maybe it was vulgar, but she still loved it!*

Buddy's affair with Zena Pickens had produced his son and disrupted the family and destroyed his first marriage. Since then, Buster had always referred to the boy as "the little half-breed bastard," but now, on seeing him for the first time, it was suddenly impossible to dismiss his own flesh and blood so cruelly. His grandson was almost a young man, handsome, serious looking, much like Buddy had been at that age, with sand-colored hair and tan skin and, surprisingly, his father's blue eyes. The boy's younger sister had Zena's heart-shaped face and black-eyed Susan eyes and the promise of Zena's voluptuous beauty.

The Shar Pei, having barked enough to bring the entire family's attention to Buster's invasion, now surrendered, curled at his feet, and stared up at him, awaiting orders. Instinctively, without asking, Buddy filled a tumbler of bourbon for his father and handed it to him.

Even in that glass-enclosed roof garden, safe from the winter winds outside, that sense of abundance: the clay tennis court, the exotic trees, the gaudy carousel, left Buster pleased yet uneasy, but he lifted his glass slightly in mock toast and winked at the little girl.

The boy couldn't contain himself any longer. "Are you Santa Claus?" he asked, eyeing the packages from FAO Schwarz.

"Hush!" Zena snapped. But Buster had gone off into

roaring laughter.

"Son, this is your granddaddy," Buddy said. "All the way from Galveston, Texas." He explained to his father that the boy was Clinton and the girl was Monica, both named for his mother's side of the family.

"And you know Zena, of course."

"Of course," Buster said affably.

He and his grandchildren regarded each other with undisguised curiosity, too fascinated to remember that staring was rude, while Buddy Garland watched his wife.

Her expression was pensive and she looked more than ever like some rebellious African queen, with her solemn, impassive gaze, her high-broad cheekbones, her full mouth and rich dark skin. Her thick black hair, pulled and braided into a sleek coil, exposed her delicate, shell-shaped ears. Her dark eyes were stormy at this sudden invasion.

Buddy had not seen her look this angry in years.

Clinton, their son, tried to engage Buster in conversation. Convinced that this white-suited giant was the classic Texas oilman, he pummeled Buster with questions about the business. Buster obliged him with old stories of his youth in the oil patch and his memories of the Texas Rangers and the night they tossed every slot machine in Galveston into the Gulf.

The winter sunlight shone on the brick and palm trees in terra-cotta planters and the painted horses on the carousel and the sound of the waterfall, while outside snow had begun to fall.

Buster had almost reached the end of his cigar and his stories—or at least the ones he could relate to a fifteen-year-old boy in the presence of his mother—but his grandchildren were rapt and even Mao did not seem inclined to move. Soon, Buster was demonstrating his Astrolabium Galileo Galilei wristwatch.

"It's like having a complete solar system," he explained. "I can tell you the time, I can predict a solar eclipse, a lunar eclipse—to the day—and I can tell you the exact time dawn comes up and sun sets and where your stellar constellations are."

Suddenly Zena stood up and raced inside, followed by Buddy, muttering some excuse and leaving Buster alone with his grandchildren.

A strange feeling came over him. The rigid sense of right and wrong that had given him the courage to banish his oldest son and take on the care of little Tammy Lynn didn't seem to apply anymore. It was one thing to issue edicts like some biblical patriarch, but a man got old. A man wanted a son. And now the sight of his grandson—one he could still mold, learning from the mistakes of the past, made him covet these two children as he had once coveted money and power.

The idea of it! That these two beautiful children—his grandchildren—were growing up in a New York tower surrounded by marble and brass and mahogany, when they could be romping at the Sand Castle, swimming in his pool or fishing in Galveston Bay, pained him deeply. He had to get them back to Galveston, where they belonged.

But Buddy Garland at that moment was not thinking in that direction at all. He had followed Zena into their second-floor bedroom, which had a large panel of interior windows looking into the living room and outward beyond to the Manhattan skyline. He found her seated on a peach-pink chair in front of a peach-pink dressing-table mirror with her head in her hands. At first Buddy thought his wife was crying, but when she looked up at him her deep brown eyes were dry.

"Get him out of here," she hissed. She knew all about the meeting in the cabin at Bull Bayou by now, but that was business. This was different. This was personal.

"He needs me," Buddy said, massaging her shoulders, but she shrugged him off.

"I don't care what you do with him," she said. "Just keep him out my house and away from my children."

241

"He's my father," Buddy said softly and went back up to the park.

By now Buster had Monica on his knee and she was playing with his watch, while Clinton was demonstrating kung fu in front of him.

"Look, Daddy," Monica said when she saw her father. "This watch has six hands!"

The dog Mao, seizing his opportunity, had jumped up on one of the wicker chairs and was nose-deep in Zena's abandoned glass, lapping up the mineral water.

Buddy wanted his father to leave.

What gave him the right to show up here and upset Zena like this? Without any warning! Without even a phone call! Had the man learned nothing during their private meetings this last year? He should have known better, he could have called, but when did Buster ever think of anyone but himself?

Buddy snapped at Clinton and Monica and ordered them to go to their rooms and start their homework. Surprised, because their father rarely raised his voice to them, they went inside without protest, after somberly shaking their visitor's hand and accepting the packages from FAO Schwarz.

Buddy poured his father another bourbon and one for himself. He suddenly felt he needed it.

"Zena isn't feeling well," he said.

Buster smiled. "No," he drawled. "I expect the truth is that your lovely wife hates my guts."

Buddy hesitated between candor and courtesy and opted for candor. "Well, yes. I expect that's it."

"You've got a nice place here, for New York," Buster said, looking around.

"The best apartment in the best building in the best location in town—to quote our real-estate broker," Buddy said.

"I never liked city living. It's bad for children," Buster said.

"My children's mother feels differently," Buddy re-

242

plied. "Besides, we have a place in Connecticut we go to on weekends."

The silence was only broken by the Shar Pei, lapping up the bourbon from Buster's tumbler this time.

"Maybe I shouldn't have come," Buster said at last. "But damn it, I miss you, son!"

Buddy reached out and playfully cuffed his father's shoulder.

Inside, one of the children was playing a heavy metal rock tape and the music seemed to go with all the metal in the apartment. The rooftop park was falling into the shade. Lights were starting to go on in neighboring towers: Trump, Olympic, the Museum of Modern Art, and the rooftops took on a wintery glow.

They sat together, father and son, saying little. Finally Buster got up to go, announcing that he would be flying home to Galveston that night. Buddy said nothing about inviting him back.

Buster walked away from Valhalla Towers sadly, thinking of all the space at the Sand Castle that was going to waste and the grass and fields and horses and the Gulf and Galveston Bay. That was where the Garlands belonged, instead of him and Valdene rattling around that big old house and the ghostly spectre of Reba Twining creeping up on him at the worst times. The house needed a *real* family.

Buddy's wife was still a problem. Better looking than he remembered, but there was no way you could pass her off as anything but a Negro. Black as the ace of spades. Black as good soil. Black as Gulf Coast crude. And beautiful, no doubt about it, even if she hated him and made no secret of it. She must have given Buddy holy hell after he left! But she'd done a good job with the children! Fine young people!

Buster sauntered up Fifth Avenue to the Pierre where he kept a suite, despising the noise and grayness and

243

hardness of the city. How could Buddy be happy here? How could he let his children grow up here? Because they'd been run out of the family and out of Galveston and he'd allowed it! Busybodies like Charlene Lurie and Carrie Clinton and Tammy Lynn's addlebrained mother had nagged him into it. Women!

Forgetting how he himself had confronted Buddy and banished him from the Sand Castle like an Old Testament prophet, Buster saw himself now as the innocent tool of vengeful harpies. He was King Lear, betrayed by ungrateful women.

Later that night, at the Westchester airport, where he kept the Garland, Inc., plane, as his pilot was preparing for take-off, Buster suddenly ordered him to wait. He grabbed the telephone and punched up Buddy's number. Prince Charles answered, but he put Buddy right on.

"Yes, what is it?" Buddy asked.

"I just wanted to say how much I enjoyed our little visit, son," Buster drawled. "You've got a beautiful wife there and she's done a fine job with those children."

Buddy was not amused. "What do you want, Dad?" he asked. "Zena and I were just going out."

"Well, I know how Zena feels about Galveston, but I don't think that girl's given the Island a chance. I was just sitting here thinking. Wouldn't those two love to come down for Mardi Gras?"

"What?"

"Mardi Gras, son. You and Zena. And the kids."

"They'll be in school," Buddy said quickly.

"Better. Then you two come down here and kick up your heels."

Buddy hesitated. He knew Zena was watching him and listening to his half of the conversation. He didn't think she would consider going, but it was worth discussing.

"I'll tell you what, Dad. How about if I get back to you?"

Buster laughed heartily. "Son, I couldn't ask you for

244

more than that!"

As he put down the phone and gave the signal for the pilot to lift off, Buster gazed out of the window with satisfaction. Yes, he was still king of the deals, no doubt about it.

Chapter Thirty

Before visiting Buster in Galveston, Belinda decided to check things out with Myles McLean. She gave him a call.

"I'm thinking about coming home," she told him.

"Home? Where are you calling home these days, Belinda?"

"You know. I was thinking of coming back to Galveston for a visit."

"I'm sure you're welcome here any time, darlin'."

"I know you feel that way. But what about my father?"

"Old Buster?" Myles said. "I think he'd be pleased."

"What about my son?" she pressed.

"Oh, excuse me. Congratulations."

"Thank you. But do you know how Buster feels about that?"

"Now, Belinda," he drawled. "Since when do you have to ask me how your daddy feels about anything? When did it make any difference to you? Come on back to Galveston where you belong, girl, and face the fiddler!"

She smiled although no one else could see it. "You're starting to sound just like Buster, Miles."

"Smart, you mean?"

"I guess so."

But she had to go back to Galveston, even if Miles tried to talk her out of it. No one would be able to change her mind. It was not just her interest in the Delancy Street building, it was a chance to reconcile with Buster. To seize the opportunity to get back in his good graces, and back into Garland, Inc.

"Will you be there?" she asked. "I trust your judgment."

He hesitated over the phone. "I thank you for the compliment, Belinda, but don't forget I still work for your daddy. When it comes to giving you informal advice, friend to friend, I wouldn't hesitate a minute. Representation's different."

"I understand," she said.

"But I'm never more than a phone call away, Belinda."

"I see," she said.

"So save those quarters, darlin'."

She said good-bye and put down the phone. A feeling of anticipation was building up in her. The fact that she was going into this totally alone only added to the challenge.

Buster had taken to visiting Mozelle Bryant at least once a week. There was something about his old flame that had endured long after the figure and the face gave way to the tides of time. He had known Mozelle off and on for more than forty years — most of his adult life.

"How come we never got married, Mozelle?" he asked one afternoon as they lay in her round, pink satin bed. Mozelle still had the taste of a bawdyhouse and, he reminded himself, the skills of one, too.

Mozelle lived in a beautifully restored Grecian Revival house in the Silk Stocking district. Inside was decorated in the red plush and rose silk and rosewood Victorian opulence that Buster remembered from the finest bordellos of his youth. Mozelle had worked in those houses, but she was a smart girl as well as a beautiful one and she had made the best of them. She always had an eye for a good investment.

247

She was bringing him his morning coffee on a little tray. He could tell by the smell of it that she'd remembered he liked it New Orleans style: with lots of chicory. She was wearing a bright green silk kimono that brought out the sea-green of her eyes. The eyes were outlined with black and her hair was still red and frizzy.

"You haven't answered my question, Mozelle," he said as he sipped the coffee.

"I guess I'm just too dumb to marry you, Buster darlin'," she said, reclining on the white wicker chaise lounge by the window. The morning sun backlit her and gave a little halo around her head. Buster was under the impression that she didn't have a thread of gray. He was a dear, but some things just went right by him, which was fine as far as Mozelle was concerned. "Maybe you're just easier to get along with when you're married to somebody else."

He started to laugh and had to put aside the coffee before he choked on it.

"You're an ornery one, Mozelle," he laughed. "I guess I just needed to be reminded. Now get back in this bed and I'll teach you some manners."

Mozelle smiled and stood up, letting the kimono fall open a little so Buster could get a flash of well-preserved leg. She was no spring chicken anymore, but you didn't sleep with someone on and off for four decades without learning what turned him on.

"We have everything we need right here," Zena shouted.

Buddy Garland watched his wife. They had been arguing like this all day. First Zena said the decision was his to make, but when he announced that he wanted to go back to Galveston, she reneged. He was angry at her and he was angry at himself because he knew what he was doing to her.

"I just thought we might go down for the Mardi Gras.

To kind of test the waters," he drawled.

She glared at him. "Never! I don't want you mixing it up in that snake pit!"

His blue eyes glinted with sudden amusement. "Worried about me? Don't think I can handle them?"

"Even snake handlers get bit," she snapped.

"Don't you think I know their ways?" he said.

"That's the trouble with snakes. You can never know what they'll do."

They left it at that, and the next afternoon Zena found herself confiding in her friend Milicent Malverne about the whole mess over lunch at Côte Basque. She was surprised and annoyed when Millie only laughed off her problems.

"Is that all?" Millie said, dismissing the whole matter like a corked wine. "Darling, mistresses are a problem. The stock market is a problem. Going back to Galveston should not be a problem."

Milicent was one of the three grand dames who ran New York's real power structure and decided who sat on the boards of the Metropolitan Museum, the Public Library, and Lincoln Center. She had inherited the billion-dollar Malverne Foundation from her late husband and was having great fun flexing the social muscle it had given her.

At eighty Milicent was also a realist, and it was an open secret in the city that she was grooming a team of young matrons to pick up her mantle when she departed this earth. Like a mother hen Milly selected their decorators, advised them on the appropriate schools for their children, used her connections to get their husbands admitted to the right clubs, and guided them on the proper charity path. She regarded Zena Pickens Garland as one of her greatest successes. Of course, Milly reminded herself, one had to have the raw material to work with. Not to mention the money.

One of the things she liked most about Zena was her taste and style. For example, the huge bird of paradise

249

pin she was wearing on her nubby gold wool Adolfo suit. The bird's body was an emerald and the bill, crown, and feathers were made up of semiprecious stones. Zena had designed the pin herself, using stones her husband had brought back from a trip to South America. The girl had flair, Milly told herself.

"It's just that we've made such a good life here in New York," Zena continued. "Buddy keeps telling me that the Island's changed, but . . ."

"I'm sure it has, dear," Milicent said. "But you know, it doesn't matter, does it?"

Zena looked at Milicent, her large chocolate eyes questioning. "What do you mean?" she asked.

"I mean that of course Galveston's changed since you lived there, dear. But don't forget, you've changed even more."

Zena stirred her espresso gently. Of course she had changed. The thought pleased her, as Milicent meant it to.

"You've changed," Milicent repeated. "And only by going back home will you be able to measure just how much. I should think you might enjoy that."

"Yes," Zena said. "Of course."

Cordell sent the Garland, Inc., helicopter to airlift Brice and Tammy Lynn from Houston for the Mardi Gras cook-off at the Maison Rouge. They shared the ride with several genuine celebrities who had been invited to add glitter to the occasion. Brice was especially impressed to meet the boxer Sven Peterson, but all Sven wanted to talk about was vitamins. He was relieved when they finally landed on the grounds of the Maison Rouge. For Brice the landing marked a triumphant return. He had been fired and sent packing like a wetback dishwasher and now he was returning an honored guest.

Tammy Lynn had arranged the whole business with

her uncle Cordell. Since Buster's marriage the old man had cut down on his workload and Cordell had assumed more responsibility with Garland, Inc. He took a special interest in the Maison Rouge, promoting this event and the ball to follow in the Garland newspapers all over the Southwest. The cook-off was Valdene's special project, one she hoped would establish her in Old Guard Galveston society, and he was anxious to maintain good relations with his tempestuous stepmother.

Uniformed bellhops descended on Brice and Tammy, their baggage was taken up to their suite, and Brice was shown to the kitchen while Tammy Lynn worked out last-minute details with Wiley Muehl.

It seemed to Brice that lately Tammy no longer spoke of he and she, but always we. "We" will make an appearance; "We" want nothing to do with that And she was doing this without even checking with him. He was going to have to talk to her.

In the more than two years they had been together, Rhonda Perillo thought she and Cordell Garland had both changed a lot. With his sister's running off and his daddy's taking a new wife, Cordell was just totally mired in running Garland, Inc., and Rhonda really felt for him. He was so overworked and tired most of the time. Sometimes she didn't see him for days. When he did come, they followed their traditional routine, with him asking her to dress up like Charlene Lurie with her jewelry and lingerie and him taking pictures. Only these days he was using a video cam and keeping the cassettes in the trunk of his car. He was always meticulous about gathering up all the tapes as well as the jewelry when he left, but Rhonda had managed to hold back one cassette for herself, as a keepsake.

It was pretty harmless, she thought, because even though the tape had a sound track, the voices consisted of Cordell giving her instructions in how to sit and

251

drape the lingerie he made her wear and her asking him "Is this all right?" Still, on the nights when he could not make it to the apartment on the Seawall, she liked to play it because she liked to hear the sound of his voice, even if it was only saying things like "Move your hand up your thigh Rhonda, honey," or "Let me see some pink, darlin'."

With so much free time on her hands, Rhonda worked at improving herself, although she and Cordell had different ideas about what that meant. At his insistence, she had begun having her hair dyed blond at Lucio's, the salon at the Maison Rouge where the handsome Italian hairdresser gave her a duplicate of Charlene's coiffure, which pleased Cordell immensely. And she had begun to dress more conservatively, studying photographs of Ann Bass and Georgette Mosbacher and Lynn Wyatt to learn from them. Cordell liked that, too. And she was wearing tinted contacts, so her naturally green eyes were now as blue as Charlene Lurie's.

The problem was that Cordell wanted her to go further, and so far she was resisting. She had a small birthmark on the inside of her thigh, and every time they made love lately, as she lay in bed, he would stroke her thigh and wonder out loud why she didn't get rid of it. At first she said she would, but she just never got around to it. There was something about the idea of such permanent change that made her nervous.

And then Cordell started on the implants, insisting that her breasts were unusually small and that her clothes would fit much better if she went from an A cup to a C one.

Unfortunately, this touched on Rhonda's greatest fear in life, for her mother had died during surgery and she was terrified of going under the knife. Fortunately, Cordell usually brought up the subject of implants when he had time on his hands, kept after Rhonda for a week or so, and then dropped it when he got distracted by something else. Lately, he was so busy he had no time to pester her about it.

Rhonda's idea of improving herself was different. She worked hard at imitating her idols. When she read in *People* that Charlene Lurie was fluent in French, she started French conversation lessons. When she read in *W* that society women knew all about Fine French Furniture and antiques, she began to visit the galleries downtown and soaked up all the details she could about the difference between Limoges and Lalique and Biedermeir and Bauhaus. She started taking a wine tasting class to learn the difference between chardonnay and chablis.

When Cordell finally asked her to marry him, and she was sure he would, she wanted to make him the perfect wife.

All this information, and so little chance to use it. For, except for Cordell's visits, she had almost no social life and they never went anywhere together.

Which was on reason why the Mardi Gras meant so much to her. And why she spent so much time on her costume and mask. And why she was so surprised when Cordell said she couldn't go to the Lafayette Ball with him.

"What do you mean, I can't go?" she repeated, stunned, after he gave her the news. "You promised!"

Cordell shook his head. "This hurts me more than it does you, darlin', believe me. But my daddy will be there and you know how he feels about divorce. In his old-fashioned eyes, I'm still married to Charlene. It would break his heart to see me with you." Cordell lied so easily he even surprised himself.

The truth was that now that Charlene was back he dreaded her finding out about Rhonda. Charlene was a vindictive bitch and there was no telling what she might do. Also, deep down, Cordell felt that as long as Charlene was around, she was a more appropriate companion for the heir to Garland, Inc., to have on his arm at Mardi Gras than some poor white-trash girl, even if

253

Rhonda had a heart of gold and was dressed up like Marie Antoinette.

"I see," Rhonda said quietly. It made her sad to see him so distracted. "I was hoping you and I . . ."

He looked a little uncomfortable. "Truth is, my ex is back in Galveston. We've had some trouble with our little girl and we need to sort out a few things."

"You mean you're getting back together?" Rhonda had always wondered about the mysterious beauty who broke Cordell's heart. She had only seen pictures of Charlene in tabloids like the *National Star* and the *Enquirer*. She looked like Morgan Fairchild and behaved like Alexis Carrington. "Will I be able to meet her?"

Cordell's shocked expression told her that was impossible. Unthinkable. The whole thing made her very sad.

"Don't you worry, darlin'," Cordell said when he left her that night. "I'll bring you back some favors from the ball and we'll have a party of our own."

"Oh, Cordell," she said, struggling to muster some enthusiasm. "That will be wonderful."

Brice already had a bunch of messages waiting for him when he got to his suite. Valdene Garland had called three times to talk about the cook-off. And there were the usual cryptic notes from his groupies. Long may they reign. He riffled through them, trying to discern by reading through the lines which looked the most promising, and wishing he had his mother's ESP.

He wondered if Belinda Garland was still around. Tammy Lynn never mentioned her aunt. All he knew was that she'd gone off and married some lifelong enemy of Buster's and left the family fold.

He gave up trying to read behind the messages, and just closed his eyes and pulled one from the pile. It was from a Mrs. Worthington. He decided to call her and see if she was worthy of a consultation.

Chapter Thirty-one

There was another reason Cordell was distracted. Charlene had moved back into their house on Oak Park Circle, uninvited and unwelcome. She had arrived with a sullen Chandler, the girl's nanny, and Chandler's pet ferret (a farewell gift from Speed Porter), bringing chaos and disorder back into his life. All because Charlene claimed she needed him to get Chandler back under control.

He didn't feel responsible for the problem at all and he had a lot more on his mind. It was all Charlene's fault that the girl had run off with Speed Porter. She was the one who had exposed his innocent daughter to a steroid-crazed muscleman.

Charlene didn't see it that way. She felt quite at home in her old house. She was touched that Cordell had made almost no changes in the decor in the twelve years since she moved out. Actually, if asked, Cordell would have told her that he hardly noticed. He spent very little time there, except to sleep. Once in a while he had brought Rhonda Perillo there, but they stayed in the master bedroom. His life these days revolved around the Garland Tower and the Maison Rouge, where he was immersed in plans for Mardi Gras which in Galveston was a solid week of balls, parades, and other celebrations.

He had not mentioned anything about Rhonda to Charlene. His ex-wife seemed to just assume there was no one else and he decided to deal with it after Mardi Gras.

Charlene had even asked her lawyers to investigate the validity of her first divorce. Was it possible that she and Cordell were still legally married?

She was thoroughly pleased to be back in Galveston again, and quickly got back into the spin, immersing herself in plans for the Mardi Gras. She gave Cordell a list of the balls they would have to attend: the Artillery Club, the Knights of Momus, the Knights of Regina, and ordered him to get tickets.

Much to her pleasure, she even got a call from Valdene Garland. At least Valdene sounded happy to have her back. She insisted that Charlene and Chandler come to the big celebrity cook-off at the Maison Rouge and to the Lafayette Ball there Saturday night.

Charlene couldn't wait to meet her ex- and future stepmother-in-law. The more time she spent in Galveston, the less she doubted that one way or another she and Cordell were going to be man and wife again. She convinced herself she only had Chandler—and Cordell's—interest at heart.

Between freshening up the house by filling it with flowers and rearranging the furniture a bit, renewing her old Island connections and planning their costumes and masks, Charlene hardly saw Cordell. He claimed he was too busy to talk. It infuriated her that he could be so indifferent. He was ignoring her and Chandler just like he used to.

After a visit to her maskmaker on Mercy Street, Charlene stopped in at Myles McLean's office to say hello, and while there she heard his secretary put through a call from Belinda Garland Lurie. So Belinda was coming to Galveston, too!

Now that would be a treat, she thought. Seeing Belinda again. Charlene wondered if Belinda knew about Claiborne and Ciprianna yet. Maybe she was coming back to the Island to discuss divorce with Myles McLean. How delightful!

Cordell also consulted with Myles McLean. Several times. He had to be reassured that his marriage to Charlene was irrevocably dissolved.

"For God's sakes," Myles exploded after Cordell's tenth call. "Don't you remember how long it took us to work out the property settlement? That divorce was a work of art."

"I just want to be sure," Cordell said.

"What's all this about?" Myles asked. "Does Charlene want to reconcile?" He'd heard that after washing out in Hollywood, she was back on the Island with her troubled daughter.

"She's moved back into our house," he answered.

"No, Cordell. It's your house. Yours alone," Myles corrected him. He regarded Buster's younger son as a pathetic wimp. No wonder Charlene Lurie could walk all over him!

Chandler Garland looked at the pastel-painted arches erected on the Strand for the Mardi Gras, and the bleachers that lined Mechanic Street. She was not impressed.

"I hate Galveston," she whined as she stroked her ferret, Mr. T. The little animal was not used to being out of his cage, and he watched from Chandler's arms with nervous anticipation, his pointed little nose twitching, his beady, black eyes alert.

"Hush," Miss Ruby warned her.

Ruby wasn't crazy about the Island, either. If they were going to be at Mardi Gras she didn't understand why Charlene didn't take them to New Orleans or, better yet, Rio. She wanted to be in a place that did it right. On this whole damn Island she couldn't find one conjure shop. But she was not about to tell Chandler that. This girl was too much trouble already. Miss Ruby would have gladly retired two years ago and gone to

257

Santo Domingo and opened a conjure shop of her own, but she felt a certain loyalty to the girl. She was a whole lot of trouble, but Ruby was afraid if she left her, Chandler would be even worse off.

"Just hush. We're stuck here until your mama says different," Miss Ruby said.

"I don't care. First chance I get I'm running away." Ruby sighed. She knew just how Chandler felt.

"Cara what do you mean you're not going to the Lafayette Ball? You already have your costume!" Lucio Cappelli, guiding genius of the Maison Rouge beauty salon, had been styling Rhonda Perillo's hair for more than a year and was well aware that she was being kept by a wealthy man, although he still had no idea who it was. Although he knew that Rhonda was deeply in love with her lover, Lucio had grave misgivings about the affair. There had to be something wrong with a man who made her dye that gorgeous red hair blonde. And hide her green eyes behind blue contact lenses. This latest development was another outrage!

Rhonda shrugged as she watched him in the mirror. "Something's come up—well, actually, a lot of things. He's involved in all kinds of plans for the Mardi Gras. He works too hard. I told you he's a member of the Artillery Club, didn't I?"

"Yes, darling, you did," Lucio nodded. He was just as impressed as she was with such a prestigious connection.

"And the Knights of Momus, and . . . all kinds of other things." She hesitated to go into more details. After all, she was supposed to be discreet. "Anyway, he says there's no way he can spend any time with me if I come to the ball anyway, so he wants me to stay home."

"Why don't you just go by yourself?"

Rhonda sighed. She had gone over all this in her mind. "I don't think I'd like to go alone, Lucio. And . . . my friend . . . has our tickets." In a moment of desperation, Rhonda had actually considered buying her

258

own ticket and going alone, but she had discovered that subscriptions for the Lafayette Ball were entirely sold out.

Being a heterosexual and Italian, Lucio Cappelli was of the opinion that there could never be too many beautiful women at a ball. Being fond of Rhonda Perillo, he wanted to see her have a good time. And being a native Roman, he adored intrigue.

"You know, Rhonda, I have a friend, an older woman, a society woman, very rich, very powerful, but still — a romantic. She buys up fifty or so tickets to this ball and likes to give them to young people, beautiful kids who have no connections or money who could never go otherwise. She says she gets tired of looking at the fat old rich."

Rhonda smiled. It was all so ridiculous. "A fairy godmother, Lucio?"

"I think she would like to be, *cara*. Believe me, I know this woman. There are no strings. She's just eccentric and likes to have a little fun with her money."

Rhonda leaned back in the salon chair. Cordell had said he couldn't take her to the ball. He'd said nothing about her going on her own. Disguised in her costume and mask, he might not even know she was there, but she could see everything.

"Well then, Lucio, I'd love to give your friend a little fun."

While Rhonda waited, Lucio went to his private phone in the rear of the salon and placed a call to his friend. Her maid answered, and then relayed the message. Soon madame herself was on the line.

"Hello? Miss Mozelle?" he said, his voice excited.

"Yes, Lucio, darling. What is it?"

He explained his friend's dilemma. Mozelle Bryant was delighted to help. Everything was arranged. Rhonda Perillo would be a guest at her table.

Chapter Thirty-two

Belinda couldn't bear to stay at the Sand Castle, and even the Maison Rouge held too many memories. She could have opened up Claiborne's Gulfside mansion, but instead she accepted her aunt Carrie Clinton's invitation to stay with her. Aunt Carrie lived in a yellow-painted gingerbread-trimmed wedding cake on Sealey Avenue. The entire house was a living museum to the illustrious Clinton family, of which Carrie and Belinda's mother Mona had been the last survivors. Now there was only Carrie, pillar of the Galveston Historical Society, the Daughters of the American Revolution, the Daughters of the Confederacy, and the Daughters of the Alamo.

"You haven't told your daddy you're here?" Carrie said with disbelief. She and Buster had never gotten along, but she still felt Belinda ought to show some respect for her daddy.

"I'll get to him," Belinda said softly. "I know how busy he is."

"Oh, my. Not at all. He's turned over so much to your brother Cordell I think he has a lot of time on his hands." Carrie looked thoughtful. "Of course, they do say that idle hands are the devil's workshop."

Another advantage to staying at Carrie's was that Myles McLean lived next door in the house he had inherited from his parents. Galveston was the kind of place where houses stayed in the same family for generations. As Belinda glanced outside Carrie's bay window

260

she could see him now standing on her aunt's front porch.

"I think you've got a visitor, Aunt Carrie," she said, just as his hand sounded the knocker.

Not waiting for her maid, Carrie herself fluttered to the door and led Myles into her old fashioned drawing room. He seemed even taller and lankier standing among Carrie's carefully arranged knicknacks. The old woman looked relieved when he settled into a large armchair and out of harm's way. She insisted he stay for tea, then went into the kitchen herself to supervise her cook, leaving Myles and Belinda alone.

"What, here alone? Old Claiborne let you come back all by yourself?" he teased.

"I brought our son and his nurse," she said. "They're upstairs napping."

"What about old Claiborne? Is he napping, too?"

"No," she said with annoyance. "And don't talk about him like he's an old man. He's ten years older than you. And extremely active."

"So I hear," Myles said dryly. He regretted that as soon as he saw the pain in her eyes. He hated to think she might actually love Claiborne Lurie or at least loved him when she married him. Charlene Lurie had hinted that her father was sighted in Paris with Ciprianna Rivers. If she knew about that, it must be difficult for her, and if she didn't know, he sure didn't want to be the one to tell her. He was torn between sympathy for Belinda and anger at her for being so stupid as to marry a cur like Lurie.

"Fayette will be glad to see you," he said, steering their conversation back to more neutral ground. "She's over at the Maison Rouge covering preparations for the cook-off tomorrow. Your stepmother's chairman, and she's over there, too. But I guess you know all about that."

"No, I didn't."

Myles was wondering how he, a man acknowledged to be another Percy Foreman in the courtroom, could be so inclined to put his foot in his mouth when he was around Belinda Garland. He still couldn't think of her as a Lurie.

"But I'm looking forward to seeing Fayette again," Belinda added quickly. "I miss her. It gets kind of lonely down on Rancho Strega."

That made him feel better. Signs of discontent. Good. An opening. He settled back as Aunt Carrie returned with a tea tray, followed by her little Mexican maid carrying another tray of homemade pralines.

The thing Buster Garland had always liked most about Mozelle Bryant was that she was one of the rare women who was just as smart out of bed as she was in. She knew when to talk and when to listen. When to throw and when to catch. Now she listened intently as he told her a little of his situation. Not everything, but enough.

"So, Buster, you're thinking that if Cordell's in charge much longer he'll draw you down the tubes," she said when he finished.

"That's about the size of it."

And then there were problems with Valdene. Mozelle was pretty sure there were problems with Valdene if Buster was here, but he had said nothing specific. It sure couldn't be because he wasn't satisfying her. Darling Buster was still the bull he'd always been.

It wasn't like Buster Garland to complain, especially about a woman. Especially when that woman was his wife. But he had begun to sense that he had made a serious mistake in marrying Valdene. He had only himself to blame, too, which didn't make it any better. That girl had fooled him from the start.

Who knew that a hillbilly preacher's wife would fall in love with the jet set? And he'd been fool enough to let himself be led around for a year like a prize steer on exhibition at a county fair while his son Cordell took Garland, Inc., to rack and ruin.

262

Oh, he'd enjoyed laying it on the line to Buddy. Putting the screws to that boy. Served him right for getting into debt with the wrong people. But the point was that Buddy belonged in Galveston and running Garland, Inc. And he had to get him back. The sooner he did, the sooner he could put the rest of his house in order.

Belinda's conversation with Myles McLean had cheered her, and while Aunt Carrie kept prodding her, she finally agreed to call Buster.

Valdene answered. Her nasal hill-country twang still grated on Belinda's ears.

"Oh, hello there, Valdene," Belinda managed to say sweetly. "Is my daddy there?"

"Oh, not right now, honey," Valdene answered just as cozily. "Don't tell me you're up here for the Mardi Gras?"

All right then, I won't, Belinda thought. "I'm staying with Aunt Carrie," she added.

"Oh, no, darlin', you know old Buster won't stand for that. He'll chew my head off if he thinks I didn't welcome you here."

Belinda would have liked to see that, but she had no intention of staying under the same roof with Valdene.

"Oh, we're all settled in. It's too much trouble to move now. But thank you."

"We?" Valdene repeated, her instinct quivering. "Is Claiborne Lurie with you?"

How she would have loved that, Belinda thought. Valdene's social ambition was so transparent. "No," she assured her. "Just the baby and the nurse and me."

"Oh." Less enthusiasm for sure. The invitation was not repeated.

"Please have Buster call me here when he gets back," Belinda said.

"Oh, sure, sure, honey. Sure."

Valdene was glad to get off the phone with Belinda. She wasn't thrilled to learn Buster's daughter was back in Galveston, but she had other things on her mind, like fittings for her costume and her mask, and all the last-minute preparations for her cook-off at the Maison Rouge.

She turned her attention back to Reba, who waited meekly for instructions.

Chapter Thirty-three

Brice was having a four-star day. The Maison Rouge had spared no expense to entertain the celebrity chefs and he turned out to be a crowd favorite, even more popular than Jacques Cartier, who had been brought all the way from Paris for the Gourmet Gala. He even had an interview scheduled with a reporter from *Paris Match*.

Much to his delight, Brice discovered that his television appearances had made his face so familiar that in a short walk he and Tammy Lynn took along the Seawall he was stopped several times by ordinary tourists. Of course, the couple from Tyler thought he was Ken Wahl, but at least they knew he was somebody.

The only one who didn't seem to enjoy their attention was Tammy Lynn. She was more possessive than ever, and gripped his arm tightly every time a halfway attractive girl approached.

"Relax," he told her. "You're mad as a hornet for nothing."

"A lot you care," she said.

The girls kept smiling.

The Mardis Gras committee had arranged a special brunch in honor of the celebrity chefs at Ashton Villa, a local landmark. There was music and dancing, but Brice quickly got bored and left while Tammy Lynn was chatting up a local banker. He walked around the grounds of the Maison Rouge. The gardens were deserted; most of the guests, he imagined, were downtown watching the parade. He wondered where Belinda Garland was. Tammy went bananas whenever he even brought up her aunt's name. It made him wonder why Tammy Lynn had arranged this homecoming. But that was like Tammy Lynn: never considering the consequences of her actions.

He was looking forward to running into Belinda again. It was a small island, after all, and their paths would have to cross sometime, even if by accident. Belinda must know by now that there was some things that even the Garlands couldn't control.

He decided to look in on the kitchen.

Charlene Lurie was restless and feeling penned in, wondering why she had ever come back to Galveston at all. Then she remembered how cute Cordell looked when he found her waiting in his living room, with his thick boyish blond hair and Robert Redford looks. If only he wasn't so wrapped up in his silly businesses and his dumb hotel so he could have some fun. After they got married again, she planned to see that Cordell learned how to relax and enjoy life.

She was a little surprised that Cordell had not yet succumbed to her, in fact he seemed downright annoyed when she moved into the master bedroom they once shared. So far, he had not slept with her, spending his nights at the Maison Rouge, but Charlene felt that only proved that Cordell was still a southern gentleman. After all, they were not married. Maybe he wanted to save her reputation. How gallant! How refreshing! How she had missed this kind of treatment in Hollywood. Show business was not for her. Give her the marriage business, she decided.

After finishing her makeup and brushing out her hair, Charlene wrapped herself in a pink satin robe and padded down the hall to her daughter's room. She wanted to be sure Chandler was getting ready, too. The girl didn't seem too enthusiastic about the whole visit.

Chandler hadn't stayed in her bedroom much since the divorce, and it still reflected the little girl she had been rather than the sophisticated little teenager who was sitting up in one of the twin French provincial beds, reading her mother's copy of French *Vogue*.

Charlene had planned to have a heart-to-heart talk with Chandler, but when her daughter looked up and caught her eye, she lost her nerve.

"Yes, Mother?" Chandler said.

"Aren't you getting ready, darlin'," Charlene said with annoyance. The last person she wanted to wait for was her teenage daughter. "We're going to miss the parade!"

Chandler shrugged. "I don't care about a parade."

Charlene thought for a minute. "Chandler, darlin', you just get yourself dressed in ten minutes or I'm canceling your charge cards."

She turned and left the room, confident that she knew the key to her daughter's heart.

Belinda had not been thinking when she made her hasty plans to come back to Galveston, otherwise she would have realized that she would be arriving in the middle of Mardis Gras. But she was here now, and in spite of herself she was drawn downtown to watch the preparations for the celebration.

It was only a short walk from Miss Carrie Clinton's to the Strand, the center of the activities, and Belinda had a chance to see all the development that had gone on since her last visit. She noticed that the Delancy Street warehouse was still vacant. That made sense. With land values down and the price of oil plummeting, it would be awfully tough to get financing for a property like that.

And yet, she was still convinced that it could be developed into a major money-maker.

She stopped in at the antique stores near the port, picked up a Haviland teapot for Carrie and a Lionel train for Alexander. He was too young to appreciate it, but she'd save it for him. She moved on to a jewelry

267

store on Tremont where she bought a silver pin for Lourdes, his nurse.

All around her, the excitement was building as the merchants prepared for the Mardis Gras. She really ought to get a costume, or a mask at least. Aunt Carrie might have something. Belinda made a mental note to ask her.

She passed the Garland, Inc., Headquarters and was tempted to drop in and see if there were any familiar faces, but she couldn't bring herself to do it. She was still angry at Cordell and didn't want to run into him. Myles had mentioned that Charlene Lurie was back in Galveston and hinted that she might be trying to reconcile with Cordell. Belinda could not help smiling at the thought of that. Charlene and Cordell deserved each other.

As she was standing outside the pink granite tower, she saw an attractive dark-haired young woman staring at her. It took a few minutes to recognize her. After all, they hadn't seen each other in almost two years, not since Buster's wedding. Then she waved, and Tammy Lynn Garland crossed the street to greet her.

While Brice was huddled with the interviewer from *Paris Match,* Tammy Lynn had gone out to see the parade. Now she and Belinda air kissed as if nothing had ever happened between them. As if they had not spoken in almost two years.

"How's everything?" Belinda asked.

Tammy Lynn smiled. "Great. Fantastic."

"Do you need anything?"

"Just a few more hours in the day. I never have enough time to take care of everything," Tammy Lynn assured her.

"You should come down to Rancho Strega, Tammy Lynn. We'd love to have you."

"Sometime." The coolness in her voice made it clear that would be unlikely any time soon.

268

"How is your friend Brice?" Belinda asked. She didn't care, but she felt she ought to show an interest. Unfortunately, it was like waving a red flag at a bull.

Tammy Lynn glared at her. For the first time, Belinda thought her niece knew about her interlude with Brice. She wanted to tell her it had all been a stupid mistake. Wasn't sainted Aunt Belinda allowed to step down from her pedestal just once in her life? But she couldn't bring herself to say more. Looking at Tammy Lynn was looking at a lit stick of dynamite. Belinda was afraid if she said any more it would set off an explosion that could never be undone.

She was tempted to tell Tammy Lynn why she really fired Brice, but put the thought aside. It would only make it worse. Besides, she didn't think Tammy Lynn would believe her.

Instead, Belinda called her niece's attention to the float going by.

"I understand you learned about cooking from your mother," the interviewer from *Paris Match* began. She was very French gamin, dressed like a young Audrey Hepburn in black sweater, black tights, and heavy gold chains around her neck and waist. She chain-smoked Gauloises, and the sweet smell of the cigarettes filled the room like incense.

Brice thought about using gold chains to tie up her wrists while he made love to her after the interview was over, then launched into the story he had by now polished through several hundred interviews. His standard interview had become a thing of beauty: amusing, inspirational. All about how his mom—a real mom—started him cooking in her own kitchen, and taught him all he knew about food, from anise to zabiglione.

"And is it true that you have never visited France?" the reporter asked incredulously.

"Yeah, that's right. What difference does it make?" He knew he sounded surly. "France is the past. I'm the future."

The girl frowned. "I understand your mother is also an American celebrity," she added, as she reached into the Hermès briefcase and produced the latest edition of the *National Enquirer*. The front-page story showed Colette in all her glory, offering predictions for the 1990's.

"I notice the name is the same. De Young—it is not common, no?" the reporter said. "And the resemblance is remarkable."

Brice looked at her, sizing her up the way he might a piece of beef, trying to decide if she was offering him a way out or intended to write about Colette, too. It was one thing to have Colette calling him up on *Oprah Winfrey,* but it was quite another to have her name linked with his in print.

And what did it matter, anyway. So he had colored his past a little. So he liked to think he'd come from a *Life* magazine family when the truth was the de Youngs were carnival Gypsies. So he said his mother was Betty Crocker and she was really more Jackie Stallone. Colette was a force of nature. The thought comforted him a little. Sly Stallone could understand about Colette.

For the first time Brice wished Tammy Lynn had sat in on this interview. He'd encouraged her to leave because he thought he might want to make this chic French girl with her short dark hair and gold chains, but now he needed Tammy Lynn's judgment. Tammy Lynn had great business judgment. On his own he was floundering. He saw his whole career going down the drain. The woman was going to make him look like a fool.

The phone rang. He leaped for it like a drowning man and sighed with relief when he heard Tammy Lynn's voice on the other end.

"Brice?" she said. Her voice sounded tentative. She knew he didn't like to be interrupted during an interview. Usually.

"What's that noise?" he demanded, recovering his composure. "I can hardly hear you."

"Oh, the parade's started. I ran into my Aunt Belinda.

270

I thought you might want to join us."

Brice wanted to see Belinda Garland around, but not with Tammy Lynn hanging on him. Besides, right now he had other things on his mind.

"The girl from *Paris Match* is still here," he said softly, then looked over to see the reporter's reaction. He knew she was listening to every word he said on the phone. Was she going to take revenge because he'd called her a *girl*. No, he reassured himself, the French were different.

"And it's not going well," Tammy Lynn said, instinctively reading the worry in his voice.

"That's right," he whispered, feeling like he was in on a conspiracy. He kept his eyes on the girl from *Paris Match,* who was watching him.

"I'll be right over. Stall her."

Brice hung up with relief. His confidence came pouring back. He probably didn't even need Tammy Lynn after all, he told himself. But he was paying her a ten percent manager's fee and she might as well earn it.

"My associate, Miss Garland, is going to join us," he said coolly. "Meanwhile, I thought I'd order something for us from room service. Do you know the Garlands? An old Galveston family. I'm sure you'll be interested in her story, too."

All thought of scoring with her had vanished. The gold chains still glittered, but for Brice they had lost their allure.

By four o'clock the parade was almost over and Charlene and Chandler were just making their way to the tail end. Charlene felt she was doing this for Cordell. He was so much a part of Galveston, and as his wife, his past and future wife, she would have to be willing to show her face at these events.

She thought of her mother's new role as Countess Ormsby and her responsibilities to the locals. Her own role in Galveston would be just like that, she thought, and the idea delighted her. It was just too bad that

Americans didn't have titles.

Countess Garland, didn't that sound nice?

"Look, Mommy," Chandler squealed, dropping her sophisticated pose and reverting to the undisguised enthusiasm of a little girl. "It's Daddy!"

Even her ferret Mr. T., hidden inside the folds of Chandler's Batman cape, peeked out to see what all the fuss was about. Sure enough, there was Cordell on top of the *Sentinel-Wave*'s pink flowered float. He was surrounded by a bevy of former Miss *Sentinel-Wave*s in one-piece bathing suits. They waved and smiled at the crowd. Cordell waved and smiled, too, but he looked very uncomfortable.

Dear Cordell, Charlene thought, and for just a minute a flash of sincere affection for her ex-husband warmed her. He was so inept! He really did need her.

"Buster, honey, Belinda's been callin' you," Valdene told him as soon as he returned to the Sand Castle.

He thanked her. He wondered if she sensed that his feelings for her had changed. He wondered if she planned to do anything about that.

He went into his study to call Belinda at Carrie's. On the private line. It rang and rang but there was no answer.

When Belinda returned from her walking tour, she found Carrie on the living-room settee, a thick scrapbook on her lap. The old woman looked up when Belinda came in, as if for a moment she had forgotten who her niece was.

"Is that you, Belinda?" she said.

"Sure is, Aunt Carrie. Sorry I've been gone so long. I got caught up in a parade. And I ran into Tammy Lynn."

"Oh, my," Aunt Carrie nodded. "It's Mardi Gras madness again." She sighed. "I'm afraid they'll never be

272

Mardi Gras like we used to have. I was just going over some pictures in this scrapbook. Come here, honey. Take a look. Know who that is?"

Belinda came over to the settee and sat down beside her aunt to get a look. All the photographs on the page were of the same slim and beaming girl, her golden hair tightly curled in the style of the 1950's.

"Mother?" she said.

Carrie laughed. "No, silly! Me! I was a Queen that year. Mona was just a handmaiden!"

She turned the pages, moving backward to the 1930's, when the costumes were even more elaborate.

"Now recognize anyone here?" She pointed at a photo of four children. The two boys were dressed like medieval pages, the two very young girls draped in feathers, jewels, and velvet. The Court of Cinderella, 1939, the caption said.

"The boy on the right looks familiar," Belinda said uncertainly.

"He better, honey. That's your husband. With his little sister Emmaline."

"Claiborne has a sister?" Belinda had never heard her husband mention any relatives besides Charlene.

"Oh, yes." Miss Carrie said, closing the book.

"Where is she now?"

An odd look crossed Carrie's plump face. "I think you best ask Claiborne that yourself, dear," she said.

Before Belinda could press for more details, there was a knock on the door and Myles had arrived to take them to dinner.

Myles had invited them to dinner at the Wentletrap, the new restaurant in the Tremont Hotel. But when he arrived at Miss Carrie's that night, he had changed his mind. "I thought we might drop in on Buster at the Sand Castle," he announced casually.

"Oh, dear," Carrie muttered, touching the fresh lace collar on her good print silk dress. She was never sure Buster welcomed her at the house. And that new wife!

Belinda was even less sure she'd be welcome and said

so.

"He called me," Myles assured her. "Couldn't get an answer here and he definitely wants to see you."

"Well then, let's go."

Carrie rushed to get a crocheted wrap—for some reason it was always cooler at the Castle lately—and insisted Belinda take one too. Then they were off.

It was one of their rare nights at home together and Valdene had planned to make the most of it. Unfortunately, as she was going over some of the plans for the cook-off, Buster walked in and announced that they would be having company for dinner.

Her first thought was that it was going to be some of his no-neck oil-patch buddies who'd stink up her house with cigar smoke and sit drinking bourbon until dawn; traces of their booming voices would linger in every corner of the Sand Castle long after they were gone.

But the truth was even worse.

"Belinda and Carrie!" she squealed. Times like this, when she was as scared as she was annoyed, she sounded more like the little girl Buster had once thought he loved. "I haven't had time to prepare!"

"Now don't go off on me, Valdene," Buster said patiently. "First of all, Belinda grew up in this house, so she's seen it every which way and doesn't give a god damn—"

"Don't swear!"

"Doesn't give a good goddamn," he said firmly, then returned to a more conciliatory tone. ". . . how this house looks. It's her home, it will always be her home, whether she wants to spend the night here or not."

Valdene put out her lower lip in the Tanya Tucker pout.

"And as for dinner, you just get on the phone to Luz. Luz was cooking here before Belinda was born, and if she can't manage to come up with something in that kitchen I spent a million dollars to redesign tell her she can go back to Chihauhau."

Buster told Luz she could go back to her hometown of Chihauhau regularly and it meant nothing to either of them, but his attitude bothered Valdene greatly.

"I don't know what you're fussin' about," she sniffed. "It isn't as if you and Belinda are close. You haven't seen her since we got married."

"I guess that's between me and my daughter, darlin'," Buster answered. Valdene caught the hint of warning in his voice and backed off.

"I think I'll go look in on Luz myself," she announced. "And I'll have Juan get some flowers from the green-house. How does a roast sound?"

Buster just grunted, and turned back to his papers until he overheard Valdene on the house phone, instructing Luz to set places for five for dinner.

"Hold on, darlin'," he shouted. "Best make that seven."

"What now, Buster? Are Charlene and Cordell coming, too?"

"No, darlin'. I guess it just slipped my mind until now, but I've gone and invited Buddy and Zena to share our little celebration. They should be arriving shortly."

Valdene stared at her husband, ignoring Luz's puzzled inquiries at the other end of the line. Now what was he up to?

Chapter Thirty-four

Even if she had not been prepared, Belinda would have known at once that another woman was now in charge at the Sand Castle. Her mother Mona had had exquisite taste, and although she had been dead more than six years, few changes had been made in the decor since her death. Until now.

A new houseman had answered the door. He obviously didn't recognize any of them, not even Belinda, but Buster was right behind him, and he greeted the three of them warmly, leading them into the living room. Belinda was glad to see her father looking so fit, and his voice still had the same strong timber, but there was something tired about him. He was paler, grayer. His hands were more deeply gnarled than she remembered and flecked with liver spots. *He's getting old* she told herself. It was as if Valdene was sucking the life force out of him.

Valdene was waiting for them in the living room. She had added a new accessory, a King Charles spaniel, a rich lady's dog. His name was Louis-Phillipe. Belinda noted that poor old Lyndon had been banished to a doghouse out back.

Everywhere she looked, Belinda could see Valdene's changes. Things like plastic flowers in the big Ming vases by the entrance to the living room. A dubious family tree purporting to show Valdene's descent from a hero of the Alamo was framed and hanging on the wall. That particularly captured Miss Carrie's interest, but she was too much of a southern lady to question its authenticity.

In the living room, the biggest change was that the big Aaron Shikler portrait of Mona Clinton Garland had disappeared, and where it used to hang over the mantelpiece there was now a new painting of Valdene in prayer robes. A Yamaha piano had been installed where a Duncan Phyfe writing desk had been, and on top of its gleaming surface was a collection of silver-framed photographs of Valdene posing with various celebrities. Some of the groupings even included Buster, looking impatient.

There was a strained, polite silence as Belinda and Myles sat on one sofa opposite Valdene with Aunt Carrie off to the side, sunk into a bergère, and Buster fixing their drinks himself at the bar.

Midway through their drinks, Valdene was called to the phone. She took it in another room, and her little dog and she were gone for some time. Buster's mood lifted visibly while she was gone, then darkened again when she returned and explained breathlessly that she was caught up in last-minute plans for her big cook-off, which was supposed to be one of the highlights of the Mardi Gras.

He knows he's made a mistake, but he doesn't want to admit it, Belinda realized suddenly. The very thought made her sad. That, more than the lined face and the gnarled hands, confirmed that her father was getting old.

She suddenly found herself missing her husband. Claiborne Lurie had a dry, snobbish humor and he would have had something mean, cutting, and funny to say about Valdene's pretensions. Time was, Belinda thought ruefully, when Buster would have been the first to laugh at her carrying-on.

This was, after all, a family gathering. Even Myles was as good as kin. But on short notice Valdene had pulled out all stops. Belinda thought she must be the terror of the kitchen staff, and they walked around her like whipped dogs. How blind could her father be, that he

277

didn't notice this? Or didn't he care?

"Oh, Valdene, you shouldn't have gone to this trouble," Belinda said politely when she saw the dining-room table laid out like a state banquet.

"That's what I told her, but she wanted to impress you," Buster said.

Valdene glared at him for just a second and then flashed her brilliant capped teeth at Belinda. "I wanted this to be special, honey. This is the first time you been back since the wedding, and I don't want you to be a stranger."

Myles squeezed Belinda's arm. She had been barely conscious that he was holding it as he led her into the dining room, but now she dared not meet his eyes for fear that she would start laughing. Valdene was so transparent. Belinda resolved to watch her back. But she felt oddly comforted, too, for she saw that she had done the right thing to marry Claiborne. With his money and his power, she did not have to depend on Buster and the Garlands. She pitied Cordell, who had so assiduously promoted the Buster-Valdene match. By now he must realize that with Valdene for a stepmother he has a tiger by the tail.

But as they entered the dining room, a sight greeted Belinda that forced her to quickly revise all her observations. The table was set for seven.

"Oh, dear," said Aunt Carrie, when she noticed the two extra places. "You're having company. Maybe we shouldn't have come."

"No at all," Buster boomed affably. "When it comes to my family, the more the merrier."

Valdene, who had looked annoyed and put out since they arrived, suddenly perked up. This made Belinda even more uneasy. Her stepmother seemed to thrive on dissension among the Garlands.

"Don't worry, ladies, I can see curiosity's just eating you alive. I've got some surprise guests for you. Yes, sir, we'll make this Mardi Gras something to remember."

Belinda flashed on the idea that he was including

278

Cordell and Charlene in this family feast but quickly discarded it. He could never look that happy at the prospect of dining with those two.

"They got here just before you folks," Buster went on. Set them up in the guest house. Told them to come up and join us when they were good and ready. I know that flight from New York can be a killer."

At that moment, Belinda could hear voices in the hallway, approaching the dining room. A man and a woman. Then they were in the doorway. Zena and Buddy. The special guests. Buster and Buddy, together again.

Buster rose to deliver a toast to the new arrivals, just as Luz brought in a steaming roast beef for his guests.

Nothing was said about Buddy's sixteen-year exile or whether this was more than just a Mardi Gras visit. But Belinda saw all her hopes about stepping into Cordell's shoes floating away in the balmy Galveston breeze.

Daddy has what he's wanted all along, she thought. *He's got his firstborn back where he wants him. And that leaves you strictly on your own.*

Chapter Thirty-five

The whole Mardi Gras experience was new to Brice and he wasn't sure he liked it. When he was growing up in Galveston he used to hear stories about the old days, before the War, when the Island had a Mardi Gras wilder than New Orleans, but he could hardly believe it.

When Tammy Lynn had first suggested they accept the invitation to come down for a Gourmet Gala, he had pictured a sleepy little off-season party, nothing like the ten nonstop days of beauty pageants, tennis tournaments, rugby tournaments, royal processions and parades, operas and exhibitions that filled the calendar, or the masked and painted partyers who filled the narrow downtown streets day and night.

It was clear that the Gourmet Gala was Valdene Garland's own special project. He was more sure than ever that Belinda Garland would turn up.

The glass-enclosed conservatory of the Maison Rouge, a huge sunny room filled with potted palms and bright pink azaleas, had been turned over to the visiting chefs. Rows of stalls had been set up on either side of the arcade. In each stall a celebrity chef was preparing his specialty on a Vulcan range, and next to each stall a celebrity host greeted the guests who strolled past sampling the fare. Almost everyone but the chefs was in costume.

There were plenty of media people there, too, from Fayette Cramer and her camera crew to stringers for the national press. They seemed to move as one, most of them following Fayette as she approached Sven Petersen the boxer and his celebrity chef, Jacque Cartier, of the famous Paris restaurant, Fantine's.

Tammy Lynn Garland was standing outside the next stall, where Brice de Young, in black tie and toque blanche, was whipping up sweet potato chips with cayenne and coriander.

Valdene Garland, in tight black lace evening gown and diamond earrings the size of silver dollars, arrived just in time for Wiley Muehl to take her around to meet the chefs as they were making last-minute adjustments to their stations. Her little dog followed close at her heels.

"Shouldn't that doggie be on a leash, Mrs. Garland?" Wiley asked.

Valdene glared at him. "That just shows how much you know, Wiley," she explained. "Louis-Phillipe is a King Charles spaniel and he knows how to behave in public."

"I hope so, ma'am. Things are going to get a bit exciting in a few minutes."

Poor Wiley did not know how prophetic he was, but at that moment the doors officially opened and the gourmet gala guests began to pour in. Little Louis-Phillipe cowered at his mistress's Charles Jourdan black lizard heels in utter terror. He had never been exposed to so many people.

Many of the revelers were coming in from the parade down on the Strand, some in costumes, some masked, some with faces painted gold. There were clowns, cats, and pirates among them, but each one of them had paid a hundred dollars for the privilege of nibbling on tidbits prepared by five famous cooks and they were ravenous.

Charlene Lurie arrived with a sulking Chandler, who had been perfectly happy watching the parade and was angry with her mother for tearing her away to come to the hotel. She had seen enough hotels in her life.

"I'm bored, Mama," Chandler whined. "I want to go home." She was wearing her Batman costume, black mask and cape and all. Mr. T., hidden in the folds of her cape, was disguised as Robin with his own cape and mask.

"Hush, darling," Charlene said. "We'll leave right after dinner."

That didn't satisfy Chandler. "I don't see why we have to come at all. I don't like it here."

"Neither do I, darlin'," Charlene assured her. "But this is Valdene's party and we have to make her happy." As part of her campaign to win back Cordell, Charlene had decided to cultivate her future stepmother-in-law, although she regarded Valdene as white trash. She looked around the room at the other guests milling around and chatting up the chefs. Who were all these people? Her father would have a fit if he saw them. He was Old Galveston, and could hardly bear to have the tourists around during the summer season. What would he think of encouraging them to come year round, she wondered.

"Charlene, darling," someone shouted, and he looked around to see who it was. A hulking blond figure in shimmering white satin track suit was waving at her from the corner, near a big magenta azalea.

"Oh, Sven, honey," Charlene said, rushing over, delighted to finally see someone who was even vaguely her sort.

Brice thought the Gourmet Gala wasn't going too badly until he looked out at the crowd and saw Belinda Lurie walking in with a stout old lady and a tall man who looked a lot like James Stewart. Belinda looked different, softer, but he would have recognized her anywhere. She looked edgy, too, as she scanned the room. Her large blue eyes met Brice's, then she turned away.

He called for more champagne.

"My, my," said Miss Carrie, as they waded through the thick crowd. "Where do all these people come from? And isn't that Tammy Lynn's beau?"

"Yes, ma'am," said Myles. "Would you like to chat with him?"

"Oh, dear no. He looks like he's working much too hard. I wouldn't want to distract him."

Belinda was relieved to hear that, and delighted when Myles suggested they go in to their table in the Maisonette.

Abandoned by her mother, and bored by the other guests, Chandler Garland was growing more and more restless. She had sampled Brice de Young's sweet potato chips and Jacques Cartier's fried mushroom pasta and Penelope Watson's ham and three cheese pasta roll and J. Alden Stanhope's oyster fritters.

She loved her Batman disguise, but the cape was awkward and she kept getting caught up in it. Feeling quite sorry for herself, she caressed her only friend in the world, Mr. T. Coming here had seemed like a good idea back on Oak Park Circle, but now she just wished she was anywhere else.

"There, there," she whispered, stroking the sleek ferret who cowered in the crook of her arm. His little nose twitched and his dark-brown eyes stared out wildly. She knew just how he felt. She hated crowds, too.

"Yoo hoo, Chandler honey, over here!"

Relieved to hear a familiar voice, even if it was her mother's, Chandler ran toward her, tripping over her cape as she did so, and crashing to the terra-cotta floor.

The crash sent little Mr. T. flying from Chandler's arms and the furry creature suddenly found himself scrambling for a grip on the tile floor, in the middle of a forest of legs. Someone screamed.

"Oh, my God, it's a rat!"

More screams.

Guests started stampeding to the exits as Valdene's

little King Charles spaniel discovered the interloper and began to bark, chasing Mr. T. into a group of potted palms. Little Louis-Phillipe was much more at home on the tile floors than the ferret who was slipping around frantically as he tried to escape, but Mr. T. had the advantage of great climbing ability and he had soon mounted a potted palm and was running along the row of chefs' work tables, sending platters and dishes crashing to the floor.

The panicked chefs deserted the room, except for Brice de Young and Jacques Cartier who remained at their stations, glaring at each other, while Sven Petersen led an impromptu posse after the two animals. Neither Brice nor Cartier was willing to concede the field by running away from a ferret and a dog.

By now they were the only people left in the conservatory and they glared at each other in silence as they tried to protect what was left of their work, while Charlene and Valdene stared open mouthed at the wreckage. And, of course, a masked Batman, still on the floor, calling in vain to the ferret.

"Mr. T. What a bad boy. What have you done?"

At that moment, Wiley Muehl arrived with two uniformed security guards. One of them rushed to Batman's side, kneeling beside the masked figure.

"Officer," he ordered. "Arrest this person."

He stripped the mask from Batman with a flourish, revealing the pale and frightened face of Chandler Garland.

With that, the little ferret, who had managed to climb the tall palm behind Cartier, lost his footing and landed with a crash into the Frenchman's stockpot. Cartier had lost his endurance contest to Brice de Young, who lifted the stunned Mr. T., his fur soaked and matted, out of the pot. All around him the rest of the chefs' stations were in total disarray.

"Well, folks," Brice said coolly. "How do you feel about scrambled eggs?"

Chapter Thirty-six

The next night's Lafayette Ball began auspiciously. The ballroom of the Maison Rouge had been decorated to resemble a French château at the dawn of spring. A thick red carpet led from the port-cochere entrance to the grand ballroom. On the way guests passed a series of raspberry lacquered screens hung with white flowers, then entered the ballroom through a pair of pedestals draped with garnet satin, supporting great crystal apothecary jars filled with white lilacs, French tulips and orchids.

The tables were covered with burgundy cloths and centered with cranberry glass vases filled with still more white lilacs, tulips, and hyacinths.

Lauren Armour was not at Aynsley Adder's table, which was filled with other politicians and his biggest backers. She had been relegated to a table nearby where her escort for the evening was one of Aynsley's aides. Aynsley was seated beside Carola Lee. Lauren was steaming.

She picked up a curried scallop hors d'ôeuvre and looked around the table. They were all Aynsley's gofers. She loathed them and knew they despised her, regarding her as a constant threat to their candidate's wholesome family image. She was a celebrity, damn it, every bit as much a celebrity as Aynsley and she deserved better.

The aides only wanted to gossip about people in

Washington and Austin. It bored her. Lauren knew she ought to be working the room the way she used to, but she didn't have the heart anymore. She noticed Fayette Cramer was taping an interview with Aynsley.

Aynsley looked wonderful. He always looked best in black tie, and of course he had a new corset for the occasion. Did Carola Lee lace him in, she wondered? Carola Lee seemed lost in her own world, staring into space, occasionally sipping from the glass she lifted to her lips with both hands. When she wasn't holding glass, Lauren noticed, her hands trembled. She had nice jewelry, though. Lauren wondered if she had inherited it. Carola Lee came from money, she knew. Aynsley had never bought Lauren a thing.

Lauren flashed on the awful thought that Aynsley could be sleeping with Fayette Cramer. Was that why he was giving her the interview? It was too painful to think about. She pushed the idea from her mind. If only she was at a better table, she could have some fun flirting. But these wimpy aides wouldn't dare put a hand on the boss's girlfriend. At least, not while the boss was only one table away.

Lauren looked at Carola Lee and she looked at Fayette. Carola Lee was in the past, Aynsley had told her so many times. Maybe Fayette was in the future. If she confronted him about it, he'd only deny it. Suddenly Lauren didn't want to spend the night alone. She looked around the room.

Charlene was dancing with Sven Petersen and she could hear the crowd buzzing. She only hoped Cordell could see them. The sight was sure to make him jealous.

She loved being held in Sven's big, muscled arms; he made her feel small and fragile and thin. Very thin. And she knew from past experience that Sven was all man and his muscles were the real thing; no steroids for him. As he had told her, over and over. He had become a real missionary on the subject, and Charlene, a great believer in better living through chemistry, was growing bored.

Someone tapped her on the shoulder and she turned around. It was little Tammy Lynn, Cordell's niece. But she wasn't so little anymore. She was all grown up and her escort looked vaguely familiar. Charlene seldom overlooked a famous face, but she drew a blank on this tall, dark stranger. His chocolate brown eyes fell on her breasts and she was suddenly glad she hadn't worn a bra. Then she recognized him. Brice de Young, the chef. Was he going to hold yesterday's debacle against her?

"Tammy Lynn, darlin'," she said, giving the debutante squeal. "How long has it been? You and your hunk come sit with Sven and me and tell us what ya'll been doin'."

"I don't care what you say," Valdene snapped as she helped herself to an asparagus tip. "That bitch put her daughter up to it. She deliberately ruined my Gourmet Gala!"

Reba Twining just shrugged. She had been trying to calm her friend all day, but Valdene had still not recovered from the ferret episode.

"Now, darlin', don't fret over spilled milk."

"Oh, shut up!"

They were not at Tammy Lynn's table long before Charlene was concentrating most of her attention on Brice. She tried to be seductive, playfully feeding him a smoked salmon canapé, but she sensed that his attention was somewhere else. She followed his gaze to a nearby table where Lauren Armour, the KLMN-TV anchor woman was seated with a gaggle of Senator Adder's aides.

Sven, too, noticed the beautiful blonde surrounded by men who paid no attention to her. What was wrong with these American men, he wondered. Besides, now that he got a better look at her, he recognized her from television. He had done his push-ups this morning while watching her pretty blond face. So, although they had not been introduced, he felt as if he already knew her. Grabbing a fresh bottle of champagne from a passing tray, Sven headed to rescue the fair damsel.

Lauren had been growing more and more irritated at being ignored by Aynsley. Then his wife stood up, and Lauren gasped. Carola Lee Adder was wearing a low-cut, flowing violet velvet gown, but it did not disguise one obvious fact. Carola Lee Adder was pregnant. Her lover's wife was going to have a baby!

She *knew* he had been sleeping with someone else, but she never suspected Carola Lee. Damn him! He had betrayed her with his own wife! The man had no scruples!

She looked into Sven's blank but sweet blue eyes. He was unaware of her connection with Aynsley and was busy telling her about the vitamin drink he had developed. Vitamins! Lauren thought. She didn't need vitamins. She needed to get laid. Or at least get high. There was no way she was going to get either from Sven. She looked around the ballroom for a more likely source, and spotted Brice de Young. Good old Brice! How long had it been? Too long! He was sitting at Charlene Lurie's table. This was her chance.

"Sven, honey, isn't that your old friend Charlene Lurie?" she asked gently. "I'd love to meet her."

Thrilled to show Charlene that he, too, knew important, famous people, Sven was delighted to oblige.

Mozelle Bryant had one of the best tables in the room, and Rhonda had a good view of the other guests, especially the ones at Cordell's table.

It was almost too good. Rhonda could see Charlene Lurie very clearly. Cordell's ex-wife was just as pretty as her pictures, and even thinner. No wonder Cordell was always after her about her diet. He really liked the thin type.

The tricolor sorbet dessert looked wonderful when the

288

waiters brought it out in an elaborate spun sugar basket on a silver tray. It looked like a cloud, floating on the tray, but Rhonda suddenly lost her appetite and pushed the dessert away.

She concentrated instead on the scene at Cordell's table: Charlene had been flirting with the big blond boxer but now turned her attention to the dark-haired man with the diamond earring.

But where, she wondered, was Cordell?

Aynsley was enjoying himself immensely. The warm reception he was getting from the crowd assured him that the time would soon be right to announce he would run for the Senate. He had not been pleased when Carola Lee announced that they were expecting an addition to the corral, but he had changed his mind. Her pregnancy—and Carola Lee always looked best when she was pregnant—would certainly dispel any ugly rumors that he ran around.

He did not have to look over to Lauren's table to sense the daggers she was sending his way. The one time tonight when their eyes met she had glared at him in silence. Aynsley was sorry he never got around to telling her about the baby, but he was a busy man and that was just not a priority. For God's sake, Lauren was supposed to be an intelligent woman. Why did this come as such a surprise to her?

Women—he could never figure them out. Oddly enough, he did not dread running into Lauren Armour tonight half as much as he feared crossing paths with Belinda Garland. He knew she had still not forgiven him for the accident that killed Arden Yates. She blamed him and always would.

Strange, how things work out. Arden was probably the only human being besides his daddy that Aynsley Adder had ever loved with a pure and abiding love. He and Belinda should have been united in their grief. But she was so damn unforgiving!

Well, he told himself, there was nothing she could do about it now.

Much to Lauren's surprise and annoyance, Brice pointedly ignored her and danced with Charlene while she was stuck with Sven who had clammy hands and kept talking about vitamins.

Tammy Lynn was also furious. She tried to hide her rage by table hopping and pretending to be pleased to run into so many old friends when she was really jealous because Brice was paying so much attention to Charlene.

Cordell was seated at the same table as his ex-wife, but he could spend little time with Charlene since he was fussing about, shaking hands and making sure that the big event went well.

Everything seemed to be proceeding as planned, at least until he noticed his father. Big Buster was table hopping himself and had paused to exchange a few words with Mozelle Bryant. To his horror, Cordell saw that Rhonda Perillo was at Mozelle's table. He barely recognized her, because her face was covered by a white feather mask, but he noticed her charm bracelet. He fancied himself a judge of good jewelry and regarded the bracelet as particularly tacky, a constant reminder of Rhonda's white trash roots.

And now she was inches away from Buster! Suppose Buster found out about their relationship? Suppose he found out about the pictures? He caught Rhonda's eye and gestured for her to meet him outside.

He found her on the terrace.

"What are you doing here?" he hissed. "I told you not to come!"

"You told me you couldn't take me, Cordell. You didn't say I couldn't come."

"Damn it, girl, use your head. Did you know that's my daddy talking to Mozelle?"

"Sure, Cordell. Everyone on the Island knows Buster Garland. But he's a nice man. I'm sure he'd understand about us. Do you want me to leave?"

More than anything else in this world, at that moment he wanted her to leave, but he did not want to arouse Buster's suspicion. Instead he sent her back with a reprimand and turned his attention back to the floor.

That's when he noticed an even more unwelcome sight. At first he thought he was hallucinating, but as he moved closer to his father's table, he saw that the two figures were all too clearly flesh and blood.

There at his father's table, talking to Valdene as bold as brass, were his brother Buddy Garland and his wife Zena.

Did Buster know about this? he asked himself. Of course, he must. They were at his table! The old scoundrel had probably been talking to Buddy for months. Pretending he was tolerating the way Cordell was running Garland, Inc., and all the time wooing Buddy and his bride to come back to Galveston.

Cordell tried not to stare at his beautiful black sister-in-law, but it was hard to miss Zena in her elaborate pink-feathered headdress. All around him he could hear the whispers: *That's her. Marrying her cost Buddy Garland millions.*

Cordell felt himself hyperventilating and thought he might just faint. And then salvation came in the form of his own personal bitch goddess.

"Are you all right, Cordell, honey?" Charlene said as she took his arm. "I thought you were going to dance with me once this evening, but now you look like you need a little rest."

"I think I need to lie down," he managed to mutter.

Charlene's eyes lit up. This was as close to a proposition as her ex-husband had come since she moved back into Oak Park Circle. In fact, it was as close as he had come to her physically in years.

"Of course, darlin'. Now didn't I hear you were keeping a suite here in the hotel. Why don't I help you upstairs and get you settled up there? How about it honey?"

291

Cordell allowed himself to be led by Charlene as he had allowed himself so many times before. In times of such upheaval, Charlene always seemed like an island of composure, a mirage for a drowning man.

Chapter Thirty-seven

Charlene and Cordell came together in bed like thunder and lightning and the last ten years of feuding were blown away by the hurricane force. Charlene was surprised that a man as stiff and rigid as Cordell could loosen up so much in bed. Well, she reminded herself, at least one part of him stayed stiff and rigid and that was all to the good.

She who had conquered movie stars and rock stars still got the greatest satisfaction from reconquering her former husband. He was hers. Once and always. Sometimes her life was better than any movie.

They stole away to Cordell's penthouse suite. He said it used to be his sister's and he had redecorated.

"This is a relief," Charlene giggled. "All this time I thought you were staying with some bimbo you had stashed up here."

She subtly reviewed the closets and drawers just to be sure, but could find nor trace of a girlfriend. Cordell was such a dear, he was still carrying a torch for her. The thought suffused her with a warm glow. She followed him into the shower and insisted on joining him.

He resisted at first, but she just started soaping him up and tickling him, too, and soon he was laughing and growing hard again.

"See?" she laughed. "You're feeling better already."

He was not one to take her on the bathroom floor, she thought wistfully as he pushed her back toward the bed and forced her down on the cover, entering her and bringing her to a swift climax.

"Cordell," she whispered. "Let's get married again."

"I'm not going to do it, Aynsley, and you can't make me," Lauren whispered, her anger turning her voice to steel.

They were in Aynsley's suite. Carola Lee had been helicoptered in just for the occasion and as soon as the band stopped she was sent back to the ranch. She understood that her husband had to stay on for his meetings. Politics was stressful for them both, but she was the most supportive of wives.

Lauren had been consigned to a room on another floor far away from Aynsley's so no one would get the wrong idea. It wasn't even a suite, and it overlooked the parking lot. Even the management of the Maison Rouge must know that she was on her way out at KLMN-TV. She felt awful and had gone back to her room hoping to just drop off to sleep. Then the call came from one of Aynsley's aides, inviting her to join them for a little party for some of Aynsley's backers. He said it was "inviting," but it sounded more like "ordering" to her. All she wanted to do was get some sleep. Even the mirror told her she needed a rest. But the aide had hinted that there might be some blow at the party, and if she passed that up she'd hate herself even more.

Now it turned out that Aynsley wanted her to make up to a tubby little Arab who was supposed to be one of the ten richest men in the Middle East. He had round, plump hands like a baby's. They were soft as a baby's, too, she noticed, as she kept pushing them off her thigh.

The suite was crowded with men from the ball. There were almost no women, just a few hookers and herself. How dare he?

The aide had abandoned her on a love seat (how cute!) beside the amorous Arab. Every time she tried to get up, the little sultan would hold her gently back. When she saw Aynsley talking to a pair of his aides, she made a dash for him.

She grabbed his arm and pulled him into a corner. "How dare you?" she demanded.

He clenched his teeth, and instead of looking at her, he looked over her shoulder, his blood shot blue eyes scanning the room. The message was clear: she was the least important person here and she was taking up his valuable time.

"If it's the package you're worried about," Aynsley said softly, "it's waiting for you in your room. I believe Wally said he left it in the soap dish in the bathroom. But I advise you to stay here a while longer."

"Why, so that greaseball can get his hand under my skirt?"

"He likes you, Lauren. He's a big fan of yours. Don't you know who he is?"

Lauren shook her head. She could never keep these dark men straight. Tommy Lasorda, Mario Cuomo, and King Hussein all looked alike to her. It was a real handicap to her in her career.

"That's Adib Jamil. He's the biggest fixer in the Middle East. We're working on a deal together and it could be worth a lot to me."

Lauren nodded. She was so tired, so wasted, she could barely think. The idea that the deal might be irregular or a bribe didn't even occur to her. The idea that Aynsley might be making a big score did. If Aynsley had money of his own, he'd leave Carola Lee, baby or no baby.

"Now be a good girl and make Adib's dreams come true," he whispered, nuzzling her ear.

As he held her close she responded automatically, embracing him and welcoming the warmth of his body. She wanted him, not that greaseball. He pushed her away gently.

"You're treating me like a whore," she pouted.

"You just be a *good* whore and stay bought," he said, turning her around and steering her back to Adib Jamil.

It took all the concentration she could muster to rejoin Adib. She decided to lie back and think about the blow

295

waiting in her room. Adib was still sitting on the loveseat, his round, smooth face darkened by a scowl. When he saw her approaching, however, he brightened. He did not stand, but merely beckoned to her to sit beside him.

She did, then put one hand on his shoulder and leaned closer to share an intimate confidence.

"You know, Adib, it's so crowded in here. Wouldn't you like to come to my room?"

Adib thereupon demonstrated the legendary speed with which he had closed so many other business deals.

"*Sí,*" said Charlene. She was still giddy from the champagne they had consumed on their way down to the border.

"*Sí,*" said Cordell, who in the middle of this crazy elopement to Juárez had had the presence of mind to wake up his chauffeur and insist that the man handle the driving while he and Charlene kept the party gong in the back.

Now his chauffeur, Franklin Delano Roosevelt Williams, was their witness.

None of them had thought of a ring, but fortunately the La Vida es Sueño twenty-four-hour marriage mill had a small gift shop where he could purchase one.

"I now pronounce you man and wife," said the small, compact Mexican who looked more like an Aztec priest than a justice of the peace. "You may kiss the bride."

Cordell took Charlene into his arms and kissed her just the way he once had under the waterfall at the Sand Castle.

She responded and they sank to the chapel floor, until the justice of the peace reminded them that this was not an appropriate place for such antics, there were other couples waiting and, besides, there was a small motel he owned available across the street. They adjourned to the motel to greet the dawn.

After Mardi Gras Belinda didn't feel much like lingering in Galveston. She had made her peace with Buster and that was enough. If he chose to bring Buddy back on board, she'd leave him and Cordell to fight it out. With any luck, Buddy and Cordell would kill each other off and she could pick up the pieces when the time came. Meanwhile, she'd put her energies where they were wanted and concentrate on her Delancy Street project.

She booked an early flight for Rancho Strega. She tried not to think of her father and Valdene. If he was unhappy it was his own fault, and he ought to do something about it. Besides, she had her own life now. Claiborne was due back from London and he wanted to see her at the ranch.

Buster had never once mentioned Claiborne all the time they were together, but Valdene kept asking her questions about him. Funny, Valdene was so curious, and Buster didn't give a damn. Belinda knew her father regarded her marriage to his lifelong enemy as a betrayal, but that was too bad. The way he favored her brothers over her was a betrayal, too, as far as she was concerned.

Buddy and Zena had left the Sand Castle at dawn, claiming that urgent business required their return to New York even while they assured Buster that they had both enjoyed the Mardi Gras and the Lafayetete Ball and, privately, Buddy assured his father that he would make a decision about his return very soon.

Now Buster looked across the breakfast table at Valdene and the ever-present Reba. Lately, if there were no guests around, they barely spoke to each other. They had little to say, but this morning Valdene had recovered from the debacle of her Gourmet Gala and was eager to rehash every detail, costume, and intrigue of last night's ball. Reba encouraged her as she dissected every guest's costume and mask and assessed the approximate cost of each. She kept asking him his opinion.

It all bored Buster stiff. And now that Belinda was gone he sensed that he might have shortchanged her. He had not even asked to see her little boy, he was so excited to have his own son Buddy on the scene. Poor little gal! He'd have to make it up to her sometime. Now that he had outlived his doctor's predictions, he was feeling immortal again.

If things were different, he told himself, he might have insisted that Belinda stay on a few more days at the Sand Castle, but he wasn't ready to invite her back into the fold just yet. He was glad she wanted to reconcile, but he could still not forgive her for running off with Claiborne Lurie. Now, of course, he saw the reason. The old goat had knocked her up, and so she thought she had no choice. The whole thing would never have happened if Mona was alive. She could have talked some sense into Belinda.

He and Lurie went back forty years, at least, and Lurie's pose as a man of the world didn't fool Buster. He knew the Luries and their kind. He might fool an innocent like Belinda, but the act couldn't last.

He only hoped that when the end came for this mismatch, and it would, it would not be too painful for his daughter.

Buster knew that Belinda blamed him because Aynsley Adder had not spent one night in jail even though a blind man could see he was responsible for her husband's death. Things were so black and white to her! He usually liked that about her, but this was one time when she ought to have trusted his judgment and let it alone. So Arden Yates was her husband, and he was too young to die. But over the years she'd built Arden up into a saint, and he was a far cry from that. He was Aynsley Adder's best friend—for Pete's sake. That should tell her something.

But Belinda was thick as a brick when she got an idea in her head. His daughter had convinced herself that Aynsley and Arden had been just two good old boys out carousing and Aynsley had too much to drink and drove off the Seawall and let his friend drown because he didn't want to get arrested for drunk driving.

298

Only he and Aynsley knew the real story, but in the back of his mind, Buster feared that that was the real reason Belinda had married Claiborne Lurie: she hoped that somehow she could use his wealth to mete some kind of justice on Aynsley Adder.

"Didn't you think Charlene looked nice?" Valdene was saying. She knew Buster hadn't been listening to a word of her commentary on the ball.

"What, oh, yes, darlin', very nice."

Valdene and Reba exchanged glances in silence.

Belinda was surprised that Claiborne had still not returned to the ranch. She was beginning to hate the seclusion and isolation, especially after the liveliness of Galveston. She found herself recalling the parades and the dancing. It had been a long time since she went dancing.

Claiborne called to say he was detained in New York. Something about an acquisition that was running into complications.

Claiborne put down the phone and turned to his complications, all of which were wrapped up in the compact form of Ciprianna Rivers.

Ciprianna did things for him that he would never dare propose to Belinda.

She did one of them now.

"You're doing what?" Buddy growled when she gave him the news. Buster had insisted they take the Garland plane back to New York and they were ensconced in the 747's cozy den.

"Going into the jewelry business. I practically design all my own pieces now. And it will give me something to do."

Buddy stared into space.

"You don't approve of this, do you?" she said.

299

"It's not that," he said. "I'm trying to decide if it's going to save me money or take what little I have left."

"Oh, Buddy, stop. I won't do either for at least five years. You have to give a business time to grow. But it will be fun and take my mind off other things."

He looked at her shrewdly. "So the deal is if I back you in this business, you'll go along with the move back to Galveston?"

Zena nodded.

Buddy grinned and put his arm around her. "You drive a hard bargain, Zena honey. You sure you're not one of the Black Garlands?"

Zena decided that meant yes.

Chapter Thirty-eight

Two days after Belinda returned to Rancho Strega, Claiborne came back from his own business trip looking fit and rested. He found her in the picture gallery. She had started to spend a lot of time alone there, studying his collection, as if by understanding his favorite paintings, she might understand him.

"The trip must have gone well," Belinda said as he greeted her.

"What? Oh, yes. The business went very well. But I haven't been able to reach Charlene. I've left messages everywhere."

"The last time I saw her was at the Lafayette Ball," Belinda said. She decided not to mention the rumors on the family grapevine that Charlene and Cordell had remarried.

"It's very irresponsible of her," he said peevishly.

"Charlene's a big girl. I expect she can take care of herself." Belinda could not say the same for her brother. What was he thinking of, to hook up with his ex-wife again? And what did Buster think? Two of his children now lost to the Luries.

"I want to talk to her about the cruise," Claiborne continued as he fixed drinks for them both at the bar. Bored with the overdeveloped Riviera and the polluted Mediterranean, Claiborne had decided that this spring they would "do" the Amazon, and Belinda was looking

301

forward to it.

Belinda hoped that Charlene would stay away and keep Cordell with her, but all she said was "I thought we would be sailing alone."

Claiborne gave her the look that meant "Don't you understand anything?" What he said was: "Don't be ridiculous. Why would you want to rattle around that big boat with only me for company?"

Belinda shrugged. "I'd been thinking it would be kind of like a second honeymoon. We never did have one."

He came closer, caressing her neck and kissing her cheek. "That's very sweet." She arched her neck at his touch, turning her lips to him expectantly, but he did not take the gesture any further. Instead, his attention turned to her sapphire-and-gold earrings. He examined each one like an appraiser.

"Very sweet," he went on. "But unrealistic."

"Then who else is coming?" she asked.

He went through a list that included the flamboyant Houston attorney Bernardo O'Higgins and his guest, a psychic named Colette; Charlene and Cordell (he assumed); the financier Joel Varney and his wife, and Ciprianna and Carl Rivers.

"Ciprianna?" Belinda said, all her antennae alerted. She had been getting funny vibes about Ciprianna for weeks.

"Now, now, Belinda. I hope you're not going to get boring and provincial about Ciprianna. She's a fabulous lady and great fun. That's all."

"And you used to sleep with her," Belinda added.

He did not wish to continue the discussion. "Is there someone you would like to invite?" he asked.

She shook her head. "I'm not even sure I want to come, Claiborne. I started looking at some sites in Galveston during Mardi Gras and I'd like to go back now that it's not so frantic and talk to some architects."

"You can do that when we come back from the cruise. Nothing's going to happen in Galveston while we're away," he said.

302

"But, Claiborne . . ." she protested, but he waved her objections aside.

"You are my wife, Belinda. And there are some responsibilities that go with the job. Not many, I admit, but there are a few and I expect you to shoulder them. You will be the hostess on this cruise and that's it."

"You know Charlene loves that kind of thing. Why don't you let her do it?"

"Never. She's too irresponsible. In fact, I hope that during this cruise you might be able to talk to her, take her under your wing."

She laughed. "Me?"

"Come on, Belinda. You two were good friends once. You were always the only one who could talk to her. And you're both family now."

"You know, Claiborne, except for Charlene, I don't know anything about your family. Does Alexander have any other relatives?"

He shrugged and concentrated on the small Constable oil that was one of his favorites. "Just Charlene and me, unfortunately. We're the last of the Luries."

"But my aunt Carrie mentioned your sister. She even showed me pictures. I think her name is Emmaline, isn't it?"

"Emmaline is dead," he said, indicating that he wanted to drop the matter. But Belinda's curiosity was aroused and she could not let go.

"What was she like?" she asked.

"She was not unlike Charlene," he said. "She was a fool."

Belinda stared at him, but he would not add anything to that. "Let's visit Alexander," he said, changing the subject. "It should be his bathtime."

The young Lurie heir was splashing in the tub, much to the amusement of his nurse.

"All right, Lourdes," Belinda said. "I'll finish him."

"He's been in three minutes, Miss Belinda."

"Soft boiled," Claiborne said dryly.

For a baby barely a year old, Alexander had amazing

303

vitality. From his chocolate-brown eyes to his little pink feet he was all noise and action. He kicked and laughed and splashed with all the joy of a baby dolphin. Round and plump, with his brown curls and triangular smile, he grabbed for the soap, his mother, and his toy duck with equal gusto.

Claiborne watched his son with interest.

"Let's hope you turn out better than your sister," he thought, then, noticing the look Belinda gave him, he realized he had spoken out loud.

Belinda had finished drying Alexander with the striped Pratesi towel and was dusting talcum powder over him. Claiborne watched her take a plump foot, examining each toe, lost in her scrutiny. All at once a deep swelling of jealousy roiled within him.

Amazed with himself and well aware of how ridiculous it was to be jealous of his infant son, Claiborne suddenly remembered urgent messages that were waiting in his study and excused himself.

Once secluded there, he called his secretary with his guest list and, that matter disposed of, he took up a new book about South America and was soon lost in contemplation of Brazil's national debt.

"Why, darlin'," Valdene told Claiborne's secretary when she called with the invitation. "You just tell Mr. Lurie we'll be at the dock with bells on."

"Well, the tarmac actually, Mrs. Garland," the secretary said. She had an eastern accent and spoke in crisp, clear tones that implied she had no time for small talk. "Mr. Lurie's plane will pick you up at the Galveston Airport and the party will be flown down to Belém at the mouth of the Amazon. The *Lone Star* will be waiting for you there to begin the cruise."

"Well, of course I knew that, darlin'," Valdene assured her.

She hung up the phone with a light heart, already planning what she would pack. How she was moving up

304

in the world! Although she was a tad surprised that Belinda's husband would invite her and Buster, Valdene wasn't going to turn down the invitation. After all, Claiborne did own Heartland's record label. That was probably why he had invited her and Buster. No, sir. She expected she'd get an argument from Buster, but he'd come around.

She looked forward to flirting a bit with Claiborne Lurie. She'd like to get him in bed just to prove he was no better than any other man. And to show up that snobbish bitch Belinda.

The more she thought about it, the more Valdene looked forward to cruising aboard the *Lone Star.*

"How could you?" Rhonda said softly.

"I wanted you to hear it from me," Cordell said.

"Then why didn't you return my calls, Cordell?" She was starting to see that Cordell was full of lies. "It's not the kind of thing you can keep a secret very long."

"No, I guess not," Cordell said. She had managed to corner him in his suite, only hours after his return from Juárez. He was getting real uncomfortable with this conversation. He wanted to tell Rhonda that there was more involved, that his interest in Charlene was as much business as sexual, but he was not yet sure himself. All he knew was that he had some foggy idea that a reconciliation with Charlene might placate Buster a bit. The sight of his brother at the Mardi Gras had shaken Cordell, and he was willing to do anything to hold on to Buster's last shred of good will.

Desperate times called for desperate measures, and he had tossed over Rhonda like extra baggage on a sinking ship. Only Rhonda wasn't taking it too well.

He was in the middle of packing to move back into the house on Oak Park Circle. Charlene was waiting for him there to renew their wedded bliss.

"How could you go back to that tramp," Rhonda screamed. "Just because she's rich?"

"She's the mother of my child. Chandler needs me," he said.

"Oh, like she hasn't needed you for the last ten years? Don't tell me what it's like to grow up without a father. I know."

He moved closely to her and tried to embrace her, but she shrugged him off. He had never seen her so angry. Come to think of it, he'd never seen her angry at all.

"It's too late for that," she snapped. "I just wanted to tell you what I think of you."

"Now you've told me," he said coolly. He was getting a little bored. Passion like Rhonda's always made him uncomfortable.

Rhonda was starting to lose her hard-earned composure. She knew that she was outmatched by Cordell and there was no way she could make him suffer the same pain she felt. At least not here and not now.

There was a knock at the door. Cordell rushed to answer it, obviously glad for an interruption and an excuse to leave her. He came back into the room with a stout, elderly black woman. She looked startled to see Rhonda there, but quickly assumed an impassive expression.

"This is Miss Ruby," Cordell said, introducing the woman. "Miss Ruby's been with my wife's family since Pluto was a pup."

Rhonda shook the old woman's thick hand, which was surprisingly soft and nicely manicured. Ruby's eyes fell on Rhonda's bracelet.

"My, what lovely charms," she said softly. She had a gentle New Orleans accent.

"Thank you. It was my mother's."

"I'm sure Miss Ruby would love to discuss estate jewelry with you, but my wife sent Miss Ruby to help with the packing," Cordell said, grinning. "She's getting restless."

"Of course," Rhonda said, recognizing the dismissal. Why had she never noticed how patronizing Cordell was before? It was going to be easy to hate him, she could see

306

that now.

She left quickly, while Miss Ruby stared after her with dark, questioning eyes.

Charlene was looking at the house on Oak Park Circle with a whole new eye, the eye of a romantic new bride. She had been pleased at first that Cordell had kept the house exactly as she left it, but now she wanted to make some changes. The decor was ten years out of date and she had a lot of new ideas.

But first she would have to call her daddy and give him the news about her marriage.

And she'd have to find Chandler and tell her, too.

Lauren woke up to find the Arab snoring beside her. He ought to be sleeping, she thought bitterly. Whatever he was paying Aynsley, he was certainly getting his money's worth. He had taken her with gusto all night long and this morning her whole body ached.

She stumbled to the bathroom and splashed cold water on her face. She looked totally wasted. Maybe she could get her hair done downstairs before she left, but it was going to take more than a haircut to help. She pulled her eyes tight. Maybe an eye job. Aynsley should pay, too. It was the stress he was putting her through that was aging her so rapidly. And her contract was up in six months. The bastard.

She reached for the soap and saw the little silver foil package sitting on top of it. Inside it were four brown glass vials of cocaine. That was all she was getting for tolerating Adib all night! Maybe it wasn't Aynsley's fault, she told herself. Maybe the aide had skimmed off some for himself. At least she had enough to get her through the morning and back to Houston if she was careful. She still had a show to do that night.

She laid out two lines and had just hoovered the first one up when the bathroom door flew open. She had forgotten to lock it and Adib stood there leering at her and then at the snow.

For one minute she was afraid he was going to grab it for himself, but he only grinned.

"Finish up quickly, Snow White," he said.

She erased the cocaine, and was so relieved, grateful, and stoned that she let him take her right there, with her ass on the bathroom counter and her legs in the air as she stared at herself in the mirrored ceiling and tried to pretend this was all just a bad movie.

"Welcome home," Charlene said, greeting Cordell at the door the way she used to in the early days of their first marriage. She gave him a wifely peck on the cheek.

Cordell stared at her. Charlene was still a beautiful woman, although much thinner than he remembered. The youthful voluptuousness that had first attracted him had given way to the society slenderness. When they consummated their remarriage (or reconsummated their marriage), her body felt downright skeletal. He could not help thinking of Rhonda's soft curves and wondering how long it would take for her to cool off so they could resume their affair.

Poor Rhonda, he thought, in a rare flash of compassion. She was a girl born to be a mistress, not a wife.

Lost in thought, he barely listened as Charlene listed the plans she had for both of them. Renovating the house, buying a pied à terre in New York, a ranch in Santa Fe. He caught something about a cruise.

"A cruise?"

"Of course," she said peevishly. "Daddy's spring cruise. It's a family tradition. Oh, darling. It will be so much fun. Lots of fun people. You remember."

Cordell was experiencing a sinking feeling in his gut, as he was starting to remember just where his first marriage to Charlene had gone wrong.

Chapter Thirty-nine

Valdene and Buster argued about the cruise for days. Buster insisted that he would not ship out anywhere with a yellow dog like Claiborne Lurie.

"But Belinda and Cordell will both be there," Valdene insisted. Not that she was looking forward to spending time with her daughter-in-law, but she knew how much he cared about Belinda even if he was still angry because she had run off and married Claiborne Lurie.

"That's exactly my point, woman," Buster roared. "I don't know what Lurie did to get Belinda to marry him and I don't want to know. And as for my son and Charlene, I always said the boy was a fool and now he's gone and proved it!"

Valdene herself was a great believer in redemption and the healing power of money. And Claiborne had lots of that. Maybe, she told herself, she had just picked a bad time to bring up the cruise with Buster. After all, Cordell had just called with the news that he and Charlene were back together. Buster would need some time to digest that.

She had recently made over the Sand Castle's glass-walled conservatory into a private chapel, and she went there now to pray while Buster headed for his office downtown at the Pink Tower.

Episodes like this morning's had convinced Buster that

he had to do something about Valdene. He had made a mistake and he was man enough to admit it, embarrassing as it would be to get in front of a judge and tell him so. When his days seemed numbered, he wanted nothing more than to spend them with Valdene. But he had outlived his doctor's predictions, and these days he felt like he could live forever.

He did not want to spend forever with Valdene.

What really kept Buster from moving was the nagging regret that he had not insisted Valdene sign a premarital agreement before he leaped into this fiasco of a marriage. Texas was a community property state, and, much as he would like to be rid of the woman, he didn't want it to cost him a bundle.

So, he sat in his office at the Pink Tower and he chewed on the big black Macanuda cigar. He wondered what Buddy and Zenobia thought of Valdene. Now, Buddy was a man who could handle her, just as Buster himself could have when he was younger. And Zena was a piece of work, too. Nothing like two cats in a fight — he'd like to see that one.

As for Cordell, well, it was clear as a bell that Valdene had his younger son wrapped around her finger and she had driven his daughter Belinda out of town. Out of town and into the arms of that yellow dog. With a baby, no less!

The baby had actually improved Belinda, however. Made her more self-confident. She sure didn't seem to be suffering any, hiding out down there at Rancho Strega. Maybe Claiborne wasn't so bad after all, he thought, then quickly discarded such a radical idea.

Buster's thoughts were temporarily interrupted by the arrival of his younger son. His heir, he thought grimly, watching Cordell as he nervously strode into the room and took a seat on a worn leather chair.

"Well, what is it now?" Buster demanded. "You want a divorce already?"

Cordell touched his tie nervously. He could never tell when his father was joking.

"You don't understand, Dad," he said. "We did this for Chandler's sake."

That really got Buster's goat. He glared at his son. Cordell started to stroke his tie and a slight tic started up in his right eye.

"Do you take me for a fool, son?" Buster asked quietly.

"No, sir."

"Do you think your daddy's getting senile, is that what you think? Giving me that horseshit!"

"No, sir." The tic in Cordell's eye was getting worse.

"That Lurie girl's got your pecker in her pocketbook and she always has. Damn it, act like a man!"

"Yes, sir. But if you only got to know Charlene—"

"Spare me," Buster grumped. "I can't help wondering what her daddy thinks of this little romance."

"Charlene's calling him today to break the news."

Bored, Buster turned his attention back to his desk. "Now if you'll excuse me, I have a business to run. Somebody has to keep Garland, Inc., going."

"Yes, sir. About that—"

Buster glared. "What about what?"

"Well, sir, Charlene asked me to take some time off to come on her daddy's spring cruise. He'll be taking the *Lone Star* out on the Amazon in a few weeks and she wants me along. You know how she is, sir."

"I do indeed," Buster said thoughtfully, his Garland blue eyes raking his son the way he might stare at a once-promising well that had come up dry in spite of a pile of geologists' reports that promised oil.

"You know, son, I haven't been fair to you. Maybe I haven't been fair to the Luries, either. And just this morning they invited Valdene and me to come along on this little old cruise. How about that?"

Cordell managed to summon his voice back through sheer effort of will. "You'll be coming, too, then?" he croaked.

"Of course. You and me, hunting and fishing together. We'll have a good old time. Maybe we'll get ourselves some of that Inca gold."

311

"That's in the Andes, Dad."

"Whatever," Buster said cheerfully.

Father and son shook hands, and Buster watched Cordell as his son went back to business. He watched him intensely, his blue eyes glittering with deep and dangerous thoughts. Then he picked up the phone and punched up the number for the Sand Castle.

"Damn it," he exploded into the phone as soon as he heard Valdene's voice. "We'll go on the cruise."

Valdene squealed. "Oh, thank you, Buster." There was a pause. But I hope you'll watch that swearing of yours when we're on the *Lone Star*."

Buster didn't answer. He had already hung up.

Claiborne was in his study at Rancho Strega. He had just finished a call to Ciprianna in New York and was reviewing some very interesting photographs his little detective had given him when his secretary informed him Charlene was on the line.

"Where are you?" he demanded. "I've been trying to reach you."

"Oh, Daddy, I just got married," she gushed.

Claiborne didn't hear her, he was ratting on about her responsibilities to him and Chandler and the Lurie name. She just kept repeating her news until it finally sunk in.

"What?" He couldn't believe what he'd heard.

"I'm married, Daddy."

"Again?"

She giggled. "Yes. You remember what you used to say when I was learning to ride: if you get thrown, you've got to jump right back on that horse."

"A husband isn't a horse. They're more expensive, for one thing," he said. "I should think you'd have learned that by now."

That made her laugh even more. "Oh, don't worry, Daddy. This one has money of his own. In fact, you know him. I just married Cordell Garland."

"Cordell? But you already married him once."

312

"Oh, Daddy," Charlene sighed. "Of course we did. But we're older now, more mature. Cordell's really grown. I'm sure it will work out this time."

"And what about Chandler?" As usual, Claiborne's dynastic concerns were first in his mind.

"She's just tickled pink to have her daddy back."

After he hung up, Claiborne tried to look at the matter realistically. As poor a choice as Cordell Garland was, at least he was not Sven Petersen or Speed Porter. At least he was white, Christian, and one hundred percent Texan. And he had money of his own.

At dinner that night, Belinda tried to talk to Claiborne, but he was morose and distracted.

"You don't seem very excited," she said.

"Excuse me, darling, but I have other things on my mind," he said. "Charlene's gotten herself married again. Did you know about this?"

"Of course not! And I don't care about Charlene, I want to talk about my own plans," she said.

"Yes, of course."

Shortly before midnight, Charlene called again.

"Twice in one day," Claiborne said dryly when he took the phone. "I can see your new husband is having a good influence on you already."

She giggled again. Marriage had put her in a good mood. Besides, she was always giddy when she was in love and she was back in love with Cordell.

"I was just thinking, daddy, about this cruise. Of course Cordell is thrilled to be coming, but I wanted to invite another couple, too. That is, if it's all right with you."

"Another couple?" he repeated.

"Maybe you've heard about Brice de Young, this hot new chef from Houston. He lives with Cordell's niece. He was just written up in *The Wall Street Journal*."

313

Charlene knew that would do the trick. Her father loved publicity just as much as she did.

"I see," he said, slowly, as if he were making a decision. But Charlene knew he would bite.

"Of course," he said at last. "By all means. I'll have my secretary call them in the morning."

Claiborne Lurie's secretary reached Brice at the Maison Rouge where he and Tammy Lynn had lingered for a few days. They were just stepping into the limo that would take them back to Houston when the call came. Brice took it in the lobby.

"Of course I'll join Mr. and Mrs. Lurie," he said evenly. The secretary asked if Miss Garland would also be coming. No, he assured her, he would be traveling alone.

There was no point in even mentioning the invitation to Tammy Lynn, Brice decided. She'd only want to come along.

Chapter Forty

There were days when Rhonda thought she would die, the ache in her heart was so bad. Her face was red and swollen from crying and she could barely bring herself to swallow anything but black coffee. She sat for days in bed wrapped in the same robe, her dyed blond hair unwashed and uncombed, staring at the television.

This went on for a week, but she soon realized that self-pity was a luxury she could not afford. She would have to go back to work soon. But doing what? She had gone from being a not very successful beauty contestant and nude model to a rich man's mistress. She knew how to keep a neurotic man happy, but that was not exactly something she could put on a job application. Besides, she thought bitterly, Cordell would never give her a reference.

There were stages to grief, and she had moved through denial and was ready for anger.

She told herself she had every right to be angry at Cordell. He had led her on all during their affair. First, he gave her a fake name, lying to her all along about everything, and when she found him in one lie he just invented another. Now he'd left her penniless.

Cordell Garland was a snake. And she wanted to pay him back real good.

She thought about shooting him. She didn't carry a gun, but in Texas it would not be hard to get her hands on one. Then she discarded the idea of shooting him because he wouldn't suffer enough.

She thought about bombing his fancy house on Oak Park Circle, but she was afraid of hurting other people along with Cordell. That was the reason she gave herself for not bombing his car or his hotel or that big building downtown he was so proud of.

She wanted him to suffer the pain and humiliation she had. High-hatting her like she was white trash!

Then it hit her, one day when she was watching palimony lawyers on *Donahue*. Suddenly it was as if new life flowed through her veins, and she pulled herself out of bed and rushed to the shower. She wanted to fix herself up for the first time in days. She wanted to look like a million dollars when she went downtown.

She was going to sue Cordell and she knew just the lawyer she wanted to help her. A nice fat palimony suit. Even if she lost the case, she'd have the satisfaction of humiliating him and dragging his precious name through the dirt. How nice!

First, though, she might stop for a rare and juicy steak. Suddenly, she was hungry for red meat.

Lauren was spending so much time with Adib Jamil since meeting him in Galveston that there were days when she did not arrive at the studio until minutes before airtime. The producer was angry and the rest of the crew glared at her, but there was nothing they could do. Everyone knew about her and Aynsley. And if anyone forgot, a few hints could remind them. He still owned the station, and if Aynsley didn't mind her seeing Adib, there was nothing they could do.

Besides, in the euphoria of Adbi's unlimited supply of cocaine, she felt invulnerable. She didn't need this lousy job or Aynsley Adder. She had Adib Jamil, the international fixer, waiting in her dressing room with all the snow a girl could ever need.

After the show, her producer grabbed her for a meeting. He was still put out because he had given her three days off to attend the Mardi Gras and she hadn't come back with one story. Everyone was talking about the elopement of Charlene Lurie and Cordell Garland, but she had barely noticed them together. And as for the other celebrities like Jacques Cartier and Sven Petersen, she had barely noticed them, either. She vaguely remembered meeting Sven, a boring blond lunkhead with clammy hands.

"So make a federal case out of it," she said blithely as she went off to join Adib.

"He's like my brother," Chandler said.

"I don't want him at my table," Cordell said.

"O, come now, you two. Can't we have breakfast in peace?" Charlene protested.

"I can't have breakfast in peace when I have to watch that filthy animal eat," Cordell snapped.

"Mr. T. isn't filthy. He's probably cleaner than you."

"He's only a ferret," Charlene said calmly. A new inner peace had descended on her since her marriage. She was, she told herself, someone who needed to be married. It was even easier to have affairs when one was married.

Her mind wandered back to plans for her cruise wardrobe. She wondered if Brice de Young was a breast man or a leg man. Fortunately, she considered her breasts and legs equally perfect.

"Look, if you have to eat with that animal, the two of you can have breakfast upstairs," Cordell was saying.

"That's just fine with me." Chandler grabbed the ferret and headed dramatically for the door. She paused in the doorway to shout into the kitchen at the cook. "Maria, Mr. T. and I will take breakfast in our room."

Charlene excused herself, too. She wanted to do the tongue trick before she went shopping.

That left Cordell alone at the breakfast table with his coffee and nostalgia for his bachelor life.

In spite of his southern airs and urbane manner, Claiborne Lurie was just another Texas trader after all. This thought hit Belinda all of a sudden and she understood that she would have to go along on his Amazon cruise if she wanted Claiborne to back her in a project in Galveston. Now that she was sure she was closed out of Garland, Inc., for good, it was more important than ever to get something going on her own.

She immersed herself in plans for the cruise. Claiborne was obsessive about details and seemed surprised and then pleased that she could cope with all that had to be done.

And that was quite a bit. Besides Captain Bellew, who hailed from Liverpool, *Lone Star*'s huge crew included an Alsatian chef, two hostesses from Limerick, an American second mate named Cleveland, and thirteen Korean seamen. They would all take their meals aboard ship, too, and food and supplies had to be taken on for them. It was a little like running a small hotel, Belinda discovered, and she knew she did that well. It was a nice feeling.

The *Lone Star* itself had already been overhauled for the trip and was being transported down to Belém, at the mouth of the Amazon in Brazil, where the cruise would begin. Claiborne had also hired Ramon Rivera y Longa, a young journalist, to act as a kind of guide and liaison with the local authorities. Recommended because he was fluent in English, Spanish, and Portuguese, he was the American-born son of an aristocratic Colombian family and was supposed to have great contacts in Peru and Brazil.

It seemed to Buster that these days the only time he had any kind of peace was when he was lying with Mozelle Bryant in her bedroom. She was a good old gal, even if she was rich. He had missed her while she was in Paris at the collections, and he arrived at her place twenty minutes early for their appointment. But she must

318

have been missing him, too, he noticed, for she was ready and waiting when the maid led him in. She was wearing that nice flowery perfume he liked and she wanted to show him some of the clothes she had bought.

"Do you have to go all that way for a dress?" he grumped.

"You do if you want to be missed," Mozelle answered, toying with his blue silk pocket handkerchief.

"Well, I missed you all right," he said, taking her in his arms. But before his lips could meet hers, he pulled back, his face a red mask of pain and sat down on the bed.

"What's the matter, honey?" Mozelle's voice was full of concern as her hands worked to loosen the neck of his shirt.

Buster was breathing deep, as if to catch his breath. In between gasps he kept insisting that nothing was wrong.

"Don't give me that!" Her concern gave way to outrage. How dare he try to tell her there was nothing wrong? "I'll have my maid call an ambulance. Hattie!"

"Now just stop that right there," Buster said, his voice gathering strength.

Mozelle could see there was no arguing with him. "Never mind, Hattie," she called out. "False alarm." She turned back to Buster. "Now suppose you tell me what's going on?"

He shrugged. Now that his strength was back, Buster was embarrassed to have shown weakness, especially in front of a woman he had known so long.

"Come on, Buster. Just how sick are you?"

Buster stared out the window at Mozelle's garden. "I've been running on bad tires for more than a year. I could kick off any day, just like that." He snapped his thick fingers.

Mozelle winced. "Is it your heart?"

He nodded.

She sat beside him on the bed and took his great paw in her soft white hand. "Oh, Buster darlin', I'm so sorry. How long have you known?"

"Doctor told me two years ago I had a year to live." He sniffed. "He as wrong about that. I been hoping he was wrong about everything."

"But what about a transplant? Have you seen other doctors? They do so much these days!"

Buster shook his head. "That stuff's for kids. I'm an old man, Mozelle. I don't want to let them start cutting me up. If I'm goin' to die I'm goin' in one piece."

"Does Valdene know?" she asked.

"No. Not my kids, either. Only Myles McLean. And now you. I suppose I'll have to tell Buddy soon. Might get him to make a decision."

"A decision?"

"I want that boy back here where he belongs, Mozelle. Back in Galveston! Running Garland, Inc., the way it should be run!"

"Easy, easy, honey," she coaxed, stroking his arm gently. "I don't want you getting excited. Now tell me exactly what's going on."

Feeling quite a bit better next morning, Buster was delighted to hear from Buddy and his son's news was good. Buddy wanted to come down to look over the business close up.

"That will be just fine, son," Buster boomed. "You and Zena come down and get your feet wet."

"What about Cordell? Have you talked to him?" Buddy did not relish the inevitable showdown with his brother, and he thought it was something Buster ought to be dealing with.

"Have no fear," Buster said cheerfully. "Cordell will be off sailing with the Luries. Honeymooning, I guess you'd call it. The coast is clear. Even Valdene's going along. Yours truly will be all alone in the big house. I'll be glad for the company."

It all sounded too easy, and Buddy sensed his father's manipulations in this, but he decided to go along. Each brief visit to Galveston had whetted his appetite. He was ready to take control of Garland, Inc.

His brother be damned.

Chapter Forty-one

Colette de Young flew to Houston as soon as she saw photographs of her son at the Galveston Mardi Gras. She was profoundly disturbed about the aura around Brice and his companion. Bad vibes all around. Besides, it would give her a chance to see Bernardo O'Higgins. They had not been together since the case ended and he was a dear man with a great aura. It was possible they had been lovers in a past life. She called Bernardo as soon as she checked into the Four Seasons, left a message for him, and then called her son.

Brice was not delighted to hear from her and tried to discourage her from coming around the restaurant, but she showed up one night with Kukla and Jan. The backroom of the old Funland snackbar had gradually grown into an exclusive dinner spot.

"We found them outside. Your mother was arguing with the maître d'," they explained. "He was trying to tell her she had to make a reservation months in advance. I don't think he understands that she's your mother."

"Chéri!" Colette shouted, throwing up her arms, which were draped on many layers of rainbow-colored chiffon so that she looked a little like a butterfly. She engulfed Brice in her multi-colored wings.

"Maman," he whispered. "What are you doing here?"

"Chéri!" What am I doing here?" she gazed around the restaurant. By now everyone had abandoned their

entrees and all eyes were focused on this encounter between mother and son. "What am I doing here? Your mother? What kind of question is that from a son to a mother? A mother who brings her good friends . . . Have you met Bernardo?" The two men nodded to acknowledge each other, while Colette raved on. "A proud mother who wanted to show off her son to a friend . . ."

"I just wish you'd called first, *maman*," he said.

"I did not have the time," she sniffed.

Tammy Lynn had left the security of her office to find out what the fuss was about. Now she was standing on the outskirts of the group, watching Brice's mother with interest. Suddenly Colette caught her staring.

"And who are you?" she demanded.

"I happen to be the owner of this restaurant," Tammy Lynn said.

Puzzled, Colette looked back at her son for an explanation.

"Tammy Lynn means she's my partner. Have you two met? Tammy Lynn Garland, of the Galveston Garlands," he said with emphasis. "Meet my mother, Madame de Young."

Colette was all grace again as she extended her hand. "Please, you must call me Colette. And have you met Mr. O'Higgins?"

There was much exclaiming back and forth as the introductions extended to include Jan and Kukla and, meanwhile, at Tammy Lynn's signal, two busboys had moved in another table and set it for Colette's group.

Now Colette was even more distracted, however, for she recognized Tammy Lynn from the Galveston pictures and still felt a bad aura between the girl and her son. How could two such mismatched people be business partners? And was there something more? Yet, even Colette was impressed by the fact that Tammy Lynn was a Garland and so she tried to overlook the bad feeling she was getting. Bernardo was calling for Cristal champagne for the table.

"You should have told me that you were going back to Galveston," she reminded Brice. "We could have returned together. Mother and son celebrities. I'm sure they had nothing like that."

"What brings you to Houston, Madame de Young?" Tammy Lynn asked.

"Please, darling. Call me Colette," she insisted. "And as you know, I'm a psychic. I've had some disturbing dreams lately and I felt I had to come. I thought something might be wrong with Brice."

They all looked to Brice, waiting for his response, but he was so angry he could barely speak. She was still using him, he steamed. Using him now as an excuse to get down to Houston so she could see O'Higgins, who was gazing at her with open admiration, as if she was a brilliant combination of Kim Bassinger and Bette Midler. Then he brightened. Maybe Colette's arrival was a godsend. She claimed she wanted to rescue him. Maybe she could rescue him from Tammy Lynn.

In the first flush of her joy at recapturing Cordell, Charlene Lurie Garland spent the morning in bed, telephoning her agent and manager to officially inform them that she was out of the business. She even managed to reach Speed Porter, who was cutting his film in New York.

"If you're looking for your daughter, I haven't seen her," he roared into the phone when he finally picked up.

"Oh, Speed, that's ancient history," Charlene purred. "Chandler tells me that you two were only friends."

"Goddamn right," he said. "The kid was lonely and needed a friend. I was just giving her a shoulder to cry on, I swear."

"And I believe you, darling," she said. "That's why I wanted you to be the first to know. Cordell and I are back together!"

He started laughing. "First? You mean the first million, don't you? It's all over the *National Standard!*"

Charlene was losing her patience. She had expected to surprise Speed and instead he was treating her marriage as some kind of trivial column item.

"Is the honeymoon over yet?"

"Why do you ask?"

"I'm up here in New York. I thought maybe you could come up and play with me. How about it?"

"You really are a sleaze, Speed," she said and slammed down the phone angrily. For a few minutes all she could think about was the sight of Speed in his pool, his rippling muscles. She really had to force herself to remember the steroids.

But the problem wasn't Speed or any of her other beaux. It wasn't even giving up her career. Now that she was back in the house on Oak Park Circle and safely married to Cordell, she was wondering why she had done it.

What in the world did she have to look forward to?

Belinda had to order new clothes for Claiborne's cruise and silently thanked whoever had invented the designer videos that saved busy women the trouble of flying to the Paris and New York collections. Too bad L.L. Bean didn't do the same. She ended with her cruise wardrobe evenly divided between Bean for day and some Ungaro caftans and party pajamas for night.

Charlene was rediscovering all the reasons why her first marriage to Cordell Garland had not worked out. And here she had given up a promising career as an actress to give Cordell another chance and to give her daughter a father. The fact that her promising career had consisted of a walk-on in the late-night television series *Heritage* hardly mattered.

What mattered was that Charlene had only been married a few weeks and she was already restless.

At least there would be two single men on the cruise: a young journalist her father had invited, and, of course, Brice de Young. She had included Tammy Lynn in her original invitation, but she was quite pleased that he would be coming alone. Too pleased to ask any questions.

Colette and her lover Bernardo O'Higgins looked forward to the cruise on the much-publicized Lurie yacht. She was thinking she had done quite well for a former sideshow fortune-teller.

"Have you told your son?" Bernie asked one afternoon as they were enjoying a cocktail at the cozy bar of La Colombe d'Or in Houston.

"No, *chéri*. I think it will be amusing to surprise him."

Charlene needed a lot of attention. Cordell had forgotten that as her husband he had to be on call twenty-four hours a day. She called him everywhere: at his office in the Garland Tower, at the Artillery Club, the Pelican Club, the gym. She didn't seem to understand that he had a job to do.

"I only wanted to be sure you knew we're leaving tomorrow at dawn," she said.

"Yes," he said patiently. "And we'll be on the river for two weeks. Unless we kill each other before that."

Charlene was pouting when she put down the phone. She thought of men like Sven and Speed. Whatever their faults, they were always there for her, but Cordell always put his work first.

She consoled herself by thinking about Brice de Young. His presence aboard ought to make the cruise a little more interesting.

Chapter Forty-two

Looking back on it later, Belinda would admit that she began to suspect the cruise might be sailing into problems when Claiborne's Boeing 727 set down in Houston to pick up Bernardo O'Higgins and Joel Varney. O'Higgins was a short, immaculately dressed man with the air of a pit bull. His traveling companion was a well-preserved beauty of a certain age, with fluffy red hair and a sensational figure who went by only one name, Colette. He explained she was a professional psychic whose second sight had recently helped him win a murder case. Belinda was tempted to ask Colette what she saw for the future of the cruise, but decided she didn't want to know. As for Jennifer Varney, the third Mrs. Varney in five years, she was very attractive, but nervous and self-conscious as if all too aware of her short husband's short attention span.

The Lurie plane next made a short hop to Galveston, where Valdene Garland boarded with Reba Twining. She announced that Buster had just that very morning informed her that he could not come with her on the cruise after all. He was tied up with pressing business matters. She had brought Reba along instead, and she hoped that Claiborne didn't mind.

Claiborne? Belinda thought. Maybe he didn't mind, but she did. She was furious that Buster had not even bothered to call her himself. And how dare Valdene just drag along Reba Twining without even asking?

Claiborne would have wanted someone a little more interesting than drab little Reba.

She looked over at him but he seemed much more put out that Charlene and Cordell had still not arrived. They ended up waiting an hour before the newlyweds pulled up with their luggage.

From there it was on to Brazil. They would pick up the Rivers and some guest of Charlene's in Manaus.

At the dock in Belém, Captain Bellew greeted them, looking very British Empire in a crisp white uniform and gold braid that gleamed in the Brazilian sun. A darkly handsome young man in a yellow polo shirt and slacks stepped forward and introduced himself as Ramon Rivera y Longa.

Well, thought Belinda, he'd certainly add to the scenery. She glanced at Charlene who had obviously formed the same opinion. Belinda hoped Ramon had a lock on his cabin door. She had best look into it.

Captain Bellew took them on a tour, proudly demonstrating that everything aboard was shipshape. It was the first time that Belinda had been aboard the *Lone Star* since that night more than a year ago when she and Claiborne had first made love, and very little had changed. Claiborne's black-and-gold stateroom looked slightly different, but she had only seen it in a dim light before and so did not realize that the difference was that the huge portrait of Ciprianna that had once hung over his bed had been replaced by a large Degas oil painting of ballerinas. One of the maids was already unpacking their luggage, and she smiled as they entered.

Yes, everything was quite shipshape.

In the week that followed, as they sailed downriver to Manaus, Charlene and Jennifer Varney discovered a mutual taste for deep-dish gossip. Joel Varney spent most of his time secluded in Claiborne's office, on the satellite telephone or at the fax. Bernardo O'Higgins and Colette de Young practiced their Spanish and Portuguese by chatting with Ramon. Valdene flirted openly with Cordell while Reba wandered up to the helicopter pad to brood.

Belinda was pleased with the way they were getting along so far and she spent her mornings sunbathing in the solarium or watching the rain forest as the *Lone Star* made its way to Manaus.

Once they were on the river, Belinda saw Claiborne, the perfectionist, go into action. Even Reba Twining's Diet Coke required fifteen minutes of preparation with a silver tray, linen napkin, and crystal swizzle stick.

Then there were the crew uniforms. The British Royal Navy whites were only for the daytime; at dinner, the staff all donned immaculate Nehru jackets and white gloves.

Sometimes, if the rains were especially heavy, they took dinner in the sumptuous dining room at the elaborate gilded brass-and-marble table, beneath a huge Gainsborough. Mostly, they preferred to dine in the glass-domed solarium under the stars.

The *Lone Star* was a floating palace, Belinda told herself. Her husband's guests were getting along and maybe, just maybe, everything would work out after all.

"Cretinos!" the tall, soignée Ciprianna Rivers shouted, following up that volley with a torrent of gutter Spanish that had everyone in the airport staring. It was seldom they saw a woman who looked quite so classy explode so obscenely, at least not in Cartagena.

Ciprianna's own porter said nothing as he pushed the cart piled high with twenty pieces of Gucci luggage, all of it bearing the gilt initials of Ciprianna Vilar Rivers. Carl Rivers, carrying his own travel wardrobe in a nondescript shoulder bag, trotted along beside them, trying to keep up with his leggy wife's brisk steps. Their twin Shih Tzus were close on his heels, barking loudly.

It had not been a good flight. They had been thrown off their Delta jet in Atlanta when Ciprianna refused to keep the little dogs in their travel kennels, and had to rebook on an ancient Colombian Airways DC-12 just to get to Cartagena.

"I'm sorry darling. It won't happen again," Carl assured her. Somewhere during their fifteen-year relationship, the power had shifted so that he, once the terror of Wall Street, was helplessly in thrall to this woman. He was her slave. He dreaded these rages of hers and would do anything to avoid them. Too late now! He could only hope she would calm down by the time they reached Manaus. But of course Claiborne Lurie would be there and Ciprianna was always on her good behavior around him.

All this high drama had wearied Carl, and by now Ciprianna was several feet ahead of him and the porter and the luggage cart. Fortunately, a limousine was waiting to take them to Lurie's helicopter. Once they were aboard the helicopter, he was sure everything would be all right.

Ciprianna immediately disappeared with the dogs behind the black-tinted windows of the air-conditioned car, leaving Carl to deal with the porter and see that all twenty pieces of luggage were safely loaded in the trunk. By the time he joined her, she had a new list of complaints which she enumerated for him while he listened in silence. The car was already filled with smoke, and he struggled not to cough. He did not smoke, but Ciprianna refused to give it up.

Carl Rivers was perfectly aware that he and Ciprianna were considered an odd couple. He suspected that Claiborne Lurie was one of the few men who understood his dilemma. Ciprianna was a slut, she was common, but she was irresistible. She had them both by the balls.

"Well?" Ciprianna demanded when she realized the limo had not budged. "Get moving. There's a helicopter waiting for us!"

"Sí, señora," the chauffeur said. "But there is one more passenger."

"Well, if he isn't here, too bad. We can't keep Señor Lurie waiting." Ciprianna meant, of course, that she must not be kept waiting, but both Carl and the chauffeur understood that.

Fortunately, at that moment, someone knocked on the driver's window and the man jumped out to put the newcomer's bags in the trunk. In another minute, a young man was joining Carl and Ciprianna in the smoky rear of the car.

"Hello there," he said. "Room in here for me?"

Ciprianna's large dark eyes widened, and her full-red lips parted in a genuine smile, all the more dazzling because it was so seldom exposed. Carl launched into a hacking cough. She ignored him.

Brice de Young, who was used to his effect on women, especially restless middle-aged ones, did not concern himself with Carl Rivers's cough, either. Soon he and Ciprianna were trading edited versions of the life stories that had brought them to this cruise.

"I wonder if you would mind not smoking when we're in the air," Brice said when they reached the helicopter. "I've got to coddle the old taste buds."

"Not at all, darling," Ciprianna said, giving him the two-hundred watt smile again as she tossed her lit cigarette onto the tarmac. They boarded. The dogs barked. The little caravan moved on.

330

Chapter Forty-three

It took the Lurie yacht seven days to sail from Belém to Manaus, stopping at Obidos, Parentins and Itacotiara along the way. At each stop the *Lone Star* took on exotic flowers and strange-looking fruits that later turned up in baskets in every guest cabin.

It was a trip of contrasts: lunching on the solarium deck on microwaved chili and frozen key lime pie, gliding by thatched hut villages while Ramon Rivera related chilling stories about the catfish fond of human flesh and insects that laid eggs in human eyes, and men who turned into jaguars during the full moon.

On the morning of the seventh day they docked at Manaus, where a man standing by the gangplank tried to sell Claiborne a baby ocelot for a thousand dollars. In the background, armed guards patroled the waterfront.

Their attention was diverted to the sky, however, by the noisy arrival of the Lurie helicopter as it landed on the *Lone Star*'s helipad.

"Oh, my God," Jennifer Varney gasped. "It's the terrorists!"

"Don't worry, dear," Claiborne assured her. "Just Mr. and Mrs. Rivers and my daughter's guest."

Ciprianna was the first to emerge from the helicopter. When she saw Claiborne Lurie, her face softened and she rushed to kiss him and launch into yet another

331

account of her humiliation at the hands of Delta Airlines.

"They screamed at me like I was some kind of criminal, darling!" she said. "You cannot imagine!"

All the while her little Shih Tzus barked at Ciprianna's heels in a supportive chorus.

Claiborne was all solicitude as he tried to calm her. He assured her everything would be better after lunch. They were all going into town to the Tropical Hotel and she would feel much better after she had freshened up and joined them there.

By this time Carl Rivers had emerged from the helicopter, followed by Brice de Young.

Belinda stared at him as they came down from the helipad to the main deck. Charlene rushed to hug him. Cordell followed awkwardly.

Belinda could not believe it. Why hadn't Claiborne told her that Brice was coming? Was this one of his games? Where was Tammy Lynn?

Suddenly Brice was approaching her, arms outstretched as if they were all friends.

"Miss Belinda! What a pleasant surprise!" He hugged her warmly, knowing perfectly well she couldn't resist without causing a scene.

He let her go, but was still smiling that enigmatic smile. His diamond earring glittered in the sun. She stepped away before he could get her again.

She needn't have worried. At that moment, Colette the psychic rushed forward shouting *Sonny* and wrapping Brice in her gauzy arms. He looked surprised and slightly embarrassed.

Belinda stared. It took a few seconds to make the connection, and by that time Charlene was very properly presenting her guest to the others. The fact that he was Colette's son was news to her, too, but she and everyone else was laughing about it and Bernie O'Higgins said it was one of those funny coincidences that made life interesting.

332

This little discovery had shifted attention away from Ciprianna, who was glaring at Belinda, as if blaming her because she was being ignored, then stamped off, followed by Carl and the dogs. Everyone else followed Claiborne into town.

Manaus was a rubber boom town built at the turn of the century by Brazilian rubber barons. The Municipal Market was a copy of Les Halles in Paris, and the town's most famous landmark, the Teatro Amazonas, was a four-story opera house with a huge dome covered in Alsatian tiles. The rise of Asian rubber plantations had left Manaus a ghost town, but it had recently been rediscovered by adventurous yachtsmen like Claiborne Lurie. The Brazilian government wanted to encourage him to invest in local industry as well.

Claiborne led them into the white courtyard of the Tropical Hotel where a lunchtime buffet was waiting for them by the circular pool. Charlene and Belinda were the first to hit the water.

After helping themselves to the Brazilian buffet, Claiborne and Joel Varney sat at a table, eyeing the women in string bikinis frolicking in the pool.

"Nice stuff," Varney remarked. "Too bad we brought our wives."

"That is my wife," Lurie said dryly. But then he remembered Ciprianna, back on the yacht, and he wondered if he had perhaps taken too much of a good thing by bringing her along.

Soon Ciprianna arrived and joined the two men. Watching the designer laughing loudly with Claiborne, Belinda could not help wondering what her husband saw in her. In spite of her grand airs, Ciprianna was really just a slut who made good, who cursed at her maids and her husband, even in public. It was as if suave, urbane, courtly Claiborne liked being around a woman who was his opposite. Yet Claiborne insisted

333

that his affair with her was long over. Belinda wondered.

When they returned to the *Lone Star,* they saw that another huge yacht had arrived in port. It turned out to be the *Half Note,* and it belonged to Sir Rodney Richards, the British record producer. He was just beside himself to be meeting genuine Texas millionaires and he insisted that the *Lone Star* party come aboard the *Half Note* for dinner that night.

Belinda was a little surprised that Claiborne accepted Sir Rodney's invitation. She had heard that the *Half Note* was a floating orgy and that wasn't Claiborne's thing at all.

She was looking forward to the outing, however, when Claiborne found her dressing in her stateroom. He looked at her with approval, the way he might gaze on the *Lone Star* or a Renoir he owned.

She smiled when she caught his eye in the mirror.

Tall, ramrod straight, with his steel-gray hair and steel-gray eyes, Claiborne radiated strength and force, and Belinda was sure other women envied her. She had seen the way the rich Brazilian women at the Tropical Hotel flirted with him. If only Claiborne wasn't so frankly cynical about their relationship. True, she hadn't married him out of any great passion, but she did wish at times that he would let her pretend.

The thought made her restless as she changed into a white silk shift to wear to Sir Rodney's. She asked him to help her with her necklace, a thick braid of colored beads, amethyst, aquamarine, golden topaz, and green malachite.

"You look lovely," he said as he stepped back to admire her, then reached into his jacket to hand her an envelope.

"What's this?" she said.

He only smiled. "Why don't you open it and see?"

But she had already opened it. Inside was a legal-looking certificate. She pulled it out and began to read it, then looked up at him. Her expression surprised him. She did not look pleased.

"This is a deed for the Delancy Street warehouse," she said.

"I know that. It's now yours. Free and clear."

"I don't understand, Claiborne. Do you mean that you've been holding on to it all this time? You're American Holding Company?"

"Among other things. I thought at the time that I might want to develop it myself and naturally I snatched it up. I've been pleased with your performance and I'm rewarding you."

"Pleased with my performance?" she repeated. "You're rewarding me? Like I'm some good little go-fer?"

"Please, Belinda, our guests will hear you."

"Is that all you care about? What about me, Claiborne? All this time you've been deceiving me. You knew how much I wanted that building!"

"Of course. But this was a matter of business. And, frankly, Belinda, you're a bright girl, but you simply don't have the ability or seasoning to put together a major project like the Delancy Street warehouse. You're still going to need my help and my backing."

Of course she was, Belinda thought bitterly. In spite of all the properties she'd looked at, none excited her the way the Delancy Street warehouse did, and now it was hers, free and clear. Perhaps Claiborne was right, she ought to be grateful. But all she was right now was furious. Slowly, as he stood watching her, she managed to control her rage and get a grip on her voice so that when she spoke there was almost no trace of anger.

"You're absolutely right, Claiborne," she said sweetly. "I'll never get the Delancy Street project off the ground without your help." And that, she reflected, was the most important thing in the world to her right now.

By the time they walked across the Manaus dock to board the *Half Note* she was actually able to manage civil conversation with her husband, but she was glad to be seated far away from him during dinner.

Tables had been set up in the ship's Grand Salon so that the two parties could mix, and Belinda found herself seated between an English rock star and a New York concert promoter. Dinner conversation was lively, but she began to suspect that many of the guests were speaking in code, with many references to Cartagena and Bogotá. Soon she realized that most of them were doing cocaine.

What am I doing here? she asked herself as she picked at the entree, a filet of beef with caviar. I don't belong here, surrounded by junkies. Even Claiborne. He wouldn't touch cocaine, but he was a power junkie, which was almost as bad.

She wanted to be anywhere else. She wanted to be back at the ranch with her son. Or in Galveston, standing on her own two feet. She wondered what Myles McLean was doing tonight. She wondered if she could ever forgive Claiborne for snatching up the Delancy Street warehouse, then handing it to her like it was a reward for being a good little girl.

She looked around the room. Everyone else was having a good time. And Ciprianna had managed to get herself seated next to Claiborne. Belinda watched the two of them together and wondered again whether her husband had really given Ciprianna up as he claimed. Brice de Young kept trying to catch her eye, but she managed to avoid him. It was funny, really, because Charlene kept trying to get his attention, and he was watching her while she watched Claiborne.

She remembered the night of Ciprianna's gala at the Maison Rouge more than a year ago. How upset Claiborne was! That was when he'd first started showing an interest in her. Had he married her on the rebound from Ciprianna, and did he regret it? Or had he never loved her at all? Suppose he married her just to hurt Ciprianna? The thought gave her shivers.

336

"The air bothering you, bubbala?" the concert promoter asked. "Can't be the air-conditioning. Sir Rodney's English. Doesn't believe in it!"

Belinda shook her head and tried to make small talk, but she was barely listening as he rattled on about his artists. If her husband was still sleeping with his ex-mistress, who was she to complain? Their marriage had been a matter of convenience for both of them.

But did he have to sleep with such a slut? And why did he have to humiliate her in public like this?

There was a streak of cruelty in Claiborne that she had never acknowledged before, and she was not going to let him use it on her. But what to do about it?

After a theatrical dessert of flaming banana crepes, they bid good night to Sir Rodney and his friends and made their way back to the *Lone Star*. Claiborne invited his guests for a nightcap in the small green salon. Most of them begged off, pleading exhaustion, so that only Colette, Bernie O'Higgins, and Brice joined them.

None of them had ever been to Rancho Strega, so Claiborne put on a video of the ranch he had recently commissioned. It began with a close-up of Alexander, then the camera eye followed him as he crawled up the porch of the hacienda.

At the sight of her son, Belinda felt a sudden pang and gasped. Then she realized it wasn't she who had gasped but Colette, who was on the banquette beside her.

"Are you all right?" she asked with concern.

Colette nodded, but she had turned quite pale.

"You look like you've seen a ghost," Belinda said, half joking. "Don't tell me you've seen my son's future."

Colette did not even smile. She just stared at Belinda with an unsettling, even gaze. "Your son is very handsome," she said as she struggled to stand up. "I think I

337

want to turn in now, thank you."

Bernie O'Higgins was on his feet at once. She waved him aside. "That's not necessary, *chéri,*" she said. "My son will show me to my cabin."

Puzzled, Brice rose to his feet and followed his mother out the door.

Brice was worried about Colette as he walked her to her cabin, although he noticed that her steps picked up as soon as they left the others behind in the green salon. By the time they reached the cabin she was sharing with Bernie O'Higgins, he was convinced Colette was over whatever it was that had been bothering her.

Au contraire. He soon learned otherwise.

"Come in and close the door, *chéri,*" his mother said without turning around. He followed her into the small sitting room. She turned to face him. Her green eyes were flashing and for the first time Brice realized his mother wasn't sick at all, she was just very angry.

"What is going on here?" she demanded. "I want to know."

He looked at her blankly. "I'm a guest, Mother, just like you."

Colette sniffed. In her rich Creole language of sniffs and shrugs, this sniff translated as pure disgust.

"I would like to know what is going on between you and Mrs. Lurie."

"Belinda? She hates my guts. It was Lurie's daughter who invited me."

"Don't give that to me, my son. Not after I've seen that child. He is the image of you at that age. The eyes, the smile, the way he moves. I should know my grandson when I see him! Now tell me what is going on."

A small suspicion was forming in Brice de Young's mind, fed by the niggling fear that his mother just

338

might have some kind of sixth sense. Could she possibly be on to something now. Maybe that explained why Belinda was always avoiding him.

"Well?" she said. "I'm still waiting for an answer."

"*Maman,* I would be happy to give you one. As soon as I have it myself." He kissed her on her powdery cheek. She smelled of patchouli.

"Just remember, Brice. Lurie is a Texan. If he finds out you are putting the horns on him, you could find yourself without your private parts."

He laughed. "Delicately put, *maman.* But I am not afraid of Lurie." No, he told himself as he left her and went on to his own cabin alone. He was far more afraid of Belinda Garland.

Chapter Forty-four

Buster was feeling very proud of himself. He had feinted both Valdene and Cordell and now they were happily sailing up the Amazon and out of his hair. It was too bad about Belinda, he was sorry to disappoint her, but that could not be helped.

His favorite son was back in the fold and he wanted them to work together, just like in the old days.

Rhonda Perillo was feeling proud of herself, too. She had pulled herself together, her hair was back to its natural red color. The blue contact lenses were gone, too, but her eyes were still red-rimmed from crying. It had taken all her courage to make her way to Myles McLean's downtown office, and now that she was alone with him she poured out the story of her long and unusual relationship with Cordell Garland.

Myles McLean said nothing, but he listened intently and, she hoped, sympathetically. He had a kind face and that helped her go on.

But when it was over, his face was impassive and his attitude noncommittal.

"That's quite a story, Miss Perillo. If you don't mind, I'd like to look into this a bit before I decide whether you even have a case." That was all he said, besides making an appointment with her to come back the following week.

As she was leaving, Rhonda noticed the stout black woman she had met briefly the last time she saw Cordell. They barely acknowledged each other. Rhonda was in no mood for small talk and Miss Ruby did not look like she was in a small talk mood, either.

Miss Ruby was curious about the familiar-looking red head, but she had other things on her mind that came first.

Ordinarily, she would have turned to her longtime employer, Claiborne Lurie, for advice, but he was away. And she trusted Myles McLean. He had a reputation for integrity.

"Well now, Miss Ruby, what brings you down here?" he asked once he had led her into the privacy of his office.

"I've got a little problem, Mr. McLean." She groped inside her ever-present tote bag and pulled out a standard envelope, handing it across the desk to Myles.

He looked it over. "Nothing here to worry a out. Just a standard 1099 form," he assured her. "Save it for your taxes."

She still looked uneasy. "It's from Garland, Inc., Mr. McLean. I never worked for them. Mr. Lurie pays my salary. Why are they saying that I worked for Garland, Inc.?"

Myles looked uneasy. He examined the form again, then assured her he would look into it.

So, he reflected, after Miss Ruby had left, he'd already had visits from two very different women this afternoon and in each story he smelled a rat.

A king-size rat named Cordell Garland.

The *Lone Star* sailed from Manaus the next morning, followed by Sir Rodney who had asked to join forces

341

with them. Claiborne was agreeable. He found the British producer quite amusing.

Late one afternoon, while they were still under sail, Belinda heard a loud banging beneath the fantail deck. The propeller. Sin, the deckhand and Cleveland, the second mate, donned scuba gear and went down to investigate, but the current was so strong it kept sweeping them away. Captain Bellew announced he was moving the yacht to an area of dead water and reanchored them about twenty feet from shore.

As the others dressed for dinner, Sin and Cleveland, stripped down for another plunge into the dank waters below.

That night, Belinda and the others, dressed to kill, stepped into the Zodiac, none too pleased about the bats that hovered above them as they headed for Sir Rodney's yacht.

"It's your flashlights that draws them," the seaman explained. But Belinda was not about to sail in the dark. She turned her light onto the shore and discovered a pair of red eyes staring at her. She screamed.

"Crocodile," Claiborne said.

The bats flapped overhead the whole way as they wove their way through floating logs and grass islands toward the *Half Note*. At least when they arrived, Sir Rodney had flutes of champagne waiting.

Sir Rodney laid out a feast, including Italian pastries from his Neopolitan chef.

When they returned to the *Lone Star* later that night, Claiborne was informed that Sin and Cleveland had still not identified the noise. They complained that the water was so dark and murky down there, they could barely see. "We had to put our masks right up against the shaft, sir, just to get a look at it," Sin told him.

"Yes, and what did you find?" Claiborne demanded impatiently.

"Nothing, sir."

"Oh, good," Belinda said. Claiborne turned to glare

at her.

"Not good at all," he said. "We may have to go back to Manaus. And even in Manaus, there's no drydock. If we can't get this straightened out, we may have to scrap the entire trip."

Suddenly, after all his meticulous planning, his entire cruise was in danger.

A half hour later, however, as he was sharing a nightcap with his guests, Cleveland appeared and informed Claiborne that the propeller problem had disappeared as suddenly as it came on.

"Well then, Captain, full steam ahead for Leticia!" he ordered.

"That's a relief," Belinda said after Captain Bellew had left.

"At least for now," Claiborne said glumly. "If the trouble comes back when we're farther upriver, we'll be even farther from a major port and the prospects aren't good."

The next morning, Brice was examining a scale model of the *Lone Star* that was inside a glass display case in the grand salon.

"You know, Claiborne, I've got an idea about this propeller problem," he said.

By this time Claiborne was willing to listen to anyone.

Brice pointed out the dorsal fin that protruded downward from the hull several feet ahead of the propeller. "I wonder if the grass and all that other debris we saw last night could pile up on this. Kind of like too many vegetables in a blender. Wouldn't that be dangerous?"

"Brice, my boy," Claiborne beamed, "I believe you've just solved our problem! I'll have Captain Bellew look into this right away."

While the crew worked, Claiborne took Belinda and some of the others in the Donzi to check out the shoreline. A farmer was cutting the slender jute reeds. Ramon explained that he would soak them in the river, then strip and dry them. The dark-haired, olive-skinned farmer was with a little blond girl about two years old who started to cry as soon as she saw the *Lone Star* group.

Valdene commented on the contrast between the dark Latin-looking farmer and his fair-skinned Anglo-looking daughter.

"You see a lot of that in Brazil," Ramon said. "Brasileros are all so mixed up by now that the European chromosomes can suddenly reassert themselves and you get blondes like that. One of nature's little jokes."

She would have to remember that, Belinda decided. If anyone else commented on her son's dark coloring, she would tell them about her Comanche grandmother. Who would challenge her?

Cordell was asking the farmer how much he made from his crop, but the man could only answer in terms of food and living supplies. He had no concept of cash. And her brother, Belinda mused, had no concept of anything else.

Suddenly the air crackled with the sound of the walkie-talkie. The farmer and his daughter stared as Claiborne talked to it. Captain Bellew was calling from the *Lone Star*.

"My compliments to Mr. de Young, sir," he said. "I've checked out his theory about the prop, and it all makes sense. We've reversed the engines to remove whatever debris accumulated on the skeg, and the problem's solved."

Brice was roundly congratulated. Claiborne throttled the Donzi to twenty knots and they sped back to the *Lone Star*, skimming over the surface of the brown water as the sun, low in the west, sparkled through their wake.

Two days later, another curious invitation arrived from the *Half Note*. Sir Rodney wondered if anyone

344

aboard the *Lone Star* would care to spend a night in the jungle.

"Why?" Claiborne demanded.

Ramon explained that the *Half Note* group wanted to soak up some of the atmosphere of the rain forest.

Claiborne frowned. "If that's all they want I'll lend them my tape of jungle noises," he said coolly.

"I think I'd like to go," Belinda said. To her surprise, only one other person was interested.

"I could go for it," Brice offered.

It was too late for her to get out of it. Claiborne only smiled benevolently. Since the episode with the propeller, he had taken a liking to Brice and didn't seem jealous at all. So, she was stuck.

Well, at least Sir Rodney's friends would be along. It wasn't as if she and Brice would be alone. She'd see to that.

When the appointed morning arrived, Belinda came up to breakfast to find everyone out on the deck watching Ciprianna's two Shih Tzus fighting over a huge beetle until Brice scooped it up and tossed it overboard. Belinda had grow up on the Gulf Coast and seen fire ants the size of her thumb, but this beetle was as big as her fist. But Brice wasn't afraid at all.

The *Half Notes* were prepared for more than beetles. Sir Rodney had an Uzi tucked into his waistband and Chili Daniels, one of his guests, had a Walther PPK in a thigh pocket. Both Donzis were loaded with food, water, hammocks, mosquito netting, insect repellent, even snake antivenom packed in ice. They weren't taking any chances.

Ramon had volunteered to join them, but he still seemed a little nervous. He explained that the area was known for the jacares—the Amazon crocodiles—that could be up to twenty feet long. He looked relieved when Sir Rodney told him that the guides were armed with 16-gauge shotguns.

They fished for piranha, paddled through the flooded

345

forest and marshes with giant lily pads, declined a generously offered native meal of catfish—head and guts attached, boiled in Amazon water—watched a hundred thousand fireflies illuminate the blackness, shuddered when bird-size insects landed on their faces, listened as the guides made the whooshing sounds that were supposed to attract the crocodiles.

That night they pitched camp in the rain forest and slept in the mosquito-netted hammocks under the stars, glistening with sweat, eyes stinging with mosquito-repellent, listening to the sounds of the jaguars in the distance.

Belinda had dozed off when she sensed someone looming over her hammock. She looked up and, seeing Brice, she sighed with impatience.

"I have to talk to you," he whispered.

"Not here, someone will hear us."

"They're all sleeping," he said. "Except for the guard, and their English isn't good enough to follow us. Or we can speak French if you'd prefer."

"I'd prefer not to speak to you in any language, ever." She struggled to sit up in the hammock. He reached out to help her, but she shrugged him off.

"In case there's any doubt, I'm not the one who invited you, Brice. And if I'd known you were coming I would have stayed home."

"With your son?" he said.

Her guard went up at once. "Keep my son out of this, thank you."

"He's a good-looking kid. I guess he takes after his old man."

She glared at him. "In some ways." In the flickering torchlight of the camp it was impossible to make out his expression, or to tell how much he knew. His insinuating manner always hinted at more. But, she assured herself, there was no way he could know the truth about Alexander. She had shared her secret with no one for exactly that reason.

346

Suddenly Ramon joined them, looking concerned.

"Is everything all right, Mrs. Lurie? Mr. de Young?" he asked.

Belinda assured him that it was and that Mr. de Young was just leaving.

"That's right, isn't it, Mr. de Young?" she repeated.

"Of course, Mrs. Lurie. Good night."

The next morning they returned to the *Lone Star* to find the entire ship in mourning and Ciprianna secluded in her cabin.

"One of the little dogs," Carl explained. "A crocodile got it."

So, Belinda thought. Those ugly reptiles were good for something after all.

Chapter Forty-five

Five days out of Manaus, and it was midnight aboard the *Lone Star*.

Cordell Garland was thinking that this cruise had been an excellent idea. He admired his father-in-law, who was everything that his own father was not. Buster was big and raw and crude, but Claiborne Lurie was sophisticated and polished. Imagine old Buster putting together a party like this, with Carl Rivers and Joel Varney on the same boat. Claiborne probably had to clear his flight plan with the SEC. Cordell laughed at his own little joke.

"What's that, honey?" Charlene called from the bathroom. She was soaking in the tub and the scent of her Poison floated out and filled their cabin.

"Oh, nothing," he assured her as he leaned back on the bed and waited for her to join him. A split of Cristal champagne, compliments of their host, was chilling in a silver cooler beside the bed. Lurie knew how to live, Cordell told himself. The man had impeccable taste.

And his friends! Rivers and Varney were heavy hitters on Wall Street. All right, maybe Rivers was pussy-whipped and maybe Varney's wives kept getting younger and dumber, but they both wielded a lot of clout on the Street. Neither of them had been caught in the Texas crash, they were too smart, too shrewd.

348

"The Street!" He liked the sound of that. Big bucks, fast pace, millions to be made in a single afternoon. The whole idea of it thrilled him. Someday soon, when the old man had gone to his reward, Cordell would be free to do wonderful things with Garland, Inc., on the Street.

He'd bring the company into the twenty-first century.

Sell off the old warhorses like the *Sentinel-Wave* and the Garland News Syndicate.

Sell off the Pink Tower and build an even bigger headquarters in New York.

Go public and make millions overnight. Real millions that he could spend any way he wanted to. He'd make Garland, Inc., a force to be reckoned with.

He would team up with men like Rivers and Varney. Launch hostile takeovers, demand greenmail, bust up whatever they couldn't buy. Kick ass the way he would never be able to do as long as Buster was alive. The old man refused to do business with Claiborne Lurie or anyone else he didn't take to. Imagine! Cordell thought such thinking was pathetically old-fashioned. Who said you had to like a man to do business with him? He sighed at the narrow-mindedness of his father. Time had passed Buster by.

"What's that, honey?" Charlene called again from the tub.

"Nothin' darlin'," he said. "I'm just waiting here for you."

"You're sweet."

He yawned. Charlene still took forever to get ready for anything, even bed. He thought of Rhonda Perillo who made him take showers with her. She used to hate to be away from him a minute. Good old Rhonda! He hoped she was doing all right, but there was no way he could see her again except on his old video tapes. Even then he'd have to be careful. Suppose Charlene or her father found out about their affair? Or Buster? His daddy was the most ornery, most old-fashioned and

349

thick-headed old coot in Galveston, which was saying something.

Cordell yearned to do great things. But his hands were tied. Buster controlled the money, and as long as he did, Cordell would never be free. Even when he was keeping Rhonda he had to try some creative bookkeeping to pay her bills. And Rhonda was not a demanding mistress. Still, it was another good reason to breathe a sigh of relief that their affair was over. He was not troubled by leaving his former mistress high and dry because it simply didn't occur to him that he had done so.

He stared across the cabin at the small Degas painting of a cotton broker in New Orleans. Something shrewd around the broker's eyes reminded Cordell of his father. As he dozed off he wondered what Buster was doing right now.

When Charlene finally emerged from her steamy bath, the scent of Poison had permeated her every pore as well as every corner of her cabin. She had pulled her straight blond hair back in a French braid and wrapped her bony frame in a peach satin robe trimmed with the kind of lace produced only in cloistered Sicilian convents.

All for nothing!

Her husband of less than a month had fallen asleep! She sat beside him and gently nudged his arm. Nothing happened. Cordell was out cold. A slap would get him up, she thought, then she had a better idea. Checking her face again in the vanity mirror, she took up the unopened bottle of chilled Cristal and tiptoed out of the cabin, gently closing the door so as not to disturb Cordell and headed down the corridor, her peach satin mules gliding silently on the plush gray carpet.

Ciprianna, too, was restless. She sat upright beside Carl in the double bed, her thick black hair hanging loose around her bare shoulders. She had not slept since losing her little dog. His surviving twin was curled up asleep at her feet.

What a cozy domestic scene we must make, she thought bitterly. While she tried to read a new biography of her idol, Catherine the Great, and Carl was deep in a study of psychic healing in the rain forest, her lover was less than fifty feet away in another cabin with his wife.

At first the idea of this cruise had seemed like a lark. Now she was not sure. Claiborne could be awfully cruel. He was toying with them both and she knew it.

She blamed herself for her dilemma. After all those years he had finally been willing to make her his bride, and what had she done? Lost her hot temper just because his fat, stupid granddaughter made her clothes look ridiculous. She had only meant to make him suffer a bit.

Had she made a mistake? Claiborne had gone off and married this blond *putana* and now they had a child. The woman was beautiful, but how could Claiborne prefer mere beauty to her? It was impossible! Ciprianna slammed the book shut. It made a loud thud, but neither Carl nor the surviving Shih Tzu stirred. They were both sound asleep. She rose from the bed and donned a violet satin robe and slippers from her new collection. When critics said she designed for rich men's mistresses, she laughed. These days, who else could afford her?

Leaving Carl and the dog in dreamland, she stole out the door.

Brice de Young was also restless and he went up to the observation deck alone to watch the jungle at night. The lights of the *Lone Star* played on the brown water,

351

lumpy with floating tree trunks and slow-moving crocodiles.

Suddenly he realized he was not alone. Someone else was coming up the ladder to join him. It was Valdene Garland, her black mane temporarily tamed into a braid and her voluptuous curves shrouded in a ruby silk caftan.

"Hi there!" she said, taking a position beside him and looking over the rail. "Why aren't you in bed?"

Brice shrugged, a little resentful of this loss of privacy. There was so much he had to sort out. Like his next move with Belinda Garland.

Valdene had moved closer to him, so that her arm brushed against him as she rested her elbows on the teak rail. He could smell her perfume. Jasmine mingled with the earthy scent of the river.

Valdene soon grew impatient. Her entire repertoire of conversational gambits drew nothing but monosyllables from Brice. How long was he going to stare at that muddy old water?

She finally went for her ace in the hole. Leaning close to him, she looked him directly in the eyes. "Brice, honey, do you know what we used to say on the gospel circuit?"

"No, Valdene. What was that?"

"OTRDC."

"What's that, some kind of mantra?"

"Sort of," she laughed, putting a soft white hand on top of his. "It means 'On the Road Doesn't Count'."

Brice looked at her, comprehending at once. He smiled. "Yes, ma'am," he said. "You come by my cabin in ten minutes and run that by me again."

Valdene watched him go, then turned her attention back to the river. She had a feeling the next ten minutes would crawl. Well, it served old Buster right for sending her on this trip alone.

Charlene had knocked first on Brice de Young's cabin door and, getting no answer, she assumed he was asleep and moved on. The ship made a sudden turn, probably to avoid a floating log and she almost lost her balance. She gripped the hall rail to steady herself with one hand while she held the champagne with the other, then plunged on. Like her daddy, she was resilient. She also knew every inch of the *Lone Star* and knew exactly where she was going next.

Unaware that Valdene had left her alone in their cabin, Reba Twining was enjoying a lovely dream. She imagined herself climbing a great golden stairs. She was wearing a flowing white choir robe and golden slippers. Golden-haired angels lined the steps and they sang as she climbed ever higher. At the top of the stairs the Master waited in golden robes, his arms outstretched.

She had had this dream many times before and she always knew what to expect: the beaming face of her spiritual guide, Prescott Sykes. But now, as she moved even nearer, she sensed something was wrong.

For one thing, this time the Master wasn't tall. Even from thirty feet away she could see that the angels towered over him. He was short and his golden robe did not disguise his portly figure.

But he beamed at her, welcoming her ever closer. And as she drew near, she discovered she was looking into the smooth round face of Carl Rivers!

Then she slipped on a golden step or tripped on her white choir robe and plunged into darkness.

That night Belinda could not sleep. Lying in the king-size bed, she could feel the ship doing strange slaloms as it swerved sharply to avoid the ever-present logs in the river. Several times she started awake from a loud bang against the hull, a little shaken, grateful for the *Lone Star*'s solid construction and for Claiborne beside her. This time when she woke she discovered that she was alone. So Claiborne couldn't sleep, either. He was probably in the library with his beloved satellite phone.

Maybe she had been too harsh about the Delancy Street property. After all, the point was that he had turned it over to her. Feeling ready to forgive and forget, she grabbed a bottle of champagne from the small cabin refrigerator and two chilled glasses. Wrapping herself in an aqua silk robe, she proceeded down the private marble-and-onyx companionway. She was going to insist he take a break.

Belinda was so intent on surprising her husband she did not even notice the noises coming from his study until she reached the foot of the companionway and then there was no turning back. She paused in the doorway. The lights were turned down, but there was no mistaking the two naked figures on the banquette. At least she recognized Claiborne instantly, but it actually took her a minute to be sure about the woman. Then the woman moaned and she knew.

Ciprianna!

She felt the bottom of her stomach drop. Shock gave away to revulsion and then disgust.

Without thinking, Belinda turned and raced back up the companionway, to their cabin. When Claiborne joined her a few minutes later, he found the door locked. By that time, it was dawn and he knew better than to bang on the door.

"Adib likes you," Aynsley said, and Lauren could sense his leer over the phone even though she couldn't see it. Aynsley must surely know that she was sleeping with Adib, too, but he didn't seem to care. In fact, he seemed to like it. He kept saying that the three of them had to get together. And tonight was the night. They were meeting for dinner at Maximus.

"Be nice to Adib," he said. "He can help us both."

A few hours later, she had joined Adib and Aynsley at the restaurant, and the three of them proceeded to get very drunk.

Lauren was annoyed because Aynsley wouldn't answer her questions. She wanted to know if it was true that he planned to sell the television station to Buddy Garland. And Adib kept telling her what a great man Aynsley was, what a great United States senator he would make.

"I will stop at nothing to see this man in Washington," Adib said.

Lauren perked up. She was sure if Aynsley went to Washington, he would divorce Carola and marry her. They could begin a new life. And a Washington base would be great for her career.

They were having such a good time, that when the restaurant closed the three of them brought the party back to her place.

Tammy Lynn Garland was not thinking of her career or much else besides Brice de Young. She had hardly left her apartment since he disappeared. Now she knew what a fool she had been.

He had just left without any explanation and she actually thought something terrible had happened to him. She had even started calling hospital emergency rooms until Tootsie Bright gave her the news. Brice was off cruising on the Amazon with Claiborne Lurie.

Damn it! She had always suspected that something had happened between her Aunt Belinda and Brice and now she was sure of it.

Spoiled, beautiful Belinda wasn't satisfied with a rich husband, she was still conniving to steal Brice! So Tammy Lynn sat alone in her apartment and brooded for days.

It turned out to be a good thing, for otherwise she would never have noticed the leak in her bathroom ceiling when she did.

When it rains, it pours, she thought bitterly as the water poured over the bathroom like rain. Whoever lived over her must have left their tub running. At three o'clock in the morning! She called the concierge and as usual there was no answer. This only fueled her anger more.

It seemed the whole world was against her: her wicked Aunt Belinda, Brice, the concierge of her apartment house, and now this idiot upstairs. Angrily she wrapped herself in a robe and headed upstairs to deal with the matter herself.

There was no answer when she knocked on the door, and then she noticed that the door was not completely closed. Gently she pushed it and it opened. Curious, she moved into the living room which was decorated a style she regarded as nouveau glitz.

Then she heard the scuffling noise. Curiosity won over caution and she moved toward the source of the sound. She found it in the bathroom. The water was running in the tub, and it was spilling out on the floor.

A woman lay on the tile floor in two inches of water. She was bound and gagged, and could only bang her knees against the wall, which explained the odd scuffling sound. Tammy Lynn automatically turned off the running water, and fell to her knees to loosen the gag, then freed the woman's hands.

"Oh, gee, thank you," the woman gasped. As she stepped up to the mirror and began to brush her hair, Tammy Lynn recognized her.

"It's my boyfriend," she said casually. "He likes to play games, and sometimes he goes too far."

Then Tammy Lynn knew her for sure: it was Lauren Armour, from the television news.

Chapter Forty-six

The next morning, as Belinda came up to the top deck, the *Lone Star* was just approaching the point where the borders of Brazil, Peru, and Colombia converged and a spectacular rainbow was breaking through the clouds. She watched it and wondered what kind of omen it might be. Maybe, she thought dryly, she should ask Colette.

The clairvoyant specialized in discerning the obscure, while she, Belinda, had been denying the obvious. For how long, she wondered. Weeks? Months? Had Claiborne resumed his affair with Ciprianna on this cruise or was Ciprianna the real reason behind all those business trips he'd been taking lately? Was it possible that he had never stopped seeing her at all?

Belinda tried to take a practical view. She had entered into this marriage without love or illusions. For her it had been a strategy for survival: she was pregnant with another man's child, and she was being forced out of the family business. A year and a half ago Claiborne Lurie had looked like a white knight. Now he looked like something very different.

No, Belidna told herself, if she had entered into the marriage with such a clear head there was no reason to leave now in a huff. She wanted to believe she was tough enough to outlast Ciprianna. She wanted to believe she could stay with Claiborne no matter how he treated her because her son was his heir, because he was going to back her development project, because it was easier to be the wife of a rich man than the daughter of one. But what she wanted to believe and what she felt in her gut were very different.

Lost in such thoughts, Belinda was suddenly distracted as Ramon rushed by looking harried, barely greeting her and explaining that he would be tied up all morning dealing with the endless forms that Brazil, Peru, and Colombia each demanded. He would not be able to go with them into Leticia and Claiborne had arranged for a local contact, a prominent *abogado,* to meet the *Lone Star* party at the dock.

She found the rest of the party having breakfast in the solarium and watching the rainbow. Her eyes met Claiborne's, but except for a hearty "good morning," it was as if nothing had happened last night. Well, she was not about to discuss it in front of the others anyway. She glared at Ciprianna, who glared back but said nothing.

Everyone seemed a little distracted, as if more than the rainbow was on their minds. Valdene was watching Brice, who was staring at Belinda. Charlene was in unusual good humor and could not take her hands off Cordell. Carl Rivers was giving the Varneys and Reba Twining the vital statistics of Brazil, Peru, and Colombia. No one from the *Half Note* would be joining them here; Sir Rodney had alluded to some previous problems with the police ("they only enforce their bloody laws against foreigners") and so was passing Leticia by. They had agreed to reunite in Iquitos in a few days.

Belinda was relieved when Claiborne suggested it was time to take the Donzis into Leticia. The two inflatable speedboats, one manned by Claiborne, the other by Brice, raced each other to the dock. Brice won. Claiborne joked that Brice would have to swim back to Texas. Everyone laughed, but it was a slightly nervous laugh.

The atmosphere around Leticia's waterfront was tangibly sinister and it was easy to believe that this was one of the major cocaine exporting towns in the world. Claiborne's friend, the *abogado*, Señor Dorado, was waiting for them on the dock near a dozen high-speed boats and a pair of seaplanes that had been confiscated from drug runners.

As they walked along the streets, an army truck passed them, plowing full speed into a pothole and splashing Charlene with slimy brown water while the *abogado* pointed out places where he had personally seen drug-world assassinations.

They stopped at a jewelry store next to the Hotel Anaconda where the owner had been murdered a few months earlier because he wouldn't sell emeralds to a cocaine exporter from Cartagena.

When Señor Dorado found out that Bernie O'Higgins was a lawyer, too, he offered to take them to watch a trial at the Leticia Hall of Justice. Bernie, Colette, and Cordell all went along for fun.

Valdene announced that before sailing on, Sir Rodney had arranged for her and Reba to lunch at the plantation of a friend of his who would be picking them up in a few minutes. The friend was a Colombian who was very anxious to break into the American gospel market. She was hoping that they would be able to discuss a new album for her.

Jennifer Varney insisted that her husband take her shopping for emeralds. How could she leave Colombia without emeralds?

Claiborne said he was returning to the ship to make a few calls on the satellite phone. He was in the middle of another one of his mysterious deals.

Ciprianna suddenly developed a headache and an urgent need to take a siesta in her cabin. She dismissed Carl and joined Claiborne.

Charlene decided she was going back, too, to change her mud-spattered dress.

359

Belinda watched them with interest and relief. At least now the whole Claiborne-Ciprianna mess was out in the open. She took a seat on a mossy bench.

"I was thinking of taking one of the Donzis," a voice behind her said and she turned to see Brice. She was so upset about Claiborne, she had forgotten Brice was in the group. Now they were alone on the plaza, and the heat of the afternoon sun was getting stronger. Belinda put on her dark glasses as he sat beside her. "Why don't you come with me?" he said.

"You mean, leave the boat for good?" she said, then immediately put up her guard again. She was not going to spill out her troubles to Brice de Young.

He smiled, that vague grin that always left her wondering how much exactly he knew. "That's up to you, Miz Belinda. I'd be perfectly happy if you just came with me to Mariposa. There's an Indian village there that hardly ever gets tourists. Ramon gave me some directions and I'm going to check it out. This Texas boy wants to see what kind of strange fruits and nuts they've got down here."

"Oh, that's right, you're a cook, aren't you?" she said, as if remembering something from a long time ago.

"I am when I'm not being fired," he said. "How about it. Do you want to come to Mariposa with me?"

He looked at her steadily, his brown eyes meeting her blue ones. She had never noticed it before, but their gold-brown color was not unlike the dark waters of the Amazon. And just as murky, she thought.

When she didn't answer, he pressed the issue. "The way I see it, Miz Belinda, you can join your brother and watch dope dealers in a show trial, you can watch Mrs. Varney try to buy up every emerald in Colombia, or you can go back on the boat and watch Ciprianna try to make your husband. But you could do all those things back home, now couldn't you?"

She nodded, and, deciding she had nothing to lose,

she got up from the stone bench. "Let's go," she said without enthusiasm.

Back in the Donzi, with Brice at the wheel, he and Belinda roared off down a narrow estuary, carried by the swift current. Flights of brilliantly colored toucans and macaws soared overhead, the air was full of the screech of howler monkeys and the loud mysterious splashes behind the cover of the jungle.

Belinda was thinking she was glad she'd come on the cruise after all, when the Donzi stopped suddenly.

"What's wrong?" she said, looking around. The estuary was very narrow and she could see the shore on either side clearly, but the thick curtain of jungle foliage, hid anything else.

"We're stuck," he said. "Ramon warned me about these natural dams. The logs and weeds just clot up and you're stuck."

"You'll have to turn around, Brice, the Donzi won't make it," she said.

"No way!" Brice started gunning the speedboat's engines. They seesawed atop the dam as his face darkened. He finally hit the throttle, sending a great froth of brown water behind them as they roared ahead at full speed.

Brice de Young, Belinda realized, had no patience with anything that stood in his way. Why hadn't she noticed that before?

"Hooray!" He laughed. "We're free!" He suddenly grabbed her and kissed her.

Yes, Belinda was thinking. Free for now.

At first Colette teased Bernardo about taking a busman's holiday by going to the courthouse, but she discovered she enjoyed the visit, too. She didn't understand the Spanish, but she could tell what was going on. It was all part of her psychic gift.

This was her first trip with Bernardo and she had

discovered that he was a good traveler. He wasn't the least bit intimidated by Claiborne's lavish yacht, or by a foreign town.

Colette hoped this trip would be the first of many.

She felt so comfortable with Bernardo, in fact, that she considered confiding her suspicions about Belinda Lurie's young son. But she held back. The whole thing was too fantastic. She was convinced the baby was her grandchild. But all she had was one of her hunches, her psychic feelings.

Besides, why tell Bernardo she was a grandmother when she didn't have to? It was bad enough introducing him to Brice.

At length, Brice and Belinda arrived at the Indian village of Mariposa. Belinda couldn't help wondering what these Indians who never saw a tourist thought of a couple of Americans in a speedboat charging down their little river.

"They'll just assume we're cocaine dealers," Brice assured her.

But the villagers were welcoming, and offered them servings from their manioc pan where the women had cooked up a mashed version of the starchy root that was the local staple. Baby pigs were rooting about, snorting up any spillover.

It was time for Valdene and Reba to get back to the *Lone Star*. Reba hated the Amazon. Too many dark-skinned people chattering away in languages she didn't understand. Too many bugs. She hated the yacht. She hated the heat. She was seasick most of the time and she wasn't one to sunbathe and she had no interest in the heathen history of the people.

Valdene, on the other hand, was in her glory. She insisted that the luncheon with Sir Rodney's friend had been a huge success. Valdene was going to send him some of her tapes as soon as they got back to Galveston.

Reba didn't like the producer or his wife, a haughty socialite who looked down on country people. Among the other guests at the lunch had been a man Reba was positive was wearing eyeliner. She was disgusted.

Reba hated every minute, and on the way back to the *Lone Star* she gave Valdene a piece of her mind.

"I think they're godless. That witch was just waiting for one of us to start eating with our hands. She's probably talking about us right now, laughing at what white trash we are."

"Who cares, Reba? That man back there wants to make me a star."

Reba gave up. Her best friend was being totally corrupted by life aboard the *Lone Star*. She could not wait to get back to Galveston. Being around Claiborne Lurie almost made her miss Buster.

Ciprianna's sundress exposed her darkly tanned skin and her strong shoulders. The big gold loops in her ears made her look even more like a Gypsy than ever. Claiborne was in his shipboard uniform: blue polo shirt and impeccably pressed chinos and Topsiders. They were in the solarium, sharing a glass of Tattinger's.

"Why doesn't your wife join us?" asked Ciprianna.

Claiborne shrugged and looked vague. "She's still off with Charlene's friend, that de Young fellow."

"Oh, yes," Ciprianna nodded sagely. "The very handsome young man. I noticed the way he watches her."

Claiborne seemed startled, then glum. Ciprianna smiled, pleased that she had planted a small seed of suspicion about his unsuitable bride.

"It's about time you got back!" Charlene cried when

363

Cordell finally returned to the *Lone Star*. Charlene was tearing up the cabin. She was lost without her personal maid, and the ship's two Irish maids didn't understand how to do things her way. And where was Cordell? He should be helping her, instead of running off with that slimy lawyer and his psychic girlfriend. No one cared about her.

Her only consolation was the conviction that her father and Ciprianna had resumed their affair. She had always disliked the designer and resented her hold on her father, but no more.

Daddy and Ciprianna were lovers again! How sad for Belinda! How nice for Charlene!

Belinda glanced at her watch. It was seven-thirty. The day had flown, and she had to admit that Brice had a gift for getting along anywhere. The villagers had taken to him at once and insisted on showing him and Belinda the local Indian ruins and demonstrating five ways to cook manioc. Unfortunately, it always tasted the same. Now the village chief was in the middle of a long story about fishing on the river. Since he spoke very little Spanish—and no English—and Brice and Belinda knew nothing of the local Indian dialect, this fable was related with a lot of sound effects and hand gestures.

"Brice," she whispered. "It's time to go. Dinner on the *Lone Star* is always at eight. Claiborne's very fussy about it."

"Just wait until Rab finishes," he insisted. But by the time the old man had wound up, it was after eight and it was so dark that two men from the village had to lead them to the shore with torches. She was furious.

Things got worse when they discovered that the Donzi wouldn't start.

"You probably stripped the gears when you jumped the dam," she said.

He shook his head. "No, we're just out of gas. But there's no way this little boat's gonna sail tonight."

"What are you saying? We have to stay here? Claiborne expects me for dinner!" Her voice was shaking.

Brice laughed.

"I'm glad you find our situation so funny," she said coldly. "You are my husband's guest, you know."

He shook his head. "Yes, ma'am. Don't worry about it. The way I see it, we have two choices: we can let the boys here take us back to the *Lone Star* in their canoe which, with the current and all, should take us about an hour and means we'll be late for dinner, or . . ."

"Or what?"

"We can stay here, you and me, sleep in the Donzi and wait until daylight when old Claiborne will come looking for us in the chopper. How about it? You and me under the stars?"

Chapter Forty-seven

Claiborne Lurie was a very serious host. Every dinner aboard the *Lone Star* was carefully planned, from the placement of the flowers to the mix of the guests. He had planned two parties for their stop in Leticia: tonight's small dinner for local functionaries and business contacts, and tomorrow's more glittering affair, which would draw guests from all over South America.

But where was his wife? His guests were beginning to arrive and Claiborne stood at the head of the gangplank to welcome them, but he stood alone.

Damn! Where was Belinda? Ever since Ciprianna's remarks about the way Brice watched her, he had resolved to keep a close eye on his wife.

When last seen she had been sailing off with that glorified cook. Was she up to something? Was she planning to humiliate him? She had been so unreasonable about the Delancy Street business! He was well aware that Belinda had seen him with Ciprianna and he had been waiting for two days for her to retaliate. Was this it? What the devil was she up to? He wanted to think about it, but he had to attend to his guests.

"Can't you hurry up, Charlene?" Cordell shouted into the bathroom. He was suffocating under the scent of Poison and there was no sign that his wife was anywhere near ready. "Can't I just go up by myself?"

Charlene peeked out of the bathroom. "No, you can't, honey. I want you on my arm when we go in. I need your support when I have to face that woman!"

"Ciprianna?" Even the usually dense Cordell had not missed the tension between Claiborne Lurie and his mistress.

"No, not Ciprianna," Charlene snapped. "Belinda. She flaunts my daddy like a diamond brooch."

"Honey, they're married, for Pete's sake."

Charlene sniffed as she came out of the bathroom. She sniffed. "She trapped him into it. Anyone who can count can see that. I'm sure he only married her because she was pregnant."

This sort of conversation made Cordell nervous. "Remember you're talking about my sister, Charlene."

"She may be your sister, but I don't trust her. I've been on to her for years. Why, I remember how she sucked up to me when we were debutantes together. Just to get close to . . ." She paused. No sense letting Cordell know that he had been her second choice. That she had been in love with Arden Yates and only seduced old Cordell on the rebound.

"Get close to whom?" he asked.

"To my daddy, of course," she said, congratulating herself on her quickness of mind. "She was after him for years. It's disgusting! Imagine doing it with a man that age!"

She had stepped into a pair of wide black chiffon pants and a halter top that exposed her bony shoulders.

"Do you think this makes me look too fat?" she asked as she eyed her skeletal figure uneasily in the mirror.

"No, honey. You're just right. Now can we go to dinner?"

Brice had never really expected Belinda to agree to

367

spend the night in the Donzi, but he got his revenge by encouraging the two Indians who conveyed them in their canoe to take their time. In sign language he convinced them that he and Belinda wanted to prolong their trip as long as possible. He liked being with her, even when she was angry.

And she was growing angrier as they moved slowly against the current, pausing every once in a while so the two Indians could maneuver their fragile canoe around the ever-present tree trunks and floating vegetation.

"Isn't there some way they can go a little faster?" she pleaded.

"Hey, Miz Belinda, this is the Amazon. The simple life. Isn't that what you came for?" Brice leaned back in the canoe. "Relax and enjoy it."

"I've never been to the Holy Land," Reba Twining confided to Carl Rivers with a faraway look in her eye.

"You haven't?" He had difficulty concentrating because he was on the alert for Ciprianna's entrance. She had banished him from their stateroom while she prepared. He knew how much she wanted to upstage Belinda and he indulged her.

"Jerusalem! The Wailing Wall! The Eye of the Needle! I'm sure it's real profound," Reba sighed. One of the stewards passed with a tray of hors d'oeuvres. She helped herself. "Valdene and I will probably go next year. Valdene is a very spiritual person."

"I can see that," said Carl.

"It's hard for her, living with Buster Garland. He's not a sensitive man. I know you understand."

"Oh, yes," he said, forgetting for a moment to watch the door and staring instead into Reba Twining's little pinched face and watery gray eyes.

"Not like Claiborne Lurie," she went on.

"You know, Reba, you are a marvelous judge of

character," said Carl Rivers.

Charlene paused in the doorway. By now most of her father's guests had arrived and he was mingling with them in the grand salon. She saw no sign of Belinda as she scanned the room. She tried the deep breathing Sven Petersen had taught her. It was important to be calm in such situations, she told herself. Instead of wasting her anger on Belinda (and how long could that marriage last anyway?) she ought to be working on Cordell, building him up.

"Oh, look, Cordell honey. There are the Varneys. Let's talk to them." Daddy's old news, she told herself. The Varneys were the future.

As they walked to the Varneys, all eyes turned in their direction. At first Charlene was thrilled, thinking they were staring at her and toward the door. Turning around, she saw Ciprianna, standing in the doorway as if expecting applause.

She smiled. She glowed. She obligingly spun around to give them the full benefit of the floral organza print of her palazzo pajamas. Her black hair was pulled back in a severe chignon, all the better to expose her fine profile, and she had tucked a huge crimson hibiscus blossom behind one ear.

Carl Rivers watched his glamorous wife until he realized that Reba was still talking to him.

"I've enjoyed our little talks, Carl," she said. "You've taught me so much. I don't think this trip would have been the same without you."

Carl looked into the shallow gray eyes as if seeing Reba for the first time.

"We had a wonderful day," Colette said as she helped herself to some beluga. She was going to miss Claiborne's unlimited supply of caviar, among other things. "The courtroom was fascinating. And between Bernie and Señor Dorado I feel I know everything there is to know about Colombian law."

"Oh really?" replied Ciprianna. She was barely listening, and her real attention was focused on the arriving women. She was counting the number of her dresses in the crowd. So far, there had been only three, and that did not help her mood.

Brice and Belinda had no trouble finding the *Lone Star,* for it was strung with bright lights and could be seen from a half mile away. It seemed to take forever to get up close though, and even longer to get the attention of Captain Bellew. One of the deckhands finally noticed them in their little canoe and fetched Captain Bellew.

"Ah, Mrs. Lurie," he said as he helped her up the ladder. "We were growing concerned."

Yes, Belinda thought. But not concerned enough to come looking for us. Nothing interfered with one of her husband's dinner parties.

"Please tell Mr. Lurie that we're back and we'll be joining him in a few minutes," she said.

"Nicely done," Brice whispered.

She drew him aside. "Should I give them money?" she whispered, indicating the two Indians.

He laughed. "Now what good would that do them? No, I promised I'd take them down to the galley and get the aluminum cans your ecologically minded husband has been storing."

"Soda cans?" She was incredulous.

"Sure! They'll turn them into fishing lures, jewelry, small cutting edges. You name it. Believe me, the cans mean much more than dollars to them."

Tables for the fifty guests and their bodyguards had

been set in the solarium so that Claiborne's guests could dine under the stars. Conversation bubbled in four languages while the stewards moved deftly among the tables. Charlene found herself next to Joel Varney. She batted her dyed eyelashes and flirted boldly. Varney was a crude little man who made Buster Garland look like Cary Grant, but the sight of those emeralds Jennifer Varney was wearing set Charlene's heart aflutter.

Her daddy was always saying she had no goals. Well, she was thinking, getting some of those emeralds for herself might be an interesting goal.

"I'll see you at dinner," said Belinda as she left Brice standing on the deck. He guessed that meant he better not join her husband's guests until he had showered and changed into something less redolent of the rain forest.

Once in his cabin, Brice pondered his next step. He still could not figure out why Belinda was so cold to him. Didn't she understand how much they had in common? He could tell she didn't like her husband's style any more than he did.

He took a quick shower and dressed. Grabbing his dinner jacket, he headed up to the solarium.

"Where have you been?" Claiborne hissed when Belinda finally arrived. She had changed into a white washed-silk jumpsuit that showed off her tan. Her blond hair was swept up in a French twist.

"Sorry I'm late, darling," she said, briskly kissing him on the cheek and taking her seat at the other end of the table. "Brice and I were stuck on the river. We had to leave the Donzi with some Indians at Mariposa, and they brought us back in their canoe."

"You're very brave, Señora Lurie," said Señor Dorado at her right. "I understand that those little canoes are fragile. They're thrown over by crocodiles all the time."

"Now you tell me!" she said. The others laughed. The tension eased. The guests were relieved that their hostess had shown up. None of them believed the Indian village story, of course, especially when Brice de Young turned up minutes later and took his seat between Valdene and Jennifer Varney. The faces of the two women brightened as they welcomed their dinner companion. He soon proved the truth of the old South American adage that anything worth having was worth waiting for.

Chapter Forty-eight

"It's good to have you back in Galveston," Myles said. "Let's hope it's not just a visit."

His old friend Buddy Garland grinned. Much water had passed under the bridge since Buddy had last occupied this office in the Pink Tower.

"I'm only sorry that I'm here on unpleasant business," Myles went on. He brought out Miss Ruby's 1099 form and explained how he came to have it.

Buddy's face turned grim and his jaw hardened as he examined it, then he looked back at Myles. "You know what this is as well as I do," he said.

Myles shrugged. "It could be a one-time thing. An oversight."

Buddy laughed. "No, I'm afraid not. I've only been here three days and I've already seen four of those things. And the canceled checks to back them up. It seems that brother Cordell's been writing company checks to these people, then cashing them himself. It's not the oldest scam in the book, but it has to be one of the dumbest."

"Do you plan to take any action?" Myles pressed.

Buddy shook his head. "He's my brother, Myles. Buster and I will settle with him our own way. And we'll take care of Miss Ruby and the others, too. Only what do you suppose he spent the money on?"

Myles decided it was time to leave. He had no

intention of discussing Rhonda Perillo with any Garlands just yet. He had still not decided whether to take her case. He didn't believe in palimony cases and the whole thing was pretty sordid. On the other hand, if Cordell Garland was going to get away with stealing from his own father's company, it would be nice to nail him for something else.

Tammy Lynn had discovered a soulmate in Houston. Since rescuing Lauren Armour, the two of them had become best friends, running back and forth between each other's apartments and trading horror stories about their lovers over pitchers of Margaritas on the terrace.

They shared the most intimate details about their affairs and generally agreed that Lauren's lover was the cruelest while Tammy Lynn's was the most indifferent.

With Brice off on his cruise, and Aynsley occupied with fund-raisers for his Senate campaign, the two women had lots of time on their hands and they spent many hours rehashing every cruelty, every abuse, physical and mental, as well as every sexual kink either lover had. (Tammy Lynn had to admit that Brice was many things, but a sexual kinkster he was not. When Lauren described some of Aynsley's favorite activities, Tammy Lynn even started to wonder if Brice might be a little boring.)

Finally Lauren even confided how Aynsley had introduced another man into their relationship.

Belinda managed to make it through dinner aboard the *Lone Star* by concentrating totally on her less than fascinating dinner companions, Señor Dorado and the Mayor of Leticia. She avoided Claiborne's eyes, but every once in a while she would look up from her conversation and discover that he was staring at her.

374

She was sure he was furious, but just as sure that he would never create a scene in front of his guests.

After dinner, someone suggested they go club hopping in town.

"Oh yes, let's go!" said Charlene. She still wanted to get Brice alone so she could find out what was going on between him and Belinda. She didn't believe that story about running out of gas for a minute. But Cordell wouldn't go along.

Struggling to follow the trial in Spanish had tired him out, and so had the necessity to keep up conversation with Claiborne's sophisticated guests. Cordell, who seldom read anything but the Garland newspapers, had a hard time following what the others were talking about. He grew tired and bored. "I'm going to turn in, honey," he announced.

"Oh no you're not," Charlene informed him, pulling him away from the other guests. "You were out having fun all afternoon while I was cooped up on this boat. Now I want to party. Besides, don't you want to know what's going on between Belinda and Brice?"

"What for?" he said.

"Damn it, how dense can you be? Doesn't it bother you that your sister's gone and married the richest man in Texas? Don't you care that she could be getting ready to get back at you for pushing her out of the Maison Rouge?"

"Ah, Belinda doesn't hold a grudge," he shrugged.

Charlene looked at her husband with contempt. "Cordell, you are such a *wimp!*"

"Don't call me that!" he insisted. "I am not a wimp!" He stared at Charlene. Her flawless peaches-and-cream complexion was flushed red with anger and her bland, patrician looks were convulsed with rage. He had forgotten how ugly she could get during one of her tantrums.

"You are a wimp, a wimp. And you're coming with me!"

Cordell sighed. "Yes, honey. Of course."

Across the room, Belinda pleaded exhaustion to Claiborne, who seemed only too happy to leave her on board, perhaps because Ciprianna was going ashore with him.

"You better stay in our cabin, Carl," Ciprianna ordered. "I don't like the way you look."

Overhearing this, Reba whispered to Carl, "If you'd like, I can bring you an American aspirin later."

Ciprianna ignored her like a great peacock might ignore a tiny flea, but Carl nodded gratefully. "Reba, that would be very kind," he said.

Joel and Jennifer Varney wanted to go. So did Valdene. And Ramon.

As soon as the group left for shore, Carl went to his cabin and Reba went to get him an aspirin. This left Belinda and Brice alone on the deck, waving to the group as they walked along the dock.

Belinda leaned over the rail and Brice stood beside her. "Well, Miz Belinda, we keep getting thrown together, whether you want it or not."

"I can stand it if you can," she said coolly. "And I do appreciate what you did tonight. You did your best to get us back in time for the party."

"No, I didn't," he said.

"False modesty doesn't become you."

"I'm not being modest. I did everything I could to slow down that canoe. I told the Indians we were lovers and you had a jealous husband."

"You what!"

"I'm not sure how much they understood. We talked mostly in sign language. But they got the part about going slow."

"How dare you?"

He stared out at the group, disappearing into the town. "I knew we didn't have enough gas to get back. I knew we'd be stranded. It was the only way I could be alone with you."

"I was right about you the first time, wasn't I? You really are a selfish pig who doesn't care about anyone but himself!"

"No, Belinda, that's just what I'm trying to tell you. I care about you. I can see how unhappy you are."

"And I'm going to be a lot more unhappy if my husband thinks I'm having an affair with you. Everyone else here tonight already thinks so."

He pulled her around gently so that she was facing him and not the shore. "Look at me, Belinda," he commanded.

"I'm looking."

"That night we made love at the Maison Rouge, did I force myself on you?"

She shook her head. "No." Even now she could recall how much she had wanted him.

"And this afternoon, at Mariposa. I could have kept you there, but I didn't, did I?"

Again she shook her head. "What are you saying, Brice?"

"Just that I won't force myself on you. I want you, and you want me. You just don't know it yet."

He pulled her closer. She did not resist. Maybe their course had been set more than a year ago, at their first meeting. Maybe she was wrong to deny it. His lips met hers. This time she did not resist.

The sudden sound of a splash in the water broke them apart.

"What's that?" she whispered, her voice still hoarse with arousal.

"Just a fish," he said, scanning the water. He took her hand. "Come with me, I want to continue this discussion."

"This is insane," Belinda whispered, but for the first time in years she felt like a giddy teenager. "Where are you going?"

377

Brice raised his finger to his lips in a gesture calling for silence. "We don't want to wake Carl or Reba," he whispered.

"We'll go to my cabin," he hissed. "Unless you want to go to yours."

"My husband . . ."

"Say no more. I hear he's been sleeping in his studio," he said.

She glared at him. Did he have to know everything? He was opening a door.

"Well here we are. It's not much, but it's home." He pulled her in. "Don't want to take a chance on being seen. Or on you changing your mind."

She lifted her chin defiantly. "I won't change my mind. This is just sex. You understand that, don't you?"

He nodded. "Just sex. Just like the last time, right?"

She stared at him.

"Look, Belinda. It may be just sex to you, but I want you to know that it's more than that to me. I wanted you the first time I saw you. I want you now."

"So you want to fuck me. That isn't love."

"How can I love you? You let me make love to you once a year. The rest of the time, you don't want to know me."

"You don't understand . . ."

"I understand more than you give me credit for. Valdene told me all about you and your father. How your brother forced you out of the business. I understand why you jumped into this marriage. But you must see by now it's a mistake. Get out of it!"

"It's not that easy. We—Claiborne and I—have a son. I have to think of him."

"Yeah. About the kid . . ."

"I'd rather not talk about him."

"Belinda, that's your solution to everything. If you don't like it, don't talk about it."

"Thank you very much for all this advice. Did you bring me here to give me a lecture?"

"Shh. Keep your voice down. You're shouting."

A wave of laughter and shouting wafted through the portholes. The partyers had returned, complaining loudly that everything in town was closed.

"I better go," she said.

"Damn! When can I see you again?"

"At breakfast."

"That's not what I mean. I want to see you alone. I want to be with you, Belinda."

"Let me think about it," she said, kissing him before checking that the companionway was clear. She hoped that she would not think about him again at all.

The following night, their last in Leticia, Claiborne tossed his big bash. This party would be classic Claiborne: some Argentine polo players, a famous Brazilian plastic surgeon, some Paraguayan generals in full uniform, a Bolivian tin heir, and a Nobel prize-winning poet from Chile. The guests started arriving by eight-thirty, and Belinda took her place beside her husband at the gangplank, welcoming them all, exchanging greetings and small talk. It was easy for her to smile. She had decided to leave Claiborne and the *Lone Star* in the morning.

Among the guests were coffee planters and cattle ranchers and men who spoke vaguely of being in the import-export line. There were bejeweled and beautiful woman said to be movie actresses, pop singers, or heiresses. Each guest brought at least one bodyguard.

Belinda knew now that she had to get away. Away from the *Lone Star*, away from Claiborne, and especially away from Brice. An affair with him now was out of the question. It didn't matter that Claiborne seemed to suspect that something had already happened between them. Let him! But he must never know the truth about their son. That was all that mattered.

She remembered the early days with Arden. How much in love they had been. How happy they were. And where did it get them? No, she told herself, it was important to be hardheaded about this.

Besides, Belinda was sure that no matter what Brice thought, her niece had not given him up. Tammy Lynn would never let him go so easily. And she was not going to get into a cat-fight with her over a man.

The night of Claiborne's party was perfect. The sky was clear, and a sultry breeze cut through the humid air. What did it matter that she did not want to be here? What did it matter that she didn't even know most of the guests, they had all been invited by Claiborne from among his extensive business and social network.

Ten round tables on the lower deck had been decorated with tropical flowers, and on the upper deck a local band was playing sambas and merengues.

When Belinda entered the grand salon, Claiborne made a short speech celebrating her virtues and handed her the long, distinctive blue kid box. She opened it and caught her breath. Inside on a bed of pale blue satin lay a necklace of glittering diamonds and sapphires linked by yellow gold. Beside it was a pair of matching earrings. Whatever else might be said about Claiborne Lurie, he did have perfect taste. He helped her put it on.

Charlene gasped. "I don't believe it!"

"Just beautiful!" said Valdene, making a mental note to have Buster buy her something just as nice when she got back to Galveston.

"Very nice," said Reba Twining politely, while reminding herself that worldly goods didn't matter.

"Gorgeous!" squealed Jennifer Varney. She suddenly feared that her Colombian emeralds might be slightly passé.

"Unbelievable!" said Ciprianna. Both Claiborne *and*

380

Carl would pay for this.

"Thank you, darling," Belinda said softly. This was his peace offering, she knew. How like him to do it in public.

It was time to welcome their guests.

Brice watched Belinda as she played the role of Mrs. Claiborne Lurie, international hostess and rich man's consort. She was very good, he had to admit it. She could even fool him.

He found her later at the bar and interrupted her conversation with the wife of a Brazilian plastic surgeon, a woman with a face of eerie perfection.

"I've missed you," he whispered.

She blushed. The doctor's wife smiled and moved on, leaving the two of them alone.

"You've got to leave him, you know."

"Leave who?"

"Your husband. Otherwise he'll just keep giving you these outrageously inappropriate gifts."

She laughed. "His guests seemed very impressed. Everyone tells me the necklace and earrings are beautiful."

"They're being polite," he insisted, touching her necklace with an appraiser's gesture. "You're too young for this kind of jewelry."

"Thank you, I guess."

"So when are you leaving him?"

"What are you talking about!"

"It's over. You must know it. You marriage is brain dead. Pull the plug, Belinda. Get on with your life."

"You mean sleep with you!"

"Anytime. I'm here for you Belinda."

"Leave me alone!" she hissed.

At that moment, Charlene passed and her ears pricked up at Belinda's command. She had consumed a lot of champagne, still steaming about the size of her father's gift to Belinda. And here she was with Brice de Young! Charlene was the one who had invited him, and he ought to be with her, not Belinda.

"My, my," she purred. "You two sure hit it off."

"I was just admiring your father's taste," Brice said.

"In some things," Charlene said, glaring at Belinda. "Is that why you told Brice to leave you alone?"

"It was a joke. Belinda and I kid around like that all the time."

"Oh? I didn't know you two were such good friends."

"Yes," Belinda said smoothly. "I gave Brice his first job in Galveston, actually."

"Yes," he said dryly. "You might say Belinda here gave me my start in Houston, too."

Charlene looked confused. Never a rocket scientist even when completely sober, it was difficult for her to follow these two after all the champagne she had consumed. Yet she sensed that there was something going on that she ought to know about. Worst of all, she sensed that Belinda and Brice were laughing at her. How dare they?

"Maybe you have my father by the balls, Belinda, but it won't last. We never had any use for the Garlands and we never will."

Belinda smiled. "Are you forgetting you're a Garland now, honey?"

Charlene was starting to feel dizzy. She needed a hit to clear her head.

"Excuse me," she said suddenly. "I think I see Ramon and I have to talk to him."

Chapter Forty-nine

Myles delivered the news to Miss Ruby with great pleasure. In the grand scheme of things, this little check was a small matter, but he was happy to tell the old woman she had nothing to worry about. He was surprised that she seemed reluctant to leave his office, however, and he realized something else was on her mind.

First she asked him about her house in Santo Domingo. The Lurie family had given her the house, deed and all, ten years earlier, and she wanted to know if there was any way they could take it back.

"No, ma'am," Myles assured her. "You've got that deed. It's all there in black and white. That property is yours."

She looked at him warily. "Even if I did something Mr. Lurie didn't like?" she pressed.

"Now, Miss Ruby, I know Claiborne Lurie has a reputation as a tough businessman, but why would he want to do something like that?"

She started to say something, then stopped again.

"No matter what you do," he assured her, "that house is yours."

"Well, I'm glad of that, 'cause I been thinking about getting something off my chest for a long time. And I think now's the time," Miss Ruby said. "It's about that girl I saw here last week."

"Miss Perillo? She's waiting for me outside now."

Ruby nodded. "I know. I saw her. I thought it was a sign. A sign that I ought to talk to her, but first I wanted to talk to you. I'm no hero, Mr. McLean. I want to tell you the story first, then you tell me what to do."

"Go ahead," Myles said, and then he sat back and listened as Ruby set out her story. It was a story with all the elements of a Gothic romance: a rich and sheltered young woman named Emmaline Lurie, who fell in love with a Galveston shrimper and eloped with him, defying her father and brother who cut her off from the family fortune until she came to her senses. But she never did, dying young and leaving behind a bereaved husband who wanted nothing to do with the Luries. And leaving behind a baby girl, too.

"I take it you think Miss Perillo is Emmaline's daughter?" Myles said.

"I know she is. She's the image of Miss Emmaline at that age. But that wasn't what first caught my eye. It was that charm bracelet. Miss Emmaline loved that bracelet."

"A bracelet can be bought and sold, Miss Ruby," he cautioned. "We'll need more proof than that."

"Oh I knew that little girl well, Mr. McLean. I tended her just after she was born, until her daddy sent me away. He was too proud for his own good, that one. But I know that girl like a map."

"Any identifying marks?"

"Oh yes, she had a little mole on the inside of her thigh."

Myles smiled and went to the door of the reception room where Rhonda Perillo was waiting to discuss her palimony case against Cordell Garland. He beckoned for her to join him and Miss Ruby. At first she looked puzzled. "Have a seat, Miss Perillo," he said. "Miss Ruby has just been telling me a very interesting story and I want you to hear it."

384

Claiborne's party had been a great success, and by the time the last of his guests left the *Lone Star* it was nearly dawn. Belinda followed him to his study. Since she discovered him with Ciprianna two nights earlier, he had been sleeping there. She didn't know or care if Ciprianna joined him. She suspected that even the crew knew what was going on, no matter how discreet Claiborne thought he was.

"I can't take this anymore," she said. "I want to leave."

He looked at her curiously, as if analyzing what she was saying. "But, darling, we'll only be on the river a few more days. Can't you wait?"

"No! If I have to go through this charade another day I'll die."

"Well, we wouldn't want that," he said, his voice smooth. She could easily be talking about new deck furniture for all the emotion he displayed. But that was her husband.

"What will I tell our guests?" he asked.

Is that all he cared about? His guests? "Tell them anything. Tell them I'm sick. Alexander is sick. There's a family emergency. I really don't care."

The beautiful necklace he had presented to her had failed to bring her around. It was time to resort to heavy ammunition.

"Wait, Belinda, before you go, there's something I'd like to show you." He walked toward the wall safe hidden behind a Manet painting and retrieved a large brown envelope. He handed it to her.

"What's this?" she asked.

"Why don't you find out for yourself?"

As she opened it, he watched her. He was very curious about her reaction to this material. "You know, Belinda, I've suspected from the beginning that there was someone else. You've seemed so unreachable most

385

of the time. You've always held some part of you apart from me, some part of you that I could never possess."

She looked up at him. "It sounds like you're talking about yourself, Claiborne. I'm not the one who's been flaunting my lover."

"No, and that's what has puzzled me. I'll admit I even went so far as to hire detectives, hoping to at least identify my rival."

"And I'm sure they told you nothing, because there's been no one else."

"Not exactly, darling. I'm afraid what I discovered was that I had the worst kind of rival: a dead man."

Now he was moving into dangerous waters. "Stop!" she warned him.

"I know you don't like hearing this, Belinda," he went on smoothly. "But you've canonized Arden Yates beyond belief. Let's face it, the man was never the saint you remember."

Belinda tried to shut out what he was saying by fumbling with the envelope clasp. But he proceeded unruffled.

"Fortunately, one of my little detectives had been retained in the past by another client who he refused to name, and although he was unable to turn up any proof of your current adultery, he did provide me with some very interesting photographs of your sainted husband."

Belinda had opened the envelope and was staring at the pictures. At the least the first two, and she could see that the others were in a similar vein, but she could not bear to look at them. They were scenes of some kind of sado-masochistic orgy, with men and women present, the women tied and bound, the men in leather masks. The photographs were in black and white, which somehow made them seem ever more sordid. In the second picture two of the men had removed their masks. She recognized Arden and Aynsley Adder.

"Well, what do you think?" Claiborne asked.

"This is what I think!" She tore up the photographs and tossed them into the air. He immediately bent down to retrieve the scraps.

"Please, Belinda. Have some sense! The servants will be here in the morning and they could piece these together!"

"Oh, Claiborne, you really are heartless!" she said, feeling she was going to be sick. "How could someone so smart be such a heartless fool! Did you think these pictures would get me to stay?"

"No, but I do think they should convince you to forget about Arden once and for all. You're a very ungrateful girl, Belinda. On this cruise alone I've given you jewelry, property, yet you refuse to cooperate."

She could not help smiling. "So you want my complete devotion while you continue to see Ciprianna," she said bitterly.

"Ciprianna is an old and dear friend . . ."

Belinda waved her hand to cut him off. "I've heard it before, Claiborne, and I've had enough. I'm leaving. I'll see you at the ranch when you get back. We'll talk about everything then."

"You'll never develop Delancy Street without my help," he shouted.

She turned and left the cabin.

He watched her go, puzzled and rather disappointed by her reaction. He had expected tears at least. Hadn't he just blown all her treasured illusions about her young husband to bits? She could hardly blame him. *He* wasn't the one at the orgy.

He told himself she would have to have time to digest the information. He had, of course, paid for the negatives and there would be no problem to reproduce more photographs should they become necessary. But he doubted that they would be. He expected that now that the shadow of Arden Yates had been removed from their marriage she would soon be brought to heel. He'd threatened her beloved project and still she

387

wouldn't bend. She was impossible!

His thoughts turned to another matter. Last night at the height of the party, Ciprianna had cornered him to complain about the jewels he had given Belinda. He would have to arrange for something of equal value to keep Ciprianna happy. Perhaps the diamond-and-platinum bracelet he had noticed at the Anaconda Hotel jewelry shop. He would send Ramon for it in the morning.

Belinda did not bother to say good-bye to anyone. As far as she was concerned, they were all Claiborne's guests anyway.

Would they even notice she was gone? She smiled to herself. Brice de Young would surely notice, but that was another reason not to say good-bye. She was anxious to put some distance between them. She didn't trust herself around him and she had a lot of thinking to do. About Arden and Claiborne and most of all, herself.

Aboard the *Lone Star* not a word was said about their missing hostess until Brice raised the matter. "What happened to Belinda?" he asked at dinner that night.

"Oh, she had some kind of family emergency and had to take the helicopter into Iquitos to get a plane home," Charlene said.

"Family emergency?" Cordell repeated. Valdene, too, looked up with concern. They were both thinking of Buster.

"Don't worry, honey," Charlene assured him as she helped herself from a silver tray proffered by the steward. "Just something with Alexander. Nothing for you to fret about."

Cordell relaxed and the steward moved on. Valdene concentrated on her fish. She did not want to choke on a bone.

After dinner there was much debate about what to do for their last night in Leticia. Charlene wanted to go dancing in town. Ciprianna wanted to gamble. The only gambling was at a private club. Señor Dorado had arranged for Claiborne to become a temporary member. They would all be his guests.

They split up into two parties: Claiborne and Bernie O'Higgins led the gamblers, who consisted of Colette de Young, the Varneys, and Ciprianna and Valdene. Ramon led Charlene and Cordell and Brice to a nightclub he knew about.

"I don't like the way you look, Carl," Ciprianna announced. "Stay in your cabin."

"I think I'll stay aboard, too," said Reba although no one had thought of her at all. "I'll look after Carl."

"Bueno," said Ciprianna. "Take care of my baby."

"Don't get into any trouble, you two," Claiborne said with a sly wink. Everyone laughed. What kind of trouble could they get into?

Reba and Carl adjourned to the *Lone Star*'s small screening room. Carl put on *Lady and the Tramp* and they settled in to watch from adjoining banquettes. When little Nutsy walked the last mile, Carl joined Reba on her banquette and offered her his pocket handkerchief to dry her tears.

The nightclub Ramon recommended was located in what had once been the ballroom of a viceroy's palace. The whole building was now crumbling and seedy, which only added to the decadent atmosphere. Ramon and his guests were led to a table near the dance floor. There was an English rock band on stage and during their breaks the D.J. played mostly American rock and roll.

"Let's dance," said Charlene, dragging Cordell on to the floor. He jerked stiffly, struggling to keep the beat. He hated dancing. He was not well coordinated and

389

had never been good at dancing or sports. His big brother Buddy, he recalled bitterly, was an excellent dancer.

While they danced, Brice looked around the room, almost expecting to discover Belinda among the crowd. But there was no sign of her. He couldn't believe she had just picked up and left without even saying good-bye.

When Charlene and Cordell returned to their table, Ramon and Brice had been joined by two Latin-looking men in perfectly tailored white suits, dripping in gold chains and each wearing a Rolex. To Brice they looked like drug dealers. They immediately started flirting with Charlene. Her smile got brighter; her laugh got louder. She was soon chattering away with them in rapid Spanish.

Cordell whispered into her ear. "Do you know what you're doing? Do you know what these guys are?"

"Of course!" she snapped, her eyes still flashing on the two dealers. "You don't think I'm going back empty-handed, do you?"

Suddenly they were interrupted by a roar from across the room. "Charlene! What the hell are you doing here?"

A hush fell on the room and even the dancers seemed frozen for the few minutes it took Harmon Lane and his entourage to stride across the dance floor and reach Charlene's table. The two dealers scattered like beetles, disappearing into the crowd. They were practiced at such quick getaways. It was a matter of survival.

"Harmon, honey!" Charlene squealed, forgetting for a moment that she was now a grand dame of Galveston and no longer wanted to act like an ambitious starlet. She even temporarily forgot about her consort Cordell who had been sulking while she chatted with the dealers.

She stood up and met Harmon with open arms. He lifted her and spun her around with such force it left her dizzy. By this time Cordell was also on his feet and extended his hand. Harmon stared at it blankly for a minute, unsure if Cordell was anybody. His bodyguards moved forward with an air of menace.

"Oh, Harmon honey, this here is my husband."

Relieved that the tall blond stranger was not just another pesky fan, Harmon shook his hand with enthusiasm.

"Me and Charlene go way back," he said by way of explanation. "Congratulations, by the way. I heard about you getting married."

Without waiting for an invitation, Harmon settled himself in one of the chairs vacated by the dealers and Charlene introduced him to the others.

"Me and the boys are down here scouting locations and doing a little research." His all-male entourage, which consisted mostly of bodyguards, settled into the tables around them, the better to watch out for potential assassins. Ramon slipped away to catch up with the beetles and do a little business.

Brice watched it all. Charlene throwing herself at the burnt-out movie star, her husband steaming with jealousy, and the two dealers conducting their business with Ramon in a dark corner of the club.

Belinda Garland was the only decent human being in the whole crowd, he thought, and she had the brains and good taste to abandon this ship. Why didn't he?

Chapter Fifty

Belinda stopped at Rancho Strega just long enough to pack some new clothes and look in on Alexander and Lourdes, then headed for Galveston.

She was still so angry at Claiborne that instead of staying at Aunt Carrie's this time, she set herself up in his gulfside mansion. They had spent most of their married life in the seclusion of Rancho Strega, and she hardly knew her way to the kitchen of the big Greek Revival house. Still, as long as they were married, what was Claiborne's was hers, and she had every right to enjoy it.

As soon as she unpacked, Belinda called Myles McLean to tell him she wanted to discuss an urgent personal matter.

It was time to file for divorce.

Now that she was back on the Island, she felt alive again. She had been hibernating at the ranch for too long. She had spent too much time trying to be the perfect Mrs. Claiborne Lurie and now she knew that was impossible. She would let Claiborne have his freedom, and if he wanted to make Ciprianna the next Mrs. Lurie, good luck to them both. They would need it! As for herself, Belinda intended to lose herself in the Delancy Street project. Real estate was a much better investment than men.

But it wasn't Claiborne who haunted her thoughts. It was Brice de Young. She found herself thinking about him at the oddest moments, like when she drove by the Maison Rouge, where they first made love. It was crazy. She knew she was attracted to him just because he was so out of the question. He was a womanizer. He was arrogant. But he had aroused feelings in her that not even Arden in the early days of their marriage had stirred. Chalk that up to the Amazon moonlight.

She was on a definite high this morning when she met with Myles in his office, and they spent two hours together, discussing her desire for a divorce and her plans for a new hotel and spa downtown. He seemed surprised that there had been no premarital agreement. "Old Claiborne must be more of a romantic than I thought," he remarked.

Belinda knew that it wasn't romance at all. Claiborne had wanted a son and she had given him one. Her son was still another reason why she should stay away from Brice. There was no way she was going to jeopardize Alexander's inheritance.

As she left Myles's office, she noticed a pretty red head in the waiting room. She looked vaguely familiar and Belinda smiled at her. To her surprise, the girl did not smile back. She just looked away.

This time when Belinda visited the Sand Castle, the reception was much warmer. Buster welcomed her with open arms, and Buddy and Zena took their cue from him. Valdene was still down in the Amazon on the *Lone Star*.

None of them asked her about Claiborne, though. It was as if he didn't exist for them. But he certainly existed for her, and now she knew just how cruel he could be. She could not forget those pictures. Why else show them to her except to hurt her? And the business of the Delancy Street property. All this time she had suspected one of her brothers had snatched it, and all along the culprit had been Claiborne.

Now she had asserted her independence by leaving him, but emotionally she was still trapped. If she wanted real freedom, she would have to develop Delancy Street, but how could she do it without seeking help from Buster or her husband.

Once Belinda was gone, the atmosphere aboard the *Lone Star* changed.

With her daughter-in-law out of the way, Valdene felt free to flirt with Ramon and Joel Varney. Cordell's opinion didn't concern her. Jennifer Varney's feelings didn't matter, either. She tried to flirt with Brice, too, but his mind seemed a thousand miles away.

Claiborne no longer bothered to hide his affair with Ciprianna. He moved back into the master stateroom and Ciprianna spent most of her time there with him.

Carl Rivers gallantly ignored the situation. He had the sympathy, if not the respect, of the rest of the party.

Reba Twining was the one exception. Watching Carl Rivers, she decided he was a true saint. A martyr to his marriage. Her respect for him grew.

Colette spent most of her time with Bernie O'Higgins. She never got tired of his stories.

Charlene was considering whether to end her own marriage. Cordell didn't travel well and he was an awful drag on her high spirits. She tried to discuss this with Brice, but he avoided her. Even Ramon seemed to prefer Joel Varney's company. Ramon and Cordell followed the tycoon around like two little puppies, eager to learn how to be great businessmen from a master.

The businessman knew what Lurie had paid for everything aboard the *Lone Star*, especially the art. Ramon and Cordell followed him from saloon to saloon, as Varney pointed out works of special interest.

He took fatherly interest in them and gave them some advice.

"Buy art," he said. "It's the hottest commodity around."

Ramon and Cordell ate this up.

"Take this little picture," Varney pointed to a small Degas ballerina that was less than twelve inches square. "Heck, it's not even a real painting, just chalk. But you know what makes it valuable?"

"It's beautiful?" Ramon said.

Varney looked surprised. "No, that's not it."

"The artist's dead," Cordell offered.

"That helps, but no. The real reason this is valuable is because it's one of three and a certain Saudi prince has the other two. When it went up for auction at Sotheby's a few years ago, the Arab's rep was authorized to go to a million for it. But Claiborne took a fancy to it and got it for one point one. I hear the prince's offered him twice that, but he won't sell. Our host can be ornery sometimes."

The three men stared at the little ballerina, pondering what could make a man spend millions for a chalk drawing.

One morning, as they neared Iquitos, Claiborne announced a skeet competition. The *Lone Star* was equipped with Remington 12-gauge pump guns in case of a terrorist attack. They were not the fine hunting guns he was used to, but they were perfectly sufficient for the contest.

Ciprianna was delighted. She was an excellent shot and, with Claiborne beside her, she blasted one clay pigeon after another out of the sky.

Ciprianna had always been fond of Claiborne. His patrician manner, his WASP good looks, his huge fortune, all appealed to her. He was also a devoted and generous lover. But he had never looked more attractive than he did since marrying Belinda Garland. The very idea that he was no longer so easily available to her made it imperative that she get him back. He must be brought to heel.

The idea of such a challenge set her hot blood burning. She resorted to her entire repertoire of sexual expertise, a repertoire gained long before she had hooked up with Carl, and employed her most arcane sexual tricks in her remaining days with Claiborne on the *Lone Star*.

As they neared their final stop on the Amazon, Ciprianna brought up the subject of marriage.

"It is ridiculous!" she steamed. "You and this . . . this—girl! You are making yourself a laughingstock! You're too old for her!"

Claiborne found her jealousy amusing. "My dear Ciprianna, what about you and Rivers? He's at least twenty years older than you. How old are you, anyway?"

"None of that makes any difference."

Claiborne, who was all logic and reason, who had great control of his passions, got a big kick out of Ciprianna's anger. Of course he privately agreed with her. His marriage had been a mistake. He would have been much happier with his longtime mistress.

"But what about Carl?"

She waved a hand, dismissing that minor inconvenience: her husband. "He will do anything to make me happy."

Claiborne smiled. "Even divorce you?"

"Of course."

"Very well, my dear. End things with Carl and we'll get married."

"What about Belinda?"

"I'll terminate our marriage as soon as you have ended yours."

The Lurie 747 was waiting for them in Iquitos and they were off to Houston.

Charlene bid a tearful farewell to Ramon and made him promise to visit her in Galveston.

Valdene said good-bye to Brice in Houston and said maybe she'd come up and visit Tammy Lynn sometime.

"Sure," said Brice without enthusiasm. He was already trying to figure out how he could reach Belinda.

Reba was delighted to be back in the United States, although she realized that she was going to miss Carl Rivers. He was so full of fascinating information. Such a brilliant man! What was he doing married to that spoiled rich bitch?

Charlene and Cordell returned to Oak Park Circle to find the house in a shambles. Chandler and her ferret were in her room, watching MTV. Charlene looked at her, sprawled on the bed, surrounded by dirty dishes and candy bar wrappers. Was it possible her daughter was fatter than ever? She would have to get the name of a good fat camp. She had heard of one in Ojai, California, that had a seven-week program. That was a possibility, unless she could find one that would take Chandler for longer. Like until she was twenty-one.

Charlene kissed her daughter on the cheek and looked at the bedspread with disgust. Empty cans of Coca-Cola were piled on the nightstand. Why couldn't Chandler at least drink Diet Coke? Didn't the girl have any pride?

She sighed. Being a good mother wasn't easy.

Manuel picked up Valdene and Reba at the airport in the white Garland limousine, but there was no sign of Buster. He wasn't waiting for them at the Sand Castle, either. When Valdene called his office at the Pink Tower they told her he was out and they didn't know where.

Something was wrong. She sensed it. And she had the strong suspicion that their bed had not been slept in while she was away.

"You know, Reba honey, I think my Buster's got somebody else," she remarked as Reba helped her unpack.

Reba shrugged her narrow shoulders. "Maybe it's a blessing in disguise," she said.

Valdene frowned. She was not in a good mood. It was one thing to have a one night stand with Brice de Young on the Amazon, it was another to have your husband cheating on you practically right under your nose. But of course Reba knew nothing about her little fling with Brice. Reba just didn't understand things like that. Sometimes Valdene wondered if poor little Reba had any glands at all.

Buster put down the phone. He was in Mozelle Bryant's cozy living room and sipping a Jack Daniel's, and now he stirred from the chintz armchair with all the grace of a bear coming out of hibernation.

"Got to be going, darlin'," he said.

Mozelle frowned. "So soon?"

"That was Manuel. He just dropped off Valdene and Reba at the Sand Castle. They'll be looking for me."

"You think so?" Mozelle's voice had an edge to it. She got along very well without Buster for many years, but now that they were knee-deep in hearts and flowers, she hated to see him go. Especially when she suspected he didn't want to leave either.

"You come back real soon, you hear?" she said as she kissed him in the doorway. His paws reached down and playfully squeezed her rump. "Hey," she said with mock alarm. "Don't waste it now."

"Don't you worry none, Mozelle," he assured her. "There's plenty of tunes left in this old violin."

* * *

No one had his number at Mozelle's, so Buster was not surprised to find the message light blinking when he stepped into the cool of the yellow El Dorado. He checked in with his office and learned that Valdene was back. No surprise. But Belinda was on the Island, too. Now what the devil was she up to, he wondered.

Tammy Lynn was waiting for Brice at Tootsie's Funland. "Welcome home," she said coolly. "Have a good trip?"

"Pretty good. Saw a lot of new fish, new fruit, new trees," he said. He ordered lunch for the two of them from the kitchen. He was anxious to see how the Funland staff had managed without him.

"What about Belinda? Did you see her?"

He glared at her. "It was her husband's boat, Tammy Lynn. Of course I saw her. Every day."

"You're in love with her, aren't you?"

"Don't be ridiculous!" he snapped, but he wondered how she could tell. If it was that obvious, how come Belinda couldn't see it? He tried to tell Tammy Lynn about Lurie's yacht, how enormous it was, like a floating palace, but she didn't want to hear it. All she wanted to know about was what had happened between him and her aunt.

"Look, Tammy Lynn," he finally exploded. "If I tell you I didn't sleep with Belinda, you wouldn't believe me."

"You're right. I wouldn't."

"Fine then, believe what you want. But the truth is that your aunt hates my guts and probably always will. Does that make you happy?"

It ought to, Tammy Lynn was thinking, so why didn't it?

Brice tried to console her. "What have you been doing while I was away?" he asked.

She was glad to change the subject and show him how well she could cope on her own. She didn't need him. "Well, I met this fabulous woman who lives one flight up from me. She's in television . . ."

"Oh really?" Brice said, without interest. His attention was already on the kitchen. The new cook would have to be told to stop overcooking the lamb.

"Oh, and I almost forgot. Waldo Brodsky has been trying to reach you."

"Waldo Brodsky? You're kidding!" Suddenly everything else, including Belinda Garland, faded away. This was serious.

"So you know him?"

"Of course I know him!" Waldo Brodsky was to the restaurant business what P.T. Barnum was to the circus, what Bill Graham was to rock concerts. He had developed the concept of dining out as entertainment and his restaurants Splendora in New York and Moonwalk in Los Angeles were notorious.

"Don't tell me he's planning to open a restaurant in Houston and wants me?" Brice said.

"Not quite, but he wants to talk to you about a guest chef gig at Moonwalk next month."

"I'll have to look at my calendar," Brice said coolly.

"Oh, don't give me that," Tammy Lynn laughed. "You know what this means as well as I do."

He could hardly wait to get to the phone so he could call Brodsky back. This was the opportunity he'd been waiting for. A week in Los Angeles at Moonwalk. He was already thinking about the menu. He'd knock them dead.

Chapter Fifty-one

The day after they returned to New York, Ciprianna insisted that Carl accompany her to her office to discuss a divorce. Traveling downtown in their limo from their Fifth Avenue penthouse to her garment district showroom, Ciprianna brought up the matter. She used the car as a rolling office, design studio, and changing room.

"Do you hear me, darling? It's over between us."

Before Carl had time to answer, she was taking a call on the car phone, and then they had reached the showroom and she was gathering up her agenda, sketchbook, and lipstick. He and the surviving Shih Tzu followed her out of the limo and up to her office.

Behind her desk, piled high with budgets, media plans, and ad mock-ups, Ciprianna looked every inch the harried executive. Only her legs, curled catlike beneath her, and the huge Helmut Newton portrait of her and her dogs on the wall behind her gave a hint of Ciprianna's other roles as wife and mistress.

While a young French woman in a smart pink uniform began to give Ciprianna a manicure, she discussed her plans with Carl. Or, rather, she listed her plans and Carl listened.

"Naturally, I want this to be fast and painless for both of us," he said.

"Are you sure you've given this enough thought?" He seriously doubted that Claiborne Lurie was going to come through with a marriage license after all these years, but Ciprianna seemed convinced. And he did want Ciprianna to be happy.

Carl noticed that she had cut her hair since they returned from the cruise. It now came to the tips of her ears, full and curly, and it gave her a younger look. A new look.

He looked around at the pink-and-mauve walls lined with framed press clips, photos of Ciprianna through the years, and ads for the myriad products her design staff conceived there: cosmetics, perfume, sportswear, all with the Ciprianna logo. His wife was a determined woman. No wonder she believed she'd finally hooked Claiborne.

A red-jacketed manservant brought in a sushi lunch on laquered trays while she explained why they would have to dissolve their marriage. She never once mentioned Claiborne Lurie. She only spoke of "irreconcilable differences" and "incompatibility."

Carl shrugged. He should be on his way downtown. The Stock Exchange would be closing soon. He had people waiting. What did it matter? When Ciprianna beckoned, he came. It was ever thus. He found himself looking forward to the single state as he had once looked forward to vacations. He was feeling his age.

Ciprianna had expected a scene. She was relieved that Carl was taking this news so well. Come to think of it, he was taking it entirely too well.

"It has to be this way," she said, wanting to be sure he understood that their marriage was over.

"Do you hear me, darling? It is over between us."

"Very well, my dear," he said. "I will have one of my attorneys draw up the papers. Unless you prefer to have your own representation."

"No, no, that's not necessary. This is perfectly amicable after all."

"Yes, perfectly amicable."

Ciprianna frowned. This was all too easy. Was it possible that her beloved Carl had someone else? Could he have been fooling her all along?

No! That was out of the question! He still adored her. He was merely happy for her. Who wouldn't be happy for her? She was about to marry one of the richest men on earth.

Nevertheless, it troubled her that Carl didn't seem the least bit jealous. What in the world was he thinking of?

Valdene was writing songs every morning. She was determined to reactivate her singing career and branch out from gospel to secular music.

She invited a few musicians out to the Sand Castle to rehearse and intended to turn the guest house into a recording studio. That afternoon she had a few out to work on her songs and jam a bit.

When Reba came in at the end of the rehearsal, she was surprised to find Valdene laughing and joking with the boys. One of them gave her a kiss that was more than affectionate, then they packed up and left, leaving Reba and Valdene alone in the guest house.

"It's coming together," Valdene said with satisfaction. "I have that old feeling." More than a musical feeling, actually. Her sexual juices were flowing after several hours in the company of these young, hot musicians. But having a fling with one of them under Buster's nose was impossible. Times like this made her appreciate Reba.

"I guess so," Reba said softly as she moved among the tables, straightening the room, collecting the cans of Pearl beer and cleaning out the ash trays.

"Why don't you leave that for the maid, honey?"

Valdene said impatiently. "You don't have to do that."

Reba shrugged.

Valdene looked at her with concern. "You haven't been yourself since we came back from that cruise. What's wrong?"

"I don't know," Reba said. "I have been feeling poorly. I sleep all night, but in the morning I'm so tired it's like I never slept at all." She was still having those disturbing dreams about Carl Rivers, but she did not recall them when she woke up.

Valdene moved closer, taking her friend by the shoulders. "Now see here, don't you get yourself all tired out, darlin'. You know how I depend on you. I need you, honey."

Reba nodded.

"After all we've been through," Valdene went on. "All we've shared. And you just wait: my career's going to be bigger than ever."

Suddenly the sound of the lawn mower came through the air. They both looked through the picture window that overlooked the grounds and they could see Felipe, the gardener, atop the tractor. He was shirtless, and his muscled arms and torso glowed with sweat. Valdene drew the curtains, cutting off the afternoon sunlight and plunging the room into darkness.

"Whoo whee, Reba, I'm so tired from all this workin' I think I'll take me a little rest. Why don't you come in to the bedroom and have a lie down with me?"

Reba stood up and followed her adored Valdene into the bedroom.

As he headed from Mozelle's house to the Sand Castle, Buster Garland was a happy man. The air-conditioning in the canary-yellow Cadillac was turned up to near freezing, Lyndon was on the front seat beside him, and the tape deck was playing Patsy Cline.

404

Everything, the air-conditioning, the Cadillac, the music, and Buster himself was going at full blast.

Things were falling into place nicely, just the way he expected them to. What did the doctors know anyway? He was feeling better than ever. His affair with Mozelle was making a new man of him. Imagine! Almost two years ago he'd thought he was dying and now he felt like twenty-two. Well, maybe thirty-two. And Garland, Inc., was in good hands. Buddy was a fine boy, who would preserve and protect everything he'd worked to build.

He chuckled to himself and the sound of his laugh startled Lyndon into waving his tail. Buster reached over and stroked the old black dog under his neck.

Mozelle had restored his confidence, his manhood. Two years with Valdene Sykes had almost broken him. She had him believing his hound dog days were over. Sending her off alone on that Amazon cruise had been a brilliant stroke. Gave him time to put his affairs in order and clear his mind. He knew now what he had to do next: He would get rid of Valdene. Maybe he'd even marry Mozelle. It was about time.

As he entered the Sand Castle, tossing his straw Panama hat jauntily onto the marble-topped chest in the hallway, a gesture which always annoyed Valdene, he called out his wife's name.

"Mrs. Garland's not here, sir," said Ramon, picking up the hat and placing it gently on the hall hatrack. "She's still in the guest house."

Buster sniffed. He had forgotten about her rehearsal. Good! If Valdene was involved in her career, she would not feel so abandoned when he gave her the bad news. In fact, he would help her launch her comeback. Delighted with his own generosity, he headed out to the guest house.

As soon as Carl Rivers returned to his own office,

he placed a call to Galveston. Odd, how he had dreaded losing Ciprianna all these years she was making a fool of him with Claiborne Lurie, and now that she was finally leaving him he felt only relief. For Carl Rivers had fallen in love: he lived only to make Reba Twining his.

Someone finally answered at the Sand Castle: a male voice with a Mexican accent, presumably a butler or houseman, informed Mr. Rivers that Miss Twining was not in at present. Carl left word for her to call him in New York.

He sighed as he replaced the phone and thought of Reba's thin little face, her watery gray eyes. He had waited years to see that kind of devotion in a woman's eyes; he could wait a few hours longer.

Valdene watched from the bed as Reba stripped down obediently in the shadowy light of the guest house bedroom. She smiled benevolently at the sight of Reba's sixty-nine-cent special K-mart white cotton pants and matching bra. They reminded her of the kind of underwear the girls at the Pentecostal home used to wear. Making love to Reba was sometimes like making love to her own self at fourteen. Reba had just never grown up.

Reba approached her, the way Valdene had taught her. She could not bring herself to look in Valdene's eyes, and her modesty and discomfort only excited Valdene more. As she drew closer, Valdene suddenly reached for Reba and kissed her on the mouth. Reba squirmed instinctively, but Valdene kept on, her warm tongue exploring Reba's mouth until she could no longer hide the fact that she was excited and began to respond. As Reba proceeded to do what Valdene had taught her, Valdene asked a question.

"Tell me, darlin', what do you think of when you're doing this I've always wondered."

406

Reba's mouth was full and she was unable to answer, but might have said: "I think of heaven."

Claiborne Lurie instructed his Houston lawyers to draw up divorce papers. Since Belinda had decamped from Rancho Strega he intended to charge her with abandonment. But the fact that he might have to share half his assets with her pained him greatly.

In his office at the ranch he studied the photographs of his wife with Myles McLean. No, there was nothing there on which to hang a divorce. Nothing to hold over her head when it came to the property settlement. And then there was the matter of Alexander's custody. Allowing the child to live with Belinda was out of the question. His son must not come under the influence of the Garland element in his heritage.

No, Claiborne thought, as he looked up at his Gainsborough. Something had to be done about Belinda. He considered the idea of something permanent.

Buster noticed that a pall had descended on the Sand Castle since Valdene's return. None of his servants said anything and yet he sensed they disliked Valdene. When he told them she would be leaving they'd probably toss a barbecue.

Feeling good, he strode down the path to the guest house. Felipe the gardener was atop the lawn mower and moving closer to the little house. The air was sweet with the smell of new-mown grass.

Inside, the living room was still in disarray, with ashtrays spilling over onto the carpet and the bowls of guacamole turning brown. The tape was playing Loretta Lynn. The room was thick with stale cigarette smoke and a pungent herby smell of marijuana that Buster associated with Mexican brothels of his youth.

Suddenly the silence of the room was broken by the

sound of a woman's moans. He recognized Valdene's voice and stepped faster toward the bedroom. The door was open. He stood in the doorway, his great bulk filling it and cutting off what little light remained. The two women sat up suddenly, both naked. Reba grabbed a sheet to cover herself, but Valdene, her dark eyes filled with rage, glared at her husband.

"What are you doing here?" she demanded.

Buster had not seen a sight like that since his youth carousing in Juárez bars, and he was not sure he was seeing it even now. He pulled out his pocket handkerchief and dabbed at his glistening brow, while his heart raced faster.

The room began to spin. The sky darkened and the first resounding clap of thunder was heard.

The days had flown by, and Belinda was barely aware that Claiborne and his guests were back from the Amazon and going their separate ways. She knew that Brice de Young was back in Houston, though. He had been calling and leaving messages everywhere, but she was not going to start up with him again.

She lost herself in interviewing architects, contractors, and potential investors. Somehow, she would develop the Delancy Street complex on her own, without any help from Claiborne or Buster.

Every day, Belinda returned from meetings exhausted, and collapsed into bed. The Lurie mansion's master bedroom had a secluded patio garden lined with oleanders and a magnificent view of the Gulf, but she hardly paused to appreciate it.

She was back on the treadmill again, determined to get Delancy Street going as soon as possible, before Claiborne pulled the plug and filed for divorce.

The first evening she had free, she was delighted to seclude herself in the master bedroom. She wrapped herself in a black silk robe, lit a fire on the marble

408

hearth, and was planning to watch the sunset, then get some badly needed sleep. Much to her disappointment, a sudden storm marred the sunset, and the only view from her bedroom was of the teeming rain, beating noisily against the French doors.

Belinda stared out at it nevertheless. There was something very primal about the darkness and the rain, the roar of the thunder and occasional flash of lightning. The palm trees outside swayed and bent with the wind. She flipped on a switch that lit the patio and suddenly the whole private garden was flooded with light.

Something—or someone—darted into a dark corner thicket of oleanders.

She knew at once with an animal's instinct that someone was out there in the darkness. Suddenly aware that the brightly lit bedroom made her an easy target, she turned off the lights, plunging the room into darkness. Outside was still floodlit, and she peered out, hoping to get a look at whoever was out there.

Belinda had relished the privacy of the mansion, but now she regretted not bringing up some of the staff from the ranch. The mansion had a caretaker, but she had given him the night off. And it was barely seven o'clock. She had not yet bothered to turn on the elaborate security system. She had never shared her husband's paranoia.

At least not until now.

Maybe, she thought, she had scared the intruder off. She drew her robe around her more tightly and looked again. It was no use, she had lost sight of whoever it was.

She noticed that the outside floodlights had a regulator, and she proceeded to dim them gradually. Maybe darkness would smoke him out.

There was a movement in the thicket. Closer. She turned to her phone. Time to get real and stop being brave. With her back to the French doors, she picked up the receiver and started to punch up 911, until she heard the frantic banging on the doors, so loud and hard over the sound of rain and thunder that she was surprised the glass didn't shatter.

With a sinking sensation, realizing the doors were not even locked, she turned to face whoever was out there.

Her stomach sank. She put back the phone and went to the door, pulling it open. "Come in," she sighed.

Shaking like a wet puppy, Brice de Young stepped inside.

"What are you doing here?" she demanded.

"I had to see you, Belinda. You never return my calls. You left the *Lone Star* without saying good-bye. I don't understand. I thought I was finally getting through to you."

Maybe you were, she thought, but all she said was, "You better get out of those wet clothes. I'll get you one of Claiborne's robes."

He grinned. "Always practical, Belinda. Always thinking of the really important things."

"Please don't be sarcastic," she said. "I can still call the police."

"And have me arrested for being sarcastic? Is that a crime?" Without waiting for an answer or the promised robe, he had begun to peel off his wet jeans and T-shirt. He stood before her. The only light in the room came from the fireplace.

Impulsively, she switched on the room lights, hoping to dispel the sensuality that surrounded him like an aura, but in the unsparing light she was even more aware of his well-muscled body and his unwavering stare. Once she had looked into those eyes and seen them full of gold and laughter. Now she saw only desire.

"Why did you fire me, Belinda? You dumped me like spoiled milk. Every time I get close to you, you

410

run away. When I cornered you on the *Lone Star* you acted like I had typhoid or something."

"You're my niece's lover."

"I am not her lover. Maybe I slept with her a few times . . ."

"Oh, Brice," she sighed. He really didn't get it.

"But I swear there's been nothing between us since you fired me."

"Brice, she's running your catering business. You're together every day. She told me so herself."

"It's business. She has a good head for business. She even lined up a gig for me in L.A. with Waldo Brodsky. I'm leaving in a few weeks. But when I come back, I'm cutting her off. I swear I haven't touched her, and believe me, it hasn't been easy fighting her off."

"But you've kept her around all this time."

He shrugged. "There was another reason."

"What's that?"

"I knew that sooner or later Tammy Lynn would lead me back to you."

Belinda looked at the ceiling in mock exasperation.

"No, really," he insisted. "And she did, too. If she hadn't gotten me back here for the Mardi Gras, I would never have met Charlene Lurie. She's the one who invited me on your husband's cruise."

"Don't tell me you've slept with that tramp, too!" The words were out before she had time to think. They sounded possessive. They sounded as if she actually cared. He caught it, too, and for a second a more calculating look flashed into his brown eyes. In that moment he knew he had her.

"No," he insisted. "Charlene's not my type." He did not want to get into a discussion of his sex life. His one-night stand with Valdene Garland aboard the *Lone Star,* his brief tryst with Lauren Armour, the parade of women he met through his work, none of them meant anything to him, but he sensed that Belinda

411

might not understand. Women like her got strange ideas.

"It doesn't matter to me, Brice. Don't you get the message? We had a fling. That's all. It happens to people all the time."

"Not with you, Belinda," he said softly. "I don't think you have too many flings."

"What about my husband? I *am* married, you know."

He laughed. A harsh, bitter laugh. "Don't give me that. Everyone on that boat knew he was sleeping with Ciprianna." He paused, fearful for a minute that he might have gone too far. Above all, he did not want to hurt her. "You did know that, didn't you?"

Belinda had turned away, so he could not see her tears. Yes, her marriage to Claiborne had been born out of a shrewd calculation, but it was still painful to be reminded that she had never been anything more than a property to him. He had acquired her and her unborn child in a package deal, scooping her up in a weak moment the way he scooped up the Delancy Street warehouse or an interesting piece of jewelry. He had never even tried to love her. At least she had tried.

Brice had moved closer to her and, gently gripping her shoulders, he forced her around to face him. His eyes met hers, and she sniffed delicately. She'd be damned if she'd blow her nose in front of him. He'd seen enough of her weakness already.

"Look me in the eye, Belinda. Look me in the eye and tell me what we had was just a fling. Tell me you haven't thought about that night we had together a thousand times, just like I have."

She looked back at him and prepared to tell him just that, but she had barely begun when his mouth was on hers, and instead of pushing him away she drew him closer. The sheer power of his heat seemed to suck her into a whirlpool as all the suppressed

412

desires and yearnings forced her to him.

"We've had this date for a long time, Belinda," he said as he gently loosened the silk cord that held her robe closed, then slipped it off her shoulders. The robe fell to the floor in a pile of black silk, like a snake's discarded skin.

His mouth was on hers, his hard, insistent lips unwilling to be put off any longer, and her own newly freed appetite welcomed him. Her hunger, so long denied, demanded satisfaction at last.

As the rain beat against the French doors, meeting the roar of thunder, his strong but subtle hands brought her alive. It was as if she became another person and shrewd, level-headed Belinda Garland could only watch in awe as a soft and pliant woman yielded to his force and then joined him in exploring each other's mysteries.

"I still think you should have let me call a doctor, Buster honey."

Buster eyed his wife uneasily, still profoundly disturbed by what he had seen going on in the guest house. No wonder he had collapsed! But now that he was feeling better, sitting up in his bed—alone—he was anxious to be up and around. But what to do about Valdene? That was a puzzler.

Of course he had been a fool to think that Valdene would somehow keep him young, buy him some time. But . . . holy heaven! Another sight like he'd come upon in the guest house and he'd surely be in his grave!

She hovered over the bed, but he waved her away. He couldn't even divorce her without the story leaking out. Damn, he had his pride! No, for the time being he'd keep Valdene and her friend Reba in the guest house. Maybe, God willing, she'd up and decide on a divorce herself. He'd just start going about providing

413

her with grounds.

He thought of Mozelle Bryant. This revenge might be very sweet indeed.

Chapter Fifty-two

Days later Belinda found herself looking at the scale model that represented her architect's plans for the Delancy Street renovation, but her mind was somewhere else. She was thinking of Brice, and the very thought of him made her smile.

"I hope you're not laughing at my design," the young architect said, only half kidding.

Belinda shook her head. "No, of course not. Only, I was just thinking . . ."

"Yes?"

"You have made plans for a restaurant here, haven't you?"

"Oh, yes, of course. Look here, it will be a glassed-in area with a fantastic view of the harbor."

"Yes," Belinda nodded. "Fantastic."

"I understand Mr. Lurie is a great gourmet. We couldn't build this project and skip a restaurant, now could we," the architect added, feeling more relaxed.

Belinda looked at him blankly. "Mr. Lurie?" she repeated.

"Mr. Lurie, your husband."

"Oh, yes, my husband," she repeated, and turned her attention back to the model. "My husband is not involved in this at all."

But she would have to do something about Claiborne, and she could not delay it much longer.

Belinda had suggested a meeting this weekend, but he

put her off, even encouraged her to keep Alexander in Galveston with her. She strongly suspected that he was entertaining a woman there. Probably Ciprianna. The tabloids were full of stories about the designer's pending divorce from Carl Rivers. It was clear everyone was waiting for the other shoe to drop: namely that he and Belinda would divorce, too, so that he would be free to marry his longtime mistress.

Belinda welcomed a divorce. Any property settlement was sure to help her develop Delancy Street that much faster.

Charlene was furious. Mr. T. had torn up her closet and found the cocaine stash she had brought back from Colombia. White powder was strewn all over her bedroom.

"Gee, it does look like snow," observed Chandler when her mother called her in to witness the damages.

Charlene realized immediately that she had made a mistake. All she needed was for her daughter to find out about her habit. Chandler would be uncontrollable.

"It's talcum powder," she snapped. "Now take that animal and go to your room."

She knelt on the rug and tried to scoop some of the powder up, but it was all gone. Fifteen thousand dollars worth of cocaine, gone. And she felt awful. Her head was splitting. Her nose was running. Her sinuses ached. She got on the phone to call Ramon.

And at Rancho Strega, Claiborne Lurie was enjoying a pleasant weekend with his beloved Ciprianna. Rather like a prehoneymoon, he decided. And what better place to spend it than at his ranch where he reigned supreme over eight thousand acres and where pesky government restrictions on off-season hunting need not concern him. Here at Rancho Strega, Claiborne Lurie ruled.

* * *
416

Brice was in Los Angeles. This was supposed to be a big break, cooking in one of Waldo Brodsky's flamboyant restaurants, but it wasn't working out that way. Tammy Lynn had arranged it, and now Tammy Lynn was sabotaging it. She had ordered the wrong supplies, equipment was missing, assistants mysteriously failed to show up. He saw what she was up to. She wanted him to fail so he'd need her. It wasn't going to work.

Since his night with Belinda, he had found Tammy Lynn more and more unbearable. Now, more than ever, he was determined to make it so that when he asked Belinda to marry him it would be clear that he only wanted her, not her money.

Although, he had to admit, her money would be nice, too.

What was he thinking? If all he wanted was money, he could have Tammy Lynn. The woman would barely let him out of her sight. Meanwhile, she was pulling the purse strings ever tighter.

He called Belinda from California. In Galveston she was deep into plans for her hotel spa.

They talked for hours, until Belinda pleaded that she needed to sleep. She had an important meeting with Claiborne the next day. He was going to fly in and she was sure he was ready to talk divorce.

Ciprianna had spent many happy hours at Rancho Strega, but she had not been a guest there since Claiborne's marriage to Belinda. This visit was like coming home.

"I feel like a bride," she said, as she and Claiborne were having breakfast in bed. It was six in the morning, an obscenely early hour for her, but she was willing to accommodate herself to Claiborne's schedule.

"Ah, yes, a bride," Claiborne said thoughtfully. "Frankly, darling, it's rather hard to picture you as a

417

blushing bride."

After all these years, Ciprianna was attuned to Claiborne's ways, and she certainly recognized this tone. It was the "second thoughts" tone she had heard so many times over the years. Before and after Belinda. She could not believe he was going to make a fool of her again.

"Don't tell me you're going to back out of this wedding?" she said.

"Darling, we'll talk about it later." He left her there while he showered in the bathroom. She could have him singing to himself.

This too was a familiar song. All too familiar. A sickening sense of déjà vu swept over her. This time there was no turning back. Carl had been entirely too happy to dissolve their marriage. At this very minute the papers were waiting for his signature. She was convinced that he had someone in the wings: but she had tolerated it because she had Claiborne. And now she didn't. Claiborne was going to betray her again.

Betrayed by both her husband and her lover! It was too much to bear. She lifted up the breakfast tray and tossed it off the bed, shattering the china. The clatter cleared her head.

Ciprianna brooded about her situation while they dressed to go hunting, and headed out to the field.

Claiborne was an expert marksman. Even at his age he did not need glasses and he liked to brag that he never missed a target. But he saw no sense in taking chances. When he caught sight of the big red-tailed pheasant, he got out of the Rover, motioned to Ciprianna to keep silent, and slowly edged up the tree as the bird came into target range.

Ciprianna watched him with her binoculars as her beloved steadied himself against a branch, positioned his rifle and fired. Then she fired, too.

The gun's retort filled the air, closely followed by another as the dry branch under Claiborne's boot cracked and he fell to the ground, setting off another shot as he hit.

Ciprianna scurried to her beloved's side. She was sure he was dead.

She calmly returned to the Rover and headed back to the house. Once there she took up the phone and dialed a familiar number. A man answered.

"Hello, Carl?" she said crisply. "I am at Rancho Strega. You must come at once. I need you."

Carl Rivers abandoned his attempts to contact Reba Twining and, chartering a plane, he hastened to rescue his wife, spiriting her quickly away from the ranch, leaving Claiborne to be discovered by a ranch hand.

Part III
Autumn 1986

Chapter Fifty-three

After his mysterious hunting accident, Claiborne Lurie lingered in a coma for six months, yet the news that he was finally dead filled Rhonda Perillo with sudden dread. Myles McLean must have expected something like this, she thought, because he had brought the news in person that morning. Her grandfather had passed away. She had never met him face-to-face and now she never would.

"What's next?" she asked. "Will I have to go to the funeral? Will I have to go to court?"

Myles spoke to her gently. "One question at a time, Rhonda. First, you don't have to do anything you don't want to do. I believe it would be a good idea to go to the funeral, though. I can go with you if you like. We'll keep the whole thing low key."

"And then?"

"Then comes probate. They'll have to submit Claiborne's will to probate. Sam Houston Lurie's will stated that the Lurie trust was to be divided among his grandchildren, but not until the last of his children passed away. That was old Claiborne. Sam Houston was pretty mad at your mother for running off and marrying Perillo. The will was his way of cutting her off. But I guess he didn't want to cut off her children."

"So, what you're saying is that Claiborne Lurie only inherited the use of his daddy's money, but he couldn't decide who to leave it to?"

Myles nodded. "You got it, girl. The probate will show just what belonged to old Claiborne and what belonged to the Lurie trust. And I believe that you are entitled to a significant share of that trust."

Rhonda's hand started to tremble, and before she could stop it, her coffee cup slipped and shattered on the terrace's tile floor.

Charlene was devastated. Poor daddy! She flew down to the ranch immediately, just to be sure Belinda did not make off with any more valuables than she had already.

Belinda felt no sadness at the news that her husband was dead. Only relief. Now she could get on with her life. Alexander's inheritance was safe. And so was her own share of the Lurie millions. She could marry Brice.

Claiborne le Torneau Lurie's funeral would have done credit to a robber baron. It was an echo of Galveston's glorious past, with a parade of twenty limousines, an honor guard of Texas Rangers, and an assortment of patricians and dignitaries that included the governor of Texas and newly appointed Senator Aynsley Adder. Radio station KGBC broadcast the service live. Galvestonians who had never met Claiborne Lurie lined the route to 22nd and Winnie where the funeral service would be conducted at the Trinity Episcopal Church that Lurie's ancestors had built.

Belinda felt no sorrow, only relief. She and Claiborne had had their differences, and their marriage was over long before his accident, but his long, drawn-out death, was not something she would have wished on anyone. And yet, if he hadn't been hurt, he would surely have tried to stop her developing Delancy Street. So, while Claiborne took six months to die, she had been free to do exactly what she wanted and the two things she most

424

wanted were to make Delancy Street a success, and to spend the rest of her life with Brice de Young.

She was not hypocrite enough to don heavy mourning, and she had opted for a simple black linen suit. Her blond hair was pulled back in a chignon, under a black straw hat. As they entered the Gothic Revival church, the men were given boutonnieres of red carnations and baby's breath. Impulsively, Belinda took one for herself and pinned it to her lapel. She had not even brought Alexander. He was too young to understand all this anyway. As far as he knew, his father was just away on another long business trip. Most of their marriage had been one long business trip anyway, she thought bitterly.

Belinda sat among the mourners, staring at the light streaming through the Tiffany window as the choir sang "Jerusalem My Happy Home" and Claiborne's white-and-gold coffin was borne out into the street. Although her brother Buddy was by her side, she never felt more alone in her life. She had asked Brice to stay away from the funeral because she feared Charlene or Ciprianna would create a scene. Sure enough, Ciprianna and Carl Rivers seized a highly visible front pew for the funeral service.

Claiborne's mistress was swathed in more black veils than his wife or daughter, and her sobs were the loudest in the church. She would miss him the most, Belinda thought. Strange that Ciprianna had never visited him while he lay dying; maybe she wanted to remember him as the man he had been.

Belinda grew impatient as the service dragged on. She was anxious to get back to Delancy Street. The renovation was almost complete and she had to start making plans for the gala opening.

On the arm of her brother Buddy, she followed the coffin outside, but on the way she noticed the same odd-looking redhead she had seen in Myles McLean's office. This time she was standing with Chandler's old nurse, Miss Ruby. The girl definitely glared at her, and

425

Belinda again wondered why. She was sure they had never met.

The mourners gathered on the lawn outside the church, and Buddy drifted away, working the crowd, as Belinda accepted condolences from a steady parade. She noticed the girl was still lingering on the fringes of the crowd. It was as if she wanted to say something, yet kept backing off. Then she turned to the man she was with and Belinda realized it was Myles McLean. She barely had time to digest that information before Myles approached her, leaving the girl standing by a palm tree with Miss Ruby.

"Belinda!" he said cheerily. "I'm sorry to see you under such sad circumstances." He took her hand as if to underline his sincerity.

"You're very kind," she said for about the thirtieth time that morning.

"If you don't mind, Belinda, there are some things I'd like to discuss with you," he said. His voice had dropped to a whisper and she had to lean closer to hear him.

"I'd like that, Myles, but my car is here to take me to the Confederate Club for the reading of Claiborne's will. I hope you understand."

"I'm afraid that's just the point, darlin'," Myles said. "There are some complications about the will that I'd like to brief you about before you hear the news from your husband's lawyers."

Her curiosity aroused, Belinda suggested Myles ride with her to the reading. Buddy looked delighted to be free of the chore. Myles followed her into the back of the limo. She was surprised that he immediately raised the window between them and the chauffeur. What could be so confidential?

Belinda thought that Claiborne had made his estate plans very clear, especially after the birth of their son. He was very anxious to preserve the vast Lurie fortune for Alexander to eventually control. Belinda would inherit half of Claiborne's estate in trust for their son. Charlene was to get the other half. But that estate only

426

represented a small part of what Claiborne had accumulated in his lifetime.

For tax purposes, most of his estate had been folded into the Lurie Trust created by Claiborne's father, Sam Houston Lurie. The root of that trust was preserved by Grandfather Lurie in a foundation controlled by members of the family, which was to be shared by his descendants.

"But isn't that the same thing?" Belinda asked, thinking of Charlene and Chandler and Alexander, even as another thought came sneaking into her consciousness. She recalled a faded photograph of a Mardi Gras queen and Claiborne's angry reaction to her questions about his family.

"I'm afraid not, darlin'," Myles continued. "You see, Claiborne had a sister . . ."

"I was afraid of that."

She glanced out of the window of the car and caught a glimpse of Charlene and Cordell as their car passed Belinda's. That was Charlene, always competitive. She thought of the car phone and was tempted to call Charlene at that moment and share this bit of news, but decided to wait. She wanted to enjoy the full impact on Charlene's face when she learned she was going to have to share one half of the income from the Lurie Foundation with a long lost aunt.

"Emmaline Lurie died years ago," Myles went on.

"Oh?"

"But she left a daughter. As we see it, the daughter is entitled to one half the income from the Lurie Foundation. Probably more, too. We'll have to sit down with Lurie's lawyers. But I wanted you to know about it first. I hope you're not disappointed."

"Disappointed?"

"It's bound to cut into your share."

"Oh, Myles," she laughed. "Just as long as it cuts into Charlene's, too."

* * *

427

They gathered in the dark, paneled private dining room of the Confederate Club for the reading of the will. And then came the news. After lunch, as Bernardo O'Higgins explained the terms of her father's will, Charlene grew more and more upset.

She had been raised as her father's only heir. Then he had gone and married Belinda Garland and fathered a child. Suddenly Charlene went from heiress of one hundred percent to a mere one-third. She bore up.

But now her father's attorneys were making her feel like she was in a strange new mall without one credit card.

"I don't understand," she repeated for the third time that hour. "Run that by me again."

"Well, Mrs. Garland, most of your father's income derived from a trust created by your grandfather, Sam Houston Lurie. There were several reasons for this. First, of course, Sam Houston Lurie wanted to avoid income taxes wherever possible."

"Of course," nodded Charlene. Avoiding taxes was certainly something she approved of.

"And he also wanted to protect the Lurie wealth from fortune hunters."

"Naturally," Charlene said, glaring at Belinda.

"Particularly your aunt's husband."

"My aunt?" Charlene repeated.

"Yes . . ."

And that was how Charlene learned she had a long-lost cousin who had a fifty percent claim to the Lurie Trust.

Belinda was explaining the day's surprises to Brice. They were in the bedroom of the penthouse suite she had taken at the Delancy Street Center. She wanted to be on the scene to oversee the final steps of the renovation. For appearance's sake Brice had taken a room on another floor. Officially, he was the consultant for the Center's restaurants. Unofficially, he was her confidant, her moral support, her lover.

When she had finished, he flashed a smile. He was lying on top of her bed, while Belinda took off the linen suit she had worn to the funeral. It had been a long day. When she saw him smiling she frowned.

"Don't tell me you think this is funny," she said as she joined him on the bed. Her hair was still swept up in the severe chignon that seemed appropriate to a bereaved widow. He reached up and removed the combs and it fell in honeyed waves around her face.

"That's better," he said. He took her in his arms and tried to kiss her, but she pulled away.

"Don't you care?" she demanded, looking into his eyes.

"Not really." He tried stroking her thigh, but she could be like a terrier when she got an idea in her head.

"But now I'm only the second richest woman in Texas!"

He just grinned. "I guess I'll just have to settle for second best," he said.

This time he was not going to let her get away. His lips met hers.

How did he do it? As his very closeness bathed her in his warmth, she barely formed that eternal question in her mind. Here with him the answer to that mystery hardly mattered. All that mattered was that she shed the jaded, shrewd, and calculating Belinda as easily as she shed her black linen suit. As his hot mouth brought her breasts alive, she was a new woman. No, not even a woman. She was an angel, a goddess. She was his.

She moaned slightly as his mouth explored a path down her stomach, and then his mouth was back on hers, even as his strong hands caressed her swollen breasts. Her long legs opened around him as he kneeled over her, his gentle touch tracing every curve of her body, bringing it alive in a way no one else ever had, ever could.

She could see that he was hard, and she reached for him, wanting him inside her, wanting to make him hers as she was his, but to her surprise, he lifted her hand away.

"No," he whispered. "I decide."

His hands gripped her hips and he moved downward again, his warm breath and wet tongue tracing her stomach, and then she could feel him on her clitoris, arousing still deeper waves of passion, until she lost track of what he was doing, where his hands and mouth were and she moaned, more loudly this time, as he entered her and he allowed her to move with him, together, as they were meant to from the minute they met.

Chapter Fifty-four

Rhonda Perillo Lurie smiled at Fayette Cramer as the star peppered her with questions about her Cinderella story. All those years she had been watching Fayette on television, and now here she was sharing her story with Fayette and the world. Fayette was so sympathetic. She really cared about how Rhonda had lived most of her life unaware that she was an heiress. Her eyes filled with tears as Rhonda related how the Luries had snubbed her mother just because Emmaline married for love and how Emmaline died when Rhonda was just a year old. And how her father, a poor but proud shrimper, never told her she was kin to one of the richest families in Texas. He was content to make his living on the Bay and wanted nothing to do with the Luries or their money.

"But you feel differently," Fayette said.

"Excuse me?" Rhonda said, not quite understanding what Fayette was getting at.

"You don't have your father's pride about taking the Lurie money?"

Rhonda blinked her green eyes to hold back the tears. "Well, you know, Fayette," she said coolly. "Unlike my daddy, I *am* a Lurie."

How nice that sounded. She was a Lurie. As much as that bitch Charlene Garland. And she was entitled to just as much of the Lurie fortune as Charlene was.

"Given the huge amount of money involved, I'm surprised the family didn't fight you more instead of caving

431

in right away." Everyone in the audience understood that Fayette knew all about fighting. Myles McLean's little sister had been married and divorced three times, before finding herself as a talk-show host.

Rhonda laughed. She was laughing a lot more easily these days. "There was never any question about the claim. I'm a poor girl, Fayette. I've lived my whole life on Galveston Island. Everybody knew me and my daddy and my aunt. All the shrimpers know each other. And of course, Miss Ruby, my mother's old nurse, saw me a few times before Mama died. I was too young to remember, but she knew my mama's charm bracelet and the little old birthmark on my leg right away." For a minute she remembered how Cordell was always after her to have the mark taken off. And here it had made her fortune!

"Do you have any regrets?" Fayette pressed.

Rhonda's eyes darkened slightly. Did a Baptist Church have a bus? Of course she had regrets! Maybe if she had found out who she was a little bit earlier she would be the one living with Cordell in that flower-filled house on Oak Park Circle. Maybe she might have never known what a weakling he was. But that was not something she was about to share with the world. Rhonda was already learning the hypocrisies of public life.

"Only one regret, Fayette," she said, her voice soft.

"Yes?" Fayette leaned closely as she waited for an answer.

"That I never had a chance to know my uncle, the beloved philanthropist Claiborne Lurie who loved my mother so much."

"Bitch!" Charlene Lurie Garland screamed as she frantically tried to change the station, but the remote control was not responding. Finally, in a fury, she tossed the control itself at the screen. It bounded off, but at least it shut down the television, plunging the room into quiet. So quiet Charlene couldn't stand it.

Her nerves were totally on edge.

This bitch, this tramp, this ex-topless dancer, this daughter of a shrimper, was going to end up with a bigger share of the Lurie fortune than she was! She was going to have to share her half of the Lurie Trust with Belinda and Alexander, while this cheap tart had her half all to herself.

Life wasn't fair.

"Easy, darlin'." Cordell tried to soothe, her, but he himself still had not recovered from the shock. Imagine! Little Rhonda Perillo, who had been so devoted to him, was now an heiress. And his wife's cousin. It made him feel a little creepy, almost like he'd committed incest.

"I've a good mind to hire a detective to find out more about this slut, Cordell. I know you're against it, but there's got to be all kinds of dirt in her past. Maybe we'd find something I could hold over her, and get her to give up her claim. We could at least keep her away from Rancho Strega . . ." One of the more galling terms of the Lurie Trust was that Rancho Strega remained a mutual property, to be shared with the hated Belinda and the despised Rhonda.

"Now, darlin'." The tic in Cordell's eye had come back, as it always did when Charlene brought up Rhonda. "I have a feeling the less you know about Miss Perillo, the better."

Tammy Lynn's prodigal father was back in the family fold, and she had discovered that he was a lot looser than Buster with the purse strings. She suspected he felt guilty about abandoning her so many years earlier, or maybe Buddy was just anxious to establish a good relationship with her now that he was going to be part of Galveston for good. Whatever, it didn't matter to her. Just as long as he kept the money coming in.

Tammy Lynn was back depending on her allowance. Her own income had suddenly dried up. Much to her surprise, and Brice's, Tootsie and Harold Bright had finally decided to sell out and retire. She wanted to keep their catering business going, or even move the restaurant somewhere else, but Brice refused. She had no illusions: he jumped at the chance to dump her. Since they closed down Funland and started excavating the property she hadn't even seen him. She still had his ten-thousand-dollar fee from Waldo Brodsky, but he was going to have to beg for it.

She had talked her father into buying her a house on West Beach where she planned to spend most of her time until she decided on her next move. Maybe she would become an interior decorator. Or a talent manager. Look at how well she had done for Brice until he deserted her.

She spent most of her time lounging by the pool deck, staring out at Galveston Bay, considering what to do with the rest of her life.

Lauren had become a frequent guest and confidante and they spent many afternoons rehashing their lovers' sins and plotting elaborate methods of revenge, especially after Tammy Lynn discovered her Aunt Belinda was now an independently wealthy widow. It wasn't fair. Belinda had everything: a fortune, a business, and Brice.

She had to think of something.

Tammy Lynn called to invite Jan Trumbo down to her beach house for the weekend.

"But, honey, isn't that when your aunt's opening Delancy Street? Don't tell me you're not invited!"

Tammy Lynn sighed. "I'm invited, but I'm not going."

"But it will be fabulous. I've been reading about it in all the papers. Aren't you dying to see what she's done with that old place?"

"Belinda's already done enough to me," Tammy Lynn snapped.

"But, honey, aren't you curious? Brice is coming by tomorrow to see me and Kukla, and we're just goin' to pump him dry for details."

There was a brief silence, and when Tammy Lynn's voice came back on the line, it was markedly cheerier.

"Maybe I'll drop by, too. Then he'll have to talk to me."
It was Jan's turn to sigh. "Honey, you're hopeless."

While Tammy Lynn's friend was talking her into going to the opening of the Delancy Street Center, Valdene Garland's friend was trying to persuade her to stay away. Buster had recovered from his mild heart attack. He had never said anything about seeing them sinning in the guest house, but Reba was sure that had brought it on, and that was why he had moved the two of them out there permanently. He claimed it was because Buddy and his family were moving into the Sand Castle, but Reba knew better and she was sure Valdene did, too. There was plenty of room for them in the big house. No, sir. Buster didn't want anything to do with Valdene at all.

Valdene had become a nonperson in the Garland family. Belinda Garland had not even had the courtesy to invite her to the Delancy Street opening.

"That don't bother me, Reba darlin'," Valdene insisted. "I'm going anyway."

Reba sighed. "I just don't know what to do with you, Valdene. Why are we staying here? Those people don't care about you. They want you out of Galveston."

Valdene's dark eyes twinkled. "My Buster's got a bad heart, honey. I don't like it down here any more than you do, but I don't think we'll be here too much longer. And when we go back to Heartland, we won't go back empty-handed."

With Cordell's help, Charlene had bounced back from the horrible news about her inheritance with amazing spirit. She threw herself into redecorating the house on Oak Park Circle. Even better, she discovered that the publicity surrounding her father's unusual legacy and her newly discovered cousin had regenerated interest in her acting career. And this time, she told herself, she was going to become a star.

Tammy Lynn and Lauren were lying beside the beach house pool, separated by a pitcher of margaritas and discussing their favorite subject: how men had ruined their lives. Specifically, Lauren recounted how she had put up with Aynsley's kinky bondage games for years, even allowed him to pander her to Adib Malouf. Now that he had been appointed to fill out the late Senator Wakefield's unexpired term in Washington, he wanted to sell the station and leave her high and dry. Tammy Lynn listened with sympathy, occasionally interjecting her own tales of how Brice de Young had used her and had an affair with her aunt.

Lauren looked at her thighs and rubbed the bruises anxiously. It was getting so she couldn't tell Aynsley's marks from Adib's. Her airtime had been cut back to practically nothing, but between Adib and Aynsley, she had no time to herself.

"You need a rest, Lauren honey. You need to get away. How'd you like to go to Mexico? You and me." Tammy Lynn started to lay out the idea that had been simmering in her head for several days, ever since the invitation to Aunt Belinda's opening night arrived. Her jealousy of Belinda's success and her conviction that her aunt and Brice had renewed their affair had sharpened all her thinking.

She started to tell Lauren about how she had run away from the Sand Castle many times when she was younger and how once she had ended up in a small Mexican town on the Pacific Coast called San Euphemia.

"We could hide out there for six months or a year and no one would find us. Everyone there minds his own business. You could get your head together, kick the cocaine . . ."

Lauren shook her head. "Aynsley would find me. I know he would."

"Suppose I told you that I had a plan, Lauren. A plan that would help you get rid of Aynsley for good."

436

Lauren's eyes widened. "You'd do that for me, Tammy Lynn? Why?"

Tammy Lynn reached over and laid her hand on her new best friend's thigh. "Because I care about you, Lauren honey. And because I want to help you." And because, she added silently, it was a way to get even with Brice and her aunt once and for all.

Step by step, she laid it out for Lauren, beginning with tomorrow afternoon when Lauren, on her way home, would drop Tammy Lynn at the Trumbo mansion in River Oaks, where she would finally corner Brice.

Her plan, she liked to think, was a work of art. The work of a true Garland.

Aynsley was in an ugly mood the next day when Lauren got back from Galveston. She had called him, asking him to meet her when she got back to her apartment. He always hated it when she telephoned him, preferring to control the times of their meetings. But this time, with Tammy Lynn's coaching, Lauren insisted that Aynsley come to her place, claiming that they had to discuss something she could not talk about on the phone.

"You're in big trouble," she said when he walked in and she handed him a cold Lone Star.

"Don't tell me you're pregnant, honeybunch. We can fix that right up."

"No, it isn't that."

Aynsley paled slightly as he considered the possibility that Lauren could have some kind of disgusting disease.

"It's Tammy Lynn's friend, Brice."

"Have you been fucking him, too?" Aynsley demanded.

"Of course not!" Lauren wondered how she could have ever taken this bloated, self-centered idiot seriously. Somehow that thought gave her the strength to go on with the story Tammy Lynn had invented for her. "I gave Tammy Lynn some snapshots of us together. Brice stole

437

them, and now he says if you don't want to buy them, he'll sell them to some tabloid."

"Shucks, Lauren, is that all? So they print some picture of me with a pretty gal. Heck, it'll bring me more votes than it takes away."

"You're very brave now," Lauren said. "But this is no prom picture. Remember that night with you and Adib?"

Aynsley sank into his chair. He sipped his long neck beer. "My, my, your friend Brice is quite the wheeler-dealer, ain't he?"

"He's not my friend, Aynsley. I just met him through Tammy Lynn."

"Don't give me that!" With that, Aynsley's hand shot out of the air so fast Lauren didn't have a chance to duck. It hit her hard against the side of her face.

"I swear, Aynsley. I had nothing to do with the picture. You know I love you. I'd never hurt you." She could already feel her cheek swelling as she rubbed it.

Aynsley held up his empty beer bottle. Lauren recognized the gesture as his command to get a fresh long neck. She rose and went to the kitchen, glad to have a chance to get some ice for her throbbing cheek. She hoped he hadn't broken anything, but she was afraid to look in a mirror and find out.

Hang on, she told herself. It won't be long. Tammy Lynn said everything would work out.

Buddy Garland had settled into his brother's office at the Pink Tower. Except for installing the big, framed photograph of a grinning Buster that hung prominently at the building's entrance, Buddy had made almost no changes in the old man's style. If anything, he reinstituted some of Buster's trademarks, revitalizing the paper and having a lot of fun doing it. He had brought back the weekly bathing beauty, Miss Galveston *Sentinel-Wave*, and he had returned the emphasis to gossip, sensationalism and self-help, which Buster regarded as the essential mix for any successful tabloid.

Buster was pleased and delighted with what Buddy was doing, but never more so than when he received an unscheduled visit from Valdene one afternoon, shortly after the latest issue had hit the stands.

She stormed into his office, black hair flying, and tossed the paper down on his desk.

"Buster Garland, how dare you?"

Buster leaned back in the chair and smiled broadly. "Now Valdene, darlin', whatever's got you all riled up?"

"This, this . . . rag." She picked up the paper and started waving it around.

"Now, Valdene. We like to have a little fun here at the *Wave,* but we only print the truth. My lawyers insist on it."

"You call this the truth?" she stormed, then opened the paper and started reading aloud. " 'Evangelist Prescott Sykes lives! Faithful followers convinced Sykes still alive. Spiritual leader Sykes sighted in Kalamazoo and Duluth!' You are libeling a great man!" She burst into tears.

Unlike most men, Buster was not unnerved by the sight of a woman in tears, especially not a woman he knew as well as he knew Valdene. Nevertheless, there was no point in getting her upset.

"Now, now, Valdene, sit down a minute. Let me get you something to drink. A Coke? Something stronger?"

"A Coke, please," Valdene said. When she realized he wasn't going to offer her a Kleenex for her tears, she scrounged around in the bottom of her Falchi bag for one and delicately dabbed at her smeared mascara.

Buster got her a Coke from his office refrigerator and poured himself some bourbon from the bottle in his desk drawer.

"Now it isn't libel, Valdene darlin', 'cause you can't libel a dead man. And we all think the world of old Prescott, wherever he is. But folks are seeing him all over the place. Just like Elvis."

"It's a lie," she snapped. "You're turning him into a joke!"

Buster looked somber. "Valdene, we like to think we report the truth in the best of taste."

"You're just trying to spoil my deal, that's all."

"What deal is that, Valdene?" asked Buster, suddenly serious.

She sniffed. "Lots of folks still care about Prescott. He was an inspiration to millions. People are after me to write a book about him. And I've been talking to a Hollywood producer about a movie about our life. And you're making a mockery of him!"

Buster's eyes widened in cherubic innocence, "Now, Valdene, we don't want to interfere with your deals." *Especially,* he was thinking, *if they would get this woman out of Galveston and out of his hair.* Nevertheless, he liked selling papers. And the Prescott Sykes stories were selling papers.

"Look at it this way, Valdene darlin'," he said smoothly. "The way these stories are pouring in, it just shows that old Prescott's gone but not forgotten."

Valdene glared at him. "You don't fool me for one minute, Buster. I know what you're up to. You just want to make it look like Prescott's still alive so our marriage won't be legal. Well, forget it. Prescott's dead, dead, dead."

Dead, dead, dead, he repeated to himself. Just as dead as his marriage.

Chapter Fifty-five

Chandler was feeling bored and lonely. Daddy was hibernating in his study, with his telephone and his fax machine, working on deals lately, like how he was going to show Grandpa Buster and Uncle Buddy that they were wrong to kick him out of the Pink Tower. Mommy was gone, too. She had flown to El Lay for a meeting with producers, but she wouldn't let Chandler come. Her mother didn't seem to like her around now that Chandler was starting to look her age. Charlene was still trying to pass as a debutante. What kind of a debutante had a sixteen-year-old daughter?

Chandler missed Miss Ruby, and now she was sorry she had complained about her old nurse and given her such a hard time. She wasn't exactly alone in the big house at Oak Park Circle, because Charlene had hired a whole new staff, but Chandler hardly knew any of them.

"It's okay, they're all bonded," Charlene assured her as she left for El Lay. All Charlene cared about was whether they might steal. But Chandler had to be around the servants all the time, and none of them talked to her. She still knew hardly anybody on the Island and she was downright lonely.

Aynsley Adder was still digesting the unwelcome news that he was being blackmailed by a worthless dog like Brice de Young. Not that he had any intentions of paying the little turd the ten thousand he wanted.

Suddenly Aynsley had to think deeply, and he was never comfortable doing that. Especially not now, when his mind was clouded with beer and cocaine.

Damn Lauren! This was all her fault.

He thought of his good buddy Arden. Good old Arden. He would know what to do. But old Arden was long gone. He would have to face this all by his lonesome.

"Tell your friend Brice I'll meet with him. Wherever he says."

"Oh, Aynsley, I know this is for the best." Lauren put her arms around him and kissed him. He pulled away. He was still not convinced she wasn't in on this, too.

"How do you contact him?" he asked.

"I don't," she said, repeating Tammy Lynn's instructions. "He calls me."

Brice was getting restless. He had put his life on hold for Belinda, but she was so wrapped up in the Delancy Street opening that he never saw her. The opening was tomorrow night and he could hardly wait.

"Look at it this way, Brice," she said. "Once this is out of the way, we can travel indefinitely."

Meanwhile, his money was running out and he was too proud to ask her for any. His fee for overseeing the opening of the Delancy Street restaurants was long gone. He longed for the money from the Waldo Brodsky gig, but Tammy Lynn was deliberately holding on to it and he'd be damned if he'd beg for it. He managed to keep in spending cash by hustling backgammon at the Pelican Yacht Club, but that was peanuts—hardly enough for a new Armani suit. Belinda didn't seem to think about things like that. She was awfully naive sometimes.

Once they were married, things would be different. He planned to launch the hottest nightclub Galveston had seen since the fifties. And the ideas were already coming. Lots of ideas. He intended to check out every club in

442

Europe on their wedding trip, getting the best ideas there, too. He could see it now: Club G. He liked the sound of that. Maybe he should consult with Colette just to be sure. With any luck, he wouldn't even need Belinda's money. With the right concept, investors would be coming to him. He'd learned so much in the restaurant business. He would select the right guests, the exactly correct mix of artists and society types, old Galveston money and young, beautiful bodies.

Meanwhile, though, Brice was restless, with time on his hands and little else. He had driven up to Houston to hang out with Jan and Kukla Trumbo and to try out some ideas he had for his club on them. The Trumbos were just back from Acapulco where they were building what sounded like the biggest house in the Western hemisphere. He listened to their plans with patience. Soon, he, too, would have that kind of money, and he and Belinda would be living in a house like the Trumbos'.

Then the maid announced that the Trumbos had another visitor. None other than Tammy Lynn Garland.

"I better go," Brice said quickly. He was no hero. "Is there a back door?"

"Stop it, Brice," Jan laughed. Tammy Lynn already knows you're here. When she called, I told her. If she can stand it, I think you can."

He could see what was going on. Jan was probably hoping to promote a reconciliation between him and Tammy Lynn. Well, he decided to go along with it. After all, once he married Belinda, he and Tammy Lynn would be family anyway.

Then she was standing in the doorway, hesitating, as if she expected him to storm out. He stood up and opened his arms.

"Tammy Lynn, darlin'. Long time no see!"

Charlene Lurie, as she was still known in "the business," was feeling used, abused, and confused all at the

443

same time. She had come out to Los Angeles in a flurry of expectation, summoned by a producer, Harold Steamfull, who was obviously intrigued by her name and recognition value, and she had been languishing at the Beverly Hills Hotel for days while he set up meetings. Now that he had her out here, he was using her name to line up the rest of his cast and backers. She could certainly see through that, and although it didn't thrill her, she was willing to go along if it meant a part in a feature film.

But what really bothered her was sitting around the Beverly Hills pool with nothing to do. Sometimes she got dressed and shopped, but none of her friends seemed to be available, and she was lonely and bored.

It was almost enough to send her back to Galveston. Almost. She understood Harold was desperate to get some kind of financing. She could tell that by some of the unsavory types he invited to have dinner with her. There were a pair of Middle Eastern businessmen — she never did find out whether they were Israelis or Arabs — and a dwarfish tycoon from New York who was even shorter than Harold and never said a word during dinner, just stared at her breasts throughout.

She decided that if today's lunch guest was another horror she was flying back to the Island. But she tried to take a positive mental attitude, dressing with special care and having an herbal wrap that morning. Harold's limo picked her up at one o'clock and deposited her at Spago at one-fifteen. She sashayed into the dining room and caught Harold's eye. He stood up to greet her. His companion, a giant of a man in a chartreuse linen suit stood up, too. Harold introduced him as the New Jersey shopping mall magnate who was going to finance the story of her life.

To Brice's enormous relief, Tammy Lynn was willing to let bygones be bygones, especially after he agreed to give her a lift back to Galveston. On the way, she even suggested that he take her to the grand opening of the Delancy Street Center that night. At first he tried to get out of it, but he couldn't without explaining about Belinda, and she still wasn't ready to go public about their relationship.

And then Tammy Lynn said the magic words: "I know I've been a bitch to hold on to Waldo Brodsky's money, but I'll have it for you tonight at the party."

"The whole ten thousand dollars?" he said. He had almost given up on it.

Tammy Lynn nodded. He kissed her on the cheek.

"Tammy Lynn, you've got yourself a date."

A few hours later, Tammy Lynn called Lauren. They chatted for a few minutes, and when Lauren hung up she turned to Aynsley, who had been hovering anxiously by the phone. "Brice knows we're going to the opening of Belinda Garland's hotel tonight," said Lauren. "He's expecting you to meet him in Tammy Lynn's suite at ten o'clock." She handed him a paper on which she had written the room number and time.

"Great!" said Aynsley. His eyes were red and he had not slept since Lauren first dropped this bombshell about the photographs, fueling himself on cocaine, beer, and rum raisin ice cream. He was prepared to do something drastic to retrieve them and ensure there would be no more where those came from.

As he stashed the paper inside his jacket, Lauren got a glimpse of the gun.

"What's that?" she said.

"What do you think it is?"

"It looked like a gun."

"Then I guess that's what it is, little lady."

"Oh, Aynsley, don't be a fool. Just pay the the ten thousand and get on with your life."

Aynsley's ruddy face turned redder. His blue eyes were a frightening combination of stupidity and cunning. He had never looked so dangerous. He grabbed her arm and started pushing her toward the door. "I'm settling things with him for good," he said. "And you're coming with me. I want to know once and for all what you have to do with this."

Armed with his daddy's old revolver and with a reluctant but beautiful woman beside him, Aynsley was really getting into the James Bond mode. He was thinking that maybe he'd made a fatal career move when he let his old daddy talk him into politics. Maybe he should have gone into the CIA. He was convinced he had all the talents for it, not to mention his good looks and way with women.

Chapter Fifty-six

Belinda had not been this nervous since her wedding night. Her first wedding night. She sometimes had trouble recalling her marriage to Claiborne Lurie at all. She was too lost in building the Delancy Street Center. And tonight she would open its doors to the world.

The redbrick exterior of the old warehouse had been left intact and it occupied most of the block. Inside had been completely gutted, so that she was able to build virtually from the ground up, exactly the way she wanted it. Delancy Street would be more than just a hotel and shops: it had a complete spa offering Chinese or Swedish massages, sauna, hot tub, and Jacuzzi, and, under Brice's direction, Belinda expected the three restaurants to rival anything anywhere else in the country.

Delancy Street Center was exactly what she had dreamed about, with all the luxuries of an absolutely first-class hotel: Frette bed linens, thick Turkish towels, and fine-smelling Chanel soaps. Fresh flowers always.

Dazzling bathrooms that were all marble and mirrors. High-ceilinged showers with glass doors and round marble bathtubs with Jacuzzis.

It had been easy to lure Wiley Muehl away from the Maison Rouge, and he had recruited an outstanding staff. They were already calling themselves "Wiley's Army."

Belinda had cheerfully agreed with Brice that it would be a nice gesture if he escorted Tammy Lynn. She was delighted that Tammy Lynn had accepted her invitation and decided to let bygones be bygones.

Now, sitting in front of the Biedermeir vanity table, Belinda made up her eyes with special care, then brushed her blond hair vigorously. She would wear her hair down, the way Brice liked it. Next came the dress. For days Belinda had been trying to make up her mind, but she finally settled on the white satin Yves Saint Laurent peplum jacket and long black wool crepe skirt. It was beautiful and feminine, like all St. Laurent's clothes, but it also looked serious, and tonight she wanted to look very serious.

She finished off the look with diamond-and-pearl earrings and a gold chain collar that Claiborne had given her early in their marriage. He had always had exquisite taste in jewelry and he knew exactly what suited her. Poor Claiborne! At least she had his jewels to remember him by.

The jewelry brought back memories of her last cruise on the *Lone Star* and the night she found out for sure that he was still involved with Ciprianna Rivers. Since Claiborne's hunting accident, the designer had reconciled with her husband. Belinda had always suspected that Ciprianna knew more about the accident than she was telling, but Ciprianna had gone into seclusion immediately afterward and avoided even the official inquiries. Belinda had never pursued it. Claiborne's condition was hopeless, what did it matter how he got that way?

Maybe of all the women in his life, herself, Charlene, his first wife Lady Ormsby, who knew how many others?, Ciprianna had been the one who truly loved him. And in his way, Claiborne had loved her. In her own way, Ciprianna had made tonight's triumph possible, and out of a funny kind of gratitude, Belinda had invited her to the gala opening. To her surprise, Ciprianna had accepted. She, too, was a pragmatist.

It just showed, Belinda reminded herself, that it was important to keep love in perspective. Even her love for Brice de Young. She was mad about him, but she had insisted on keeping their affair under wraps for as long as Claiborne lingered in his death-in-life. Even Brice was not worth missing out on a billion-dollar fortune, one that would make her independent once and for all. Now that Claiborne was gone, she still delayed going public. She did not want publicity about the romance — or speculation about when it had begun — to overshadow the opening. As far as her family and the world at large was concerned, Brice was merely the restaurant director of the Delancy Street Center.

It was one of life's little ironies that Claiborne's long dying had freed her to develop her massive Delancy Street project in a way that never could have happened while he was well. The divorce papers he ordered had been drawn up but never signed, and she was still Mrs. Claiborne Lurie, with access to Claiborne's wealth but free of his control. For the first time in years, awash in building the hotel, and nourished by her affair with Brice, she was a genuinely happy woman.

Down the hall from Belinda, Brice paced the floor of Tammy Lynn's penthouse suite nervously. She was really going to make him earn his ten thousand, he could see that now. And he wasn't going to see a penny of it until she had gotten her money's worth by parading with him in front of Belinda's assembled guests. Well, he didn't care, and he was sure Belinda didn't, either. He had already told her about Tammy Lynn and she actually thought it was a good idea. It would help family harmony, she said.

If they ever got there.

He looked around the suite, admiring the renovation. It was very similar to Belinda's, with a living-room ceiling that was two stories high, and a sweeping staircase that led to the second floor and a balcony that overlooked the room. The two bedrooms were upstairs, and he supposed Tammy Lynn was preparing a dramatic descent to impress him.

He tapped his foot impatiently.

Before going downstairs to join her guests, Belinda looked in on Alexander. He was sleeping in his crib. She stood over him, admiring how perfect he was. He was the most beautiful baby she had ever seen and he was hers. She stroked his soft arms and plump legs. He wriggled and opened his eyes. Great chocolate-brown eyes stared up at her. He blinked. His angelic little face suddenly screwed up like a gargoyle. He started to cry.

And cry. And cry.

Belinda picked him up to try to calm him.

He wriggled angrily in her arms. His little face turned red.

Hearing her little charge wailing, Lourdes came running in. She looked at Belinda and then at the baby. At the sight of her, he stopped crying.

"Let me take him, miss," she said.

Reluctantly, Belinda handed her son over to his nurse. Newly calm, his color faded to baby pink. Soon he was smiling and gurgling as Lourdes cooed at him.

"What was wrong?" Belinda asked.

"He just didn't recognize you, miss," Lourdes said.

Very nice, Belinda was thinking. She'd been so wrapped up in her own empire-building that she was a stranger to her own son. How could she have let this happen? Fortunately, it was not too late. And she had an option. She had laughed off Buster's offer to buy her out, but now she saw that it was the perfect opportunity. She and Brice and Alexander would stay in Italy for at least a few months and the three of them would live like a family.

Which, after all, they were.

"This beats the Motel Six," said Buster Garland, who was a genuinely happy man, pleased that his only daughter had done so well on her own.

450

Zena Garland agreed. She was wearing a short jade-green silk crepe dress that exposed her ebony shoulders and legs to great advantage. Her only jewelry was a pair of intricate jade-and-diamond ear clips that she had designed herself.

"Little sister is quite a woman," Buddy Garland added.

"Yes," Mozelle Bryant agreed. "Your daughter is a woman of many parts."

The four of them were standing beneath the great Baccarat chandelier in the main lobby of the Delancy Street Center. They had been among the first to arrive. Buddy was anxious to demonstrate that there was no family rift, at least not between him and his sister. He knew that all of Galveston was buzzing since he had virtually fired Cordell, but he had no quarrel with Belinda. In fact, he admired her for breaking out on her own like this.

At first he did not take her seriously. He had been away from Galveston for so long that in some ways he still thought of his sister as a naive kid who wanted to play with the big boys. Certainly that was the way Buster talked about her. But Belinda had been through a lot and she learned from it all.

"Here she comes now," said Zena.

"Don't she look pretty?" said Buster with pride. By now he had completely and conveniently forgotten that he had refused to help her acquire a property of her own.

"A beauty," Buddy agreed.

Chandler Lurie Garland had cut the hair on one side of her head so close to her scalp that she looked like a refugee from a concentration camp. The other side was long, blond and straight. She was also wearing a small earring in her nose. The whole look was supposed to make her look like Cindy Lauper but did not quite work. Her progress through schools in California, Switzerland, New York, and Galveston had prepared her for the same

451

life as her mother: that of a Texas debutante. Chandler could judge a horse, a diamond, or a piece of china at a glance, but she knew nothing about the measure of a man. Being sixteen, she had no idea of this, of course.

She had dressed for Aunt Belinda's big night with special care. She liked her Aunt Belinda, who was the only grown-up in the family who talked to her like a person. She really missed Miss Ruby, who used to talk to her all the time. Funny, she used to wish Miss Ruby would leave, and now that the old woman was gone she missed her all the time. All of a sudden, she upped and announced she was going to work for someone else, her new cousin Rhonda, but Mommy and Daddy were so furious they wouldn't talk about it. Miss Ruby still checked up on her, though, calling her up and reminding her to be good.

Belinda walked toward Buster and Buddy, but her smooth progress was halted as she was stopped by various guests who wanted to congratulate her or compliment her. She finally reached Buster's party which had settled into a banquette, where she joined them.

"I can't stay," she said, and they understood that she had to work the room. Then she noticed Chandler.

"What happened to your nose?" she asked. Belinda was used to Chandler's unusual fashion sense, but the strange black growth on the side of her nose was something new.

"It's a nose ring," Chandler explained. "My mother hates it."

Belinda was not going to be lured into talking about Charlene. "How come you don't have one for Mr. T.?"

"Oh, you can't pierce a ferret's nose!" Chandler looked at her aunt. "Oh, I get it, you're kidding. Very funny, Aunt Belinda."

"Thanks, Chandler. You look very nice, by the way. Where are your mom and dad?"

"Oh, Daddy's around here somewhere." There had already been a scene at home with Mama calling from El

452

Lay to say she could not possibly come back for Aunt Belinda's opening and Daddy insisting that he had to make an appearance. She finally agreed that Chandler could go with Daddy, but only for a few hours, and only on the condition that she would watch to see if her Aunt Belinda had a boyfriend.

Chandler had no intention of being a sex spy for her mother, and as soon as they arrived she slipped away from her father and moved alone through the crowd, feeling very adult in her mother's short black velvet sheath and long red silk gloves. She was no longer the chubby little girl Speed Porter had felt sorry for and treated like a little sister.

Later, as she roamed through the crowd, she noticed a handsome dark man staring at her. An older man. He had to be at least twenty-five. When he caught her eye he winked. She tried to wink back, but she probably didn't do a good job because he laughed.

That really got her annoyed, and she stormed over to him, her blue eyes steely with anger.

"Excuse me," she said haughtily. "Do you know who I am?"

Ramon Rivera blinked, then laughed. "Are you speaking to me?" He truly had no idea why a child who looked like Cindy Lauper would be addressing him.

"Of course I'm speaking to you. You just laughed at me, and I want you to know that my aunt owns the Delancy Street Center and all I have to do is snap my fingers and you'll be out on your ear."

Far from being insulted, Ramon felt a warm glow come over him, for he sensed his luck was about to change. This enchanting little girl was a sign of it. An omen.

And it was about time, for things had been mostly downhill for him since he sailed on Claiborne's Amazon cruise. He had hoped that Lurie would sponsor him, he had hoped to sell his articles about the cruise to *Rolling Stone,* he had hoped to see Charlene Garland again. So many hopes, so many disappointments! Nobody wanted

453

his articles. Nobody wanted his contacts. Like Charlene Garland, they only wanted two things from him: sex and cocaine. He was being forced to deal drugs just to stay alive. People seemed to expect it of him, just because he was young, handsome, and Colombian. Fortunately, Joel Varney had arranged a membership for him in the Pelican Yacht Club. He played tennis there often, and he hoped to make the contacts that would propel his career as a journalist. But so far nothing had happened.

Now this charming girl was threatening to have him thrown out. But perhaps there was hope.

"You've told me everything but who you are," he said kindly.

"I'm Chandler Lurie Garland."

"And I am Ramon Rivera y Longa and I'm most pleased to meet you. Has anyone told you that you resemble Cindy Lauper?"

"Do you see who Chandler is talking to?" Belinda asked Brice. They were dancing. The band was playing "Nightime."

"Don't worry about that kid, she can take care of herself," he assured her.

It was easy to forget about Chandler. Belinda had a lot on her mind. The launch of the Delancy Street Center was a great success.

"Let's go up to your room," he whispered. "You should be celebrating."

"Later, Brice. Right now your date's getting anxious."

Tammy Lynn had been dancing nearby with Myles McLean, but Belinda was conscious of her niece's angry glare. Brice had assured her Tammy Lynn wanted to let bygones be bygones.

She wondered, and was almost relieved when the music ended and she could send Brice back to her.

"Oh, look, Reba, there's Ciprianna and Carl." Valdene waved at the couple who were dancing, but they didn't

454

notice her. Lots of people in the room didn't notice her lately, since the news had spread that her days as Mrs. Buster Garland might be numbered.

"You know, darlin', I think that Carl Rivers took quite a shine to you on old Claiborne's cruise. Did you know that?"

Reba was watching the Rivers dancing, too. "No," she said softly, but her voice sounded very far away.

"Oh, there you are. I wondered where you'd gone," said Belinda.

"Oh, Ramon and I have been checking out the arcade, Aunt Belinda. You've really turned this place into a palace!" With her dewy skin and soft features, Chandler looked very sweet and very young.

Just then Wiley Muehl appeared to tell Chandler that her father's car was waiting to take her home. She turned to her aunt for a reprieve.

"Aunt Belinda, say I don't have to go home! I'm just starting to have fun!"

"I'm sorry Chandler, but you have to do what your daddy says."

To Belinda's relief, Chandler went along without complaint. This was so unlike her that Belinda suspected she had already lined up a midnight date with Ramon. Actually, it was because Chandler had managed to slip her phone number to him before leaving and was quite sure she would be hearing from him again.

Belinda continued to work the room, accepting congratulations from her guests. Everyone seemed to be having a good time, raving about the band and the decor and the food. She paused at the table where Cordell had joined Buddy and Buster for a temporary truce. Even cousin Lamar had come in from the West Coast with a bevy of beautiful young women. At first Brice had insisted that he ought to sit with Belinda and she insisted just as strongly that he could not.

"But I thought you and your brothers made up. I thought you were all one big happy family again," he said.

"Sure, but you don't know my family if you think I trust them to leave it that way."

She was relieved that Tammy Lynn had asked him to be her escort. She didn't feel the least bit threatened and it would keep him busy. She just hoped Tammy Lynn had gotten over her infatuation with him. She felt better watching them dance together. How much trouble could Tammy Lynn make on the dance floor?

Cousin Lamar rose to go. His entourage rose with him. "Well, folks, I guess I'll turn in. The girls need their beauty rest."

The girls giggled.

Buster and Mozelle also rose to leave. Buster grinned at Belinda. "Congratulations, darlin'. You've made me very proud."

After Buster had left and Belinda had moved on to welcome more of her guests, Valdene wandered over to greet Cordell. Since everybody knew Buster, and Buddy had fired him, Valdene thought they might have something in common. They had both been tossed out by the Garlands.

Giddy with champagne and malice, Tammy Lynn was feeling absolutely wonderful as she danced with Brice in the ballroom. Poor Brice! What she had done to his reputation! Aynsley Adder thought he was a scheming blackmailer and Aynsley was such a hothead, that tonight he would probably kill him. Or Brice would kill Aynsley. With any luck, the two of them would kill each other and save the State of Texas the cost of a murder trial. Lauren had called her frantically from Houston just before she left with Aynsley. She wanted to warn Tammy Lynn that

456

Aynsley was bringing a gun. As if Tammy Lynn would be surprised!

She had left word with the hotel desk to let her know when Lauren and Aynsley had checked into her suite. Then she'd send Brice back up. He would be expecting money, and Aynsley would be expecting a blackmailer.

Everything was going to go according to her plan. She might not be as beautiful as Aunt Belinda, but Tammy Lynn was sure she had the brains to be just as successful. It was only a matter of time.

In Hollywood, Charlene Garland was concentrating all her personal charm on Harold Steamfull and Winston Weinstein, her producers, with only occasional trips to the ladies' room for a restorative hit of cocaine.

This time, when she returned to the table, only to find that a young, cheap-looking blond with silicone tits that were falling out of her low-cut black leather bustier had joined Winston and Harold. They introduced her as Jessica-Jennifer.

"One of the Brat Pack's biggest talents," said Harold with enthusiasm as he stood to let Charlene inside the banquette.

Charlene eyed Jessica-Jennifer with distaste as she sat beside her. She noticed the girl was staring at her, watching her closely. She couldn't tell if Jessica-Jennifer was nearsighted or stoned. Or was she a lesbian?

Dinner was strained, and before coffee was served Winston Weinstein announced that he and Jessica-Jennifer were expected at a party in Malibu and had to get going. Charlene was sorry to see Winston go, but she couldn't say the same for the starlet. The girl was pure white trash. She made a mental note to invite Winston to Rancho Strega real soon. The two of them, alone in that unspoiled country, would have lots to share. She wondered what he was like in bed.

She realized Harold was talking to her about the slut.

457

"Jessica-Jennifer wanted to meet you. She wants to study your character."

"My character?"

"Yes, didn't I tell you?" Harold laughed. "I guess it just fell through the cracks. Paperwork."

"Tell me what."

"You're off the picture, Charlene. We're going with Jessica-Jennifer."

Charlene was pinned inside the banquette or she would have stormed out of the restaurant. *How dare he have this piece of white trash play her on the screen?*

"How can you hire her when you could have me, the real thing!"

"I'm sorry, Charlene, I truly am. But we've decided to go with a Charlene Lurie type."

"A Charlene Lurie type! But I'm Charlene Lurie!"

Harold glanced around to see if anyone had overheard her. He hated scenes, and fortunately everyone else in the restaurant was engrossed in their own conversations. He took her hand and looked into her eyes. His lovers always told him he had eyes like a lost puppy.

"Charlene, listen to me. I'm telling you this with love. Go home. Go back to Galveston. You're too good for this town. Go back to Galveston where you belong."

Lauren didn't know how Ansley managed to get them to Galveston without an accident. He was weaving through downtown like a maniac, ranting and shouting, and she was sure he was going to get them both killed. He made her lay out lines for them while he drove, then hoovered his up at 85 m.p.h. It was a wonder the highway patrol didn't stop them. She had dreaded getting to Delancy Street Center, yet when they pulled in front of the big redbrick building she felt only relief. At least she'd be out of the car.

She had barely put her hand on the car door when Aynsley was out and around to her side, yanking it open

458

and pulling her out. She almost lost her balance and he gripped her even harder to keep her upright.

"Please, Aynsley, you're hurting me." He ignored her and tossed his car keys to the parking valet.

"I'll hurt you a lot more before this is over," he said, turning back to her. "You're not going to make a fool out of me."

"Aynsley," she pleaded. "I had nothing to do with this."

"Sure, right. I want to hear this Brice's side of this story. Then we'll see."

Lauren was miserable. Her sinuses ached, her nose was running, and she knew she looked awful. She hoped with all her heart that things were going to go according to Tammy Lynn's plan. It had all made perfect sense when they talked about it back at Tammy Lynn's beach house, but somehow reality seemed to be a little different. At least Tammy Lynn didn't sound a bit worried that Aynsley was bringing her along to buy the photographs back from Brice.

Lauren watched Aynsley check into the suite Tammy Lynn had reserved. The lobby was crowded with people there for the opening gala, but he was so upset, he wasn't even concerned about them being seen in public together. Once upon a time that would have made her very happy. As they ascended in the elevator, Lauren prayed that Tammy Lynn knew what she was doing, because she sure didn't.

Brice and Tammy Lynn were sharing a flute of champagne on the terrace when the bellhop brought her word that Aynsley and Lauren had arrived and gone up to the suite. She almost hated to send Brice away, because he had been on his good behavior all night. That ten thousand must mean a lot to him. She knew she didn't.

Of course, she had not told him about Aynsley and Lauren, just that Lauren was bringing his money. And now she informed him that Lauren was waiting upstairs, and pressed her room key into his hand.

"Aren't you coming up to see her?" he asked.

She shook her head. "Tell Lauren to come down and join the party. I've got to visit with my kin. You go up and get your money. You deserve it."

She smiled and kissed him on the cheek before sending him off, then turned to go chat with Aunt Belinda.

On his way up in the elevator, Brice started talking to a middle-aged Hollywood type surrounded by a bunch of giggling movie starlets and missed his floor. They invited him to party in their suite, but he was in a hurry to pick up his money from Lauren. When he finally found Tammy Lynn's suite, he was surprised that the door was slightly ajar. He could hear a man and woman arguing. He pushed it and stepped into the living room.

"De Young?" a man shouted.

Brice looked up. A beefy stranger was standing at the top of the stairs waving a gun.

He tried to measure the situation. The man was angry, drunk, and looked out of shape, but the gun gave him a definite edge. Brice raised his hands to show him they were empty.

"Who are you?" the man demanded.

"Whoa there, buddy," Brice said coolly, while his stomach felt like it had dropped to his knees. "I've got no gun. See? Did I come at a bad time?"

At this point he noticed the blonde who had been arguing with the man. He expected her to be relieved, but instead she looked dazed. It took a few seconds for him to recognize her.

Lauren Armour!

She had dropped about twenty pounds, which had not improved her looks at all. She looked haggard and drawn and about sixty years old. Her eyes were glassy and her nose was running. She looked like a hard-core junkie.

Jesus Christ, he was thinking. What had he

gotten into?

"You still haven't told me what you're doing here," Red Face was demanding.

Brice looked around the suite uneasily. The sight of Lauren Armour up on the balcony, half dazed, appalled him. She didn't even seem to recognize him. And where was Tammy Lynn?

"I was invited," he said coolly as he ascended the stairs. "Were you?" He was starting to sense that Red Face was a bully, and it was important not to show fear when dealing with a bully. Especially one who was waving a gun.

"I am a United States senator!"

A light went on inside Brice's head. Aynsley Adder had been pointed out to him around Houston and Galveston. Funny, him showing up here in Tammy Lynn's suite. He tried to remember the story; it seemed that Adder had something to do with the death of Belinda's first husband. But then, he supposed any enemy of Belinda's was automatically a friend of Tammy Lynn.

"Senator Adder, of course," Brice said, extending his hand.

Adder looked confused, as if he couldn't decide what to do with his gun if he shook Brice's hand. He finally seemed to grasp that he could put it in his other hand. Then he gestured to the wreck that had once been Lauren Armour.

"I believe you know this lady," he said.

"Hi there, Lauren," Brice said, trying to sound casual. She gazed at him foggily. "Brice?" Then a shadow of her smile broke through. She looked almost like the old Lauren as her face brightened. That was enough to enrage Adder. He reached for her and yanked her to her feet, shaking her out like an old coat.

"Don't act like you don't know what's going on," Adder shouted. "I guess you and this bitch thought you could blackmail me into buying back your pictures. You've both

461

got another thought coming."

The gun was back in his right hand now and he held it to Lauren's head. She looked too stoned to understand the danger she was in, but the sight of the shining metal against her blond hair horrified Brice.

"Hey, you've got to stop this," he insisted, moving toward the enraged Adder.

Adder stepped back, pulling Lauren with him. Brice followed. It was as if they were dancing.

"Here, give me that," Brice said, reaching for the gun. If he could just get it away from Adder until he sobered up . . .

But Adder was too fast for him and, releasing Lauren, who fell facedown in a heap on the carpet, he moved away again.

Now that Lauren was free, however, Brice had no reason to be tentative, and he had the edge on Adder in age, weight, and general condition. He leaped at him, once again going for the gun, but Adder waved it away. The impact of Brice against his chest knocked Adder over onto the floor.

The two men rolled around the balcony as Brice struggled for Adder's gun, until they had reached the top of the stairs. Instinctively, Brice pulled back, but Adder, too drunk to realize where he was, went rolling down the stairs. As he tried to get back on his feet, his gun slipped out of his hand, exploded a shot, then clattered behind him down the marble steps. He landed in a heap at the foot of the staircase.

Lauren moaned.

Brice looked at her, and then at the door.

Tammy Lynn was standing in the doorway, her eyes quickly taking in the sight of an unconscious Lauren crumpled on the balcony while Brice stood over Aynsley Adder at the foot of the stairs.

"What's going on here?" she demanded. "I heard a shot."

Brice stared at Adder's lifeless body, trying to make

462

sense of what had just happened. The gun must have gone off as it fell down the stairs. That seemed like a lifetime ago. He looked down at the senator now. There was no sign of a wound, but there was no mistaking Adder's condition.

"He's dead," he muttered. "It was him or me."

"Did you shoot him?"

Brice shook his head. "No. He's not wounded. He must have had a heart attack as he fell. He didn't look like he was in great shape."

To his surprise, Tammy Lynn looked almost — satisfied. He wasn't sure she understood what had happened.

"It was an accident, Tammy Lynn. He came at me, we struggled, and he fell down the stairs," he added. "Lauren saw the whole thing."

Tammy Lynn looked up at her friend collapsed face-down at the top of the stairs. From time to time Lauren moaned slightly, as if she was having a bad dream.

"I don't think she's going to remember much about this, Brice honey. She's coked out."

"What are we going to do?" Brice asked. No matter where he tried to look in that vast living room his eyes fell on the hulking corpse of Senator Aynsley Adder.

Tammy Lynn smiled. Brice, honey. I haven't seen you so upset since Aunt Belinda fired you from the Maison Rouge."

"That's ancient history," he snapped. *Why was she bringing Belinda up now?*

"Not to me."

"Look, Tammy Lynn, let's talk about it some other time. Right now we've got a body to get rid of."

Her smile had turned nasty. "Why look at me, Brice? You're the one who killed him."

"I'll just tell them it was self-defense. I was trying to help Lauren."

"And what were you doing here?"

"But I was here to meet Lauren. To get my money. You fixed it up."

"Did I?" Her face was suddenly a mask.

Brice was starting to get an ugly feeling inside. He wondered if this was what Colette's premonitions were like, because he was sure getting a premonition here. He was starting to comprehend a very unpleasant fact: little Miss Tammy Lynn Garland did not wish him well.

And he had never needed her more.

Chapter Fifty-seven

After gallantly bringing Miss Mozelle Bryant to her door Buster reluctantly left her there and returned to the Delancy Street Center. His little granddaughter Tammy Lynn had asked him to drop by her suite for a chat and he did not want to refuse her. It was so seldom lately that all the Garlands got together under one roof, he wanted to make the most of it.

On returning, he spied Belinda in the lobby and invited her to come along. At first she demurred, claiming that Tammy Lynn might want a private talk.

"Nonsense!" he insisted, and took her arm before she could protest. Besides, the guests had started to leave and there was no need for her to stick around. Everyone agreed that the Delancy Street Center was a roaring success.

Belinda was still glowing from her triumph and she sensed that Buster wanted to talk to her about it, but as they stepped off the elevator on the penthouse floor she knew immediately that something was wrong. The corridor was too quiet, but Buster said nothing about it and she did not want to alarm him.

They reached the door to Tammy Lynn's suite and knocked. The door opened a crack and Tammy Lynn's little pinched face appeared.

"Oh, Grandpa Buster, thank God you're here," she said, pulling it open wide. "Brice just went crazy. He tried to kill me."

Belinda stared at her and stepped into the room. Tammy Lynn had been so intent on getting her story out that she hadn't noticed her until now, but she merely smiled.

Her triumph was complete! She wouldn't have to wait for Belinda's reaction, she was getting it right now. And Belinda looked sick.

Belinda saw Brice standing behind her niece. He looked stunned.

"Tammy Lynn, what are you talking about?" he demanded.

Bit by bit, Belinda took in the rest of the room: the body at the foot of the stairs, the woman collapsed on the balcony. Tammy Lynn was rattling off some story to Buster about a fight with Brice over money and how Aynsley Adder had tried to protect her.

Aynsley Adder? Now she knew Tammy Lynn was lying. Aynsley never protected anyone but himself in his whole life. But did Buster believe her?

Belinda moved toward Adder's body and touched him. He looked like he was asleep but he was very dead. It was a moment she had longed for, yet it was strangely unsatisfying. She never thought she would wish that Aynsley Adder was alive, but at that moment she did.

Brice had followed her and was standing over her. "You've got to believe me, Belinda," he whispered. "He fell down the stairs. It was an accident. She set me up."

Yes, she could see how Tammy Lynn had planned it, but did Buster? She looked over. He was listening intently to Tammy Lynn's story, nodding, but his eyes, too, were taking in the room.

Tammy Lynn seemed to get more and more wrapped up in her story, as if by piling up details she could make it more believable. But Buster had had enough. He gently put his hand on her shoulder, and at his touch she stopped.

"Whoa, darlin'. Pause for a breath. You're gonna need your strength."

"Oh, Granddad, I'm so glad you're here," she sighed,

collapsing in his vast arms.

He patted her on the head. Of course, I don't believe a word of this, and neither does your aunt, but that's no never mind. I find my niece in a hotel suite with a dead yellow dog and a mongrel pup and I don't ask but one question. How can I return this scene to some measure of respectability?"

"Huh?" Tammy Lynn stared. He was not reacting according to plan. He was supposed to rage and storm and have Brice thrown in jail. And Belinda was supposed to be crying by now. Instead, Brice had his arm around her and they were watching as if Tammy Lynn was the one in trouble.

"Where's the bedroom?" Buster demanded.

"There's two," she answered automatically. "I've been using the one at the right of the stairs."

"Good," he snapped. "Then we'll use the one on the left." He turned to Brice for the first time. "Young fella, you're in better shape than I am. Give me a hand getting this worthless carcass up the stairs."

"Yes, sir." Brice snapped to attention, relieved that Buster seemed to know what he was doing.

The next few minutes were a blur to Belinda. She watched as the two men dragged Aynsley's body up the stairs. By the time they had settled him in bed, Lauren had started coming to, and Buster and Brice spent a few minutes in quiet conversation with her. When the men rejoined Belinda they looked quite relieved.

"I'll just have to call up my friend the sheriff, but I think we can handle this thing. Poor Aynsley had a fatal heart attack while engaging in man's favorite sport, that's all. I don't think that'll hurt your hotel's reputation any, do you, Belinda?"

Her hotel! She'd been so worried about Brice she hadn't even thought of the impact of a scandal on her hotel. Leave it to Buster to come up with the perfect coverup.

"Back in the oil patch, we used to call it dying in the saddle," Buster said as he picked up the phone. "I think

467

old Aynsley would have wanted it that way, don't you?"

Brice took Belinda's hand, while Tammy Lynn glared at them. Buster saw her.

"And you, young lady. I think it's time you went away for another good long rest. Maybe with your friend Miss Armour up there. Don't you agree?"

Overnight, the Delancy Street Center became a Galveston institution, just as Belinda had expected. She had proved she could have a success completely on her own. Although, she had to admit, Buster had saved the day by foiling Tammy Lynn. And he'd sent her off to San Euphemia with Lauren Armour for a long vacation. Belinda thought she ought to be in a sanitorium, but Buster wouldn't hear of it. Maybe he was right. Tammy Lynn had been in others and they didn't seem to have done any good.

Buster certainly knew what he was doing when he created the cover story for Aynsley's death. The official cause was listed as a heart attack, but rumors were flying that he had died while making love, just as Buster had expected. That only enhanced the reputation of her hotel.

In just a matter of days, the grand ballroom had been booked solid for the next year with charity galas, debutante balls, and society weddings. Names of local luminaries like the Moodys, the Kempners, and the Mitchells were appearing regularly in the reservation books for the three restaurants.

So what next? That was a question Belinda asked herself every morning. She was ready for a bigger adventure. A new challenge.

She was not totally surprised when Buster invited her to lunch to talk business. He suggested Gaido's for old time's sake. They hedged and sparred throughout the meal, until he came to the point.

"You done good, darlin'."

"Thank you." She did not add that it was without any help from him, but she couldn't resist at least a little

468

needling. "You sound surprised."

"Pleasantly surprised, darlin'. Pleasantly surprised."

Belinda smiled at him. She was enjoying this; it was quite nice to see Buster eating crow.

"Yes, indeed," he went on. "I was just telling Buddy how pleased and proud I am of you. And we agreed that there was no sense in letting your fine business brain get out of the family."

"I'm flattered," she said coolly.

"Yes, ma'am. We want you on our side. We want you back."

Belinda toyed with the blackened redfish. This little encounter was sharpening her appetite. It was sharpening all her senses, and she was wary of her father's next move. Wary and curious at the same time.

"And what do you and Buddy have in mind for little me?"

Buster smiled. If he noticed her sarcasm, he had decided to ignore it.

"Darlin', we want you on our team. We're family. We want you back at Garland, Inc. Running the Maison Rouge and Delancy Street both."

Belinda started to laugh. "I see, Daddy. You want me to give up my independence, come back into the family fold, and start taking orders again from you and Buddy."

Buster looked slightly dismayed. That was exactly what he wanted, but he didn't like the way it sounded when put like that. "Now, darlin'," he soothed. "We have your best interests at heart."

She reached over and touched her father's gnarled hand. "I know, Daddy. I know. You and Buddy are looking out for me and I appreciate it. But if you don't mind, I'll just let things be a while."

Buster's blue eyes narrowed. "How about if we wanted to buy you out? You could name your own price. How about that?"

"That's certainly a possibility," she said coolly. "I'd have to think about it."

She was thinking about it even now: how sweet it was

469

to have Buster offering to take over the business she had built on land he wouldn't even help her buy. Still, she could not resist a dig.

"All of it could have been yours," she said.

But Buster was too happy to be offended. His blue eyes merely twinkled, and he smiled broadly. "You're my daughter, Belinda, and everything you have is mine."

Belinda thought she finally understood her father.

Epilogue

On the last day of April, near sunset, Buster Garland sat under an oak tree, not far from the terrace of the Sand Castle. He told himself that when the gnats got too bothersome he would go inside, but in the meantime he relished the glory of twilight. In one thick hand, with its unusually long fingers and almost delicate oval nails, he held a fine Macanuda cigar. His lined face and thick white hair were hidden by the broad-brimmed Panama hat.

He was serene in his kingdom; a Gulf Coast Texan in high cotton. Old Lyndon lay at his feet. These days the poor old hounddog barely summoned enough energy to follow his master, but he remained steadfast. In the pool nearby his grandchildren's toys floated.

He had not felt his age since his mild heart attack more than six months ago. Separation from Valdene had renewed his vigor, and the return of Buddy and Belinda and their families gave him a faith in the future that his son Cordell had almost destroyed. All his rancor, toward Buddy, toward Belinda, even toward Cordell, had faded.

Although he still kept the master bedroom at the Sand Castle, he had turned over most of the house to Buddy and Zena. Valdene was holding out in the guest house. She was determined to outlive him and to die his widow.

Well, let her. If his days were numbered, he would rather spend them with a good woman than with a lying degenerate wildcat.

It took less than twenty minutes to reach Mozelle's house in his yellow Cadillac. Here even old Lyndon was welcome, and the dog started panting as soon as they hit Broadway. The dog could barely contain himself as Buster parked the car, and when he opened the door, Lyndon bounded to Mozelle's door with the spirit of a young pup.

Mozelle gave Buster a big hug, scratched Lyndon's neck vigorously, and led them to the rear of the house where dinner for her and Buster had been set in the garden. The plot was small but thick with oak and oleander, with all the privacy of a forest grove.

The time he spent with Mozelle was just plain restful, and as the evening passed, marked by good food, good bourbon and good talk, he resolved once again to see if something could not be done about their relationship. He was old-fashioned enough to want to make an honest woman of her, but shrewd enough to know that she'd be insulted if he even brought it up. He would wait until the Valdene issue was settled once and for all.

Meanwhile, Buster was a happy man. He watched as Mozelle rose to clear the table. She had given her staff the night off and they were alone in the house. Lyndon was curled up asleep by the outdoor fireplace. Buster took her hand, and held it.

"That's a real southern lady's hand, Mozelle," he said. "Soft and fragrant as a lily."

Her green eyes twinkled. "Why, thank you, Buster. Are you trying to get on my good side?"

He laughed. "I hope I am by now. If not, I guess I'll keep on trying."

He had not let go of her hand, and now he took the other one, pulling her into his lap.

"What's this? What will my neighbors say?"

"You know me better than that," he said. "Besides, it's dark now." The only light was from the candles on the table which played on both their faces, bathing them in a youthful glow. The years slipped away with the evening light and suddenly they were two kids again.

His lips met hers.

472

"When was the last time you did it on the grass?" he said hoarsely.

Mozelle seemed to read his mind. "You know, Buster honey, that's something I'd like to do once more before I die."

Now it was her turn to take his hand as she led him to a secluded corner of the garden, draped by honeysuckle and night-blooming jasmine. There was a swing big enough for two.

"Let's sit here a while," she suggested. They sat there like two shy teenagers from another era, their era. Then he took her in his arms again. This time she responded with even more passion.

Soon he was leading her down onto the grass and they were laughing and fumbling and then they were one and forgot about the night and the heavy-scented air and the wet grass and the spring chill and thought only of each other.

And when it was over, and Mozelle lay there, with Buster against her warm breast, she sensed an ugly coldness steal over her lover.

But it was too late. She lay there until dawn, crying and rocking, crying and rocking as she held the body of Buster Garland for the last time.

Coming Headlines from the
Sentinel-Wave:

GALVESTON MOURNS DEATH OF
BUSTER GARLAND

TEXAS WEDDING OF THE CENTURY:
GARLAND HEIRESS WEDS FORMER FRY COOK

BRICE DE YOUNG ANNOUNCES OPENING OF
HOT SPOT "CLUB G"

COMING SOON—THE WORLD PREMIERE OF
"TOXIC TEXAS TERROR" STARRING
CHARLENE LURIE

MR. & MRS. BUDDY GARLAND DENY RUMORS
THEIR MARRIAGE ON ROCKS

CORDELL GARLAND FORMS RESORT DEVELOP-
MENT COMPANY: DENIES MAFIA LINK OF PLANS
TO COMPETE WITH GARLAND, INC.

CINDERELLA HEIRESS RHONDA PERILLO-LURIE TO WED MYLES MCLEAN

MORE PRESCOTT SYKES SIGHTINGS!

MYSTERY SERIAL KILLER TERRORIZES GALVESTON!

MY DAYS AS A SENATOR'S SEX SLAVE BY LAUREN ARMOUR, AS TOLD TO TAMMY LYNN GARLAND